MW00589358

CHERISH THE DREAM

GEMMA JACKSON

POOLBEG

This book is a work of fiction. References to real people, events, establishments, organisations, or locales are intended only to provide a sense of authenticity, and are used fictitiously. All other characters, and all incidents and dialogue, are drawn from the author's imagination and are not to be construed as real.

Published 2023
by Poolbeg Press Ltd
123 Grange Hill, Baldoyle
Dublin 13, Ireland
E-mail: poolbeg@poolbeg.com
www.poolbeg.com

© Gemma Jackson 2023

© Poolbeg Press Ltd. 2023, copyright for editing, typesetting, layout, design, ebook

The moral right of the author has been asserted.
A catalogue record for this book is available from the British Library.

ISBN 978-1-78199 4900

All rights reserved. No part of this publication may be reproduced or transmitted in any form or by any means, electronic or mechanical, including photography, recording, or any information storage or retrieval system, without permission in writing from the publisher. The book is sold subject to the condition that it shall not, by way of trade or otherwise, be lent, resold or otherwise circulated without the publisher's prior consent in any form of binding or cover other than that in which it is published and without a similar condition, including this condition, being imposed on the subsequent purchaser.

www.poolbeg.com

About the Author

Gemma Jackson was born in Dublin, Ireland, one of seven children born to Rose and Patrick Jackson. The world Gemma was born into is now described as a world of poverty, deprivation and desperation – but not to the people living it at the time.

Gemma was born in the tenements of Dublin. Yes, she remembers going to bed hungry. Yes, new clothes were something you received only at Easter and Christmas and toys were few. But the abiding memories from her childhood are of love, laughter and music.

Imagination and dreams were an escape from the real world – sitting around the fire huddled under a hairy blanket while listening to stories of exotic places and people. Everyone had a story to tell.

Perhaps it was these stories that sent Gemma out into the big wild world at the age of seventeen to "see what is out there".

Gemma admits to being intimately acquainted with poverty. She has a passing knowledge of wealth but the love, music and laugher of her childhood has never left her.

Now her stories are being told in book form. What more could she want?

Also by Gemma Jackson

Through Streets Broad and Narrow
Ha'penny Chance
The Ha'penny Place
Ha'penny Schemes
Impossible Dream
Dare to Dream

In the Krista series

Krista's Escape
Krista's Journey
Krista's Choice
Krista's Chance
Krista's Dilemma
Krista's Doubt
Krista's Duty
Krista's Deeds

Published by Poolbeg

Acknowledgements

Thank you to my readers and those who take the time to share their enjoyment of my books with me and in book forums.

We have all come through difficult times but again, music, story-telling and wonderful writers kept me sane – or as sane as I can ever claim to be.

Thank you to my daughter who never fails to keep my addiction fed – tea – it could be a lot worse!

The world of radio is a constant joy to me. The music and banter keep me company while I type away at my stories.

Libraries and librarians have also been a constant in my life – the rich world available to all of us with just a visit to the library. Thank you.

Thanks to the people at Poolbeg Press for allowing me to live my dream. Paula Campbell who like a Fairy Queen granted me my wish – I am indeed a published author. Gaye Shortland, my editor, who waves her magic wand over my work and makes it sparkle and shine.

I awake every morning – and after checking to see I am still here – I smile. My world is full of wonderful people and fabulous stories. Thank you for allowing me to share them with you.

To the daughter and the dog. The daughter for keeping me supplied with tea. The dog for forcing me to step away from my computer and enjoy the beauty of the world around me.

Chapter 1

Percy Place
Dublin, Ireland

November 1899

"Richard, I am at my wits' end," Georgina Corrigan-Whitmore said. "It is so difficult to prove that one is alive!" She looked across the hearth at her friend and financial advisor Richard Wilson. "Do you have any idea of the number of people who have greeted me with the cry 'But you are dead!' It is quite demoralising."

The two friends were in Georgina's sitting room, a fire blazing cheerily in the hearth.

"I have been giving some thought to the matter, my dear." Richard wanted to free his friend from the coils left by her unlamented late husband, Captain Charles Whitmore. The man had delighted in causing upset for Georgie when alive – even in death he appeared to have left her nothing but trouble.

"I wish you would share your thoughts with me." Georgina stared into the flames.

Her husband had died in a very public manner aboard a train – with a woman listed on the passenger manifest as his wife by his side. Georgina, his legal wife, was suffering the consequences of that act.

At least something good had come from her abusive husband's

demise. Her parents, before their death, had been forced to see the true nature of the man they had chosen as a husband for their only child. They had tied up their estate in such a way that she could not access the funds while married to Captain Whitmore. With his death she was free to receive the monies held in trust for her by the Wilson firm. She no longer had to worry about paying for the coal to heat this house. She could afford to pay her staff. The removal of the constant worry about funds was a great relief.

"I believe, during this difficult time when you have a need to establish your identity, you should carry with you at all times at least three notarised letters from people of unimpeachable standing in society. You have friends in high society, Georgie, use them."

Georgina cringed. "I have not felt truly a part of society for many years, I'm afraid, and I so dislike asking anyone for favours." Her late husband had systematically separated her from everyone she could depend on during their marriage. She had become a shadow of her former self under his cruel fists and demanding ways, creeping around trying desperately not to draw attention to herself – and now this – *her name in the newspapers.*

"You cannot be too delicate in this matter, Georgie. You have recently assisted both the Dowager Duchess of Westbrooke and the Earl of Camlough. You are on first-name terms with a great many prominent people – now is the time to turn to them and ask for their assistance. I do not think the Dowager Duchess and the Earl will quibble about supplying you with written proof that you are the widow and were the legal wife of Captain Charles Whitmore. My father, as your man of affairs, should supply the third affidavit. I'm sure the Earl can request his friend Judge Hartlepool to notarise the documents. You would then hold letters proving beyond doubt that you are indeed who you claim to be, saving you the embarrassment you have experienced lately."

"It all seems so sordid."

"Nevertheless, Georgie, it must be done."

"I will do as you suggest." She had to do something about the situation she found herself in.

Her late husband had died in a train derailment while travelling in a private carriage in the company of the Earl of Castlewellan who had also died in the crash. The accident – which had claimed the lives of many – had received a great deal of attention from the newspaper reporters and updates on the matter appeared frequently in the dailies. A woman, who had been her husband's close companion for a long time before the accident – and indeed was referred to by many as the Captain's wife – also travelled in the Earl of Castlewellan's private carriage. The unfortunate woman's body was identified by the crash investigators and the newspaper reporters as the wife of Captain Whitmore. The legal ramifications of the situation for Georgina were causing ripples that seemed to spread daily.

"I am sorry if it upsets you, Georgie, but the matter must be handled. I believe notarised letters would be ideal. I am sure you will have no trouble getting those you ask to agree. Now, to other matters – Elias Simpson has heard from Whitmore's sons."

"That poor man!" Georgina felt nothing but sympathy for her late husband's man of affairs. He had been left with a legal mess on his hands.

She had been her late husband's third wife, his two previous wives having predeceased him. He had five sons from his first two marriages – sons she became stepmother to – although three were older than she. Four of them were travelling on the high seas in their father's ship – seeking their fortune as it were. Their father had intended to make the voyage with them but was prevented by a terrible accident which led to the amputation of his legs.

"The late captain's sons have decided not to return to Ireland at this time. They have sent Elias a notarised document leaving their affairs in his hands – under the supervision of their brother Edward."

The eldest of Whitmore's sons from his second marriage, Edward had remained in Ireland to safeguard his own inheritance as the future Earl of Camlough. Richard was glad he himself was not tasked to handle these matters – Elias had looked quite worn the last time he'd seen him.

"Charles Whitmore was a miserable husband and to his shame he was not much of a father either." Georgina had suffered through ten years as stepmother. "It doesn't surprise me to learn that none of the sons he sent off on that epic sea voyage he plotted and paid for would bother to return to lay him to rest."

"Edward will have a great deal to handle in his brothers' names," Richard said.

"His grandfather, the Earl of Camlough, will ably assist him I have no doubt." Georgina was grateful to be free of that burden. Her stepsons had not treated her kindly.

"Elias Simpson has asked for a meeting with us two, to discuss your inheritance from your husband."

"I would be surprised if that man hasn't written me out of his will entirely." Georgina wanted nothing to do with her husband or his affairs. She stifled a sigh. She had no option in the matter. She had been married to the man, after all. It was her duty to see his affairs put in order. If only for the five men he had sired.

"I will set up a time to meet that we can all agree on. Now, tell me, what of your strange household?" Richard wanted to change the subject. Georgie had agreed to ask for letters of character and to meet with Elias. He could now relax. He had been afraid she would baulk at the necessity.

"Let us order tea and I shall answer your question." Georgina stood to pull at the embroidered cord and summon a servant.

They waited in silence until Bridget, one of her three orphanage-trained housemaids, answered the bell.

"Tea for two, Bridget, and perhaps Cook has some little treat that Richard would enjoy?"

"She always has!" said Bridget, smiling.

When the girl had departed, Georgina turned to Richard.

"My household?" She laughed. "I sometimes feel I am living in a lunatic asylum. There never seems to be a moment without drama of one kind or another."

"You were forced by circumstances into opening your home to strangers. Do you regret it?"

"There are matters I would and will change. I can appreciate the positive aspects of many of the changes I was forced to make. I was drifting in a strange world during my marriage. I can see that now. I was so afraid, Richard – sure that one of the many beatings I received at the Captain's hands would be the end of me – that fear ruled my every action."

"You were isolated from all of your friends." Richard had tried on many occasions to see Georgina and been rebuffed. He'd stopped trying, much to his shame. He'd had no notion of the life his poor Georgie was living.

"But enough of that. I have the funds now to change things. You know my housekeeper and cook are past retirement age …"

"You surely do not mean to put them out to pasture?" Richard interrupted. "It would break their hearts."

"Not at all." Georgina had been giving a great deal of thought to the matter of servants for her strange household. "Those two women have been with my family since long before my own birth. They have amassed knowledge and skills that they can share with the women who will pass through this house."

"Then you do intend to continue with your work for the BOBs?"

A knock sounded before she could answer.

"Come in!"

Bridget entered with a tea tray. "Sponge cake hot from the oven!" she said.

"Perfect! Thank Cook for us."

Georgina waited until Bridget had placed the tea tray close to hand and left the room before continuing.

"Yes, indeed, I do intend to continue my work with the BOBs," she said as she poured tea into delicate china cups.

"I'm glad to hear it." Richard and his father donated generously to the BOBs. It was a worthwhile cause and something both men believed in passionately.

Georgina could not refuse to help women who needed to escape a difficult home situation – not with her own experience at a less-than-loving husband's hands. She had seen and heard a great deal of the difficulties faced by females since becoming actively involved in the work of the BOBs.

The BOBs, a secret society, was established when the fashionable ladies of the ton had decided to assist members of their gender and class who were in difficulty. Brides of Breeding, BOBs for short, had set up a system which helped women escape into a new life.

Below stairs, the staff and residents of the Percy Place house were busy with the daily chores. Housekeeper Lily Chambers and cook Betty Powell were sitting at a table in the kitchen alcove. The two elderly women – both in their seventies although they would never admit their ages aloud – were enjoying a well-earned pot of tea.

"Do you think the mistress will employ male servants now?" Lily leaned forward to ask.

"Well, she has the money now to employ more servants," Betty answered. "But, you know, Lily, I don't like having male servants under foot. Now, I don't say I haven't missed having footmen and a butler to take some of the work off our shoulders. I'd be a fool to wish more work onto us but … I have enjoyed living in a women-only household – apart from young Liam of course! What would we do without him?" Liam was the house boot boy.

"I'm in two minds about male servants." Lily sipped her tea and looked with fondness around the large kitchen area. "Of course, the installation of those bathrooms and indoor toilets has been amazing – it has reduced a great deal of the work for the maids and boot boy." She shrugged shoulders clad in black bombazine. "Still, I do miss the old days, I will say, and I thought I'd be delighted to have a full staff under my hand again, but …"

"The new way of doing things is not all that bad." Cook knew just what her friend meant. They'd had to learn new ways of working in order to survive with untrained staff and women who came and went through the house.

"I don't know if I'm up to any more changes," Lily said softly. "I'm feeling my age."

"Go away out of that, Lily Chambers! You're not more than three years older than me and I'm feeling full of the joys of life. You've years yet in those bones."

"My bones are aching, Betty," Lily said. "There are days when it hurts to get out of bed." She thanked God daily that her room had been moved from the attic to the basement. She could not have kept on climbing those stairs morning, noon and night.

"More tea, Mrs Chambers?" Ruth Brown asked.

Ruth was one of the three orphans in the house who had been trained by the nuns of the Goldenbridge Orphanage to enter into service in a large household. She was trained as a kitchen maid, Sarah Black as a seamstress while Bridget O'Brien was deemed suitable to serve as a maid of all work. The three young girls were obligated to serve four years of unpaid service – their wages being given to the nuns in part repayment for their years of care. They would receive no wages until they reached the age of sixteen and were placed in permanent positions. In the meantime, they worked for Georgina and slept in the attic of the Percy Place house.

"A fresh pot of tea would be nice." It was Cook who answered. It gave her a tingle to see how fast the kettle boiled on her new gas cooker.

"So many changes!" Lily loved the fact that water was now pumped into the house. No more hauling buckets around. It cut down on the maids' work and her worries. But was she up to dealing with more changes? She didn't know and that was a fact.

"You're like the Mother of Sorrows today." Cook looked at her friend with worried eyes. "What's really bothering you?"

"I hate to leave this house," Lily said slowly. "I've been here since I was a young lass of twelve. The place is my home but, Cook, I don't think I have it in me to keep working for much longer."

"Never!"

"I was thinking of asking Agatha Hancock to take over my duties. She's a trained housekeeper, after all."

Agatha was one of the many women who had found their way to this house seeking help. In Agatha's case, the help she sought was not for herself but a young housemaid in her charge. It was a long and complicated story – one of many the staff had seen since their lady, Georgina, was forced to open her home to waifs and strays.

"She won't do it." Cook shook her head.

"Why ever not? She was a housekeeper for years before she helped Helen Butcher run away. Surely she'd be glad to take up her old profession?"

Agatha and Helen had arrived at the Percy Place house in great distress. Helen was in the family way, having been taken advantage of by the young master of the house where she worked as a maid. Agatha and Helen, like all who found themselves living at the Percy Place house, were expected to lend a hand in the chores needed to keep the house running efficiently.

Cook sat back and waited while Ruth removed the soiled dishes and set the table for a fresh pot of tea. As soon as the young kitchen maid had returned to her duties, she leaned forward to say: "You've noticed how Agatha hangs around that baby? You'd think it was her own son!"

"She's helping Helen." Lily hadn't thought that strange at all – after all, the woman had given up everything she knew to get Helen the help she needed.

"No, she is not." Cook had her own opinion. "Agatha won't be remaining here when that baby leaves this house – you mark my words. That little lad might be only four months old but he has Agatha Hancock wrapped around his little finger." She slapped the table top, rattling the crockery, to emphasise her words.

Chapter 2

Castlewellan
County Down
Northeast Coast of Ireland

"*REBECCA!*" The irritated male voice practically shook the timbers of the old building. "*Where is that girl?*"

Leo Purdey pushed his head deeper into his pillow. Could his son not leave the poor girl alone for even a minute? She was Percival's niece, for goodness' sake! The daughter of his dead sister, a fact he seemed able to forget. Suit him better to shift that lazy lump of a son of his. Rebecca worked harder than any man on the place – the Good Lord knew, she was smarter than all of them put together.

"*FATHER!*"

Leo stifled a sigh. Could Percival not speak in a normal tone of voice? Why did he always have to yell at the top of his lungs? He listened to heavy work boots pounding up the uncarpeted wooden staircase. He tried not to jump when the bedroom door was pushed open with so much force that it beat off the whitewashed wall of his room.

"*Is she here?*" Percival Purdey stood in the doorway, his brown eyes almost burning in his angry face. He was a stocky man, short and muscular like all of the Purdey males.

"I am not yet ready for the Last Rites, son," Leo said softly. "To my knowledge I still have all of my faculties. I am not deaf. Would you mind not shouting and stomping around the place like a bull in a china shop?"

"*I'm looking for that girl!*" Percival was conducting a visual examination of the large master bedroom. He wouldn't put it past the old man to hide the girl. "If I don't keep my eye on her she'll be off somewhere daydreaming."

"Would you care to search under the bed?" What mischief did he think the poor girl could get up to? With her duties as field hand, childminder and nursemaid to an old man, when had the poor girl a minute to call her own? "Perhaps I have her stashed in my dressing room?" He raised a trembling hand and pointed towards the door leading off the room. He hated growing old. How he would love to jump from the bed and box his son's ears for his impertinence! He would do it too if only he was sure he wouldn't fall over and make a fool of himself.

The grandfather clock in the hallway struck the hour, the sound of ten musical chimes carrying up the stairs and through the open door of the room.

"Rebecca will be here shortly to tend to me," Leo said when the last chime sounded. "She is never late in completing her morning chores." He tried not to defend his granddaughter too much – that would only cause more problems for the girl.

"Only because you made her that ridiculous gift of a golden fob watch." Percival grunted and turned to leave the room. He had things to see to. "Tell her to search me out as soon as she has finished here." He stomped off, leaving the door standing open.

Leo closed his eyes at this discourtesy. His son was an angry man and appeared to enjoy sharing his displeasure in life with all around him. It was time to take action. He was being selfish keeping the young woman who brought joy into his life tied to his side. Time to let the bird loose from her cage.

"Your uncle is looking for you, Lady Rebecca," Mrs Agnew, the Purdey family head cook, said as soon as Rebecca stepped into the kitchen.

Rebecca had left her muddy boots in the back hallway, and the knitted toes of her socks peeped out from underneath her heavy brown woollen skirt. She'd spent time in the hallway brushing the caked muck from her hem. How she wished she could wear trousers like the men – so much more convenient when working the land.

"I'll see him later." Rebecca removed her leather gloves, pushing then into her skirt pocket while walking into the scullery.

She greeted the young maid who was washing a veritable mountain of pots and pans. She used some of the warm water from a bucket standing by the sink to wash her hands and face. The family had not yet modernised the house so running water was not available. She dried herself on a piece of towelling the maid passed to her and left the scullery with a smile of thanks.

She strode back into the kitchen, her long legs kicking her skirt forward. "I'll take Grandfather's tray up now, Mrs Agnew."

She looked forward to the time she spent with her grandfather. It sometimes felt like the only time in the day when she could breathe freely. She pressed a hand to the reassuring solidness of the gold fob watch she kept pinned hidden inside her brown cardigan. She checked its position several times a day, terrified of losing something so dear to her. She couldn't leave precious objects in her room – her cousins, since her grandfather's decline in health, appeared to be of the opinion that anything she possessed belonged to them – this was not an attitude she wanted to encourage.

"Someone," a voice announced as the door into the kitchen from the main house was pushed open, "has marched up and down the stairs in muddy boots."

The housekeeper, Hilda Savage, let the door swing shut at her back as she strode into the kitchen, her eyes examining every inch of the space. This large area was the gathering place of the household staff. Maids rushed around while footmen sat at a long table pushed against one wall, polishing silver and crystal.

"Milly," she ordered one of the under maids, "see to cleaning the stairs."

"Yes, Mrs Savage." Milly hurried to obey.

"Lady Rebecca." Hilda put a hand to her thin chest. With a name like Savage and the appearance of a crow, her black uniform covering her from neck to ankle, one could be forgiven for thinking the woman harsh. One would be wrong. Hilda's thin bosom hid a heart of gold. She was very fond of the little cuckoo in their nest. She had watched Lady Rebecca Henderson grow from babyhood into a charming, caring woman. There was little she could do about the difficulties of the life the young woman lived since the master had taken to his bed – but that didn't stop her trying. "Is it time for the master's morning snack already? Time passes swiftly."

She watched Mrs Agnew put the finishing touches to a tray set for two, barking out instructions to her helpers as she worked.

"I had the girl put a tray in your office, Mrs Savage," Mrs Agnew said. "It only needs a fresh pot of tea."

"Thank you, Mrs Agnew." Hilda was satisfied that all was running smoothly. "You had better get that tray up to the master, Lady Rebecca. I know he enjoys having you share a mid-morning break with him." She refused to call the son of the house "master" while the old man still ruled the house from his bed.

"I too enjoy the time we spend together." Rebecca picked up the laden silver tray with no sign of difficulty.

"Don't forget your uncle wants to see you!" Mrs Agnew called after the young woman.

"I won't!" Rebecca had no intention of seeking her uncle out. She'd let him find her.

"Grandfather, why on earth is your door standing wide open?" Rebecca hurried to place the tray on a trolley parked neatly under one of the many windows in the room. She closed the door with a snap. "You'll catch your death of cold." The sickroom had a fire that was kept burning brightly but the draughts in the old house could chill a body.

Leo watched Rebecca push the trolley over to the side of the bed. He enjoyed the sight of the beautiful young woman bustling around the room, seeing to his comfort. The weak winter sun seemed to dance over her golden hair – he envied the strength and grace in her long lean young body.

"I don't have much time – I have much to do today," she said, teasing her grandfather while consulting her watch with pride. Her green eyes glistened with laughter when she caught his eye.

"You have as much time as I say you do!" Leo snapped. He was still master of this house, no matter what his son believed.

"Feeling our mettle today, are we?" Rebecca held the old man's body forward with one hand while struggling with the bed pillows with the other. She bunched the thick feather pillows high, allowing her grandfather to sit up in the bed without strain.

"I'll have none of your sass, young lady," Leo grumped. He adored the cheeky grin she gave him at his words.

Rebecca poured the tea. Taking a smaller, lighter tray from the lower shelf of the trolley, she placed a cup of tea and a buttered scone on it and placed it on Leo's lap. She had been on the go since early morning and was glad of a chance to sit down by the trolley and enjoy sharing the food Mrs Agnew had sent up to tempt the invalid's appetite. She ignored her grandfather's curses while he struggled to eat and drink, but lent a hand without comment whenever he'd allow it.

"Sit close by me," Leo said when the trolley had been returned to its place under the window, the chair back in its place by the bed.

"I have to go, Grandfather." Rebecca didn't want her uncle to catch her slacking.

"*Sit down, I said!*" Leo had been putting off this talk for years but it was time – and past time – to tell this young woman the truth.

"My uncle –"

"I'll deal with my son. I'm not dead yet. Sit down."

He waited until she sat on the chair beside his bed and took his trembling hand. He looked at the long, elegant fingers wrapped around his own roughened, swollen ones. The lump in his throat was almost choking him.

"It is time for you to leave this place," he forced out through lips that felt frozen.

"Leave!" Rebecca gasped.

"You must." Leo closed his eyes, unwilling to see the pain and bewilderment on her beautiful face.

"But why, Grandfather? What have I done?" Rebecca bit her lower lip to stop it trembling. Had her beloved grandfather lost his mind to the dreadful disease ravaging his body? Why on earth would he say she needed to leave the only home she had ever known?

"You were always asking why when you were little." He fought the unmanly tears. "It almost drove me wild at times."

"*But why …*" She wondered if she should have the housekeeper summon the doctor. Her grandfather was behaving very strangely.

15

"Your cousin Peregrine is to marry Lavinia Carson." Leo ignored the horror Rebecca was unable to conceal. "I know what your life has become in this house, child. Do you think I am blind and deaf?" He was so angry at the treatment his grandchild had received at the hands of his family since his illness. She was a lady born and they were attempting to turn her into a servant. The sheer gall of his son and grandson infuriated him. There was little he could do about it, however, as he withered away in this bedroom that had become his prison.

"I could protect you from my son and his family when I was still hale and hearty." His deep sigh shook the body that no longer followed his commands. The shaking disease had eaten away at his body and his pride. "But I will be unable to protect you from the cruelties of your cousin and his fiancé. He will use you – use your knowledge of this property and the business that has supported this family in fine style for generations. I spent years forcing knowledge on the running of this property into your head!" He smiled with delight when she glared. "Lavinia will abuse you – while smiling charmingly – we both know it! *I will not have it.*" He clenched his teeth while his body shook uncontrollably.

"Do not upset yourself, I beg of you." Rebecca hated to see her beloved grandfather reduced to this shaking wreck. What a horrible disease to rob a man such as her grandfather of his dignity! "Grandfather, why do they hate me so?" She had asked many times before without ever receiving an answer. She wanted to know why – she deserved to know that at least. "What have I done?"

"Oh, my sweet child," Leo choked, "you have done nothing. You are the innocent in all of this." It was not her fault she was beautiful, titled and wealthier in her own right than her cousins.

"Please explain, Grandfather," Rebecca pleaded. "I need to understand."

Chapter 3

"Clive Henderson, the Earl of Castlewellan is dead," Leo said, his voice whisper-soft.

"Has his death been confirmed?" Rebecca asked. The neighbouring and much larger estate belonging to the Earl had been in an uproar for weeks, with gossip and conjecture flying around the local area. To her knowledge no official statement had yet been issued.

"Yes, his private railway carriage was involved in that terrible train derailment some weeks ago."

"How will his death affect me?" She knew who the Earl was – she had worried and wondered how his death would affect her ever since hearing news of the accident. She had hidden her fears, not wanting to upset her grandfather.

"He was your father." Leo had never tried to hide the connection – how could he when the man insisted on visiting his child? He had controlled those visits – by heck, he had – the man was never allowed to be alone with the child. The Purdey family might not be as high up the social ladder as the Earl but they were wealthy, respected landowners. He had protected his grandchild to the best of his ability.

The Earl had been a danger to Rebecca when he was alive – in death he posed an even bigger risk. She could now be used as a pawn in the legal battle to secure his estate.

"My late mother's husband." Through the years Rebecca had been told bits and pieces of her origins. Was she going to hear the full story at last?

"He sired you, child, and there is nothing either of us can do to change that fact." He waved one trembling hand from her head to her toes. "Look at you – you are the very image of him." Though he thanked the Lord nightly that she had never shown any of the evil that man's beauty hid inside.

"Grandfather ..."

"Hush, child," Leo closed his eyes briefly then snapped them open again to stare into her beloved face. "It was the worst mistake I made in my life, allowing my youngest daughter to marry that man – you know this – I have told you often enough through the years." He rested back against the pillows, longing to escape into sleep.

"You have never explained to me, though, why you feared the man." Rebecca had always known that the Earl was her sire. He had visited her grandfather's estate throughout her childhood, bringing with him fear and upset – but she had never known why!

"Listen then." He refused to close his eyes. He wanted to see her face when he told her of the mistakes of his past. "Clive Henderson, the Earl – though he had not come into the title then – laid siege to my poor Delores' heart." He sighed as he remembered. "She was such a silly little thing but I didn't mind that – she was female – she was supposed to be silly or so I had been raised to believe." He hadn't made the same mistake with his granddaughter. He had insisted on her being raised to use her natural abilities. No daydreaming about ribbons and ball dresses for Rebecca! "My mouth is dry, child."

18

He waited while Rebecca poured a glass of water from a nearby urn. He suffered the indignity of her holding the glass for him while wishing for something stronger to drink. There would be time enough for that when he had set his plans in motion.

"Their courtship was the talk of the county," he continued when he had moistened his mouth. "Your grandmother could not hide her delight that one of her daughters had caught the eye of such a worthy suitor. It was a step up socially for the Purdey family and my wife revelled in her new status. It was all balls and picnics. The neighbourhood celebrated the joyous event in style."

"It sounds delightful," Rebecca prompted him when he seemed lost in thought.

"We did not see our daughter for some time after the wedding but we were not concerned." He cringed when he remembered his failure to protect his child. "We were not concerned," he repeated. "They were very young and newly married – such a perfect couple – or so everyone believed."

"Grandfather …"

"Get me a whiskey, child. I cannot tell this tale on water …"

Rebecca almost ran to the table that held the decanters of strong spirits and glasses. She poured a generous measure of whiskey and carried it back to the bed.

"That's better!" Leo smacked his lips as the strong spirit burned down his gullet. He continued with his tale. "Delores appeared on our doorstep one day." He fought tears and won. "She was a shadow of the child we had watched dance down the aisle." His daughter had been carried to the door in the arms of a servant – wrapped like a package in a cloak belonging to Mrs Daniels – a formidable woman who was a close neighbour. Mrs Daniels had forced her way into the Earl's house when refused access to the new bride one too many times.

"Mrs Daniels … your godmother …" he signalled for more whisky, "it was she who rescued your mother." He had never forgotten the big-eyed stares of young Allegra and Horatia Daniels – as they sat in the family carriage, listening to their mother berate him. They were only babies then – how quickly the years passed!

Rebecca didn't try to speak as silence fell once more on the room. What could she say? She had known none of this.

"That man had abused my daughter in a fashion I could never have imagined and wish to God that I had never seen."

At first, Leo had thought to send his daughter back to her lawful husband. She belonged to him as the law of the land stated. That was until Mrs Daniels had insisted on showing him the scars that covered his poor daughter's scantily clad body. He tried to close his ears as his daughter told of the horrors inflicted on her by a man who was supposed to protect her. The words had made him sick to his stomach but he couldn't deny the evidence of his own eyes.

"I summoned a doctor and a skilled local female artist to record my girl's injuries. I couldn't send for the Justice of the Peace – that position was held by the old earl – but I did send for him in his role of father and demanded he chastise his son. I showed him the evidence of his son's crime against his wife. It did no good. That young man stood before us quite unaffected by our shock and horror. I threatened him with scandal and he laughed. The old earl would not consider divorce." The drawings of his daughter's wounds were stored in his safe. He had never been able to look at them but he kept them close to hand in case of need.

Rebecca could well imagine the scene. The Earl had been everything that was charming – if slightly condescending – to her during his visits. It was obvious – to her at least – that the man was accustomed to all around him bowing down before him.

"I demanded and it was agreed your mother would recuperate from her injuries in my house." Leo had wanted to pound the young man into the ground but did nothing.

Later, Mrs Daniels had told him of an organisation that would help to make his daughter disappear – get her safely away and help her make a new life for herself. They had put plans in place to make that happen. Mrs Daniels had been a tower of strength and support to him in his hour of need. The situation with his daughter was outside his sphere of experience. He needed all of the help he could get to correct the mistake he had made in giving his child into the hands of a monster.

"Then it was discovered Delores was with child," he continued.

They couldn't tell his daughter of their plans for her. She became hysterical whenever the subject of her future was mentioned.

"I argued for Delores to remain with her family while she carried what might well have been the future heir to the earldom."

He'd been surprised when the old earl allowed this but he had argued long and hard to keep his child by his side. The man had not only damaged her body, he had ruined her mind. His child had to be tended to like a baby – forced to eat – forced to dress – forced to even leave her bedroom. She was like a ghost of her former self, drifting from day to day never seeming really to be aware of the world around her. It had broken her mother's heart.

"My mother died giving birth to me," Rebecca whispered.

"So she did." Leo agreed with her words but in his heart he believed his daughter had died the first time that man had carved into her flesh with a knife. She had never recovered from his cruelties.

Mrs Daniels had offered to take the baby away but he couldn't bear to part with her. The first time Rebecca had gripped his finger in her little hand and smiled at him he'd lost his heart to her. She was his from that moment on.

21

"I've been selfish, child."

"Grandfather, no!"

"*Yes!* I should have sent you away when I was still a fine figure of a man. I couldn't bear to part with you. Now …well, child … it is time for you to flee." He held up a shaking hand to stop her speaking. "Plans have been in place since you were sixteen years old but I kept putting off this moment. You are nineteen years old, Rebecca – a woman grown. I had prayed to remain sound of mind and body until you reached your twenty-first year – alas, it was not to be."

"I don't want to leave you, Grandfather." She took the empty glass and put it on the bedside table.

"Listen to me!" He grabbed her hand. "The doctor wants me to agree to take laudanum."

"You are in a great deal of pain, Grandfather. The laudanum would help."

"If I agree to take the dread concoction, I may as well agree to lose my mind. I have already lost my body." He had not done well by this child of his heart. How many young swains had he sent on their way with a flea in their ear? It would have been kinder to allow her to make her own choices but he hadn't dared. Not while her father lived. The Earl would never have agreed to a union he had not sanctioned and that might well have removed Rebecca from his life altogether. Selfish – that's what he was.

"Grandfather …"

"I grow weary …" Leo couldn't bear to drag out this moment any longer. "You are to ride over to Mrs Daniels. You must be sure to take your horse and your dog with you. They were gifts from her, after all." He tried to hide the trembling in his voice – this was breaking his heart.

"Why must I do this? I don't understand, Grandfather!" Rebecca tried not to wail.

"You are a wealthy young woman. So wealthy, in fact, that it would not matter to some if you were ugly as a newt. You, my dear, are a prize plum on the marriage market. I have hidden you away with a great deal of difficulty. You must flee or find yourself the object of every fortune hunter in this area, not to mention London." He sighed deeply, remembering the many arguments he'd had with the Earl about presenting Rebecca to polite society. "You should have had a London season upon your eighteenth birthday and been presented at court. My son, your own uncle, will not hesitate to make coin off the wealth you would bring to any suitor who claimed your hand in marriage."

"I have no wish to marry and leave you, Grandfather."

"You must leave while I still have full use of my mind" He could bear no more of this soul-searching. "I had Mrs Savage assist me in packing the jewels you inherited from your mother and some of your fancy clothing, puss. Mrs Savage is a wonder, as you well know. Under my supervision she managed to pack two chests and, in a way we have never discussed, she had those two chests delivered to the Daniels house as soon as rumours of the Earl's untimely death began to circulate in the area."

"You have been busy, Grandfather." Rebecca had noticed the disappearance of her best clothing but thought the maid had removed the garments – she had outgrown most if not all of them. The jewels were kept in her grandfather's safe in his study, the combination for opening it known only to him as far as she was aware.

"You must leave now. I want to know you are safely away before I give in to the doctor's appeals."

"What of the estate?" She had been a part of the Purdey family business for years and almost in total control since her grandfather had taken to his bed.

"My son and his family were given the same instruction and education as you. It is not your fault nor mine that they choose to waste their days in idleness. They can sort out the business between them when I am gone. You and I will not be here to see it."

"Grandfather …" She didn't know what to say or do.

They stared at each other, neither willing to end what might be the last time they were ever together. Rebecca wondered that the sound of their breaking hearts did not echo around the room.

"Ring the bell for Mrs Savage." Leo gestured towards a long board affixed to the bedroom wall. The silver bell-pulls set into the board were kept highly polished. There was a similar board in the wall of the kitchen. Each bell-pull had a staff position written underneath. A bell would chime in the kitchen, signalling the master's call. "Someone needs to remove that tray and carry hot water up here and I have need of my valet."

"I can —"

"No, you cannot." Leo didn't want to give his son a chance to lay hands on Rebecca. While she was in his room, she was safe. "We have servants for fetching and carrying."

Rebecca went to obey her grandfather's order. She was frightened. She had been born on the Purdey family estate – lived all of her life here – what was to become of her?

Chapter 4

"Where do you think you are going?"

Rebecca almost groaned aloud at the sound of her uncle's shout. She had almost made her escape. It had broken her heart to leave her grandfather and creep down the servants' staircase and out of the house. Now she would have to face this – her final time, she prayed – of butting heads with her uncle.

"I left word I wanted to see you – were you not told?"

Rebecca wondered often if her uncle was suffering from hearing loss. Surely if his hearing was sound, he would know how unpleasant his constant banging and shouting were to those around him.

"I'm in a hurry, Uncle." She ignored his demand. She was not answerable to her uncle. "Mrs Daniels sent word that she needs a display of dahlia for her table and entryway." She had gathered the beautiful autumnal blooms herself and wrapped them in moist hessian for the ride over to the neighbouring estate.

"Waste of good money – bloody fruit and flowers." Percival Purdey took a deep breath, preparing to lecture yet again on his disdain for the family business. "Sheep and cows, that's what we should be raising not bloody flowers!"

"As you say, Uncle." Rebecca wondered what would happen to the flower, fruit and seed business – set up by her maternal ancestors – when she left. "I need to deliver these flowers while the blooms are still at their best." She saw the stable boy lead her saddled horse from the barn and almost groaned. She had been so close to escaping.

"*I want you back here in quick order!*" her uncle shouted. "*There are things we need to discuss, girl. There will be changes made when I take charge here, I can tell you. No more running all over the countryside making special deliveries for you, my girl! I'll soon put a halt to your gallop. See if I don't!*"

"Yes, Uncle." Rebecca looked at the flowers in her arms. It was fitting somehow that they were the very last of the blooms. She'd nurtured them carefully to make the flowers last in the cold. She was aware of her uncle's ranting but wasn't listening to his words. She was heart-sore and didn't care what the man might have planned for her.

"Taunton is coming to pay his respects to you tomorrow. You better be dressed all fancy and waiting for him." He watched her follow the stable boy to the mounting block.

She put the flowers in a contraption she'd had made to carry them. The horse stood still while she fiddled about, making sure the flowers were protected for their journey. When she was seated – side-saddle as was only decent – and her skirts arranged, she stared down at him with those witch-like green eyes.

He longed to slap the horse hard and pray the fool woman would break her neck. She'd been a thorn in his side for years. But things were changing. The old man couldn't last much longer. He'd soon have this cheeky upstart where he wanted her. See how she liked it then!

"Yes, Uncle." Her stomach heaved at the very thought of greeting that old man with his sweaty hands and foul-smelling breath. "*Dandy!*" She whistled for her old dog.

"And that's another thing, girl." Percival had to have the last word. "That old dog does nothing but eat and sleep. I'm not paying for his feeding anymore."

"Yes, Uncle." Rebecca gave her mare its head, glad to escape her uncle's presence.

"Rebecca!" Josephine Daniels turned at the sound of the horse's hooves. She'd been enjoying the cold but bright day – taking the time to ensure that her beloved garden was safe in its winter sleep. She removed her gardening gloves and dropped them onto the trowel at her feet. She had been expecting this visitor ever since she heard of the Earl of Castlewellan's death.

"Godmother, I have been ordered by my grandfather to disappear!" Rebecca said dramatically.

"Is it that time, my dear?" Josephine's heart broke for the young woman but this day had been a long time in coming. "*Tim!*" she shouted for her devoted jarvey.

He quickly arrived and Rebecca waited until he had a close grip on the reins before she dismounted.

"Take the dog with you, Tim," Josephine ordered. "I shall have more instructions for you soon no doubt – stay close to the house."

The two women were sitting in a private sitting room on the first floor of the Daniels' home. The windows overlooked the entrance and would give them warning if anyone approached. Josephine's family knew not to disturb her when she had closed the door to this room. It was her business office and one had to receive an invitation to enter.

"Now, tell me all." Josephine said.

"Grandfather …" Rebecca had to stop as her chest hurt. "He has ordered me to disappear. He said you would know what needs to be done."

"Indeed, we have been planning this day for a long time, your grandfather and I."

"My uncle knows I am here. He discovered me in the stable yard – I pretended I was preparing to deliver flowers to you."

"Those beautiful dahlias?" Josephine had long been envious of this young woman's ability to grow the most stunning flowers. "You need to make floral arrangements for the house. I have no doubt your uncle or one of his servants will arrive on my doorstep when you do not return home. I must have something to show him when I explain you were here but left."

"Very well. I am at a loss as to why I need to disappear. My uncle is trying to marry me off to old Mr Taunton. Imagine! But surely I can say no and be done with it? Why must I run away – and now – with Grandfather so ill?" Rebecca had to force herself not to wail like a baby.

"Oh, if only it were that simple!" Josephine was mentally planning what needed to be done to keep this young woman safe. "You, according to the rule of the land, are under the control of the males in your life. No one is free to aid you." She leaned over and pressed one hand over the white-knuckled fists clenched in Rebecca's lap. "You will have to say goodbye to your horse and dog, I'm afraid." She couldn't offer to keep the animals here.

Rebecca could swear she felt her heart break further.

"I advised your grandfather to discuss these matters with you, but he was adamant in his refusal." Josephine hated to see the decline of such a good man. That dreadful shaking disease could take years to destroy the body it had invaded. She sighed deeply – such was life and one simply had to learn to live with it. "I have a great many documents and instructions for you, my dear, but not today." She stood and offered her hand to Rebecca. "Come along – you need to arrange those flowers and then, my dear – I am so terribly sorry – but you must bid farewell to your pets. They must be removed from my estate before any can think to look for you here."

"What will happen to them?" Rebecca felt numb.

"I have an old friend a goodly distance from here who will be glad of their company."

"Dandy is not fit to walk a long distance." Rebecca felt immense pain at the very thought of leaving her pets – how much more would she be forced to bear?

"Tim will take them in the horsebox but he must leave soon." Josephine sighed. "We must hide you."

The Daniel's family home had a well-concealed priest hole, situated between the bedrooms of her two daughters. Allegra and Horatia knew of their mother's work with the BOBs. They would assist in keeping their friend hidden.

Rebecca lay on a mat positioned on the floor of the small space set aside to conceal priests when they were being persecuted in the old days. She had refused food and drink, wanting only to be alone to wallow in the sorrow she had been forced to endure this day. Sleep was impossible as she wondered and worried about her future.

Why had she never planned for this day? She should have known this day was coming. When her grandfather took to his bed and her uncle and cousins began to treat her with open contempt – why had she never considered leaving?

Before being hidden away in this dark, damp hidey-hole she had brushed and groomed her horse and dog with tears streaming down her face – unable to bear the fact that she would never see them again. Folly, the mare, had been with her for years. Dandy, her beloved rascal of a dog, had long been her faithful companion. They wouldn't

29

understand why she had disappeared. She prayed that they would be treated with love and kindness in their new lives.

She worried about the fate of the family business. The families of their tenant farmers had worked for the Purdeys for generations. How could she not worry about people who had served her grandfather faithfully? The women who tended the flowers and seedlings. The men who tilled the earth. The drivers who delivered their fruit and flowers to the railway line early each morning. Their loyal customers. What would happen to them if her uncle carried out his oft-repeated threat to plough under all the blooms and seedlings his family had spent generations nursing?

She bit down on her knuckles. The very thought of the destruction of such sweet-smelling beauty caused her actual physical pain. Surely her uncle would not be foolish enough to destroy a well-established family business that had supported him and his family for generations? At the very least he would keep their famous orchards. Or would he? Her uncle was such an angry man. He was capable of anything while in one of his furies. Would he even wait until his father died before destroying his own heritage? If she'd had the time, there were so many cherished cuttings and seedlings she would have carried away with her.

She was desperately trying not to think of her beloved grandfather. He would be at the mercy of his son now. It had hurt so much when he commanded her to leave. She had grown up following on his heels. It was his work-stained hands that covered her much smaller hands as he taught her to plant seedlings. He had encouraged her to care for and love the land and its bounty. The days spent with him – in memory – were always sunny. He had taught her so much. She had looked up to him – thought him a giant amongst men. How they had laughed when she grew taller than him!

How was one expected to live through so much pain? She imagined she could feel her heart bleeding in her breast. How would she survive?

She owed it to her grandfather to make the best of her life. To take all he had taught her and flourish in the new life she was to step into – so he had commanded. But, oh dear Lord, how could she bear it?

She heard Allegra and Horatia preparing for the evening. It must be later than she thought. There was no light in this little space but the sound of maids jumping to obey their mistress's demands carried through from either side of her. The two young women she had studied music, art, and dance with knew she was there but not for a moment did their words and actions reveal that knowledge.

Chapter 5

Percy Place
Dublin

Georgina blew gently over the cup of steaming chocolate in her hand. The five older women of the Percy Place house were sitting in the staff sitting room, enjoying hot chocolate before retiring for the evening. Georgina, Lily, Betty, the lodger Dorothy Lawler and Flora Kilroy, the youngest by far of the women and a distant relative of Georgina's, had fallen into the habit of enjoying a hot drink and conversation at the end of the day.

"Ladies, the Babington-Hawthorns, while having a marvellous time appearing to the world as barge folk, wish to leave Dublin and resume their place in society." The couple had arrived in Dublin on a barge and had delighted in playing the role of barge folk until the arrival of cold weather took the pleasure out of it and they fled to other accommodation.

Ethan Babington-Hawthorn was the natural father of Helen Butcher's child. Ethan had been drugged and tricked by his own father into accosting their housemaid. The Babington-Hawthorns – a delightful couple mortified by the circumstances – offered to adopt the baby who was the result of that shameful act and raise it as their own. They had offered Helen a goodly sum for her troubles.

"What's going to happen to Agatha and Helen when the Babington-Hawthorns leave?" Lily Chambers wondered aloud. Agatha had stopped joining them in the evenings since the birth of Helen's child. "It will break Agatha's heart if they take that baby away from her. Then there's Helen …" Lily didn't wish to speak ill of the young woman who'd had her fair share of heartache but, dear Lord, she did enjoy her tragic position within the household. She'd been paid well to give up her baby to a couple who could give him a far better life than any of them had ever known. She'd been paid richly to act as wet nurse for her own child – a child she'd never wanted.

"I had thought to eventually offer them both positions within this household," Georgina said. "But … now I'm not at all sure if that would be suitable."

"Should I be here for this?" Dorothy asked. "I am, after all, only the lodger." Dorothy, the mother of adult twin sons, was desperately trying to recover her financial security after the death of her husband. She was in Dublin to take control of the factory that had been in her family for generations. She too was a refugee seeking comfort in the Percy Place house.

"You are a member of my strange household," Georgina replied. "And, as such, your opinion is valued."

"Well, then …" Dorothy enjoyed these evening chats and tried not to let her acerbic personality reign here, but she'd had quite enough of Miss Helen Butcher and her many problems. "I believe Agatha will offer her services to the Babington-Hawthorns. As Lily has stated – Agatha will not wish to be far from that baby. Helen, however, is a different kettle of fish altogether. I would not employ her but the need for qualified staff in your home is glaringly obvious."

"I have tried to talk to Helen about her future." Flora didn't understand the woman. They were of an age but vastly different personalities. She felt great sympathy for Helen – after all, there but for the grace of God went she – it could so easily have been her with a baby she didn't want or feel able to care for. But she'd like to believe she'd have been more active in deciding her own future. "Molly," she mentioned another young woman residing in the house, elder sister to Liam their boot boy, "believes Helen is vastly enjoying her starring role in her own tragic opera!" She almost giggled. Molly had no time or patience for the woman she shared a room with.

"She has a good head on her shoulders, young Molly." Dorothy was paying for Molly to lodge and study in this house. She took an interest in the girl's progress. "I think we need to consider Helen's changed circumstances. She has been given a nice little nest-egg. Surely we can find her a husband who will cater to her every need?"

"That is certainly an option I hadn't considered," Georgina said when the silence in the room stretched uncomfortably.

"I believe Billy Flint would be the person to consult on the matter," Dorothy said.

Cook felt the need to say something. "What would we do without that young man? He can't be more than one and twenty, yet he has an old man's head on his shoulders."

"I will give all you have said careful consideration." Georgina paused for a moment and looked around at the women whom she considered friends. "As to the matter of staff – I agree that this house is in dire need of trained staff. It is no longer necessary to work ourselves to a standstill every day." There was no need to explain to everyone that the money she could now freely access came from her parents. It was an unusual bequest, but Richard and his father had tightly held those funds in trust for when Georgina might need them.

There were polite noises, but no one commented.

"I did not wish evil upon Charles Whitmore." Georgina stared into her cup. "I am having difficulty accepting that the death of that man – a man I exchanged marriage vows with – has brought good fortune to my door. His death – the nature of it – has brought a great many problems also."

Flora had assisted in the writing of letters to request written proof of Georgina's identity. She'd seen how difficult all of this was for her relative – a woman who had taken her in on her word alone. She felt a great debt to this woman who had opened her door to someone she had never met who claimed a family connection.

"I'm sorry," Dorothy didn't want the conversation to degenerate into wails and moans, "but what has this to do with staff shortages?"

"It means that I can now afford to employ the additional staff we need." Georgina sat up straight in her chair. "Thank you, Dorothy."

"For ..."

"The gentle kick in the rear!" Georgina almost laughed. She had discovered that this woman – her lodger – accepted no shilly-shallying. "Now, the matter of staff. Do we wish to employ male staff?"

There was silence as each woman waited for someone else to speak.

Finally, it was Flora who spoke. "I can offer no opinion on this matter. I have never been in a position to employ staff." The story of Flora's life before coming to this house would bring tears to the eyes of a corpse. She had never allowed that to keep her from improving her circumstances when given the chance.

"Betty and I were talking about this just the other day." Lily had hoped to have this conversation in private with her mistress. "If you are employing more staff, Miss Georgina ..." Since the death of her husband her young mistress had insisted on being referred to as "Miss Georgina" – she had no wish to be reminded of her ill-fated marriage. "I think it's time you found a new housekeeper." She was forced to

35

put her cup on a nearby table as her hands shook too much to hold it.

There were murmurs of surprise and shock.

"This house would cease to function without you, Lily." Georgina wanted to hug the older woman but didn't dare. She could tell Lily was holding on to her composure by the skin of her teeth.

"I'm feeling me age, Miss Georgina." Lily kept her eyes on her hands clenched in her lap. "I'm not up to the work anymore." She lifted her eyes to stare at the woman she'd seen grow from a tiny baby. "I don't want to let you down."

"Does this house require a butler and footmen?" Dorothy interrupted before the room could be reduced to tears. She thought the staff were handling the running of the house admirably. "Surely having live-in male staff would cause problems in a house set up for women fleeing difficult situations? I have enjoyed living in an all-female household." She thought it would be a shame to change things. "Men, no matter their rank or situation in life, appear to believe that their word is law."

"That's a fact." Betty's chins wagged in agreement with her nodding head. "Them footmen and that butler we had before everything changed – they thought they were a step above everyone else."

"Ladies," Georgina tapped a fingernail against her cup, "we are getting off topic." She looked around the gathering.

"We need trained housemaids," Lily said. "We've put too much on the shoulders of those three young maids – not to mention young Liam. We need staff who know what is required to run a gentlewoman's household." She'd been longing for someone to take some of the weight off her shoulders. "I had thought to ask young Helen but …"

"That young woman is fine if you tell her what to do, where to go,

36

what to think." Dorothy hadn't asked to be part of this discussion but, since she was, she'd have her say. "She has no 'get up and go' – young Bridget has more sense in her head than Helen ever thought of having." She was convinced a good man was what Helen wanted and needed.

"I agree with you." There had been times when Lily wanted to box that young woman's ears. Surely she hadn't always been as dozy as she appeared. Yes, what happened to her was sad, but she wasn't the first to be taken advantage of and she wouldn't be the last. "I had thought to speak with Agatha, but Cook had her say on that!"

"As we've already said and I believe, Agatha will follow wherever that baby goes," Betty said.

There were nods of agreement.

"So, if we are to employ more staff we will have to look outside this house," Georgina said. "Molly," she mentioned a young woman presently being trained in the house, "has already informed me that she has no intention of going into service." It would have been ideal to employ Helen and Molly – the two young women already living in the house – but that was not to be.

"Anyone you employ will have to learn a new way of doing things." Dorothy had been shocked at first by the running of this household. The three young maids ordered and instructed the young women who passed through the door. "I'm afraid employing staff for your household will not be an easy matter – maids are not usually encouraged to think for themselves."

"There are also the concerns about secrecy." Lily had thought of that in her desire for additional staff. "If and when we increase the number of household staff – we also increase the danger of the happenings of this house being spoken about amongst the new staff members' cronies. That is not something we desire."

"You have all given me a great deal to think about." Georgina was tired. "It is late and I am wanting my bed." She stood and put the empty mug on a nearby tray.

"Everything will look better in the morning." Betty stood to gather the mugs. "At least, that's what I've always heard."

The women spent time restoring order to the room before wishing each other goodnight.

Chapter 6

"Thank you for agreeing to meet with me," Elias Simpson said as he was shown into Richard's city office. He looked from Richard to Georgina. "I must apologise for the delay in contacting you about your husband's affairs, Mrs Whitmore." He still wasn't completely sure he had all the facts and figures at his fingertips. The late Captain Whitmore had played fast and loose with the laws of the land in his financial dealings. He'd been a canny operator. The estate was giving him and his accounting staff nightmares.

Richard stood to greet his guest and they shook hands. "I've ordered tea to be served, Elias. I hope we will not have need of something stronger."

"I am sure we will get through this together – without resorting to strong drink," Georgina said, greeting her husband's man of affairs with a smile. If Charles Whitmore hadn't driven her to strong drink while alive, she refused to allow him to bedevil her now he was dead. She waited while the two men walked across the room to join her at the long table pulled up to the tall windows. The table would be needed for what she imagined would be a small mountain of papers.

Elias began to empty his bulging Gladstone briefcase onto the end of the table furthest from Georgina. He would need the space. "Captain Whitmore's last will and testament is a rather simplistic document in light of recent developments." He pulled at the stiff collar of his shirt. He hated to be unsure of his findings. He needed this woman's assistance in handling some of the documents left in his care.

"Perhaps it would be easiest if you first told me how I have been placed with the death of my husband?" Georgina didn't expect to inherit anything but headaches from her husband's estate. "The man did have five adult sons after all."

"That's just it, dear lady." Elias almost fell into the chair placed by his side.

He was grateful for the knock on the door and the chance to collect his composure that the entrance of a servant with the requested tea gave him. He wanted to drop his aching head into his hands and groan but contented himself with watching the tea tray being placed close to Mrs Whitmore's hand.

He continued after the servant had left the room. "The wording of the will is such that I am unsure of my late client's wishes. He added a rather nasty codicil concerning Georgina Corrigan ..." He held up one hand when the lady looked like speaking. "However, there is a great deal of property purchased and registered in the name of Mrs Captain Charles Whitmore and all here must agree – legally that is yourself."

"Dear Lord!" Georgina paused in the pouring of tea, aghast at this latest development.

"What concerns you about this?" Richard took a cup of tea and saucer from Georgina and passed it to Elias. He accepted a second cup and placed it on the table in front of his chair.

"I do apologise, dear lady," Elias said, "but Captain Whitmore escorted a lady around proclaiming to all that she was his wife – now there is no paperwork to substantiate this claim – however, there may well have been grounds for this woman to claim a portion of the estate as the Captain's recognised common-law wife. I believe at the time of the writing of this will that the Mrs Captain Charles Whitmore mentioned in the last will and testament of my client is in fact this other woman." He wanted to bang his head off the table in frustration. How was a man supposed to deal with something this unsavoury?

"The unfortunate woman who died in the crash with him." Georgina shuddered at the thought.

"That may well be the case," Richard said, "but Georgie was the Captain's legal wife and as such those properties now belong to her." The man had probably used Georgie's dowry money to purchase those properties. It was the kind of thing that would have amused him. He, however, was determined to see that Georgie received something for the years of abuse she had suffered at that man's hands. "Has someone come forward to make a claim against the estate?"

"Not at this time." Elias had insisted the poor woman's name appeared in an altered list of those who died in that terrible train crash. He had issued cheques monthly in the woman's name for years.

"If you can tell me – without going into any details – how were his sons left?" Georgina had not been treated kindly by her husband's sons but nonetheless they deserved something from their father's estate.

"The expedition your late husband funded was very expensive." Elias felt it would not be a breach of confidence to share some of the details. The Whitmore men had left Dublin in a ship funded by their father. The late captain believed that a vast fortune was to be made on the planned voyage. "The two eldest sons, Charles and George, have been left equal shares in the ship. The three youngest,

41

the children of his second marriage have each been left sums of money and a memento, but the bulk of the estate is deeded to Mrs Captain Charles Whitmore." Elias gulped the cooling tea.

"For goodness' sake!" Georgina gasped. "What does that mean?"

"The properties, monies, bonds and investments," Elias pulled at his collar again, feeling heat rise to his face, "are all to go to Mrs Captain Charles Whitmore. I drew up the document. The," he coughed politely into his fist, "lady was present when the document was drawn up and insisted on seeing the final typewritten version. I had the strong impression that she had somehow coerced the Captian into writing the will." She had talked openly of the Captain's plans to divorce his weak weed of a wife. That woman had her eye very much on the prize. If he understood anything about this outrageous affair, she believed she would one day be legally Mrs Captain Charles Whitmore. She was, he felt, what Dubliners would call a 'cute whore'. She had insisted on seeing that she would be well cared for if something were to happen to her – well, whatever the Captain had been to her. The law – because of the number of royal children born outside a legal union – had been forced to recognise 'unusual' arrangements in a way not discussed in polite society.

"It is all so dreadfully sordid." Georgina buried her face in her teacup – mortified.

"I did not, at that time, believe my client was going to let the document stand!" He was sure that Whitmore had bowed to the woman's demands simply to keep her quiet and planned to change the document at his earliest convenience. That had not occurred before death claimed him – and now Elias was left with the nightmare of sorting out this nasty tangle.

"So," Richard passed his cup to Georgie for a refill, "as it stands Georgina Corrigan Whitmore, his legal wife, inherits everything." He

42

wanted to laugh aloud. The man had been caught in a trap of his own making.

"I agree." Elias thought Georgina deserved everything she could get for the abuse she had suffered while married to that abusive man. He had witnessed the result of some of that abuse himself.

"My head is whirling," Georgina said. "This is not at all what I was expecting when this meeting was arranged." She looked at Richard. His family firm handled her finances.

"I have documents that require your signature." Elias gestured towards the mound of papers on the table in front of him. "I would advise you to consult your man of business before signing anything, however."

"If Georgie agrees," Richard said, "you may leave the documents with me. I will consult my father. He is a man of vast experience in these matters. I have no doubt he will wish to study the items in detail."

"Richard's family firm have handled my family's finances for generations," Georgina said, in case Elias was unaware of this fact.

"I would appreciate the advice of someone of your father's experience and reputation, Richard." Elias didn't feel qualified to handle the tangle left by Captain Whitmore, but unfortunately it was his bounden duty to do so.

"This is a fine kettle of fish," Georgina said as soon as Richard returned from seeing Elias Simpson out. The poor man had looked exhausted.

"Would you prefer that you and I go over these documents before I bring them to my father's attention?" Richard stood over the papers on the table.

"Let me remove these dishes and we can spread the papers out." Georgina stood to collect the china.

"Leave those, I'll call my servant." Richard was staring intently at the papers he had picked up from the table. "I'll order a fresh pot of tea. We're going to need it."

"No wonder poor old Elias almost ran out of here!" Richard had been reading the documents left in his care.

The servant had removed the used tea things and carried in a fresh pot of tea and chinaware while Richard remained standing by the table shifting through papers. Georgina had moved from the table to take a seat by the fire and wait to hear what Richard had to say.

"There is nothing illegal in these papers as far as I can see but there is certainly a great deal of very inventive accounting." He walked over to join Georgina by the fire.

"You have been training me and the women of my household to handle our own financial affairs." Georgina watched him pull at the impeccably pressed crease in his trousers and slowly take the seat across the fire from her. "Don't fall at the first fence now, Richard. I assure you I am capable of understanding financial papers."

"I have no doubt of your capability, my dear Georgie." Richard leaned forward to stare at the Persian rug at his feet. "Those papers …" he said after a long moment, waving in the direction of the table, "I have only glanced at them but even so," he looked up to stare into her eyes, "they're a record of some of the most creative fiscal shenanigans I have ever seen."

"Was Charles Whitmore an outlaw?" Georgina stood and walked over to the tea tray sitting on the long table.

"You have been reading too many of those penny dreadfuls from America, Georgie!" Richard barked a laugh.

"Tea?" she asked without turning.

"You enjoy your tea, my dear. I am going to have something

44

stronger." He walked to a nearby table which held crystal decanters and glasses. "I feel in need of strong drink." He poured a measure of brandy into a crystal goblet.

"What has you so worried, old friend?" Georgina asked when they were both once more seated on either side of the fireplace.

"I want to study those papers in detail – with my father by my side. From the brief glance I gave them," he again gestured towards the table under the window, "the man you married had some unique ways of handling his finances."

"How?" If two men of business were worried by her late husband's paperwork, what chance had she of making sense of matters?

"He told you he sold off all of the dowry properties you brought to the marriage, didn't he?"

"To fund the sailing expedition he planned to take with his sons," she said.

"He did not, in fact, sell them. He used the properties as collateral against a loan he took from the Earl of Castlewellan."

"I beg your pardon?"

"He took out an insurance policy with Lloyds of London to cover the cost of the voyage he planned." He ignored her surprise. "The policy paid out if something should stop Whitmore completing the voyage. When he had his accident and lost his legs, the policy paid out the monies owed. He used those funds to repay the loan and the properties returned to Whitmore's estate."

There was silence as they sat and simply stared at each other.

"Your dowry properties have returned to you, Georgina. They form part of Whitmore's estate which has now passed to you."

Before she could speak, before she could even gather her thoughts, a sharp rap on the office door sounded and the door to the room was pushed open.

Walter Wilson, Richard's father, walked into the room, positively beaming.

"That telephone is really the most marvellous invention," he chirped with a broad smile. He was one of the first people to have a telephone installed in his place of business. "I have just received a telephone call from Belfast. Imagine!" He rubbed his hands together in glee. "A message from the North of Ireland only takes moments now – isn't that a wonder?" He looked around, waiting for them to share his joy. He didn't appear to notice the stunned looks on the faces of his audience. "I'm glad you are still here, Georgina. The news concerns you."

Georgina wasn't sure she could handle any more news today.

"Take a seat, Father." Richard stood to allow the older man to sit in front of the fire.

"No, no." Walter pressed his hands onto his son's shoulders and pushed him back into the chair. "I have matters to see to. I knew you were meeting with Georgina this morning and wanted to catch her before she left." He smiled at Georgina, waiting to see if she would comment. When she remained silent, he continued to share the news he had only moments before received. "There is to be a special service held for the victims of that terrible railway crash." Again, he waited, and when both of his listeners remained silent, said, "This will be followed by a service to be held at the Castlewellan Estate, open only to invitees." When he again received no reaction, he clapped his hands. "Surely you see, my dear Georgina, that this will be an ideal way to establish yourself very firmly as the widow of Captain Charles Whitmore!"

Chapter 7

Daniels Home
Castlewellan, Co Down

"Rise and shine, darling daughter!" The sound of handclapping was followed almost immediately by an explosion of light as the heavy curtains were pulled back from the window. "There are plans to be made."

"*Mama!*" Allegra, her hair tied up in thick ribbons of fabric to encourage curls to form overnight, pushed the bedcovers away from her face to gape open-mouthed at her parent.

"Your sister is awake and waiting for you in the blue room. You may join us in your night attire." Josephine swirled towards the servant almost panting on her heels. "Kearns, you have your orders." She clapped her hands again. "Do hurry along, everybody! The day is wasting."

Kearns, with a swish of her petticoats, left the room.

"*Mama?*" Allegra hissed.

"Your father and brothers are breaking their fast in the dining room." Josephine glared at her daughter while holding a finger before her lips. "We will not disturb them. Come, come, dear, we must make plans. Do get up!" She crossed to the open bedroom door and, stepping out into the hallway, throwing her arms dramatically in the air, she exclaimed, "Must I do everything myself?"

Allegra sat on the side of the bed, waiting. She was sure her mother was up to something.

In only moments she was proved correct when Josephine stepped back into the room, closing the door at her back and hurrying across the thick carpet to lean and whisper in her eldest daughter's ear: "Get poor Rebecca out of the priest hole, for goodness' sake!" There was an opening into the priest hole in Allegra's dressing room. "She will need to refresh herself, the poor dear – you must loan her something of yours to wear. I have cleared this floor of servants and will continue to berate you loudly for your tardiness. Now come along, dear – we have much to do."

Josephine Daniels glanced at the three young women taking hot chocolate with her in her blue withdrawing room. Her two daughters were enjoying the drama of the situation. Poor Rebecca, however, was looking distinctly wan.

"How long will I need to remain hidden here?" Rebecca couldn't bear to stay locked up in that priest hole. She had only spent one night locked away, it was true, but already she was on the point of despair. She would go insane sitting in that dark hole.

"Kearns told Mama that your uncle has instigated a search for you." Allegra sipped chocolate, staring at her friend in sympathy. What would she do if she were to be ejected from everything she knew? It did not bear thinking about. "He claims you must have been thrown from your horse and expresses great concern for your welfare."

"He sent an extremely nosy and unpleasant groom here to enquire as to your movements."

Josephine had never cared for the Purdey men. The women –

Rebecca's aunts – had escaped that household into marriage as soon as they came of age. That said something, she'd always believed, about the nature of the house and its inhabitants. She was content to wait until her own daughters found gentlemen they could be sure would seek to ensure their well-being – they had no need to rush into marriage.

"The groom had the impertinence to question my servants." She would have enjoyed sending the man away with a flea in his ear but had played the concerned friend extremely well, if she did say so herself. She had to think carefully. The eldest Purdey son was no fool, for all his blustering. He would have this estate watched. It was well known locally that Rebecca had free run of this house from her earliest days.

"Your uncle is offering a generous reward for information concerning your whereabouts." Horatia hated to see her friend so pale and listless. Rebecca was someone who needed to be out in the air to flourish. She had never been a hothouse plant.

"I trust my servants but truly the money on offer could tempt any one of them," Josephine said. "I pray not, but they are not saints and have concerns of their own."

"I am sorry to bring these problems to your door." Rebecca felt dizzy for a moment, her world figuratively spinning around her head. "I had a thought last night in that dark hideaway. If Aubrey Whittaker had been at home I would have sought his advice about disappearing. Aubrey was always up for an adventure and my uncle would not have thought to seek me there."

"Dear Aubrey," Horatia agreed. "He always led us into such wild adventures."

"Aubrey Whittaker was a bad influence on my family!" But Josephine smiled. How could she be angry at a charming young man who had joined her sons and daughters in enjoying their young lives. She was awfully fond of Aubrey and had hoped for a connection between Aubrey and Horatia but, alas, it was not to be. They were as brother and sister.

"Aubrey would be the very person to secret Rebecca away," Allegra said. "He would stare down anyone who dared to question him. But since he is not available to us, why not consult Rebecca's Great-aunt Lady Caroline?"

"The late earl's aunt has never expressed a particular interest in me." Rebecca was astonished at this suggestion. "I have met her, of course. Why would you suggest we consult the woman now?"

"Lady Caroline has far more strings to her bow than you might think," Allegra stated mysteriously.

"Excellent suggestion." Josephine nodded at her daughter, ignoring Rebecca's comment. "Horatia, go request Rory join us, please."

"Oh, Mother, must I?"

"Do not be silly, I beg of you. Alert Rory to the situation and ask that she join us but, for goodness' sake, remind her to bring her infernal notebook and eyeglasses. The woman is getting so forgetful." She gestured towards the door.

"Well, this is a fine how do you do!" Aurora Daniels, her short plump body tightly encased in black bombazine, bustled into the room with Horatia at her heels. "I thought you would be here, child." She wrapped her chubby arms around Rebecca and hugged her so closely the breath almost left her body. "Someone, pour me a cup of chocolate," she demanded, releasing Rebecca to take a seat at the table. "What's to do?"

Horatia put the notebook and eyeglasses she carried on the table close to her aunt's hand.

"We need to get Rebecca away from here as quickly as possible." Josephine admired her husband's sister who had been a member of her household since the day she married. The woman had her own wing in the house and lived independently. Aurora Daniels was no one's dependent. "Allegra suggested we take her to Lady Caroline."

"Did she indeed?" Aurora, or Rory as she insisted on being called, kicked her heels in delight. "Gets her brains from me. that one does!"

"Indeed!" Josephine tried not to laugh but really her sister-in-law was irrepressible. What would she have done without her company and sage advice through the years?

"Why don't you marry?" Rory demanded of Rebecca. "Lord knows it wouldn't be difficult to find a man to take you. You have beauty, not to mention the funds you would bring to the union. That would solve your problems. You could let some man do your thinking for you." And create many new problems, Rory knew, but she needed to see what the girl was made of. She was a winsome chit and had been from birth, but did she have the backbone needed to take control of her life?

"I have given no great thought to marriage." Rebecca kept her eyes down. How could she tell these women that the thought of being tied down by the daily chore of taking care of a house and servants, paying duty calls to people she didn't have anything in common with, and putting up with the demands of a husband filled her with horror.

"That father of yours should have taken you to London to make your bow to the Queen." Rory sucked her lips tight against her lips in disgust. "You are Lady Rebecca Henderson, daughter of the Earl of Castlewellan. You should have been out in society, not digging in the dirt like a common labourer." She beat her hand against the table top. "And so I said to that father of yours many times – good-looking rogue that he was. I shall miss him." She had never understood why

51

everyone seemed to think the late Earl of Castlewellan was such a devil. He had never been anything but charming to her.

"It is unfortunate your father died without a male heir." Josephine blotted her lips with a linen napkin. The chocolate pot was empty. She had no intention of ringing for another. There was no time to sit gossiping. There were matters to attend to. Rebecca could not linger in that priest hole – they had to get her away from here without being seen. That was, after all, why she had sent for Rory.

"Are we to whisk you away then to your Great-aunt Caroline?" Rory stared at Rebecca, waiting for her to decide. It was her life, after all.

"I am rather at a loss as to what to do." Rebecca tried not to cry. When had she had the opportunity to plan for her own future? Was it not the females' lot in life to be told what to do by the males who controlled the finances? Besides, she had spent the past two years caring for her grandfather, staying out of the way of her uncle and his family, and practically running the Purdey flower and fruit business. She knew no other world. "I would greatly appreciate any advice or suggestions you might make."

"We need reliable information." Rory put her elbows on the table. "We cannot run about like chickens with our heads cut off. Do we even know for a certainty that Rebecca must run for her life? Is it possible that we are all of us making a mountain out of a molehill?"

"My Uncle Percival has invited Mr Taunton to pay his respects to me." Rebecca felt her gorge rise at the thought.

"He is as old as your grandfather!" Horatia exclaimed. "And the smell of his breath is foul."

"Still, you could be a young widow," Rory said. "That old goat cannot last much longer."

"*Rory!*" Josephine shouted.

"And my cousin Peregrine is to marry Lavinia Carson." Rebecca ignored the reactions of the others, too lost in the mire of her own thoughts.

"Lavinia would delight in having you under her thumb." Allegra shuddered.

Rebecca did not want to discuss Lavinia Carson. They had grown up with her and she was everything that was pleasant to anyone who could advance her place in life. She saved her disdain and spite for those she considered beneath her station.

"Great-uncle Thomas – the new Earl of Castlewellan – has repeatedly demanded that I should return to the Castlewellan estate," she said.

"He is a widower with five young sons and three daughters, I am told," said Rory.

"He cannot be thinking of a marriage between himself and Rebecca, can he? He is her great-uncle after all. Is that not forbidden by the law of the land?" Josephine looked to Rory for an answer.

"I'm not sure of the legal position but when has that ever mattered when money or power is involved?" Rory barked. "Consider the queen and her children. Victoria has married off her children into the royal houses of Europe – all of whom have blood ties that are far too close – in my humble opinion."

"You humble, Rory?" Josephine laughed.

"Surely what you are thinking of is unnatural, Mama." Allegra cringed at the very thought.

"He does not need to marry Rebecca," Horatia said slowly. "He simply needs to prevent her marrying anyone. Keep her under his thumb and a member of his household. He would have easy access to her funds then, if that is what concerns us."

"We need information, as I have already stated." Rory jumped to her feet. "I have never cared for the Reverend Thomas Henderson – all sanctimonious lectures and false smiles while he drools over the contents of one's bodice. The man's a hypocrite – eight children – good Lord!" She had never supported the idea of large families. She stood with her hands gripping the back of her chair. "Lady Caroline will be able to supply us with information about Thomas and his plans." She looked at the women gazing up at her. "And she may well be able to help us make any plans that are needed."

"There is to be a public service for the people who lost their lives in that terrible train crash," Josephine said before Rory could leave. "I received notification yesterday." She stared at Rory meaningfully. "Everyone who is anyone is expected to attend."

"That may very well work to our advantage!" Rory clapped her hands.

"Could you take Rebecca to your section of the house, please?" Josephine asked. "I receive far more visitors than you and I worry her presence here may be detected."

Rory nodded. "No doubt half the neighbours will be calling to discuss the upcoming event."

"We don't often have grand public gatherings. The gossips will have a field day."

Chapter 8

Dublin

Georgina stood on the bridge, staring into the waters of the Grand Canal. A lone swan drifted on his way under the bridge, capturing her gaze for a moment. She had left Richard's office building in Mount Street Crescent, planning to take a moment to think in St Stephen's Church. Her feet had refused to carry her inside the tall white building – she needed air – needed to breathe. Her mind whirled in such a fashion that she longed to clutch at her throbbing temples and scream. She could not afford to lose her composure. She had to think. Had she invited Richard to dine with her this evening? She didn't know – could barely remember leaving the office.

Was there anywhere she could just escape to and think? She could not remain in Richard's offices – he had business to attend to. Her home in Percy Place held more problems than solutions. She almost envied the old horse plodding along the rim of the canal – one foot in front of the other – towing the heavy barge along the canal in the direction of the bridge she stood upon.

She laughed aloud – slightly hysterically – clapping one black-leather gloved hand to her mouth. She glanced over her shoulder, praying that none of the passers-by had noticed her unseemly behaviour. She turned and crossed the bridge, avoiding the steaming deposits of horse manure. She wanted to see again that swan and the old horse travelling away from her now. Was she going mad? She had thought to go to the church to think, yet had been drawn to the canal. Was the vision in front of her an answer to an unspoken prayer?

She reached the other side of the bridge and stared at the swan drifting seemingly effortlessly into the distance – while all the time the webbed feet were almost certainly paddling frantically as he fought the power of the water pouring from the nearby open floodgates. The horse, head down, plodding placidly along as he pulled a weight many times his own size. There was her answer. There was how she needed to go on. She would present an image of calm grace to the outside world while frantically trying to handle the problems that were being thrown her way. Yes, the weight might be backbreaking – but if she put one foot in front of the other and carried on she would eventually reach her destination.

She looked towards the heavens and smiled while mentally whispering a prayer of thanks. She straightened her shoulders and turned towards home.

"Is that yerself, Miss Georgina?" Lily Chambers hurried down the long basement hallway. She had been listening to hear her mistress turn the key in the doorway leading from under the granite steps at the front of the house. "You were out before the streets were aired this morning. You shouldn't have gone out alone, Miss Georgina. What were you thinking of leaving the house without a maid or companion by your side? I was that worried! Who knows what could have happened to you?"

"I'm fine, Lily." Georgina stifled a sigh. "It's a very short walk from this house to Richard's office." They'd had this discussion before Georgina left this morning. "And I had Dorothy with me when I left." She had been glad of Dorothy's company leaving the house. The woman walked to the factory she'd inherited from her late father every weekday morning. They had parted company as soon as they reached one of the nearby bridges that crossed the canal.

Georgina walked down the hallway, removing her gloves and stuffing them into the pocket of her hip-length woollen jacket and loosening the ribbons of her bonnet with Lily chirping her complaints in her ear.

"The post is sitting on the table," Cook said when Georgina stepped into her kitchen. "There is something there we all recognise." She gestured towards the table in the alcove where a large brown envelope was sitting amongst a scattering of white ones.

The letters from America went to the BOBs' Dublin address and were redirected to Percy Place in a fresh envelope to conceal their origins.

"I had to almost throw my body over the letters from America to keep them safe," she said. "No doubt we will be receiving a visit from the Dowager Duchess soon. That woman doesn't like to be left out of things. She'll be wanting to know what was in them letters. You mark my words." Without pause she continued, "Ruth, take Miss Georgina's outside clothes up to the hall and hang them on the hallstand. Sit yerself down, Miss Georgina, I've the kettle on and it won't take me a minute to have a pot of tea on the go. I daresay you got nothing to eat since you left the house. I'll have something for you in the shake of a duck's tail. Now sit yerself down. Yer making me place look untidy." Cook too had been worried about her mistress – imagine stepping out without a maid! What was the world coming to?

Georgina passed her outdoor clothing to Ruth while her eyes

examined the post on the table. Ruth left the kitchen to carry out her orders.

"Has Liam set the fire in my sitting room upstairs?" Georgina asked. "And where are the others?"

"Liam has set all of the house fires, and he is at this moment polishing the brass fenders throughout the house," Lily said. "Sarah is in the washhouse with the washerwoman. They are sorting through the chests of discarded servant uniforms. I had two of Billy's men carry the chests down from the attic. It is far too cold and dark up there to examine the garments carefully. The young women are at their deportment lessons with Madame Arliss."

"Yes, of course." Georgina had used the excuse of not taking one of the women away from her lessons to escape the house alone this morning. How silly of her to forget that. "And Agatha?"

"She has the baby in her charge in your old playroom," Cook supplied.

"Ruth," Georgina said as the cook's helper reappeared, "serve Mrs Chambers and Cook a pot of tea, please." She picked up the post from the table and with this in her hands walked towards the door. "I'll ring when I'm ready for refreshments, Cook."

In her sitting room Georgina dropped the mail onto her desk. She took a box of long matches from the mantel and, quickly striking a match, lit the tightly packed paper in the grate. She watched with satisfaction as the paper caught. The fire would soon be blazing.

"It takes little to please you," she said aloud.

Removing items from her desk drawers, she put her golden fountain pen in the indentation at the top of the desk, a notepad by her hand in case she needed it, together with the silver letter opener. She pulled the mesh wastepaper basket from under the desk and placed it nearby before pulling her chair close to the lip of the desk and taking her seat. She could hear no noise from the dining room which was set up as a schoolroom for the times Madame Arliss visited.

She put the silver letter opener into the flap of a thin envelope with the crest of the Goldenbridge Orphanage on it, wondering what her great-aunt the Reverend Mother wanted of her now. The few lines of the note drew a groan from her lips. The lines were shaky, not at all her great-aunt's usual style.

My dear Georgina, the note read. *When you receive this note I will have already been laid to my rest. There is a box, our family heirloom, packed and sealed by my own hand, waiting for you at the convent. Pick it up as soon as you may.*

Georgina pushed away from her desk and went to lean on the mantel, staring with unseeing eyes into the fire. The news was not unexpected. The old nun had been ready to go and meet her Maker – as she put it – for some time now.

A little while later she went back to her desk, blowing her nose on the handkerchief she'd taken from her skirt pocket – crying always seemed to block her nose. She'd said her prayers silently for the repose of her relative's soul. "Now, make a note," she said. She took up her fountain pen, a gift from the Reverend Mother, and noted that she needed to make a visit to the nun's home at Goldenbridge. She thanked heaven she now had enough funds to make a generous donation to the convent. The nuns would expect it. She needed to request a cheque from Richard and carry it with her when she went. She kicked the desk in frustration at being unable to access her own funds – because she was female. She made a note to remind herself to ask Richard if that had changed now that she was a widow?

Georgina continued to open envelopes, keeping the letters from America for last – as a promised treat to herself. She frowned at the contents of one envelope. The letter was written in an uneducated hand – a Miss Sally Mulligan requesting a meeting at her earliest convenience at an address in Baggot Street. What on earth was that about? She put the letter to one side, making a note to herself to deal with the matter later. Then, finally, she was ready to open the letters from America.

The note from Jenny contained more of her wonderful hand-sketched drawings in the margins and on the envelope. It was a wonderful way of sharing her world with those at home. "Thank goodness I opened this alone," Georgina whispered.

Jenny had included a private note for her.

The news of the Earl of Castlewellan's death has been reported with great fanfare in the newspapers here. I have considered the matter until my head aches and have decided that the death of that man can have no bearing on my life. I would, however, ask that you do what you can for the daughter of his first marriage. She should be a young woman now and may need your assistance. I enclose her details.

Georgina took note of the name – *Lady Rebecca Henderson* – and other details provided before she crumpled the note and hurried to throw it in the fire. She stood watching it burn. She took the fire iron and raked the coals, hiding any sign of the note. Jenny had once been Eugenie, Countess of Castlewellan. Surely the death of the Earl would considerably change her circumstances? How could it not?

"What does she imagine I will be able to do about that man's daughter? I was not aware that Eugenie was his second bride," she whispered into the flames of the fire. How had their lives come to this, she wondered? She had grown up with Eugenie, they had been close friends planning their futures and whispering of adventure. Where had all of those youthful dreams gone? They had bowed down to parental pressure and both made disastrous marriages at far too young an age.

60

"Ladies, ladies!" Clapping hands sounded in the hallway outside Georgina's door.

She looked at the clock on the mantel, unable to believe so much of the day had gone.

"Please remember, grace and dignity at all times!" Madame Arliss was releasing her students from their studies.

Georgina continued to open envelopes, refusing to feel guilty as she enjoyed the news the letters contained in peace. She would share the news at the lunch table and leave the letters in the hallway for everyone to enjoy. It was selfish of her, she knew, but she did so enjoy the adventures the ladies in America shared in their letters home.

Georgina had become involved in the BOBs when a place was needed for the first of the women being sent to America. The women had lived with her while they were trained to take control of their own destiny – everything from finances to physical safety was covered in the months the women lived at Percy Place. They had tried to prepare them for the chance of being sent to the Americas to become "Harvey Girls" who worked in dining cars and railway stations across the Americas. It was considered suitable employment for gently reared young women. So far, the system seemed to be working wonderfully well.

What a good idea it was of the Dowager Duchess's to insist she pay the postage on the letters from America. It relieved the women of having to wait till they had the funds to send letters such a long distance. It was more expensive to accept cash-on-delivery envelopes certainly, but the Dowager Duchess could afford the expense.

Chapter 9

"There will be no gulping down of my good food." Cook slapped the table, glaring at the young people. Ruth, Sarah, Bridget, and Liam stopped shoving food into their mouths. "Miss Flora will read the letters from America to us – like always – so there is no reason not to enjoy the food I've taken the time to prepare." She tutted and shook her head at the impatient youngsters. "I'll be giving you lot nosebags like the horses if you don't take care."

Flora tried to hide the fact that she had been as guilty as the youngsters of trying to hurry the meal along. The practice of one person reading aloud the letters from America – slowly and clearly – had come into place when too many hands grabbing at the lightweight, tissue-thin paper designed for long-distance post to reduce the cost of postage had become dangerous to the fragile documents. Everyone loved hearing about the adventures of the ladies who had left this house to travel so far from home.

"How went the lessons this morning, ladies?" Georgina asked from her seat at the head of the table.

There was silence as Flora, Bridget, Helen and Molly looked at each other, waiting to see who would be brave enough to answer. It was Flora who spoke up.

"I thought we were all making improvements, but Madame Arliss may not agree with me." She waited to see if anyone else had something to say before adding, "Our hands, nails and handkerchiefs passed inspection. Our grooming was tolerable. We knew the names and correct greetings for the nobility and each of us walked and sat with grace and dignity."

"You forgot to mention our diction." Bridget placed her knife and fork carefully on her plate as she'd been taught. She used her linen napkin to wipe her lips. "Madame Arliss has been teaching us the correct pronunciation of words and we must practise them. We must also practise the sound of vowels. Today, we play-acted greeting each other and engaging in polite conversation." She threw back her head and laughed, the sound of her enjoyment bringing smiles to everyone's face. "I had to be a duchess." She buried her face in her napkin and giggled.

"I thought you made a very fine duchess!" Molly, who had been given the chance to change her life and never ceased to thank whatever fates had brought her here, laughed.

Agatha mentally nudged Helen to add something to the conversation but the girl remained mute. What was to be done with her? Agatha was at her wits' end. She glanced over to the Moses basket placed carefully out of all draughts in one corner of the staff dining room and stifled a sigh. Helen hadn't even glanced at the baby when she'd entered the room. She had left everything she knew to bring Helen to this house. It had turned out better than she could ever have expected for Helen and her unwanted child, but it was time for Helen to think and act for herself. Some might say long past time.

"We owe a debt of gratitude to the Dowager Duchess for finding such a qualified lady to teach you," Georgina said.

"It doesn't feel that way at times," Flora said. "Madame Arliss is very strict. There is no time for levity in her classroom."

"Nonetheless, I have noticed a marked improvement in all of you."

Polite conversation out of the way, they each applied themselves to their meal, all eagerly anticipating the reading of the letters from America.

"We'll clear the table —" Cook began. "*No rushing!*" she barked when the three maids and Liam pushed their chairs back with force. "I'll not have me dishes broken. Miss Flora, you're excused from clean-up duty. Just this once we'll leave the dirty dishes lie and have our tea after Miss Flora has read to us." She too was desperate to hear the latest from America.

"This first letter is from Jenny Castle." Flora was standing at the end of the table, across from Georgina, very aware of her audience hanging on her every word. "It has all of the delightful sketches we've come to expect." She looked over the top of the letter to say. "I'll leave the letter in the hallway for all to see — but it needs saying: please be careful when you touch it. It is very delicate." The letters from America were kept in a glass-topped cabinet in the long basement hallway.

Flora began to read.

"*Dear Everyone — It is difficult to know how to address these letters. The naming of each person would take up far too much room on the page, I fear. I like to think of you all sitting in the staff dining room listening to my letters being read aloud. Georgie has written to me of your keen interest.*

Bridget, my dear, you will have to be very careful in the placing of my current position on the map I've been told so much about."

She and Flora had drawn a large-scale map of America on the white wall in the basement corridor. With each new letter the map was updated so that they could all follow the adventures of past pupils with keen interest.

"I have been sent to La Castaneda in Las Vegas, New Mexico. It is Mr Harvey's very first hotel and the pride of the Harvey line. I have drawn an image of the hotel, a building very strange to my eyes, I am sure you will all agree when you see it. The landscape is very foreign to me. I am surrounded by desert, and something called cacti – very strange plants. These too I have drawn for your information. The hotel and railway tracks are placed in land that belonged to the native people. I have seen Indians. I have sketched these too.

I regret to say I have been guilty of staring in open-mouthed astonishment at almost everything I see around me. It really is a strange new world, but fascinating.

The work of a Harvey Girl is not as difficult as I'd been led to believe. It is not at all different from being in service. The trains – great steaming monsters – pull into the station as many as ten times a day and we serve a delicious three-course meal to the passengers in under thirty minutes – the time allowed for the train to stop and refuel. It is all very exciting, and I am fascinated by the people who pass before me every day. I intend to purchase a sketchbook at the earliest opportunity and record my impressions of the world around me.

Felicity, Verity, and I have promised to keep in touch. We are fortunate as Mr Harvey has arrangements in place for our correspondence to be sent by rail to our location – at no charge – this is a great boon to all three of us. It can be lonely being the new girl until one finds one's feet.

I will close now as I find I am yawning over my notepad. I hope all of you are well and please give my regards to everyone. Your friend, Jenny Castle."

There was pandemonium when Flora laid the letter on the cleared table. They all jumped to their feet, wanting to see the drawings. Flora had to speak very sharply, to remind everyone to be careful.

"That's never the hotel!" Cook's finger hovered over the drawing of a long building with open-arched upside-down U-shaped areas running along its front. "Is that a bell tower?"

"That plant looks like a green man with many arms." Helen pointed to a drawing in the margin of one page.

"Jenny notes it is called a Saguaro cactus," Flora said.

There were *oohs* and *aahs* as a world far away from their own was revealed to them.

"Look," Lily clasped a hand to her breast, "is that an Indian man, do you suppose?"

"Flora," Bridget was almost dancing in place she was so excited, "do you think we could ask the librarian to find us books about New Mexico and all of these strange-looking plants?"

"We must." Flora too wanted to know more.

"Ruth, Liam, give me a hand making and serving the tea. I'm gasping for a cup."

The rest of the people didn't even notice their leaving, each one wanting to make sure they had seen all the drawings on offer.

Agatha walked over to check on the baby. She wanted to pick him up, but he was sleeping so soundly it would be a shame to wake him. She glanced over her shoulder at the people who continued to exclaim and marvel over the wonders of a strange world. What did they know about anything? Had they ever asked her how she was coping with the strange world she'd wandered into?

She was from the country – born and bred on a vast estate. This Dublin was a strange new world to her – but did anyone care? She missed the miles of beautiful green fields. The air in Dublin tasted strange. She had never seen the like of the many smoking chimneys and the poverty. Why, you couldn't even cross the streets without watching for deposits of filth that belonged in the stable-yard – not out where anyone could step in it. She longed to see fields dotted with cows, horses, and sheep. She missed her duties at the Big House. She'd had a list as long as your arm to complete every day there. There was never a moment to wonder and worry.

"The next letter is from Felicia," Flora remained standing while everyone drank their tea and listened to her. She could make a fresh pot of tea for herself later. "*My dears*," she says, "*I have so much news to share with you all. I have seen my brothers. Is that not a marvel? Here in this vast country, I was able to travel by train – at no cost – because I am a Harvey Girl – oh, the thrill of even writing those words! I was granted permission to visit my brothers before taking up my duties. I was beside myself with excitement, longing to share my good fortune with my beloved brothers. They did not share in my delight. I became quite cross with them when they continued to insist that the work of a waitress was not a suitable occupation for their sister. I closed my ears to their complaints and determined to enjoy my visit with them.*

Bridget, for your map, Kentucky is a beautiful state with miles of lush green fields. There are horses everywhere, it seems to me. The state seems obsessed with horses and horse racing. My brothers are very much at home there. They wanted me to remain in the role of their housekeeper. The role of their unpaid domestic help being more in line with what they believe should be their sister's place in life! Thank goodness for the teachings of Percy Place. I was quite sharp in my refusal of their offer.

I have now arrived to take up my position in Topeka, Kansas – the very first of Mr Harvey's railway restaurants. Isn't that delightful? I plan to make myself a distinguished member of staff and work hard towards advancing my opportunities with this fine company. I have now spent so much time as a passenger aboard trains that I feel quite informed as to the needs of passengers. I am so newly arrived at Topeka that I have not seen a great deal of the area. I shall write more when I may.

I shall stop now. I want to get this letter onto the mail train. I hope all are well in Percy Place. Please keep writing. It is wonderful to receive your news.

Your friend. Felicia."

"There now," Cook sighed. "Imagine travelling all over the place by train – and it not costing a penny!"

"Shame her brothers do not support her in her efforts to improve her lot in life." Flora decided to take a cup of tea before continuing. Her mouth was very dry.

"Her brothers offered her a home," Helen said. "That was generous of them. They would have taken care of her."

"We are endeavouring to teach women to care for themselves in this house!" Georgina almost snapped.

"I'm ready to continue." Flora hastily gulped her tea before an argument could develop.

"*My Dears,*" Verity says. "*I am in another world. I have taken up my first posting with Mr Harvey – Dodge City, Kansas, can you imagine?*

I am learning a new language. They have 'cowpunchers' and 'chuck wagons' and 'feed lots' and a whole host of other terms that are unfamiliar to me. But I shall learn.

Vast herds of cattle stroll the streets here. They do not tell you in the books we have read of the heat … and the dust. My dears, the dust! One fights it constantly. The area is rough, I cannot lie. It is a land time seems to have passed by. The train station and the growing town appears to my eyes to be a hastily erected tumbledown of many different buildings. They do not even have sidewalks.

However, I am loving every moment of my new life. It is vastly different from being a poor relation to the Dowager Duchess, I do assure you. Mr Harvey has a rule that no one may dine without a jacket and tie. This does not please the cowboys. It is the duty of the Harvey Girls to insist they don one of the many jackets and ties Mr Harvey keeps on hand. I am becoming expert at judging a gentleman's size. Quite shocking!

I have regular customers who remain drinking coffee long after the trains have departed. They know of my fascination with what they call the 'old days' and freely talk to me of the glory days of the past. Quite thrilling.

The days pass so swiftly. There is never the chance for tedium. The work is familiar to me now and I can move and serve with great speed. I have received more praise for my efforts in the months I have been here than I ever received in my years with the Dowager Duchess. It is very satisfying.

The Dowager Duchess writes of her intention to someday visit this part of the world. I fall into hysterical laughter at the very thought. I would pay money to see her deal with some of the characters I am coming to know.

I am living in a world I never dared dream of, ladies, and I am being paid to do so. My life has changed in so many ways. The world is opening to me. I feel very fortunate.

I will write more when I have time. I think of you all fondly. Do keep writing to me. Your letters are much appreciated.

Your friend, Verity."

"Her writing voice is very different from the cool calm young woman who stayed here," Lily remarked into the silence that had fallen.

"There is no letter from Mia this time," Flora was speaking of Euphemia Locke-Statton, another of the women who travelled to America. Mia, as she was now known, had remained in New York having entered into a marriage with a wealthy young man she'd met on the ship travelling to America.

"No doubt we will hear from Mia another day." Lily Chambers shook her head at the miracle of hearing from the young women who had travelled so far away from home. The modern world was a different place to the one she'd been born into.

"I must update the map." Bridget looked to Georgina for permission.

"The table needs to be cleared and the kitchen cleaned!" Cook said before anyone could lose themselves in plans to update the map. There would be time for that later.

Chapter 10

Castlewellan
County Down

"This clothing will never fit you, Rebecca." Tabitha Garwood, the lifelong companion of Aurora Daniels, held a cotton day dress aloft. It was one of many they had pulled from the trunks delivered to the Daniels home for Rebecca.

"Your body shape has changed from a child to a young woman," Rory Daniels pronounced. "And I do believe you have grown taller since you wore these garments, my dear."

Rebecca grimaced as she surveyed the clothes. Her wardrobe had not been updated since her grandfather took to his bed. She had practically forgotten she owned such frivolous garments.

The three women – Rebecca, Tabitha and Rory – were gathered in a large guest bedroom located in Rory's wing of the house.

"We must consult Monica. She is a skilled seamstress." Tabitha, tall, lean and greying, was the physical opposite of her friend Rory but the two were inseparable. "She may be able to let down the hem on these dresses, although the style is frightfully youthful for someone of your advanced years." She smiled at the frowning Rebecca.

"Am I not to be kept hidden away like the mad aunt?" Rebecca asked.

"Your grandfather should have taken steps to protect you long before this!" Rory practically barked. "That man – it is sheer male vanity that has caused him to take to his bed. The poor cannot afford to lay down arms when struck down with the palsy."

"Now, now, Rory!" Tabitha objected. "Imagine being struck down with palsy after enjoying great good health all of your life!"

"*It is vanity, I tell you!*" Rory snapped.

Rebecca wanted to defend her grandfather but these two women intimidated her. She kept her thoughts firmly locked behind her teeth while mentally steaming with anger.

"Not so, my dear." Tabitha pressed her fingers into her forehead, trying to remember the name of the doctor who had written such a fascinating article for the medical journal. "I read an article written by Dr James Parkinson – it was some years ago now – he wrote that the palsy that makes people lose control of their body is actually caused by a problem of the brain. It attracted my attention particularly as I have always been fascinated by the workings of our brains."

"Tabitha should have been a doctor." Rory smiled fondly. "It was not to be, however."

"I have my potions and lotions to occupy my mind," Tabitha said.

"Hey ho, nothing we can do about that now. Do sit on the bed, Rebecca." Rory indicated the large four-poster bed placed centrally in the room. "Tabby and I will sit in the chairs by the window. You must stay away from the windows at all times. We do not want anyone who may be passing to catch even a glimpse of you."

"Rebecca my dear," Tabitha took a seat by the table pulled beneath a long window that overlooked the garden, "we do not yet know what to do with you." She held up a hand when Rebecca was about to speak. She had been given the details available about Rebecca's situation. "It is a good idea to consult Lady Caroline, your great-aunt.

She of all people will know what the situation is on the Castlewellan estate. We are not party to the private circumstances of the new earl, but his sister surely will be."

"Rebecca, you do not need me to tell you that my sister by marriage is your godmother." Rory sat across the table from Tabitha. She stared out the window. Was it her imagination or were there a great many more servants loitering about than usual? "Josephine has in her possession papers dealing with your inheritance. She has not yet had time to share these with you. There is much that can be done to assist you, but we need further information."

"Are you aware of an organisation called the BOBs?" Tabitha stared at the young woman sitting on the bed.

"My grandfather has mentioned it from time to time but in no great detail," Rebecca replied.

"The BOBs was set up by bored young women seeking a distraction from the tedium of their lives," Rory said.

"Now, Rory," Tabitha patted the plump dimpled hand resting on top of the table between them, "the BOBs do a great deal of good." She turned to Rebecca. "The women and indeed the men of this house are ardent supporters of the BOBs. Our treasured seamstress Monica came to us through the good offices of the BOBs. We would be lost without her."

"I'm sorry but I do not understand how this concerns me?" Rebecca said.

"Ah yes," Tabitha said with a nod. "You are of an age when the world revolves around you and your cares."

"Tabby!" Rory objected.

"The BOBs, young lady, are the people we must consult if – as it appears to be – you must be spirited away from all the people wishing to lay hands on you." Tabitha leaned forward to stare at Rebecca.

"I do not wish to appear dense, Miss Tabitha," Rebecca leaned her aching head against the mahogany bedpost nearest to her, "but I am having difficulty understanding what my life has become. I awoke one morning to my life as it has always been – then my grandfather ordered me to flee – I obeyed his command as I always have – but I fail to understand why or indeed how this," she waved her hand frantically about the room, "has come to be. Can you please explain matters to me in a way that I can understand?"

"You poor child!" Rory sighed.

"Rebecca," Tabitha too sighed, "you have the fortune or indeed misfortune depending on your point of view, of being young, attractive, and wealthy. Your grandfather Purdey sheltered and protected you while he could, but his health is failing." She hated to see the silent tears that flowed down Rebecca's pretty face, but one had to be brutal sometimes.

"My dear, you cannot help but be aware," Rory took over, "that your Uncle Percival has resented your presence in his life from the moment you were born. He will attempt to make money from you as soon as his father quits this earth. Your cousin Peregrine too believes that you stole his grandfather's attention and affections from him – the heir – and will delight in seeing you fall."

"Your great-uncle, the new Earl of Castlewellan, cares not a jot for you as a person," Tabitha said. "He sees you as a walking source of income for his family. In addition, as your father's daughter – you are also an impediment to him taking complete control of the Castlewellan estate. He needs you under his thumb. You are much admired among the workers of both your father's and grandfather's estate. That, in his little mind, cannot be allowed."

"How could I not be aware of all of this?" Rebecca had known how her Purdey relatives felt about her – how could she not? – but to think people she had never even met wished her ill – it was past all understanding. "Have I slept the days away?"

"My dear," Tabitha shook her head, "you are female. You were born to sit in a corner looking pretty and sewing a fine seam while the men in your life controlled your every thought and movement. That is seen as the lot of the female of a certain class. The poor do not have the luxury of raising their females to a life of pretty uselessness."

"That does not sound fair," Rebecca said.

"Nothing in this life is fair, child," Tabitha replied. "There are those of us who fight what is seen as the natural order of things, but we are few."

"The discussion of the female lot in life is for another time!" Rory snapped. "We must discuss Rebecca's situation but, as I seem to have said ad infinitum, we need information."

"For the moment," Tabitha slapped the table, "we will send Velma and Monica to you, Rebecca. You need to bathe and wash your hair. Thank goodness for indoor plumbing. When you have completed your toilette, I suggest you take a nap. It cannot have been comfortable sleeping in that dusty priest hole. While you are doing that, Rory and I will travel to visit Lady Caroline and seek her assistance. We will know more when we return." She stood up. "For heaven's sake, child, stay away from all windows."

"Thank you, Velma." Rebecca closed her eyes as the older woman scrubbed her hair.

"If you don't mind me saying, Lady Rebecca," Velma Harris examined the thick golden hair under her hands, "your hair is a right mess."

"Is it?" Rebecca leaned forward in the bath of hot water and almost groaned in pleasure. When was the last time she'd had the time to simply relax and be tended? It was wonderful.

"Oh, to be young and pretty!" Velma laughed softly.

"I do not feel very young at the moment, Velma."

"No, I daresay you don't." Velma applied some of the shampoo that Miss Tabitha made in her herbal room to the well-soaked hair.

"Are you not tempted by the reward being offered for information about me, Velma?"

"Indeed, I am not." Velma scrubbed fiercely at the hair under her hands. "I am well paid for my services here. That is not to say that extra money is not always welcome. But I wouldn't sleep easy knowing I was taking what I consider blood money." Her fingers continued to dig into the hair, massaging the scalp. "Lean back."

Rebecca obeyed the command, closing her eyes and mouth tightly, as Velma poured water, from a bucket she'd placed by the side of the bath, liberally over the shampoo-soaked hair.

"I'll give it another scrub, Lady Rebecca." Velma examined the hair. "You have not been taking care of it as you should."

"Who has the time, Velma?" Until two days ago her days had been filled with chores and duties.

"Well, if we can keep you safe from the many nosy parkers who have taken to strolling about the estate gardens, you'll have nothing but time on your hands."

"I am sorry to bring this trouble to the Daniels family," Rebecca said.

"It's no fault of yours. Everyone in the neighbourhood knows you are a close friend of the family and it's known this is the last place you visited. That lot out there," she jerked her chin in the general direction of the outdoors, "are just taking a chance that you might be here. I'd like to give all of them Nosy Nellies a piece of my mind!"

"Ladies." Power, Lady Caroline's butler, accepted the calling cards the two ladies handed to him. He held the door of the manor house open.

"If you would care to wait in the orangery. Lady Caroline is presently occupied with a guest."

This large manor house sitting in its splendid extensive grounds served as a way station for the BOBs. The staff were devoted to their mistress and held her secrets close. Many females had been smuggled into and out of this house under Power's watchful eyes.

"I always enjoy visiting the orangery." Tabitha stepped into the hallway.

Rory joined Tabitha. "Surely we were expected, Power?"

"Lady Caroline is, of course, always delighted by your company," Power responded. "But the Earl of Castlewellan has deigned to pay an unannounced visit on my lady his sister."

He led the way into the drawing room that allowed access to the orangery, a large, heated glass building, sitting close to the house. One gained entrance to it through a glass walkway from one of the four drawing rooms or directly from the grounds.

Power opened the large double floor-length windows that led to the orangery walkway.

"Would you care for coffee to be served, ladies?"

"Thank you, Power," Tabitha said, "but no. We will explore the orangery. I do so enjoy seeing Lady Caroline's latest acquisitions." The lady was renowned throughout the world for her collection of rare trees which she imported and nurtured in her orangery and on her grounds.

"Ladies …" Power held the doors open for the two ladies to enter, closing them at their backs. It wouldn't do to allow any of the heated air of the orangery to escape when the doors at the other end of the walkway were opened. He hurried away to retake his place in the servants' hallway that traversed the house. The hidden hallway allowed the servants to move freely about the manor house without being observed and disturbing the inhabitants unduly. It also served as an excellent location for a spyhole. His mistress knew of this and had requested that he listen to her conversation with her younger brother – the Earl.

"Really, Caro, you are being most disagreeable."

The soft pious-sounding tones were clearly to be heard when Power silently slid the covering from the spyhole – cleverly concealed on the other side of the wall of the yellow drawing room.

"Because I won't pander to your greed?"

Oh, his mistress was in fine form! Power would run for the hills if he caused that bite to enter her cultured voice.

"I do not consider asking you to allow my third son to study under you an action of greed." Thomas soft voice was almost sibilant – like a snake. "Aloysius has always had an interest in nature." He walked over to the windows overlooking the grounds. "Who better to train him?" He waved towards the view. "There is nothing but trees as far as the eye can see."

Caroline wished she could have this upstart thrown out of her house, but she needed to know what he was about. She had not seen him in over thirty years. Those years had not been kind to him. She'd been twenty years old when he was born of her father's second or was it third wife – who could remember? He had entered the world, it appeared to her at the time, wanting what everyone else had. He was a whiny demanding infant, and it would seem not much had changed. If she was not mistaken, he now had his eye on her estate.

"I have no interest, nor indeed is it in my nature, to have people study by my side. I have written and published numerous books on my subject. Let him study those. I have not the patience to be a teacher." Caroline pushed to her feet, using the side of her chair and her walking stick. She knew Thomas hated that she stood taller than he. She might well be old but her back had not bowed. She stood for a moment, staring down at him. "If you insist on staying, I suppose I must offer you refreshments." She pulled the embroidered cord that hung to one side of the enormous fireplace. She almost smiled, thinking of Power dashing from the servant hallway to be available to respond to the bell. She returned to her seat, inwardly delighted to have metaphorically cocked a snoot at this little twerp.

"You are still everything that is gracious." Thomas swept the tails of his morning coat aside before taking a seat uninvited.

"Let us dispense with this mockery of civility." Caroline had no desire to spend time with this little man – little in stature and nature. "You have your eye on my estate for one of your sons. *Allow me to continue!*" she snapped when he looked like interrupting her. "We have never been close. I was already married and had my own home when you arrived into this world. I feel no family sentiment towards you or your issue." She shook her head. "Five sons and three daughters, Thomas. Is that not a little excessive for a man of the cloth?"

"The Bible –"

"Yes, yes, but does the Bible pay to support such a large household?"

"You come perilously close to blasphemy, sister."

A knock sounded on the door.

"Come in!" Caroline responded. The man was proving even harder to converse with than she would have imagined. The only good thing her nephew Clive had ever done, as far as she was concerned, was to run this little man out of Ireland. Thomas had been terrified of Clive for some reason – although they were of an age.

"You rang, m'lady?" Powers stood in the open doorway, presenting the perfect image of a butler.

Chapter 11

Percy Place
Dublin

"Whatever is the matter, Georgie? You do not at all appear your usual self." Richard sipped brandy from a crystal balloon, regarding his friend across the hearth.

He had enjoyed yet another entertaining and delicious meal served in the servant's dining room off the kitchen in the basement of Georgie's house. After which they had retired to her sitting room to enjoy a relaxing brandy – just the two of them. The strictest of society matrons would be horrified at the very thought of an unrelated male and female enjoying a moment of ease unchaperoned – but Georgie was a widow now – did that count?

"I fear I could be having some kind of attack of the nerves." Georgina sipped her brandy, staring into the fire.

"Is there anything I can do to help?"

"I feel I have been running in place for too long, Richard."

She continued to stare into the fire without speaking and was grateful when her old friend simply waited for her to gather her thoughts.

"Charles Whitmore," she refused to call that man her husband, "dismissed my staff and left me penniless. I daresay he found it amusing to think of me floundering." She swirled her drink. "A woman I never knew assumed my identity and ran up enormous debt around town. You know all of this, Richard – you were by my side through all of it."

"It gave me great pleasure to assist you, my dear," he said.

"When I was approached to assist the BOBs, I agreed – not out of any wish to assist my fellow man – although perhaps I should say woman – but because I was offered cash I so desperately needed. I had just taken custody of Sarah, Ruth, and Bridget, the three young orphans, and had no way of paying their stipend. I had Lily and Betty, my loyal retainers, to think of – I took in a lodger to further aid my finances – then Flora turned up on my doorstep."

"Are you now wishing them all to Hades?" Richard stood to replenish his brandy.

"I don't know what I wish, Richard. That is the problem." Georgina drank the last of her brandy, wishing she was bold enough to fling the snifter into the fire. She imagined she would enjoy the explosion that would follow.

She shook her head when Richard approached with the brandy decanter but he ignored that and replenished her glass anyway.

"Does this have anything to do with the fact that you found out this morning that you are wealthier than you could have imagined and no longer have any financial worries?" Richard asked as he sat down again. He didn't know what else could have cast her into the doldrums. "Do you wish you could turn back time?"

"Turn back time to when – a time when my parents lived and everything looked so promising – or when Charles Whitmore lived and I crept around this house beaten and bruised, terrified of every shadow? Turn back time to when, Richard?"

"My dear …"

"There are so many demands on my time and attention. How am I supposed to split myself into a dozen pieces so that I may handle all that is demanded of me?" Georgina wanted to just collapse and wallow in her own concerns for a moment – was that so wrong?

"Georgie, at the table this evening there was much talk of engaging staff." Richard had been entertained and amused by the many opinions offered as to the wants and needs of this strange household.

"Yes …"

"In my humble opinion you have a great deal of the help you need close to hand. Hear me out," he pleaded when she looked ready to object. "You have Billy Flint and his army of Smiths and Joneses living in your carriage house. Those men are ready to tend to your every need. You have Lily and Betty who between them have a lifetime of experience in running your household. You have Flora who is desperate to pay you back for giving her a home. You have help, Georgina. You must simply learn how to ask for the assistance you need. And then there is me …"

"You have always been the best of friends, Richard."

"Georgie …" No, it was too soon to speak of his feelings for her. She had only just escaped Whitmore's coils. She needed time. Not too much time. He had missed his chance with her once before. He would not step aside again. "You must learn to delegate, my dear. The help you need is there – use it."

"I have feared to state my opinion and needs for so long, Richard." It sometimes seemed to her – in the dark hours of the night – that her late husband had beaten the fire out of her. How could she recapture the woman she had once been? "How does one seek assistance from those in their care?"

"Speak with Flora!" Richard laughed. "Have her make one of her infernal lists. Make a list of everything you feel is hanging over your head – the chores that you feel only you can deal with – and then examine them."

"And when I find myself buried under this long list of chores – what then?"

"Delegate, my dear. Do we need to make it the word of the day as we did in our youth? *Delegate*."

The following morning – after an excellent night's sleep – due perhaps in large part to the brandy she had consumed – Georgina felt ready to take matters in hand. She enjoyed an excellent breakfast with the members of her household and now sat in her drawing room making a list of matters that she felt needed immediate attention. A knock on her door signalled the first of her visitors. The door opened when she shouted enter and Billy Flint put his head inside.

"You sent for me, missus?"

"Come in and take a seat, Billy, please."

Georgina looked at the tall handsome young man as if she had never seen him before. The changes in his appearance since she had first met him were marked. He stood taller, his shoulders pulled back, displaying his manly form – a form gained through hard physical work. His caramel-coloured hair was spotlessly clean and windswept, his handsome face close-shaven, emphasising his strong jaw. The wicked gleam in his cobalt-blue eyes almost brought a blush to her face. Billy Flint was a man to turn female heads. She had offered this stranger the use of her carriage house in return for services rendered. She had never imagined how many times and in how many ways she would call upon those services.

"How can I help you, missus?" Billy prompted when he'd taken a seat and the lady of the house just stared at him.

"Billy," Georgina picked up an envelope from a nearby table and opened it, "I received a letter – no, rather, let us say a note – written in an uneducated hand – a Miss Sally Mulligan is demanding my attention …"

"Demanding?" Billy sat forward in the chair.

"That is certainly how it appears to me." Georgina passed the note to him. "Do you know this address?"

"I do – it's just a good stretch of the legs from here." Billy knew the address and knew it was not somewhere a lady of Georgina's sensibilities should ever visit.

"I would like to employ you to take care of this matter …" She held up her hand when Billy looked ready to interrupt. "You have carried out so much valuable work for me, Billy. I don't know if I have ever really thanked you for all you and your men do around here."

"You gave me somewhere decent to live, missus." Billy shifted on the chair, embarrassed to be thanked. "What me and my men do around here is nothing to what you offer us. We eat well, you had indoor plumbing installed in the carriage house. I can be warm and clean and owe nothing to no man. That is beyond price in my world."

"Nonetheless, I am aware of what I owe you." Georgina said. "My own situation – from a financial viewpoint anyway – has vastly improved." There was no point in standing on her dignity with this young man. He had known from the day he met her that she was practically penniless.

"I am happy about your good fortune," Billy said with a wide smile.

"Billy, I now wish to offer you a salary …"

"No offense, missus, but I don't want to be tied down to a job." He could make more money ducking and diving around. He intended to make something of himself.

"No, no, you misunderstand." She was making a mess of this. "Let us say instead a retainer. Something you should already have been paid but I simply could not afford."

"We have helped each other out." Billy squirmed on his seat. "I am not unhappy with our bargain." He was enjoying living in a comfortable home, with a better address than he had ever had, and indoor plumbing to boot. This house and its many changing inhabitants were teaching him how to go about in society. Why, thanks to this woman he knew a duchess and an earl, by God!

"Billy, I need help. I need your help. I am no fool. I know where that address," she nodded towards the note he still held, "is located. I know the late Captain Charles Whitmore was not always what I would consider an honest upright gentleman."

"No …" Billy didn't know what to say.

"I want you to handle matters such as this." Again she indicated the note. "I will pay you a monthly retainer to handle this affair and any others of this nature that might occur. You have been a mine of information and assistance to the women of this house, Billy. I am simply asking you to continue to be so — starting with whatever the writer of that note, this Miss Sally Mulligan, is demanding of me. Can you do this?"

"No better man." Billy knew just who to ask about this. Georgina knew the person in question too but he'd keep that close to his chest.

"I will pay you a guinea a month …"

"Plus, the use of the carriage house?" Billy tried not to fall off his chair. That was a bloody fortune.

"What would we do without Billy Flint at the bottom of the garden to run to?" Georgina laughed.

"We have a deal." Billy stood and broke the rules of society by offering to shake hands with a woman. He didn't know and he didn't care. A handshake sealed the deal as far as he was concerned.

"Thank you, Billy." Georgina's smile was wide as she shook hands with someone for the first time in her life. She found she liked it.

"Can I keep this?" He held up the note.

"Yes, indeed," Georgina passed him the envelope. "I will be glad to get it off my desk."

"Leave it to me." Billy took the envelope. "I'll get back to you as soon as I know something."

"Thank you. Now, would you be so kind as to tell Agatha I wish to speak with her?"

"I'll do that."

Billy took his leave and Georgina sat back in her chair. First item off her list.

"Agatha ..."

"Before you say anything," Agatha Hancock was sitting stiffly by the fire in Georgina's drawing room, almost glaring across at Georgina, "if you are thinking of offering me the position of housekeeper, I thank you for your consideration, but I want to return home."

"I rather thought that would be the case." Georgina had never believed this woman would stay. "Do you believe your old position in Limerick on the Babington-Hawthorn estate will still be available to you? And has Helen offered to share any of the monies she received with you?" She could not in good conscience let this woman go without at least knowing what, if any, plans she had made.

Agatha shook her head sadly. She had been bitterly disappointed in that young woman. She had tried so hard to help her in her hour of need – given up everything for her – because she was the daughter and the living image of the man Agatha would always love. She mourned his untimely death still. "I am ashamed to say that Helen thinks only of herself. She may well look like her dearly departed father, but she has her mother's hard heart."

"What then are your plans?" Georgina ignored the remarks on Helen's character.

"Mr Ethan Babington-Hawthorn has discussed the situation at length with me. I am once more to swallow my pride and return to Babington Hall, head bowed. With Mr Ethan's blessing, I will concoct a story that will delight the old master – claiming I ran away to protect his grandchild for him." Her sigh seemed to shake her body. "I will return to my previous position and pray the old master doesn't linger on this earth much longer. I will not be alone in my delight when Mr Ethan takes his rightful place as Master of Babington Hall."

"You have made arrangements then to leave us?" Really, what else could Georgina say or do?

"Mr Ethan has given me the money for my train fare back to Limerick and a little extra. I will arrange transport back to Babington Hall from there."

With that, she stood to leave.

"Let me know if there is anything I can do to facilitate your leaving," said Georgina.

"Thank you." Agatha was unsure of herself. Was she supposed to thank this woman for taking them in?

"Please send Molly to me with tea for two and scones if Cook has any to hand," Georgina said to Agatha's stiff back.

"Molly, I need advice."

Georgina was sipping the tea Molly had delivered and joined her to drink. The scones had been appreciated and soon disappeared. She enjoyed listening to Molly's delight in everything. Her view of matters was vastly entertaining.

"From me, missus?" Molly was surprised.

"Yes … Helen …"

"Before you say anything, missus!" Molly jumped to her feet. She had been enjoying taking tea with the mistress like the gentry. Trust bloody Helen to ruin it. "I need to walk about. I cannot sit still and talk about that one – she fair does my head in. And having to share a room with her is a nightmare!"

"I had thought you would have some sympathy for Helen. After all, you too came to us to escape being forced by a man you detested."

"And I get down on my knees every night and thank God for you and this house, missus. You saved my life and no mistake – but bloody misery-guts Helen – I fair want to slap her upside the head at least twenty times a day."

"Molly," Georgina interrupted what could very well turn into a rant, "has Helen made any mention at all of her plans for the future. Surely she must have some ideas?"

"Missus …" Molly returned to her seat. "I think – and it's only my opinion, mind – but I really think the bawld Helen thinks the money she will get for that baby is enough to allow her to sit here, in your house, for the rest of her days, enjoying her own drama."

"Oh, dear!" Georgina gasped.

Chapter 12

"Well, well, well – '*The dead arose and appeared to many*'! Billy Flint, what are you doing at my door? I thought you'd forgotten all about the little people now that you're going up in the world."

The woman known locally as Granny Grunt stood in the open doorway of her basement room, staring up at the young man she'd known since birth. Hadn't she delivered him into the world?

"Put the kettle on, Granny!" Billy laughed. "I have a bit of business for you."

"Give me a minute. I don't normally invite people into me room." Granny shut the door in his face.

Billy stood with his back to the basement door, looking out on a yard with a free-standing tap. Barefoot and in some cases bare-arsed children who lived in these tenements ran around. This enclave of poverty, known locally as The Lane, was hidden amongst the wealthiest Dublin streets. It was just a short stroll from Percy Place and across the canal weir into this well-concealed area.

The door opened at his back.

"Come on in then but wipe your feet." Granny was known for her wisdom and herbal knowledge, but she would turn her hand to most things to make a penny. A woman had to keep body and soul together.

Billy made a show of wiping his feet on the bare cement before following her into her room.

"Sit on the windowsill – there's not enough room in here to swing a cat."

There was one comfortable chair in the high-ceilinged room and that was Granny's. She had the room divided with a curtain that went from halfway up the high wall to the floor, hiding her bed and chamber pot and anything else she might have. That curtain was pulled closed now.

Billy didn't take a seat on the narrow windowsill – it would pinch the arse off him – instead he sat on the floor, close enough to her chair to have a quiet conversation with her. He watched and waited while she prepared tea over the open fire.

"I don't suppose you've been drinking out of enamel mugs over there in Percy Place." Granny passed one of the mugs of tea she'd poured to Billy before sitting in her chair with a sigh. "I've no milk so you'll have to drink it black."

"What, no slice of lemon?"

"Get away with you, you cheeky article!" Granny blew on her tea. "Now, tell me what you want with me. It's hale and hearty you're looking so you don't need one of me herbal tonics."

"I need information and, depending on what you tell me, your company." Billy knew if anyone could help him with Georgina's problem it would be Granny. He might well need Granny to accompany him to the address he'd been given.

"What's in it for me?" It didn't do to give information out for nothing.

"This to start," Billy raised one butt-cheek off the floor and searched in his pocket for one of the silver shillings he'd put in there before leaving his place.

"A shilling!" Granny had expected a penny or perhaps a threepenny piece, but this did surprise her. "You want me to help you rob the Crown Jewels?"

"Give over, Granny," Billy said. "This is serious."

"I can see that." Granny stared at the silver piece in her open hand.

"What do you know about Sally Mulligan?" Billy asked.

"*Aah!*" Granny closed her hand over the coin. She'd earn this. "I wondered when she would raise her head up."

"Tell me what you know, old woman." Billy tried to find a comfortable position on the hard floor.

"Sally – do you know her?"

"I might know her face but not to put a name on it." Billy knew a lot of people by sight.

"Well, Sally Mulligan is the younger sister of yer one that swanned around Dublin claiming to be Mrs Captain Charles Whitmore. Lord, she was a hard-faced cow, but she didn't deserve to die so young. Still, she was where she didn't ought to be, I suppose – in the Earl of Castlewellan's private carriage, on that train that crashed and killed everyone." Granny shook her head.

"Well, this Sally Mulligan wants something with Miss Georgina. She wrote to her and almost demanded a meeting. Any idea what she might want?"

"Well," Granny sucked on her mug of tea, "Sally and her sister ran three houses for Whitmore up and around Baggot Street."

"*What?*" He had never heard anything about this. How was he going to face Georgina and tell her something like this?

"I never did tell Georgina what I knew. That poor woman had more than enough to handle with Captain bloody Whitmore and his brood of ungrateful sons. She was under their thumb and beaten down. Why should I bring more worries to her door?"

"But – three houses – all around Baggot Street?"

"In that general area, not next door to each other," Granny said. "You wouldn't want the redcoats taking a notion to raid a street, now would yeh?" Ireland had been under English rule for centuries. The streets of Dublin fairly heaved with red-coated soldiers supposed to keep the peace.

"Are they all brothels?" Billy asked.

"Oh, nothing so vulgar, Billy. No, no, you make more money if you put a bit of class to the place."

"Well, what are they then?"

"I only know this from keeping me eyes and ears open and me mouth shut." Granny fingered the shilling. "If they are the houses I am thinking of – and I'm not sure of me facts – one is a gambling den, but only for the better class of customer – one is used to rent clean rooms by the hour – and the other supplies services for people with – let us say – out of the ordinary tastes in their delights."

"What kind of delights?" Billy felt as if he was getting an education here.

"Men who like to be hurt – or men who like to hurt – take your pick. Sally runs that house."

"Name of God!" Billy was wide-eyed.

"You don't know everything, young Billy."

"What will I tell Miss Georgina?"

"Nothing, you will tell her nothing … yet. Now, you listen to me, Billy Flint." She leaned over and lightly slapped his cheek. "It is not our place to judge how people make a living. There is many a one that puts food on the table for their children and a roof over their heads working in those houses and others like them. Who are we to judge?"

91

"Name of God!" Billy ran his hands through his hair.

"Now if you'll take my advice …"

"Gladly."

"You will go home and get yourself dressed up like a Little Lord Muck. I've seen yeh and I know you can do it. You will go meet with Sally and you will learn everything she has to tell you about those three houses. There is a fortune to be made there, lad, for those who have the stomach for it. Those that take the cream off the top keep their hands clean and rake in the cash. You go see what Sally wants and learn from her. She and that sister of hers had good brains behind their pretty faces. Take yourself off now and make yourself gorgeous before you go to see Sally. But keep your wits about you, young Billy, for that one could buy and sell yeh."

"I'll do that." Billy's head was spinning. He pushed off the floor to his feet. He put his hand in his pocket and took out another shilling, offering it to Granny. She had more than earned it.

"What's that for?" Granny stared at the coin in his hand.

"For my education."

"I would like to speak with Miss Mulligan," Billy raised his hat to the man who opened the door. A butler – well, what passed for a butler. He knew the man by sight. Billy had run the streets of Dublin for years and knew many more than would ever know him. This man had been a bare-knuckle boxer in his heyday – as his battered face could attest.

"Your card," the man mumbled.

"I do not have an appointment." Billy raised an eyebrow and stared the man down. His card, indeed! That was taking the thing a bit too far. He opened the leather briefcase he carried and removed the letter – one of the few items in the briefcase – and held it up. He didn't want to give this man a reason to lash out. "I have come in response to a letter Miss Mulligan sent to my employer."

"If you would care to step inside." The muscled butler checked the street as he opened the door wider, allowing Billy to enter. "If you would wait in the green drawing room." He opened a door off the entrance.

Billy followed, removing his hat. He stepped into the green drawing room, barely biting back a whistle. This place looked like a home of repute. Certainly, the decorations were just a tad vulgar in comparison to other homes he had seen but only just a tad. The number of mirrors placed all around the room was startling. He resisted pulling at his white collar. He was not comfortable in these surroundings.

The door to the room opened. A slim woman, clad entirely in black with a square of black lace covering her blond hair, entered and shut the door at her back. He knew her to see. She wouldn't recognise him as the snot-nosed child that once ran wild around these streets.

"You wished to see me." She stepped forward.

"Are you Miss Sally Mulligan?" Billy felt as if she'd undressed him, her examination of his person was so detailed. This was not a woman to trifle with.

"I am." She waited.

"I am here in response to a letter you sent." Billy had not returned the letter to his briefcase and now held it out for her view. "Could we perhaps sit down?"

"Not in here." She turned on her heel. "This room is for guests. Come into my office." She walked out without checking to see if he followed.

Billy put the letter in his breast pocket and followed her out in silence. There were no staff to be seen but then perhaps houses of ill repute operated on a different timescale to homes. Who knew? He didn't.

"I hope you have at least had the decency to bring me a cheque!" Sally snapped as soon as the door to her basement office was closed. She waved at a chair in front of the desk which Billy took, putting his briefcase, his hat on top, onto the floor by his feet.

"Miss Mulligan, you sent a rather demanding letter to the home of a lady." He stared at her. She hadn't taken the seat behind the desk. He didn't like her staring down at him. He was playing poker with a viper. He needed to hold the winning hand. "That lady in turn passed it on to her man of business, having no idea who you were or what it was you were demanding. Her man of business – understanding the matter – has sent me to make enquiries." Well, that was as clear as mud.

"*I need funds!*" Sally almost roared. "*Do you think these houses run themselves – I have staff to pay!*"

"You realise that with the death of Captain Charles Whitmore matters have been in disarray." Billy couldn't believe the words coming out of his own mouth.

"*My bloody sister!*" Sally kicked at the desk. "Always so sure she knew what she was doing. Always so certain she held the winning hand. Well, she's dead now and I am left to deal with the fallout." She began to cry. "She was sure and certain she could talk that old man Whitmore into signing these houses over to her – especially after he lost his legs – bloody pandered to him she did. *And for what!*" Tears were running down her face.

Billy didn't know how to react.

A knock sounded on the office door and, without waiting for permission, the butler stuck his head around the door he held open.

"Everything all right, Sally?"

"Come in, Dad." Sally collapsed into the chair pulled up to the desk.

"Dad!" Billy wanted to clap his hands. If he wasn't very much mistaken, he was in!

"What's going on?" Sally's dad stepped into the office, glaring down at a seated Billy.

"Miss Mulligan, Mr Mulligan …" Billy decided it would pay to be polite. He needed the information these people held. "I am sorry for your loss. It is difficult, I am sure, to lose a daughter and sister." He didn't know how it might feel, he was glad to think, but it sounded good. "With the death of Captain Whitmore and your daughter matters have fallen into – quite frankly – a muddle. Tell me how I can be of assistance?"

"*We need money,*" Mr Mulligan bit out.

"Dad …" Sally dropped her head into her hands.

"Well, does he think these bloody bawdy houses run on fresh air, Sally? That lot are getting all the money and you're worn to a bone trying to keep up."

"I know, Dad – I've told him so."

"Pardon me," said Billy, "but couldn't you remove the funds you need from the cash in hand?" He figured these houses must be a goldmine.

"*What bloody cash?*" Mr Mulligan roared, his fists clenching. "Everything is done on credit round here – no filthy money must pass through our hands. It lowers the tone, don't yeh know?"

Whitmore, you clever bastard, Billy thought. No cash, so no danger of any thief getting it into his head to break in and rob the place and with no cash the people who worked for you couldn't rob you blind either. By God, that man had been a 'cute whore' as they said in certain circles.

Chapter 13

The following morning a sharp rap on the exterior basement door of the Percy Place house sounded. The household were at breakfast and for a moment everyone looked at everyone else. Who in the name of goodness came calling this early in the morning – and at the back door? Though, technically, it wasn't that early. Each member of the household had a cup of tea and a piece of bread first thing in the morning but there were a great many chores to complete around the house before the Percy Place household was ready to sit down to the first full meal of the day.

"Liam, see who is at the door." Cook ordered. She wasn't moving away from her breakfast. She'd only just sat down.

Liam shoved a piece of bread dipped in egg into his mouth before pushing away from the table – still chewing – and ran to the back door.

"Good man!" Billy Flint didn't wait for the door to be fully opened to him. He pushed the door wide open gently, forcing Liam back into the hallway that was off the kitchen leading to the back door. "I'll just step in for a minute. You go back to your breakfast, lad." He almost laughed at the food decorating the lad's face. "A growing boy needs his food."

Liam didn't need to be told twice. He turned and dashed down the hallway, back to the staff dining room where he sat down and attacked his food again.

"Were you born in a barn, Liam Mulvey?" Cook demanded. "You didn't shut the door behind you – and who was at the door? You never said."

"Billy Flint and some woman." Liam was more interested in his food.

"What woman?" Lily Chambers asked.

"Ladies," Billy Flint put his head inside the door, "sorry to disturb you but I found someone loitering around the grounds this morning."

"You …" Lily started to rise.

"No, no, don't get up." Billy stepped into the room. He was looking for Georgina, but she wasn't there. "Look who I found." He stepped to one side, revealing the figure of a short stout woman hiding behind him.

"Ermatrude Willowbee!" Cook exclaimed. "As I live and breathe, what are you doing out and about so early in the morning?"

"I'll leave your bag here." Billy put Ermatrude's briefcase on top of one of the sideboards in the room – not the one covered with food.

"I am so sorry." Ermatrude or "Erma" as the BOBs had renamed her – was one of the original group of women sent to this house by them. She dithered in the doorway. "I know it is frightfully early to pay a social call," she wrung her hands, "but I just wanted to get out of that house for a moment."

"Sit yourself down," Cook said. There was no need for introductions, Erma had lived in this house for long enough. "There's a couple of spare chairs. Miss Georgina wanted a lie-in this morning." And, as usual, Dorothy had already left for her work at the nearby factory. Cook looked around the room as if seeking divine intervention. "Flora," she ordered, "put another cup and saucer on the table."

Erma sat down.

Agatha had hoped to mention her plans to travel back to Limerick after breakfast, when everyone was gathered around the table. She'd keep her tongue behind her teeth and her news to herself until they found out what this latest brouhaha was all about. Helen carried on eating, having nothing to add to the moment. Molly was waiting to see what was about to happen – there was never a dull moment in this house, it seemed to her.

"I'll leave you to it, ladies." Billy didn't want to hear what this was about. He had enough concerns of his own. "I'll get back to my own breakfast. Mrs Chambers, if you would ask Miss Georgina to make a time for me to speak with her privately sometime today, I'd appreciate it."

"Yes, of course, Billy." Lily looked from Billy to Erma – what was going on?

"Here, Erma." Flora put a cup and saucer in front of Erma. "Have you eaten?"

"No, no, I haven't." Erma gave a weak smile to all at the table.

"Then fill a plate for yourself," Cook said. "There is full and plenty. Flora, get her a plate."

Lily looked at the youngest members of the household. They had their heads bent to their plates, stuffing food into their mouths, but she knew their ears would be wagging, wanting to hear every word said. She wondered if she needed to remove the youngsters from the room. Was whatever was about to be said suitable for their ears?

"Ruth, Sarah, Bridget and Liam," she began. "If you youngsters have finished –"

"There is no need to send them away, Mrs Chambers," said Erma, who was at the sideboard filling a plate with breakfast food to overflowing. She could imagine what concerned the housekeeper. "I have not brought bad news to your door. I am merely having what one might well call an attack of the vapours."

She brought her plate and a knife and fork to the table and took a seat. She bent her head to her food and said nothing more.

Cook and Lily exchanged glances but, with nothing to do or say, began to enjoy the food that was before them. Time enough to find out what had brought Erma here.

The meal was over and the youngest were being encouraged to clear the table under the watchful eye of Lily Chambers.

"Flora," Cook had matters to attend to, "if you would take charge of Erma while we get our day organised."

"I am frightfully sorry for any trouble I have caused you," Erma again apologised.

"You go with Flora," Cook stood up. "I must send a tea tray up to Miss Georgina. The dishes need to be washed and the day planned. We will meet in my kitchen alcove later and share a pot of tea if you need to talk to me and Mrs Chambers."

"Thank you." Erma hung her head. "The meal was delicious as always, Cook."

"You go along now with Flora. She'll soon sort out what's what." Cook hoped this was true.

"There is no need to bother, Flora." Erma sighed hugely. "Would it be possible for me to read the letters from America – please. Somewhere quiet and out of the way. I never get a chance to really study them when in company with the Dowager Duchess." Erma, through the good offices of the BOBs, had been employed as secretary to the Dowager Duchess. "I long to learn the news about the women who went to America. I did, after all, come to this house in their company."

Cook nodded. "Flora can help you there."

"Come along, Erma." Flora put her hand on Cook's arm and held her in place for a moment. "I will take the tea up to Georgina, Cook. Just give me a moment to get Erma settled."

"Georgina, Georgina, you need to wake up!" Flora stood over the bed and waited to see if Georgina would budge. Poor woman, it sometimes seemed to her that this distant relative of hers had the worries of the world on her shoulders. "*Georgina!*" she fairly hissed.

"*Huh!*" Georgina tried to snuggle into her pillow. "*G'way.*"

"Come on, Georgina!" Flora urged. "Rise and shine."

"What time is it?" Georgina struggled to awaken. She had been enjoying a blissful sleep. She begrudgingly pushed herself into a sitting position, swiping a hand at the hair falling in her face – not for Georgina fabric strips to encourage curls – she could not be bothered fussing with that piece of vanity.

"I brought up a tea tray – we let you sleep as long as we could," Flora said. "I know how you hate tepid tea. So, let's be having you as they say around here."

"What is going on?" Georgina braced herself for whatever might be coming.

She allowed Flora to place the tray across her lap and pour her a cup of tea from the small delft teapot wrapped in a knitted tea cosy that sat on the tray.

"Ermatrude Willowbee is downstairs weeping and wailing." Flora stood over Georgina while she sipped gratefully at her tea. "She is reading the letters from America with a damp handkerchief clutched to her heaving bosom."

"Would you go away out of that!" Georgina used one of Cook's favourite phrases while staring over her teacup. "You should be writing fiction, you rascal!" She couldn't prevent the smile that touched her lips. "What is really happening?"

"Erma really is downstairs." Flora sat on the side of the bed, being careful not to upset the tray and scald Georgina. "She arrived early this morning, claiming she was having some sort of crisis of the nerves. I didn't ask her what she meant – nor did anyone else. That is all I know. But, as you well know, if Erma is here, the Dowager Duchess and her cronies can't be far behind."

"That is all I need to start my day." Georgina poured the remains of her tea into the slop bowl sitting on the tray under the tea strainer. She poured herself a fresh cup of tea, added milk, and waited.

"You had to know we would be invaded by the BOBs once that batch of letters arrived from America," Flora said. It was the usual thing in this house now – letters from America arrived and shortly afterwards the Dowager Duchess and her companions came to visit.

"I did, of course, but I could pray for an extra day …"

"Well, it doesn't look like you are going to get it." Flora wasn't unsympathetic but one had to face facts. "So, you need to rise and face the day." She went to stand when she suddenly remembered. "And Billy Flint stepped in to say he wants to arrange a private meeting with you sometime today." She slapped her knees and stood. "There now, I've given you all the news."

"I am taking a long hot bath!" Georgina snapped. "If the Dowager Duchess happens to arrive before I have finished, you can tell her I am about my ablutions." The nod of her head had her hair falling once more into her face.

"You've been mixing with high society too much, my girl." Flora stood with her hands on her hips, smiling widely. "Ablutions, indeed! What's wrong with telling the old girl you are giving yourself a good scrub?"

The pair giggled at the very idea of saying something of the sort to the very proper Dowager Duchess of Westbrooke.

"There now," Flora said. "It does the heart good to start the day off with a laugh." She headed for the door. "I'll let you get about your *ablutions*." The sound of her laughter carried into the room as she closed the door at her back.

"Oh, for goodness' sake," Georgina muttered to the empty room. "That means I will have to make an effort with my dress." She sighed deeply. It wouldn't do to appear before the Dowager Duchess in anything but her best clothing. I had planned to speak with Flora today, she thought.

She almost swore when she discovered the small teapot was already empty.

Chapter 14

Georgina hurried down the stairs, suitably groomed for greeting any guests. She was tightly corseted, wearing a shirt top with a high neck and puffed sleeves in pale blue and a waisted skirt in navy blue — perfect attire, she hoped. Her damp hair in a loose chignon was secured at the back of her neck. She checked the gold fob watch she wore on her chest, gasping slightly at the time. The sound of voices carried from the rooms on the first floor. Flora must have started the household dusting in preparation for their uninvited guests.

"Flora! Bridget!" On reaching the first floor she put her head around the door to the drawing room. The pair, covered in sacking aprons to protect their dark work clothing and wearing headscarves, were busily dusting. "I need you to stop what you are doing."

The pair turned to stare at her.

"Flora, if you would change into something appropriate, please. I would like you to join me in speaking with the Dowager Duchess and company. Bridget, your best uniform. You may open the front door to our guests and carry out whatever duties Mrs Chambers gives you."

Ruth and Sarah came into the hallway from the dining room on hearing her voice. They too were covered in sacking aprons and wearing headscarves to protect their clothing from the cobwebs that had to be brushed regularly from the ceiling gaslight fittings.

"Where are Helen and Molly?" She would have expected that pair to be assisting in the cleaning.

"Agatha is preparing to pack her belongings," Flora answered. "Did you know she intended to leave?"

"This is not a prison, anyone who wishes may leave. Agatha mentioned something to me about her plans to return to Limerick. It was nothing definite as far as I was concerned."

"Well, she is upstairs now packing her chests, being soundly berated by an extremely irritated Helen for even thinking of deserting her." Flora grimaced. "There has been much weeping and wailing. Molly is taking care of the baby."

"I cannot turn my attention to that drama at this moment in time." Georgina wanted to bang heads together but now was not the time. "Flora and Bridget, if you would quickly change. Ruth, if you would carry the cleaning supplies down to the basement, please, and ask Cook to prepare a small plate of bacon and eggs, with toast and a large pot of tea for me. I will eat in the staff dining room. Sarah, check the ladies' water closet – a polite term for the toilet and washbowl set up on this floor for the use of guests. "Be sure everything our guests might need is close to hand."

The four, so ordered, scattered.

"Flora," Georgina's voice halted Flora for a moment on the stairs, "where did you put Erma?"

"Erma was in the staff sitting room the last I saw of her." Flora continued up the stairs.

"Thank you." Georgina wondered how long it would be before the Dowager Duchess arrived. There was only so much they could do and, really, when people insisted on visiting without so much as a by your leave – well, they could take them as they found them. The thought didn't do much to quell her anxiety.

Liam stepped through the doorway that led from the basement to the first floor of the house. He had a well-filled bucket in each hand. His skinny shoulders bowed under the weight.

"Bless you, Liam. Have you cleaned the fireplaces on this floor?" Georgina hated to see a child so worn down.

"I had all the fireplaces in the house cleaned out before I sat down to my breakfast, madam." Liam was very aware of his importance – being the only male in the house. "I am going to set the fires on this floor now. Did you want me to put a match to them?"

"If you would, Liam," Georgina said as she hurried away. If she was lucky, she could escape into the staff dining room before Erma saw her. She wanted to enjoy something substantial to eat and a large pot of tea before having to deal with anyone's woes.

Georgina blotted her lips with her linen napkin, sighing in delight. The meal as always had been delicious – Cook was a marvel.

Flora, after a quick rap of her knuckles on the servants' dining-room door, stuck her head in to say, "The carriages have begun to arrive. The Dowager Duchess's in the lead, of course."

"Let me see you." Georgina leaned back in her chair. She refused to jump up every time these ladies deigned to visit Percy Place.

Flora entered then twirled to show off her finery.

"That shade of bronze looks wonderful on you," Georgina said.

"I am not wearing corsets." Flora ran her hands down the blouse she wore. "It is ridiculous – in my opinion – to force your body into something that cuts off your breath."

"And you've gone for the shorter length of skirt too." Georgina ran her eyes over Flora's outfit. "Very daring."

"Every time these women visit, I find myself running up and down stairs at their beck and call." She pulled out one side of her bronze-coloured skirt, revealing more of her brown-leather laced-high boots. "This new length allows me a greater freedom of movement."

"Bridget will open the front door." Georgina pressed her hands against her eyes, trying to think of everything that needed to be done. "Please awaken Erma. It wouldn't do for her employer to find her asleep. Then, if you could take the letters from America upstairs and share them with the ladies of the BOBs. That should keep them entertained. I will be upstairs momentarily."

"Take your time." Flora turned to leave. "No doubt this lot will want to see the places mentioned in the letters on our map." The map was much in demand when the ladies visited. As the map was painted onto the basement wall and could not be moved, Flora would take the ladies out the front door of the house and down the granite steps to the basement entrance concealed under the steps. The basement door led directly into the hallway where the map was situated, so there was no need to bring the ladies into the kitchen area of the basement. "Here is Erma now," Flora said as she stepped out, leaving the door open at her back.

"Oh, Georgina, whatever must you think of me!" Erma hurried into the room all of a flutter. "If Sarah hadn't awoken me I daresay I would be in disgrace." She stared around the room and with a gasp put a hand to her bosom. "Thank goodness, there it is!" She put a hand on the briefcase Billy Flint had carried in for her and left on the sideboard. "I couldn't think what I might have done with it. I didn't even take the time to restore order to my appearance."

"I want to enjoy another cup of tea." Georgina waved a hand towards Erma. "You take the time to step into the servant's bathroom. We will go upstairs together."

"Thank you, I won't be long." Erma spun on a heel. "Do not leave without me. I do not want the Dowager Duchess to believe I have been derelict in my duties."

"Hurry along, Erma. Time is passing."

"Yes, yes, I will be right back."

Georgina leaned back in her chair, closing her eyes. The tea was too tepid now for her taste, but she would just sit here and collect herself.

"Ladies!" Georgina stood on the granite stone landing, at the top of the steps leading up from her front garden to her door. She stood for a moment directly in front of the main entrance, her hands folded at her waist and watched the parade.

Bridget, with the Dowager Duchess holding tight to her elbow to steady herself on the steps, led the way up the granite steps to the entrance door. Lady Arabella, Lady Beatrice and Flora followed close on their heels. Bridget was beaming at the pleasure Georgina knew she found in wearing her best uniform – dark skirt wide with petticoats, black bodice, gleaming white apron with frilled straps that crossed over her shoulders and down her back to button at her waist – with her golden curls pinned under a lace cap.

When they were halfway up the entrance steps Georgina turned and entered the house, leaving the door open.

When the top of the steps was reached, the Dowager Duchess dropped Bridget's arm. The young maid stepped to the side out of the way, head lowered. In deepest purple, looking every inch the society leader, the Duchess stepped through the door and into the hall where Georgina waited. Lady Arabella Sutton, in deep pink, was next in social standing and followed her, with Lady Beatrice Constable, wearing lemon, next in line. Flora brought up the rear.

"Georgina, we have been to view the map in your basement," the

Dowager Duchess said as she entered the hallway. "I must have one of those maps. I say it each time we visit but today I am determined."

Georgina smiled and waited.

"We have much to discuss and decide today. But where is Erma? She left a note with my butler to say she was travelling ahead of me this morning. My carriage driver informs me he left her at your home – at a ridiculously early hour of the morning for visiting – where is she?" The Dowager Duchess stopped to draw breath.

"Georgina, wonderful to see you," Arabella said, smiling.

"Thank you for having us – yet again," Beatrice added.

"Ladies, shall we step into the drawing room?" Georgina watched Bridget hug the wall as she tried to work her way around the ladies unobserved and open the drawing-room door. The hallway was becoming ridiculously crowded, the wide skirts the women wore taking up a great deal of space.

"No, no," the Dowager Duchess stated. "The dining room – we have a great deal to discuss. Erma has the paperwork we need for our consultation – where is that woman?"

It was Flora's turn to hug the wall on the opposite side of the hallway from Bridget, heading towards the dining room to open the door.

"Erma is already in the dining room, arranging the paperwork on the sideboards," Georgina said, turning towards the dining room.

"Georgina, we will be taking up a great deal of your time today." The Dowager Duchess stepped through the door held open by Flora. "Erma, there you are!"

"Your Grace!" Erma jumped, almost dropping the papers she held.

The Dowager Duchess took the chair Flora held for her, at the head of the long dining table.

"We must –" she began.

"Constance, allow us time to organise ourselves." Lady Beatrice addressed her in the familiar fashion it had been decided they should use when conducting the business of the BOBs. With so many titled ladies in the room it became tedious to constantly refer to someone as 'Your Grace' or 'Your Ladyship'. They did not have the time to stand on ceremony.

"Yes, of course." Constance allowed Flora to arrange her chair. "There is simply so much to do, and I am eager to begin."

"Are refreshments needed at this time?" Georgina stood to the side of the table, watching Flora and Bridget seat her guests.

"If Flora could remain with us to assist Erma with the paperwork," Constance said, "tea and a snack would be most welcome."

"We each had our chefs prepare a basket of foodstuffs." Arabella took her seat. "Not to insult your household, Georgina, but we cannot expect your staff to prepare all that will be needed today."

"We have a great deal we wish to achieve," Beatrice said from her place at the table. "It was decided that we would each supply foodstuffs since our servants too will require nourishment throughout the day."

Octavia White-Gershwin, one of the first women to be placed by the BOB's in Georgina's house and now employed as companion to Lady Arabella, had made the suggestion that a contribution to the household might be appreciated.

The women expected their maids and their carriage staff to wait for them. That also meant caring for their horses and drivers. It would demand a great deal of the few staff members that Georgina had available.

"We may well be here all day," Constance said, much to Georgina's well-concealed horror.

Chapter 15

Georgina, smiling serenely, reminding herself to think of the swan floating on the canal, stepped out of the room. She waited until the door was closed at her back before picking up her skirts and running down the hall, through the door, down the stairs and practically exploding into the crowded basement.

"*They may well be here all day!*" she wailed. "*What in the name of goodness are we going to do?*" She didn't wait for a reply. "Sarah, Ruth, best uniforms, quickly. You will no doubt be needed to serve."

"I can't spare Ruth." Cook stood with her clenched fists on her hips. "Have you seen this lot?" She waved one hand at the three enormous baskets taking up space on her kitchen worktable.

"Tavi, nice to see you." Georgina allowed a moment to greet Octavia White-Gershwin, a pretty strawberry blonde who stood to one side of the kitchen, smiling broadly. Octavia, on discovering her brother had gambled away the family fortune had turned to the BOBs for assistance.

"Georgina, I have placed the maidservants who accompanied the BOBs in the servants' sitting room for the moment," Tavi said. "If I could borrow something to protect my clothing, I could assist Cook." The spoiled, bitter aristocrat who first came to this house would never have thought to offer assistance. "I can still remember Cook's lessons."

"Come with me." Lily Chambers couldn't refuse help. "I will find you one of Cook's large wraparound aprons." She stopped for a moment to say to Georgina. "Billy Flint has the carriage drivers and their horses in hand. The men will come into the house to eat and warm themselves in relays, he informed me." She led Tavi from the room.

"The ladies want tea and a snack served now, Cook." Georgina, while mentally thanking the Good Lord once more for Billy Flint, almost cringed at the look Cook threw her.

"*Liam!*" Cook barked. "Get that fancy uniform on you! You can give Bridget a hand with the tea things."

"Bless you, Cook." Georgina backed towards the exit.

"Now to the first order of business." Constance held out her hand towards Erma. The Dowager Duchess swung the long rose-gold chain, attached to the bosom of her top with a pair of gold rimmed pince-nez attached, from one finger as she waited for the correct file.

The women were gathered, tea and a snack served by Bridget and Liam with the assistance of Erma and Flora, around the dining-room table.

Erma, who mercifully knew which file Constance wanted, placed the brown cardboard-covered file on the table by the her elbow.

"I have received a letter from Miss Judith Babington-Hawthorn …"

"My godmother," Beatrice reminded everyone at the table.

"Indeed." Constance put the pince-nez on the tip of her nose with one hand while opening the file with the other. "Miss Judith Babington-Hawthorn is too much of a mouthful to read here so we will simply refer to her as Miss Judith." She expected no objections and waited for none but continued. "It would appear that someone has approached Miss Judith concerning the whereabouts of one Helen Butcher." She stared around the table. "Is that not the servant girl who was brought to this house in distress?"

"It is indeed, Your Grace." Georgine dreaded to hear what was coming.

"Now, now, Georgina dear, no titles when about the business of the BOBs," Constance said with a smile.

"I apologise. Do you wish me to send for Helen?" Please say no, she thought rather frantically. Helen would faint and tremble in this company, she was sure.

"No, no, there is no need for that." Constance didn't raise her head from reading the file. "I have had Erma make a copy of the letter which I will leave with you. You will need to discuss the issue with this Helen Butcher and send a response as soon as possible to Miss Judith. I know I can leave this matter in your capable hands, Georgina."

"May we know what is happening, Constance," Beatrice asked. After all, it concerned her godmother, did it not?

"Haven't I said?" Constance looked up.

"No, dear," Arabella said. "You have not."

"Well, it would appear this …" she had to consult the file again, "Helen Butcher was stepping out with a young man by the name of Ernest Cunningham who was, and still is, in service at the same house in Limerick." She looked around the table. "This is why fraternising between the servants is severely discouraged. He is making rather a nuisance of himself, according to Miss Judith. He wants to know where Helen is and to be given the opportunity to approach her."

"Does he indeed?" Georgina wondered if this could be an answer to her prayers. Helen had been offered a sum of money to give her baby up to its natural father. Would this young man consider marrying her?

"It is all rather fascinating," Constance said. "The young man has been in training for years with the baker and cake-maker at this estate in Limerick – apparently the 'Big House' provides bread to all on the estate. Well, that is not unusual – what is unusual is that this young man has a relative in Canada who wishes to pay his way to travel out to join him with a view to opening and operating a bread-making factory – have you ever heard of such a thing?"

"That is fascinating." Georgina wanted to jump up and dance. Surely Helen would agree to go with her young man – surely?

"I would not dream of purchasing bread manufactured in a factory," Arabella said.

"Not everyone has a personal chef and baker," Beatrice remarked.

"That is none of our never mind," Constance said. "Georgina, if you could pass on Helen's response – that should be all that is needed." She passed the file back to the attentive Erma. "Next." She held her hand out, waiting for the next file to be placed in it.

While this was going on, Flora moved to refresh the teacups.

"Ah yes!" Constance said when she opened the next file. "This concerns you most, Arabella." She gave the file back to Erma. "Pass that along, please. Arabella, you can deal with this while I enjoy my tea."

"Is this the file with Petunia's letter?" Arabella opened the file Erma had placed on the table. She glanced over the letter inside before closing it again. She put a hand across her mouth and bowed her head.

Everyone paid attention to their tea while Arabella gathered her composure.

Arabella raised her head and with bright eyes stared across the table at Georgina. "Petunia Wallace-Mountford, at a very young age, was my dear companion and governess. She is a marvellous educator and I owe her much." She took a deep breath. "Petunia accepted a position at a lady's academy in Paris. She was delighted to be permitted to educate girls …"

"Do continue, dear," Constance prompted when Arabella stopped speaking.

"Georgina," Arabella went on, "this is not at all the usual BOBs case – Petunia is not seeking our assistance with a placement. She desires at this time somewhere that decent women may stay while they ponder their circumstances."

"Are there no ladies' hostels to be found in Paris?" Beatrice asked.

"Petunia Wallace-Montford has been of inestimable help to the BOBs through the years," Constance put in. "The woman and her family, while having no money to speak of, have the widest of social connections. Petunia has made those connections available to the BOBs. She has helped so many and never asked for anything in return. This is the very first time that she has asked for anything for herself. I would like to help her if it is at all possible."

"Wait, ladies. Let me refresh my memory of the details." Arabella opened the file again and read. Then she looked up and took a deep breath. "There are, in fact, three ladies seeking shelter. The school where Petunia was employed has been having financial difficulties for some time. It has become more fashionable to send young ladies to Switzerland. That is neither here nor there. Petunia and her friend," she consulted the letter once more, "Miss Susan Templeton – who has served for years as the school's cook – wish to remain together. Petunia's niece – a student at the school – will remain in Petunia's care at this time. Therefore, Petunia is seeking somewhere for the three of them to reside until such time as they may make plans."

"Arabella," Georgina looked into the other woman's eyes, "I opened my home to Dorothy as a lodger at a time when my finances were desperately strained and I needed her rent. That situation, thankfully, no longer exists. Now I have no need to turn my home into a lodging house for ladies."

"You misunderstand," Arabella said. "Petunia cannot afford to pay for three ladies to rest somewhere in comfort while they sort out their future. She asks that the BOBs help finance their stay in a home open to the ladies the BOBs assist – not to sit around in idleness – but to offer their services in any capacity needed while they try to come up with a situation that will allow all three of them to remain together."

"Is this not the very situation we are educating our young ladies to avoid – offering their services freely for a roof over their head?" Georgina said.

"Petunia and Susan fully intend to place an advertisement in the *Lady's Journal* magazine offering their services as companion and cook to a respectable lady – preferably somewhere by the sea. They both wish to return to Ireland. The problem is Thelma – the niece. She has been a student at the school in Paris. As has already been stated, the family have great connections within society but not a great deal of money – they have never been what one might call a family of means. Thelma's father – Petunia's brother – has leased out the family estate and his house in London. He cannot offer his daughter a home at this time. Petunia needs time to organise her affairs. She asks that we find her lodging within a house that supports the BOBs. I immediately thought of you when we heard of Petunia's plight."

"Me," Georgina said.

"You are desperately pressed for staff," Beatrice put in. "That is obvious."

"You need help, Georgina," Constance said.

"But these ladies are not seeking employment in my house," Georgina objected.

"As I said, they are prepared to work for their lodgings," Arabella said. "Think about it, Georgina." Arabella was practically begging. "You need help. Susan has cooked for young women for years. She might perhaps know of someone seeking employment. She could at the very least help in interviewing cooks for this house. Petunia grew up expecting to run her own household and was trained accordingly. She has had the training of young minds for years. She is skilled in knowledge of the domestic duties needed to run a home. She could assist you. She too would be an ideal person to offer help and advice on the hiring of servants. Georgina, please consider opening your house to these ladies! The BOBs will, of course, pay the usual amount for their care."

How could she refuse? If she had three women willing to lend a hand, surely that would relieve some of the pressure on her own household? Then, too, she had the three orphans she was supposed to be training. Bridget was a special case, of course, but the other two seemed determined to spend their lives in service. These women could help her deal with that issue.

"Allow me to think on the matter," she finally said.

"You do not have much time!" Arabella almost wailed. What would she have become without the guidance of dear Petunia? The woman had guided her steps into her role as a modern woman of means. Why, she might have ended up like dear Beatrice, forced into a marriage that brought her nothing but sorrow. Petunia Wallace-Mountford had taught her the importance of standing up for herself and the skills to do so and manage her own affairs.

The women busied themselves with the business of enjoying the tea and the snack that were being neglected. Flora and Erma stood back – hands clasped at their waists – trying to be practically invisible.

"Very well." Georgina felt she could do nothing but agree. She hoped she wasn't making a mistake. "I am prepared to offer shelter to the three ladies."

"Thank you," Arabella said fervently. "You will not regret it."

"Excellent," Constance said. "Erma, make a note to yourself. Contact Petunia post-haste. Also, we should determine if there is a trading vessel offering passenger cabins travelling between Cherbourg and Dublin. If so, purchase cabin tickets for the ladies. It will save an enormous amount of time hauling luggage between train stations and whatnot. It is the least Petunia deserves of us."

"That is extremely kind of you, Constance," Arabella said.

"If we have reached a natural stopping point," Beatrice said, "I wish to visit the ladies' water closet."

"Capital idea." Constance too needed to visit the toilet.

Chapter 16

When the ladies reconvened, after a visit to the necessary, Constance insisted a brisk walk in the open air would freshen their minds and relieve the pressure of their corsets. It would also incidentally allow staff to clear the dining room.

There was a great deal of running around by the ladies' maids before the three titled ladies were suitably attired to step out into the fresh air. Together with Georgina, they set off to enjoy a gentle meander along the banks of the Grand Canal.

When they returned to the house they were glad of the heat being provided by the blazing fire in the dining room – which Liam had taken the opportunity to rake out and reload with coal. The table had been cleared of anything to do with tea. It now held a hand-embroidered centre piece with a crystal decanter of water, slices of lemon floating in it. Four glasses stood close to hand in case of need. Four chairs were pulled away from the table, awaiting the return of the ladies.

A bulky brown file sat at the head of the table.

Flora and Erma had been given permission to leave the room and seek their own refreshment.

"Ah, well done, Erma!" Constance stood by her seat at the table, patting the file on the table. "I requested she leave this file close to hand."

"Is this why you cleared the room of servants?" Arabella leaned against a sideboard. Not simply because, as a matter of social etiquette, she couldn't sit until the Dowager Duchess did – but also because standing was far more comfortable than sitting when one was so tightly corseted.

"I did wonder." Beatrice held her hands out to the fire, enjoying the warmth but careful to keep her full skirts away from the flame.

Georgina wished they would get on with it. She needed to check on her household.

"I wanted us to be private when I opened discussion on this matter," Constance said.

"Is it a particularly disturbing situation?" Beatrice turned from the fire and joined Arabella by the sideboard.

"Not in the way you mean," Constance said. "At least I don't think so." She gave another pat to the file. "I received not one, not two but three letters from people deeply involved in the BOBs about this situation." She sighed deeply and looked at each woman in the room. "They can have no idea of the can of worms they have opened for all here."

"You are being awfully dramatic, Constance," Arabella said. "What on earth do you mean?"

"The three missives concern a young female." She paused for a moment. "Lady Rebecca Henderson, eldest daughter of the late Earl of Castlewellan …"

"Oh, heavens!" Beatrice put one trembling hand to her breast.

Georgina's eyes widened as she remembered the note from Jenny concerning that girl.

"Our chickens have come home to roost," Arabella, who spent a great deal more time on the grounds of her family estate than anyone knew, used a farming analogy.

"What exactly is the problem for this Lady Rebecca Henderson?" said Georgina. Should she mention Jenny's note? Perhaps not – she would wait and see.

"According to her grandfather – a man who has generously donated to the BOBs for many years – Rebecca is the most wonderful female who ever drew breath. However," and here she paused to once again stare at each woman, "she resembles her late father the Earl greatly. She has the same golden hair, green eyes and striking good looks …"

"Oh, Lord!" Georgina didn't care if she was committing a social faux pas – she fell into the nearest chair. "You are surely not thinking of asking me to house this girl!" She shook her head violently. "*I cannot.*"

"Lady Rebecca is not yet one and twenty." Constance began to pace around the table. "She is young, beautiful and most damaging of all – extremely wealthy."

"With her father dead," Beatrice gasped what they were all thinking, "she has no one to protect her. The poor woman is a target for every grasping opportunist in the land."

"Indeed." Constance continued to pace.

"Who were the other missives from?" Arabella thought to ask. "You have mentioned her grandfather – who else contacted the BOBs?"

"Lady Caroline Wormsley – aunt to the late earl and one of our most devoted members."

Beatrice and Arabella groaned aloud – Georgina simply stared, having no idea who the lady was.

"Mrs Josephine Daniels – her godmother …"

"The chit is certainly well connected!" Arabella gasped.

"Ladies," Georgina put in, "I am at a loss."

"Lady Caroline Wormsley – aunt to the late earl – is a woman of great personal renown. She has travelled the world both with her late husband and alone collecting samples of trees never seen in Europe. She then imports, plants, and germinates the trees in her own extensive grounds. She is considered a leading authority on tree germination and care. She has written many well received books on her subject. Her gardens are visited by thousands of renowned gardeners from around the world." Beatrice was a great admirer of the lady.

"She also provides shelter in her home and grounds to the ladies the BOBs send to her and has done for years," Constance added.

"Mrs Josephine Daniels," Arabella said, "is everything one could wish from a supporter of the BOBs. She not only takes in and hides a great many females – she also holds a yearly charity ball – with all proceeds going to the BOBs."

"Could one of those not hide the young woman?" Georgina asked.

Constance, who was still standing, opened the file on the table. She removed a document and held her pince-nez in front of her nose for a moment. "Mr Purdey, the young lady's maternal grandfather, is extremely ill with that dreadful shaking disease that I daresay we are all aware of. He does not have many good days, I am told." She picked up another document. "Mrs Daniels cannot take the girl because she is her godmother, and it is well known she considers the girl another daughter. Lady Caroline – while being a blood relation – has had nothing to do with the girl. However, her estate marches cheek by jowl with the larger Castlewellan estate. It would not be safe to hide her there."

"So, they must remove her from her home." Georgina stood and gazed around for a moment as if lost, before walking over to stand staring into the fire. She understood the danger this young woman was in. While she herself had never been a renowned beauty, her inheritance had made her a very attractive target – not only to the grasping man she had married but others. The girl would be safe nowhere her name and fortune were known.

"According to the letter I received from Mrs Daniels, the girl has already fled her home. She was forced to leave her grandfather – a man to whom she is devoted – her horse and the dog she has had as a companion for most of her life ..."

Gasps sounded at the distress the young woman must feel.

"One's animals are sometimes closer than family," Beatrice said softly.

"The girl – again according to Mrs Daniels and her grandfather – has not led a sheltered life. She has worked by her grandfather's side since she was very young. She has been educated to take an active part in the Purdey family business. Which is something to do with fruit and flowers, I believe." Constance shrugged. She knew nothing of labouring in a business. "Mrs Daniels insisted the child should receive dancing, art and music appreciation but the young girl truly loves working the land."

"It sounds to me that this young girl is a chip off the great-aunt's block." Arabella too enjoyed working the land and overseeing the family estates but had to do so largely in secret. A lady was not supposed to do anything that might resemble work. "Lady Caroline had to fight every step of the way for her right to travel and pursue her own interests."

"This is not a girl who should be locked away like the mad aunt until she comes of age – even then she will never be safe from the

122

fortune hunters that litter society." Beatrice shook her head sadly. "If she has spent her life outdoors working the land, it would be evil to expect her to sit indoors sewing a fine seam." There was a trace of bitterness in Beatrice's words that no-one there understood.

"Should we then address the 'elephant in the room'?" Georgina said.

"I am afraid we must." Constance sat down with a flurry of skirts.

"Bridget ..." Arabella and Beatrice said together.

There was silence as each waited for the other to speak.

"If Bridget were not a factor," Constance said slowly, "Lady Rebecca could be educated in this house – much as we educate the ladies we have sent to Mr Harvey in America. While waiting to be old enough to touch her own funds, she could be educated in how to handle her own affairs – here in this very house. But there is Bridget ..."

"Who has been treated disgracefully." Arabella almost flounced into a chair.

"What could Eugenie do?" Beatrice protested. "The situation she found herself in at the time was such that it was not thought she would survive. She was at death's door, for goodness' sake!" She had taken an interest in the case when she met Jenny in this very house. She had interviewed some of the older women of the BOBs, seeking information about the woman now known as Jenny Castle, formally Eugenie, Countess of Castlewellan.

"I was not a dowager duchess then." Constance shook her head sadly. "I was involved with the BOBs, of course, but not to the extent I am nowadays. I heard and knew of the case. What that man had done to the woman who was his countess – it was never revealed in polite society but the BOBs knew the details – and one would have had to be deaf not to hear the whispers. The disappearance of the Countess of Castlewellan was a nine-day wonder."

"The BOBs of the day did the best they could. It would not have been easy to hide a woman who was thought to be fatally injured. Jenny was not expected to survive the birth. Everyone involved was endangered but they did what they could to keep the mother alive until the babe was born. The countess survived against all the odds. It took much careful planning to get Jenny and then her new-born babe to safety. The fuss the Earl was making at the time hindered every stage of the venture. From reading the files and speaking with some of our older members – this was one of the most difficult cases the BOBs ever handled. They did what they thought best – now Bridget is reaping what has been sown."

"They kept mother and child alive!" Constance slapped the table-top. "Let us not forget that. They were kept alive at great risk to all involved. The law was on the Earl's side. She was his legal wife – he could do what he liked to her."

"I remember those days in my nightmares." Georgina joined the ladies around the table. "Eugenie was far too young to be handed into the care of the Earl. We spoke of running away together but we were too young and knew no one who would or could help us. Clive Henderson, the Earl of Castlewellan, was the catch of the season. He was so good-looking, young and charming. No one understood Eugenie's reluctance to be his bride." She shook her head as if she tried to shake the memories away. "I care deeply for Bridget. If things had been different, I would have stood as her godmother."

"She is the legitimate daughter of the late Earl of Castlewellan and his countess," said Constance. "She was born to their union. She is a lady and should be recognised as such. She should never have been turned into a maid of all work." She struck the table with the side of her fist. "Lord knows Eugenie paid enough monies to those nuns to raise the babe in silk and satin."

"I don't believe there is a record of her birth anywhere." Georgina thought then of the box her great-aunt the Reverend Mother had left for her at the Goldenbridge Convent – could that clever old woman have thought of a way to see that Bridget came into her rightful inheritance? She wouldn't put it past her. She really must make time to go and fetch whatever the nun had left for her.

"We are indeed on the 'horns of a dilemma', ladies," Constance sighed. "It would appear we must occupy ourselves with the two daughters of the late Earl of Castlewellan."

"It has been suggested to me," Georgina began while her brain was frantically trying to sort out the problem, "that I should attend the special services to be held in the grounds of the Castlewellan Estate – home to the Earls of Castlewellan – for those lost in the train crash that took the Earl and my husband's lives. It would – it has been pointed out to me – establish me firmly as the widow of Captain Charles Whitmore – which all here know me to be. I can't think how … but I wonder if my presence could somehow be worked to Rebecca's advantage in this situation …"

"What a splendid idea!" Constance clapped her hands. "I will accompany you. You must take Flora with you as your companion. We will pay our respects and at the same time provide cover to smuggle the Lady Rebecca away! Truly, it is divine intervention!"

"I shall not attend," Beatrice said. "Not to be thought crass but, Georgina, I didn't like or respect either man. I can see no reason to attend."

"I too will not attend," Arabella said, "but I will place my carriage and driver at your disposal, Georgina. You will need more than one carriage. Constance has never been known to travel lightly."

"That is kind of you, Arabella," Constance said, "but we shall not be travelling by horse carriage. We will travel by train – a journey that could take days will pass in hours aboard the train! Leave it with me. I shall instruct my staff to arrange to have my private rail carriage attached to the Dublin to Belfast train. I am sure we will need to change train-tracks somewhere along the way – my staff will handle that. So we will travel in every comfort."

"Surely planning such a journey is beyond Erma's capabilities?" Georgina didn't want to denigrate Erma, but she simply couldn't see her plan such a complicated journey.

"No, no," Constance said with a laugh. "Erma is responsible for the work of the BOBs only. My social secretary and companion – a fiercely efficient woman – will organise everything down to the last little detail. I would be lost without dear Letitia to organise my life."

"Letitia will handle everything," Arabella said, nodding.

"You will travel safely with Letitia McAuliffe at the helm," Beatrice agreed.

Georgina had never met or heard of this Letitia before – but then she didn't move in the same social circles as these ladies.

"We must make plans," Constance said. "There is no time to lose. We will attend this service, establish dear Georgina's bona fide legal status and spirit Lady Rebecca away. What could be more satisfactory? We will face the problem of the half-sisters Rebecca and Bridget when we have to, ladies, and not a moment before." She pushed to her feet, practically dancing in place. "I do love to be involved in matters of skulduggery." She laughed. "Come, we will refresh ourselves before calling down to the kitchen for lunch. This really is splendid, ladies. We have achieved much."

Chapter 17

Georgina was draped inelegantly in a chair pulled close to the fire in her study, legs stretched out, toes pointing to the ceiling, heels keeping her braced in the chair, arms hanging over the sides of the chair to the floor, head thrown back — completely and utterly exhausted in mind and body. It was far too early for an adult female to retire to her bed — but, dear Lord, this day had felt as long as a year.

A baby crying somewhere in the house brought a pain to her heart. At one time she had thought it would be her child or children crying and laughing around this house, but it was not to be.

She heard Sarah, Ruth, Bridget and Liam making their way up to their beds in the attic. They must be exhausted. So much had been demanded of them today. The barely heard hissing conversation going on between the foursome sounded disagreeable but she couldn't bring herself to care — not at this moment in time.

She desperately tried to ignore the knocking on the study door. She did not want refreshments. She did not want company. She did not want conversation.

Whoever was knocking was not going away.

With a grunt of displeasure, she pushed on her heels, held the arms of the chair tightly, and pushed her aching body upright.

"*Come in!*" she barked out. She amused herself for a moment by imagining that she could shoot flames from her eyes. She would reduce whoever was at the door to ash.

"I'm sorry." The door opened and Billy Flint stuck his head through the opening. "I know the last thing you want is company, Miss Georgina, but," he stepped into the room, closing the door at his back, "what I must talk to you about can't wait. I really am most terribly sorry to disturb you."

"It is I who should apologise, Billy." Georgina waved to the chair across the hearth from where she sat. "You asked for a meeting with me, but I was invaded."

"I know." Billy sat. He too had been frantically busy. "I had boys and men running madly around the place, handling all of them horses." He shook his head. "What must it be like to travel somewhere and expect everyone to jump to attention? Three carriages, Miss Georgina, all the horses – what did they expect those men to do with all of them horses, I ask your sacred pardon?"

"What did you do with them, Billy?" She had felt immensely grateful to him but had not found the time to thank him.

"I had the men walk those carriages and horses across to the stables in The Lane. Those horses were warm, dry, and well fed in the Ryan stables, I can assure you. Old man Ryan was almost in tears, thinking of the money he could charge for stabling fees. The carriages were out of the weather too."

"I will see those fees are promptly paid," Georgina promised.

"I know you will." Billy looked into the fire.

"That is not why you disturbed me, Billy. You know well I will pay promptly for today's services. What is upsetting you?"

"Why would you think something was upsetting me?" Billy liked to think he kept his thoughts to himself.

"It is written on your face." Georgina smiled. "Besides, you asked for a meeting with me – did you not?"

"I did …"

"Well, what is it?"

"I went to see the woman who wrote you that note … Sally Mulligan …" Billy could feel his cheeks heat and hoped she'd think it was from the fire.

"Billy," Georgina sighed, "is it a brothel, as I feared?"

Billy ignored her question for the moment. It was what he had thought himself to begin with, after all. "Sally Mulligan – the woman runs or ran three houses for the Captain." He had decided to use her late husband's title rather than name.

"Three!" Georgina gasped, staring at Billy in horror.

"They are not bawdy houses as such." Billy pulled at the neck of his jumper. He was determined to get through this. "One house is set up as a gambling den – for the better class of gentlemen. The place, from what I heard and was told, is a gold mine. Georgina," he leaned forward to say, "the three places run by this woman are making money hand over fist. The amount of money taken nightly made my eyes water. It's like the pot of gold at the end of the rainbow."

"That it should come to this!" Georgina, her elbow propped up on the arm of her chair, rested her cheek on her clenched fist. "Me, Georgina Corrigan, owner of three bawdy houses!" She glared at Billy. "No matter how you try to dress it up, Billy Flint – they are bawdy houses."

"That employ a great number of local people behind those doors." Billy waited.

"Poor women …"

"No," Billy stopped her. "I know it is not what you are used to, Georgina – far from it you were raised – but those women are not poor innocent country girls being beaten and drugged into prostitution. I doubt any of those poor girls woke up one morning and decided to make money from catering to a man's needs – but these women have made that decision, Georgina. They are businesswomen and proud of it."

"Proud!"

"If you will forgive my cheek, Miss Georgina –" Billy was fighting for his life now – he had to make her see reason, "the Captain beat you bloody, used your body and took your money. Those women do the same thing to the men who visit one of the houses in particular – men of strange inclinations – and are well rewarded for it."

"Billy Flint, you are totally reprehensible!" But, when she thought about it, Georgina was forced to concede his point – even if only silently.

"Miss Georgina," Billy learned forward again, "those houses employ cleaners, cooks, waiters, and barmen. They have front-of-house staff that act as maids and butlers, if you can believe it. They are a hive of activity every evening. They support a lot of people."

"But what of the watch?" Georgina referred to the red-coated soldiers who paraded through Dublin's streets and were supposed to enforce the law of the land.

"The redcoats are well paid to look the other way," Billy said. "Then, too, their commanding officers are some of the best customers of those three houses."

"Dear Lord, it is another world! No wonder it is referred to as the underbelly of society!" She shook her head. "Billy, I can't keep houses of ill-repute open. I cannot profit from what is perceived to be the misery of others."

"Miss Georgina," Billy insisted, "the men and women who work in those houses keep a roof over their kids' heads and food on the table. The customers are all well-placed members of Dublin's upper crust and visiting gentry. The Captain and the two women he employed to run those establishments knew what they were about."

"Two women?"

Billy almost flinched. He should have kept his mouth shut but it was out now, and she deserved the truth.

"The woman the Captain presented to others as his wife was Sally Mulligan's older sister." He grimaced apologetically.

"The woman who died in the train crash with him?"

"Yes."

"I see." What could she say?

The two were silent for a moment, staring at each other – each wondering what to say next. Finally, it was Billy who broke the uncomfortable silence.

"Miss Georgina," he looked into the fire, "there is a fortune being made by those three houses. Sally told me that the Captain had been approached more than once to sell one or all of them. She is afraid – deathly afraid – of what will happen to those houses now. The Captain ran a tight ship – you should pardon the pun – but Sally knows some of the toughs of Dublin have had their eyes on those houses. She does not want to see all that she and her sister worked so hard to establish fall into disrepair."

"You have given me a great deal to think about, Billy." Georgina knew nothing about bawdy houses – not their customs – nor indeed their customers. She didn't want to, but she did know people who had very little money. It would be a crime to jettison a profitable business. Wouldn't it?

"Sally needs money now," Billy said.

"Could she not use the money you claim is pouring into those houses?" Georgina would have thought there was a great deal of cash floating around houses of that nature.

"That is the beauty of it, Miss Georgina – no cash changes hands – it is all handled by account." Billy shook his head, still impressed by the handling of those businesses.

"In the name of God," Georgina stared, "are you telling me someone writes up an invoice and sends out statements regarding the activities of *bawdy houses!*" She practically screamed the last.

"Yes." Billy tried not to laugh.

"Who," Georgina demanded, "handles the accounting for such a thing."

"Elias Simpson has an accounting firm. His staff handle all of the invoices."

Billy thought Georgina was going to faint – her eyes practically jumped from her face.

"Elias Simpson! That beggars all belief!"

"It is clever, Miss Georgina," Billy insisted. "There is no cash on any of the premises. No thief would be tempted to burgle the place. The staff can't dip their fingers in the takings. It is pure genius." He shook his head admiringly. "Sally needs to be paid, Miss Georgina. The woman has expenses she must cover. Sally has been sending demands to Elias Simpson and pawning items from the houses while she waits to hear from you. She can't keep going while you decide what to do."

Georgina could feel a headache coming on. "Tomorrow morning, I want you to contact Elias Simpson and instruct him to pay Sally Mulligan whatever is owed and enough to redeem whatever items she has pawned. You will request the accounting books for a possible interested buyer to peruse. Tonight, well, tonight I want you to sit down with Flora and tell her everything you have told me."

"I beg your pardon?" Billy flushed at the very thought.

"This is what I want you to do." Georgina's mind was frantically whirling. Flora was struggling, floundering. There had been talk of her assisting Dorothy but that had not turned out as they wished. The men of the factory resented such a young pretty woman trying to become involved in their affairs. It had made matters more difficult for Dorothy. Flora had no wish to travel to America and become a Harvey Girl. She was instructing Bridget but that did not occupy all her time. Georgina had the impression that Flora had resigned herself to the role of poor relation – always on hand to aid Georgina in any way required for the roof over her head. That could not be. It would be wrong on so many levels.

"You know the alcove in the kitchen – by unwritten law Cook's domain. I want you to use your charm on Cook and politely request that she allow you to speak with Flora in that alcove. I am sure the household are all in the servants' sitting room at that time. You should have peace to conduct your business. Tell Flora everything you have told me. I will meet with you tomorrow when you return from Elias Simpson's offices with the ledgers. At that time, I will tell you my decision. I have some thoughts on the matter, but I would like to sleep on them."

"Tell Flora everything?" Billy wanted to be sure he understood. "But she is only a young girl!"

"Flora has been through more than you could possibly imagine, Billy Flint." Georgina had the germ of an idea. But she needed time to think. She had her best ideas while she slept. "Just do as I ask. Tell Flora everything. I will speak with you both tomorrow once we have the business ledgers from those three houses at hand."

"I'll do as you ask, Miss Georgina." Billy wondered what the next day would bring. But first he had to look across a table and tell a young woman details that would put him to the blush.

Chapter 18

At breakfast the following morning Georgina looked around the table at the people gathered in the servants' dining room.

"I want to thank everyone here for the work they did to keep this house running smoothly during the invasion of yesterday." She smiled around the gathering. "If anyone here has a problem or needs my attention, now is the time to speak. Within the week I will be travelling up to County Down in the northeast of the country by train in the company of the Dowager Duchess. She appears to believe we can make the journey in one day. I am not so certain. So, speak now as I will be busy packing an overnight bag and organising my widow's weeds to wear."

There was silence as everyone looked at everyone else to see who would speak.

"I …" Flora leaned forward.

"I know of your need, Flora," Georgina quickly put in. "We will meet in my study after this meal."

She looked around the table, waiting. When no one else spoke, she sighed inwardly.

"Agatha, have you made arrangements for your return to Limerick?" Georgina ignored Helen's pained cry of disbelief and shock.

"I have almost completed my packing and am waiting." Agatha glared at Helen in a most unloving way. Matters had truly taken a turn for the worst between those two. "I need to be certain about the care of the baby before I leave. Granny Grunt is to instruct us on the use of baby formula. If the baby takes to the formula, he will have no more need of Helen and be able to leave this house. I was wishful to wait until we knew all about feeding the little lamb from a bottle."

"Helen, are you familiar with ..." Georgina had to search her mind for the name, "an Ernest Cunningham?"

Helen's eyes grew wide. "We ... we were stepping out together."

"You were what?" Agatha practically roared.

The eyes of everyone at the table were moving between the two women. They were being vastly entertained by the commotion.

"I didn't spend every moment of my time taking care of my mother's family." Helen glared at Agatha. "Why should I? I wanted a life of my own." She wailed, *"All that is ruined now!"*

"You were stepping out with young Ernest?" Agatha was having a difficult time processing this information. "Young Ernest from the bakery kitchen – the red-headed youngster who bakes bread?" How could she not have noticed what was going on under her very nose?

"We began work at the Big House together." Helen sniffed and stared around the table, disgusted with the lack of sympathy she was receiving. Didn't they understand – her life was ruined. *"We helped each other!"* Her voice had risen to a wail again. *"We became good friends – Ernest is lovely!"*

There was more than one pair of eyes that rolled at the wail the girl issued.

"Would this Ernest not have married you when you found you

135

were expecting a baby?" Molly Mulvey asked in all innocence. It was the done thing after all.

"I will leave you all to deal with this!" Dorothy Lawlor pushed away from the table. Really, Helen would give a saint indigestion. Did she have to enjoy her own melodrama quite so much? "I am needed elsewhere." She had work to do and stubborn men to deal with – Helen was big enough and bold enough to sort her own life out. It wasn't as if she hadn't been offered copious amounts of help. "Cook, thank you for a wonderful meal." She ignored the wails of despair issuing from Helen's throat. How the girl wasn't constantly hoarse from all her weeping and wailing, Dorothy did not know.

"I'll make another pot of tea." Cook was glad to escape the noise for a moment.

The two women left the servants' dining room together.

The four youngsters, Bridet, Sarah, Ruth, and Liam were delighted. It appeared the breakfast break would be extended today, and they could rest their weary limbs.

"Was there a reason you mentioned this young lad, Miss Georgina?" Lily Chambers too was glad of the rest. Yesterday had taken it out of all of them. She dreaded to think of the mountains of housework waiting beyond the door.

"The young man –" Georgina began only to be interrupted by Helen.

"*Ernest would have married me!*" Helen screamed at Molly. "*He wanted to run away with me!*" She gloated for a moment. "But I couldn't tell him I didn't want the thing growing inside of me. How could I? He'd never understand. He would think I was a monster – just like all of you do!" She pushed to her feet, throwing her arms wide dramatically. "Don't think I don't know what you all think of me!" She dropped back into her chair, sobbing.

The sound of a baby's wail carried into the room. The baby had been left warm and dry inside his basket in the servants' sitting room with the door propped open while breakfast was served. It would appear the young man was awake and ready for his own breakfast.

"Somebody, go get that thing – it will be hungry – and dirty too, I daresay," Helen continued to sob. *"I hate my life! I wish I were dead!"*

"That can be arranged." Molly stood abruptly – her hands clenched into fists. "There are times when I could willingly kill you." She walked over to Helen and took her by the upper arm, pulling her to her feet. "Come on, you moaning Minnie, that poor little fella didn't ask for you as a mother. He needs feeding and you are getting paid to do it. So shut yer gob and come along." She began to pull Helen from the room.

No one objected. They simply sat and stared at the carry-on.

"No one move me plate!" Molly said over Helen's wails. "I'm hungry and thirsty still! I'll supervise the baby and bring him in here when he has been seen to, but I want more food and I'm gasping for a drop more tea!" She continued to haul Helen towards the door as she spoke. With a grunt she opened the door from the servants' dining room into the kitchen and pushed Helen in front of her.

"Well, we can safely say 'all human life is here'," said Georgina. "Breakfast will be a much quieter event when Helen and her baby leave this house."

Flora, a tray of tea in her hands, followed on Georgina's heels into her study. The two had made their escape when Molly returned with the baby fed and changed. Helen was nowhere to be seen.

"I didn't get a moment to tell Helen that her young man wants to see her." Georgina carried the table from underneath the window and placed it by the fire. "You can put the tray there. We can be comfortable in front of the fire while we talk."

"Liam is a little treasure, the way he keeps all of the fires in the house burning." Flora put the tray down carefully.

"Pour us both a cup of tea," Georgina took one of the chairs by the fireside. "We have much to discuss."

"I thought Billy Flint would go up in flames last night when we were talking – at your insistence, I believe," Flora said as she poured tea into one of the porcelain cups. "He was blushing that much – the poor man was mortified. Why did you wish me to know about those houses?"

When they both had their tea and Flora was settled in the chair across the hearth from her, Georgina said, "Flora, it has become obvious to me – in the time you have spent with us – that you feel tainted by what was done to you."

"You believe I should work in one of those houses?" The cup in Flora's hand shook in its saucer. She'd been awake half the night wondering and worrying about this very thing.

"Good heavens, no!" Georgina gasped. "That is the very last thing I thought or would expect." She was horrified that Flora had thought such a thing even for a moment.

"Then why did you insist Billy Flint tell me all?" Flora's stomach had been churning with anxiety.

"Flora ..." Georgina put her tea on the table. She rose, took the cup and saucer from Flora's trembling hands and placed them on the table. Then she took both of Flora's hands in her own and stared into her startled eyes. "Let me try and put my thoughts into words."

"I didn't know what to think!" Flora practically sobbed.

"Billy Flint has explained to you what those three houses are and how I became the not-so-proud owner?" She waited for Flora's nod and squeezed her hands before releasing them and going back to sit in her chair. "Those houses – let us call them businesses – I have been informed they are gold mines." She sighed deeply but continued to speak. "It has been pointed out to me that they employ a great many people. I do not want to be responsible for putting people out of work, the good Lord knows, but I cannot be the mistress of what I consider bawdy houses."

"What do you want of me?" Flora pleaded.

"I have watched you these past months, Flora. You are suffering from what Granny Grunt likes to call 'the misery of being done good to'."

"What does that mean?"

"You don't believe you deserve to have a good life. You don't believe you deserve to be happy and fulfilled."

"That is not true!" Flora objected.

"Is it not?" Georgina waved a hand before Flora could respond. "You need to spend time thinking about what I have said but, in the meantime, I have to get ready for my journey to the North. It was suggested that you should accompany me – but that would never do. The train stops in Drogheda, Dundalk, and Newry – places where you may be recognised if the man who caged you has people searching the area for you. I will not expose you to that danger." She shook her head. "But I digress – the bawdy houses." She leaned forward to stare at Flora. "I have asked Billy Flint to request the ledgers from each business. I want you to study them. You have an exceptional brain, Flora. That you have informed us is one of the reasons you attracted the attention of the man who kept you caged. I want you to use it. I want you to study each business and assemble a report for me. I want to know everything there is to know about those three houses. If indeed there is a fortune to be made – why should it go to strangers?"

"You want me to run those houses." Flora stared at her.

"No, not exactly." Georgina sat back. "You and Billy Flint share a shame of your origins. He is bastard born and all know it. His mother makes no secret of being the mistress of a rich man. Billy wants to establish his own life – he wants to walk proudly about, knowing he has achieved something of his own. I think – from watching you – that you share the same ambition."

"And?"

"I want you and Billy to make a study of those three businesses. I want you both to know everything there is to know about those three houses and what goes on inside them. Write me a report. Advise me as to what I should do. One thing I will mention to you. If, as Billy has informed me, no cash changes hands in any of those houses – if indeed they write invoices and send out statements – how do they know the men or indeed women have the funds to pay their bills?"

"Billy and I wondered about that very thing."

"Someone is providing financial, and it would seem social information. Who? What does he gain? You need to study the business ledgers, Flora. Learn everything you can and then you must pick Sally Mulligan's brain. The woman knows it all. Ask if she needs more help. She can hardly be responsible for all three houses. Increase her salary. Offer her a percentage of profits. But learn, Flora. If there is a fortune to be made here – why should you not be the one making it?"

"Me?"

"Being without funds is a miserable existence, Flora," Georgina said. "I suffered from that condition for only a short while and even then I had a roof over my head. You have a chance here – you and Billy. You will need him by your side. You will have need of the muscle he always seems to have available to him."

"I would be a known madam!" Flora didn't know whether to laugh or be horrified.

"Indeed, you will not!" Georgina snapped. "You hardly think the wonderful Captain Charles Whitmore was known as a sordid purveyor of flesh – heaven forfend! You must learn, Flora. I will expect a detailed report when I return. And for heaven's sake do not become romantically involved with Billy Flint – that would not do at all."

Chapter 19

"The train will be stopping in Dundalk to take on additional coal, Your Grace," Bates, the Dowager Duchess's butler, stepped into the carriage to announce.

Georgina was trying desperately not to appear stunned by the level of luxury surrounding her. The private railway carriage was decorated in a fashion she imagined would suit a Fairy Queen. It was unlike anything she had ever experienced before. The pale-blue velvet furnishings, the silver accents, the Arabian silk carpet underfoot. The beauty of the interior took her breath away. She'd put her hands behind her back to stop herself from reaching out to stroke the luxurious fabric on the wide armchairs. She wanted to pass her fingers through the prisms of light cast by the coloured glass lampshades attached to the walls. The highly polished timber tables situated between each pair of blue velvet armchairs gleamed and seemed to reflect light around the carriage. All in all, it was breathtakingly beautiful. What a way to travel!

There was a connecting carriage for the butler, cook, footmen and maids who accompanied the Dowager Duchess.

"If you would care to take a turn in the fresh air while the train is at a standstill, Your Grace?" Bates, while taking in everything in the carriage, appeared to have eyes only for his mistress. "I am informed it will take up to twenty minutes to refuel."

"Fresh air, Bates?" Constance exclaimed. "With the smoke and smuts from the engine? I think not."

"Very well, Your Grace." The man bowed from the carriage.

"I would like to step out if that is not too inconvenient, Your Grace." Georgina was about to boil. She had dressed for the winter weather and travel on a train. She had expected to be assailed by smuts from the engine and draughts from badly fitted windows. Constance's carriage was beyond all her expectations. The braziers pumped heat into the luxurious space, adding to Georgina's discomfort. She was sweating and the uncomfortable widow's weeds that she wore were not helping the matter.

"I believe we should all step outside." Letitia McAuliffe, a tall rail-thin lady of uncertain years seemed to glide along by Constance's side. She appeared to anticipate her every want and need. She spoke softly but her words were heard.

"Is there really a need, Letitia?" Constance said. "I am most comfortable."

"It would do you good to stretch your limbs, Your Grace," Letitia said.

"Oh, I know I am in disgrace when dear Letitia addresses me as 'Your Grace'." Constance laughed. "Very well, have someone fetch my furs. I have no wish to catch a chill."

Georgia sat back, keeping her feet well out of the way of the traffic that suddenly seemed to fill the carriage. There were maids to change Constance's shoes so she wouldn't get her feet wet, her dresser to organise her clothing and check it was warm enough and footmen standing with rich furs draped over their arms. Georgina thought the carriage past belief and could happily live in it — but the constant fussing of servants would drive her insane.

"Your carriage will be shunted off to one side when we reach Newry, Your Grace," Bates ignored the hustle and bustle to state. "The carriages will then be attached to a local engine which will take us to Newcastle, a seaside holiday town, I believe. The nearest railway station to our final destination."

"I have arranged for rooms to be made available to us at the new luxury Slieve Donard Hotel in Newcastle," Letitia said. "It is but steps from the railway station, I am reliably informed."

"Very good." Constance waited until her butler was in place to assist her from the carriage.

In Castlewellan, on that same day, Lady Caroline Worsley called for the horses to be hitched to her carriage. She wanted two outriders saddled and waiting to accompany her. She had a most important errand to run.

When the carriage was standing waiting on the apron at the front of the house, outriders at the ready, Lady Caroline emerged from the house, attired entirely in black as befitted the occasion and leaning heavily on her cane. She kept her coachman standing, holding the carriage door open for her to enter, and the driver's lad at the horses' heads, holding them steady, while she continued to give instructions to her butler Power.

"I hope you have notified Aurora Daniels that I require her coach to be put at my disposal for all of today!" Lady Caroline did not bother to lower her voice as she called over to Power who was standing tall on the steps of the manor house.

"I have indeed, milady!" Power said.

"I have no idea of the number of people who will accompany Her Grace the Dowager Duchess of Westbrooke. I can only hope that two carriages will be sufficient. It is most vexing. Who knew that someone of Her Grace's social standing would be attending what should be, after all, a private service for my nephew?"

"Indeed, milady."

"It truly is most vexing!" she reiterated while stepping up into her carriage.

"Yes, milady," Powers said to the disappearing carriage. He waited until the carriage had reached the road at the end of the driveway before stepping back into the house and closing the door.

When Lady Caroline's carriage made the turn into the Daniels' wide entrance from the road, she used her cane to slap the roof. Her driver's lad pushed back the partition that opened in the roof of the carriage.

"Yes, milady?" The young man turned his ear to the opening to better hear the lady's instructions.

"Go around to the side of the house," Lady Caroline ordered. "We will be stopping at the west wing."

"Yes, milady," was uttered before the partition was closed.

On approaching the west wing, a bulky travelling coach standing on the apron that ran around the house came into view. Aurora Daniels, dressed in black, was standing outside the closed entrance to the wing.

"*No, no, no, no, no!*" Lady Caroline didn't wait for her carriage to reach a stop before she lowered the window of her carriage door to shout out. "*Aurora, what were you thinking? The travel coach — for a duchess! Have you lost your senses?*"

Aurora Daniels, sticking her chin out and rolling up the sleeves of her knitted black cardigan, approached the open window. She ignored all of the men standing about taking care of the horses.

"Have *I* lost my senses? What were *you* thinking, Lady Caroline? This family too will be attending the service. How do you think we were going to reach your family's private chapel – walk – or perhaps ride? We have need of our carriage. As it is, it will be a great squeeze. My nephews and brother will have to ride alongside our own family carriage. You are lucky we are allowing you to borrow the travel coach. We could have made use of it ourselves today of all days."

"But I am to escort a Dowager Duchess!" Lady Caroline shrilled.

"I daresay she can travel in your fancy rig. Her servants or lesser beings can use the coach and be glad to have it."

"Oh, this is past believing, Aurora! I distinctly told you I needed the Daniels' family carriage." She pointed one hand out the window – finger raised in the direction of the bulky travel coach. "Not that monstrosity!"

"You have the use of our travel coach and four horses to carry whoever needs to be shifted." Rory put her hands on her hips. "Be glad we are gracious enough to loan it to you."

The servants stood around in the cold, wishing the women would just get on with it. The horses stamped their hooves impatiently.

The travel coach was not designed for speed. It was a big bulky thing with a large rolled protruding section at the rear to allow for travel chests to be stored securely for long-distance travel.

Lady Rebecca Henderson was twisted up inside this protruding section, holding on tightly to the leather straps that hung down to ensure the luggage did not move in transit. Her hands were warm inside padded leather gloves covered with knitted ones to disguise their feminine shape. She prayed the straps would hold her in place without too much shifting. She listened to the women argue, shivering with both excitement and dread.

146

She had been hidden inside the luggage section of the carriage for hours. It felt like days. She had crept out of the house before dawn, wearing the clothing of a local fisherman – dark trousers, a bulky jacket over a knitted jumper with a high collar that came up over her chin, boots and a knitted hat pulled down to her eyebrows over her braided and tightly pinned hair. The clothing gave her some measure of warmth, but she'd had nothing to eat or drink this day and, now that the moment was upon her, she wished the ladies would just get on with it!

"Oh, very well," Lady Caroline conceded. "But I dread to think what Her Grace will have to say about this."

"Pity about her!" Rory glared. "If she is that fussed, she should have brought her own carriage."

"Her Grace is travelling by private railway carriage to Newcastle. It is little enough to ask of us to arrange for her to travel in comfort from Newcastle to Castlewellan." Lady Caroline sighed dramatically. "Very well, let us away. I shall speak with you later, Rory. I am not at all pleased."

Rory turned to the Daniels' driver and ordered him up on the box. He was to follow Lady Caroline's rig.

"The Dowager Duchess is stopping to freshen up at the Slieve Donard Hotel if you should happen to fall too far behind my driver!" Lady Caroline shouted in a very unladylike manner to the driver when he was up on the box, reins in hand.

Rory stepped away to allow the coach to move. She had to force herself to walk calmly towards the house. Rebecca was on her way. She could do no more but perhaps a little prayer for her safe arrival wouldn't go amiss.

In Dundalk, Georgina was staring transfixed at a printed notice, safely out of the weather behind the glass of a noticeboard, on the wall of the railway platform.

"Good, isn't it?" a male voice at her shoulder almost had her jumping out of her skin.

"I beg your pardon?" Georgina turned to see a railway worker, his navy uniform tidy, peaked cap pulled down. He held a green cloth flag attached to a wooden post in one hand and a red flag in the other. Some sort of signalling, she supposed.

"That there picture." He nodded towards the notice Georgina had been staring at. "Haven't happened to see that young woman, have you?"

He didn't give her time to respond – thankfully – since she felt incapable of forming words just now.

"They fair pulled this station apart looking for that one!" He jerked his chin in the direction of the noticeboard. "I never saw her and, if I didn't see her, stands to reason she was never here. Not to mention having half the men in the county out beating the bushes. Never found hide nor hair of her – long gone if you ask me. Still, there be the reward." His attention was grabbed by something happening down the platform and, touching a flag to the peak of his cap, he left her side.

"What has attracted your attention, Georgina dear?" Constance, on Letitia's arm, came to stand at Georgina's side.

"I was admiring the quality of the painting in this notice." She pointed to the painting of Flora that stood out from the ragged pieces of paper advertising services on offer in the region, stuck behind the glass of the noticeboard. "The printer must be most skilled in his craft, the image is so clear."

"Indeed." The Dowager Duchess's voice couldn't have been less interested. "Come along, dear. We need to stretch out our limbs before returning to our stuffy carriage."

The three women turned away from the noticeboard to stroll almost in step along the platform.

"One mustn't grumble of course," Constance continued. "The train is so much faster than travelling by horse-drawn carriage. Progress – we must embrace it."

The three figures, dressed in unrelieved black, were well aware of the attention they were being paid but strolled on regardless.

Georgina's knees were trembling. She was so thankful that she hadn't brought Flora with her on this journey. She could not have denied bearing a startling resemblance to the woman in that notice. She was aware of a whispered conversation being carried on by her two companions but could not force herself to pay attention. Dear Lord, that monster was still searching for Flora! Where else had that notice been posted? Had it been posted in all of the train stations along this line? She had been so impressed by the private railway carriage awaiting her in Dublin that she had paid no attention to her surroundings. She would ask Billy Flint to send one of his men to check out the Dublin railway stations. They needed to know how much danger Flora was in while out and about in Dublin. She sighed deeply. That was a worry for another day.

Chapter 20

Rebecca, her booted feet braced against the rear of the luggage-storage space – her arms wrapped in the hanging leather straps, her back to the carriage body, tried to anticipate the movement of the coach. She tried to force her stiff body to relax. The journey of less than five miles would be a long, long journey, if she didn't move her body with the sway of the heavy vehicle.

An argument being carried out up on the box was just a murmur of voices to her over the sound of the horses' hooves hitting the ground, but it was comforting in a strange way. She wanted to shout and scream in frustration – not at the situation she found herself in – but at her own stupidity. How had she allowed her life to come to this?

It had been decided by the women of the BOBs that the special service being held at the Earl of Castlewellan's Estate – a service to honour the late Earl – Rebecca's own father – would be an ideal time to spirit her away from the people wishing to lay hands on her – well, not on her personally – but on her fortune.

Clive Henderson, the late Earl of Castlewellan, had been her sire.

Yes, she had feared him in life but she should be standing at the front of the chapel today showing her respect – and where was she? The daughter of an Earl – hiding in the luggage compartment of an old coach, praying for deliverance.

How had she managed to close her ears to the many, many lectures she'd received about planning for her own future? Her grandfather, Mrs Daniels, even her friends Allegra and Horatia Daniels had tried to interest her in planning for the future. True, her friends had been mostly interested in the males presented to them – they had a list of requirements for any male seeking their hand in marriage. But not her, oh no, she'd gone blithely on her way, closing her eyes and ears, ignoring all the advice from those older and wiser than herself. It was her own fault she found herself in this predicament. To the sound of the horses' hooves, she felt tears of self-pity flowing down her face.

"Did Aurora Daniels not even think to put lap rugs in this ugly great thing?" Lady Caroline's voice was trumpet-clear.

Rebecca released the leather straps and turned to fit her body along the lip of the luggage space as best she could.

The closures on the luggage cover were snapped open, the sudden light almost blinding Rebecca, but she had no time to think – just act. She put one long leg out carefully onto the cobblestones at the railway station front. With great speed she removed her body from the luggage space and on all fours crawled under the rear wheels of the carriage. While this was going on the snaps were locked back in place.

While Lady Caroline continued to make a nuisance of herself – opening the coach doors – demanding the attention of the driver of the carriage, Rebecca checked the area around the railway station – the way appeared clear. It would appear all attention was being paid to the engine pulling the unusual railway carriages along the seafront and towards the station. She rolled clear of the coach, came to her feet and with her gloved hands pushed into the big pockets of her jacket, chin buried in the neck of the fisherman's jumper, she tried to walk in a manly fashion towards the railway station. She had her railway ticket in her pocket – the BOBs thought of everything.

As ordered, Rebecca reached the station before the train. She stood with her back against the wall, her eyes lowered – checking everything out through her lowered lashes. There were local dignitaries on hand to greet the visiting duchess it seemed. A red carpet was being rolled from the street into the station with shouted instructions being given by a sweating man who seemed to like the sound of his own voice – how much instruction was needed to roll out a carpet? It would appear a great deal of fuss was to be made of the Dowager Duchess. The train came to a complete stop, belching out clouds of smoke. One of the doors to the gleaming silver-and-blue carriage opened and the crowd surged forward. Rebecca stood away from the wall and began to manoeuvre around the crowd which paid her not the least attention. She headed towards the second train carriage.

Letitia McAuliffe had been keeping her eyes peeled for this figure. She had been informed that the young woman would be dressed in the clothes of a sailing man. Thankfully this figure was the only one so dressed. It would have been difficult to spot her otherwise. The disguise was perfect to the casual observer.

"There are two doors to each carriage."

The feminine voice in her ear almost gave Rebecca a heart attack. A hand in the small of her back pushed her towards the nearest door which was slowly opening in the second carriage. While this was taking place, a door further down the carriage opened and a bevy of uniformed servants, loudly chattering, exclaiming over the delights of a day by the sea, practically exploded out of the train.

"Come quickly!" another feminine voice hissed.

Rebecca was pulled into the train before the door was fully open. The door was pulled closed at her back and, as she glanced behind, she saw the woman who had pushed her inside join the crowd, a white lace handkerchief fluttering towards her face.

"Get out of those clothes, quickly."

Rebecca was having difficulty seeing in the darkness. The leather blinds were pulled down over the carriage windows.

"Come along, girl!" the voice snapped. "We don't have much time. The Dowager Duchess can only hold their attention for so long before she must leave to attend the service."

The fisherman's outfit was pulled from Rebecca's shivering body and a dress made of very rough fabric pulled over her head.

"We have no time to do anything with your hair!" the voice said. "Pull out all of those pins and shake your hair about your head."

One of the window blinds – further down the carriage from where Rebecca stood – was opened slightly, allowing a smidgen of light to enter.

Rebecca watched the shadowy figure move about the carriage with confidence.

"Oh, dear, that simply will not do – your hair is far too thick and bright in colour. Pin it back up!"

When Rebecca had obeyed her instructions what she thought must be a mob cap was pulled over her hair and down to her ears, while soft hands made sure all her hair was underneath.

The excited chatter from outside continued to rise and fall while Rebecca was transformed from a fisherman to a serving maid. The fisherman's clothing was roughly shoved into a storage box attached to the carriage wall. A wooden platform was unlocked from the wall over the storage box. The platform had a thin pad attached: it appeared to be a bed of some sort.

"Quickly, put a foot on the storage-box lid and climb up onto the bed." A hand on her derriere gave Rebecca a push. "We have not a moment to lose." The woman was almost panting. "Quickly, girl, lie down, do as I say."

As soon as Rebecca was stretched out on the plank bed a rolled curtain was unsnapped from the ceiling and pulled down, concealing the bed and its occupant. "Lie still and say nothing. You are unwell."

"What ..."

"*Shhh*, this little drama is not complete yet!" the woman hissed.

They remained like that, Rebecca behind the curtains, the woman moving around the carriage. Rebecca could hear her rolling up the leather blinds.

The curtain over Rebecca's bed lifted slightly in the breeze from the open door of the carriage. She pressed her body into the cold wall at her back.

"I am sorry, madam. No passengers are allowed in the carriage while it is being shunted and turned."

"Is there a problem?" said another voice – a male voice this time.

Rebecca didn't know who the voices belonged to but could only wait to see what happened.

"Oh, Mr Bates!" Rebecca's guardian cried. "I must stay here with the sick young maid. This man says I can't – but I can't be responsible if we have to move her – you know what she has been like so far today. I can't say I am best pleased to miss a stroll by the sea in your company – the sea air would have done me a power of good, I have no doubt. But I know my duty. I will remain here while everyone else enjoys their day out at the seaside." The misery in her voice was clearly heard.

"I am sorry, sir, madam, but no one may remain on the trains in the shunting yard. It is against the rules." The guard once again tried to enforce railyard law. "This is a busy railway station, don't you know.

We have the rich and famous coming to enjoy the sea air and the trains from Belfast bring holidaymakers even in this weather. We need the tracks clear. We can't be responsible for people who might take it into their heads to wander about. Now let's be having yeh, missus."

"*Oh, Mr Bates!*" the wail this time was almost ear-piercing. "*You know what's been happening!* I've spent all of this journey on me hands and knees cleaning up this young maid's mess. I don't like to complain but the smell – well, Mr Bates – you know yourself – you couldn't help noticing – it was enough to turn anyone's stomach."

"Indeed," said Bates.

"I don't like to complain," the woman continued, "but I gave her laudanum – just a touch, mind – I couldn't stand the noises she were making – it wouldn't be safe to move her and I can't leave her here alone – how can I? What if she were to throw up again and no one about? Why, she could die, Mr Bates! You read about it in the newspapers. People choking on their own vomit. I couldn't have that on me conscience, Mr Bates. Oh, no, not me!"

"The young maid really is frightfully ill," Bates said to the guard. "I was tempted to throw her off the train in Dundalk but, as butler to the Dowager Duchess of Westbrooke, one is expected to behave in a certain manner – the Dowager Duchess demands high standards from all of her staff. Please allow these women to remain on board the train. I can assure you they will not leave the carriage and wander around the tracks. The Dowager Duchess has reserved staff rooms at the Slieve Donard Hotel, so should there be any problems you can contact me there. Take this for your trouble."

"Oh, thank you, sir! Well, I really shouldn't – but since the carriage is owned by a duchess – well, what is a plain man to do?"

The door was closed and no more was said.

The noise on the platform continued but in the servants' carriage all was silent. When the carriage began to slowly pull away from the platform Rebecca sighed with relief. She had been so afraid that she would be discovered. Her heavy sigh was heard from behind the curtain covering the sleeping platform.

"Do you fancy a drop of tea?"

When the carriage came to a complete stop the curtain over the bed was rolled up into the roof and a smiling face beamed between raised arms while busy hands locked the curtain in place. Then the woman with dark silvering hair and honest grey eyes set into a pretty face stood for a moment waiting.

"Tea?" Rebecca repeated as if she had never heard of the brew.

"I never introduced myself." The woman lowered her arms and held a hand to her chest. "I am known as Mrs Morgan – a title of respect – I've never been married – but you can call me Jane." Jane Morgan looked at the pretty young woman huddled on the plank bed with something like pity in her heart. "We should be safe here. The carriages have been shunted into the railway yard. We would not only see but hear anyone approaching. So, I repeat, fancy a cup of tea?"

"Mrs Morgan, I would love a cup of tea," Rebecca said.

"I'll get the kettle on." Jane turned away from the bed. "We have a spirit stove for brewing tea and I have a large picnic hamper that hasn't been touched. I daresay you are hungry?"

"I am both hungry and thirsty, Mrs Morgan, thank you." Rebecca was close to tears. She had been so frightened. She was not out of danger yet but somehow the efficient Mrs Morgan gave her the confidence to relax – if only slightly. She hadn't slept at all last night and the lack of sleep was catching up on her. She yawned widely.

"The kettle's on." Jane opened cupboards, pulling the necessary items for tea-making and serving from them. She put the items on the tops of the cupboards. "It wouldn't do for you to run around the carriage, but it should be safe to speak – if we do it softly."

"I can't thank you enough for doing this for me," Rebecca said. "Are you truly disappointed not to be able to enjoy the sea air?"

"Bless you, no!" Jane sat on a cupboard top across the carriage aisle from where the kettle sat on top of the spirit stove. "I was up half the night helping to get these two carriages ready. When we have had a cup of tea and something to eat, I'm going to pull down another one of the beds and take a nap. All the comforts of home these carriages have, and Jane Morgan is not a one to refuse a bit of comfort. We can both have a good long sleep in the warm – while everyone else runs around freezing their bits off."

"You sounded very convincing." Rebecca took a flat pillow she'd only just noticed and put it between her back and the metal of the railway carriage.

"I had to be. I thought that guard would never leave but when Mr Bates – the Dowager Duchess's butler – crossed his palm with silver he soon shot away." Jane was keeping a close eye on the kettle. She didn't trust that spirit stove not to fall over and set the place on fire.

"The Duchess brought her butler along – whatever for?"

"To make a splash – impress the locals." Jane stared for a moment. "And to hide the fact that we were smuggling you onto this train."

"Everyone has been so kind," Rebecca sighed.

"It is difficult, isn't it?" Jane stood to check the stove. "I was in your position once – so I do understand – better than most."

"Really?" Rebecca hadn't imagined anyone suffering as she had the last few weeks.

"Oh yes." Jane stood by the spirit stove, her back to Rebecca. "Life is strange. We were in very similar situations: I was pretty but poor, you are beautiful and rich, yet we had the same problem – yes, indeed – men and what they wanted to do with us."

Chapter 21

"But – but all believe the Captain's wife died by his side in the railway crash!" a stout matron exclaimed in horror upon being introduced to Georgina by Lady Caroline.

"The lady who died alongside the Captain and the Earl of Castlewellan while travelling in the Earl's private railway carriage was not Mrs Captain Charles Whitmore – I have the honour of that title." Georgina wondered in how many ways and how many times she would have to say the same thing. She longed to scream and run from this place. However, a great deal of effort had been put into this farce and she must prevail.

The Earl of Castlewellan's palatial mansion, sitting on a rise overlooking his estate, was the venue for a social gathering, held after the church service. The ballroom held a great number of titled people and members of the local gentry. Lady Caroline had taken Georgina under her wing. Georgina was besieged by people eager to make her acquaintance.

The service held in the private chapel on the estate had been long and, to Georgina's ears, rambling. The crowd attending had spilled out into the grounds surrounding the chapel, trampling the flowers on the Henderson family graves. Those invited to attend the gathering at the palatial home of the Earl had sat warm and dry inside the chapel, of course.

"Such a shame, Lady Caroline, that your brother Thomas does not enjoy the good looks of the former Earl of Castlewellan," the stout matron simpered.

Georgina couldn't remember her name – she had been introduced to so many people today – remembering everyone's name and title would have been impossible.

"Thomas has yet managed to do something my nephew Clive never accomplished!" Lady Caroline snapped.

"Pray tell, Lady Caroline," the stout matron leaned in to ask. "What has he achieved? I confess that my attention wandered somewhat while he delivered his sermon."

Sermon, Georgina thought. It had been the most outrageous piece of self-aggrandisement she had ever been forced to listen to. She would venture to guess that half the congregation had fallen asleep while the new earl twittered on about his many blessings.

"Thomas has managed to produce five sons in his image." Lady Caroline stared across the packed ballroom as if she could see the new earl and his family – an impossibility with the crowd packed into the ballroom. "The Henderson family have no need now to worry about the succession." The thought of the dull-witted young men sired by her brother inheriting her family title and estates was not something she could endorse – but what did it matter – she was female and had no say in the matter.

"Indeed, indeed," said the stout lady but she was speaking to Caroline's back as she had taken a firm grip on Georgina's elbow and was pulling her away.

"Excuse us, I see someone I must speak with." Lady Caroline didn't wait for a response but continued to pull Georgina along, ignoring the people who tried to catch her attention. "I hope you don't mind, Georgina." Lady Caroline pulled Georgina towards one of the open ballroom doors. "I need to escape this madhouse if only for a moment."

"Georgina, there you are!" Constance, wrapped warmly in her furs with Letitia by her side, walked around the side of one of the mansion's crenelated towers to the spot where Georgina and Lady Caroline huddled out of the wind, staring out over the extensive lawn. "A servant told me I might find you here."

"Ah, one is never hidden from one's servants!" Lady Caroline puffed on a cheroot – the cheroot supplied possibly by the very servant who had, no doubt, been eager to inform the Dowager Duchess of the whereabouts of the Henderson family rebel. "Have you reached the end of your legendary patience, my dear Constance?"

"I have indeed, Caroline. I have a long journey ahead of me, but I couldn't leave without saying goodbye to my hostess."

"Is that what I am – the hostess?" Caroline drew strongly on the cheroot. "I don't know if I was aware of that fact."

"I consider you so," Constance said. "As such I sought you out to say my farewells. I am sorry for the great loss your family has suffered, Caroline." She put her hand on Caroline's shoulder and squeezed briefly. "I am sorry my visit was under such sad circumstances." She shrugged. "But such is life."

"Indeed." Caroline threw her cheroot onto the grass. "It was good to see you, old friend. Thank you for coming. I will have my driver bring the carriage around. I daresay you will not object to Mrs Whitmore and Mrs McAuliffe travelling with you?"

Letitia and Georgina had travelled to the Castlewellan Estate in the Daniels' travelling coach.

"I have no objection to such pleasant company," Constance said. "I enjoyed the chance to converse with you on the journey to this estate, Caroline. One so seldom gets the chance to speak in private." There had been no private conversation held in Lady Caroline's carriage, but the fiction would explain the two coaches needed. "I will enjoy a brief rest at the hotel while my butler gathers up my staff and my railway carriages are set up for the return journey. No doubt the young maids are enjoying their day by the seaside even in this brisk weather."

The women turned to walk back towards the mansion, each hoping they could escape without anyone delaying them.

"The loss of so many young lives! So many children lost their lives in that train crash, it does not bear thinking about."

Constance, her maid by her side, was behind a tall Chinese lacquered screen.

The women were gathered in the luxurious lounge of the suite that had been secured for her use in the Slieve Donard Hotel – a tall redbrick edifice standing proudly on land leading down to the ocean. The views from the windows all offered a view of the grounds and down to the grey, foaming Irish Sea.

Georgina and Letitia were sitting in front of one set of long windows, gazing out at the gas-lit gardens. They had refused an offer of refreshments.

The black outer clothing the Dowager Duchess had been wearing was thrown over the top of the screen. This was soon joined by her whale-boned corsets – gleaming white – decorated with lace – and trailing the many cords that bound them to a lady's figure.

"Georgina, Letitia, you should both change." Constance's voice continued to issue from behind the high screen. "There is no longer a need to suffer the discomfort of our stays. It will be late and I daresay most of Dublin will be asleep when our train reaches our destination. We should travel in comfort, don't you think?"

After the refreshing and enjoyable stop at the Slieve Donard Hotel, the Dowager Duchess's party was gathered in the Newcastle train station, waiting for the engine and twin carriages to be brought to the departure platform. Bates and Letitia ensured that everyone and everything they had brought with them was accounted for, while the staff climbed aboard the train. Constance arrived last, waiting until the red carpet had once more been deployed.

Jane Morgan had everything in the servant's carriage locked down and ready to be shifted when the engine came to move the carriages into position. Rebecca remained hidden behind the rolled-down curtain over her bed. She had slept deeply and long and was once more awake and shivering in dread of what might be before her.

The journey from Newcastle to Newry passed without incident. Rebecca remained stiffly alert and holding on to the edge of the platform bed.

The Dowager Duchess's carriages were smoothly connected to the Belfast to Dublin train in Newry. The beds in the servants' carriage were pulled down and with Bates on attentive guard the maids and footmen lay down to sleep. Their day would start very early in the morning despite the late hours they had remained on duty today.

In the Dowager Duchess's carriage the footrests of the comfortable armchairs were pulled out, allowing one to lie prone, thick covers were draped over the occupants of the chairs, the lamps were blown out and all settled to sleep – except of course the few servants whose job it was to remain alert and ensure all was as it should be.

"We will be stopping again at Dundalk." Bates was balancing – a foot on each side of the platform created over the open divide between the two carriages – his leather gloved hand holding tightly to the bar secured to the exterior of the carriage. His body moved with the motion of the train.

"Well, these monsters eat a great deal of coal," Jane Morgan, well wrapped up against the cold wind making its way into the open area between the two carriages, said.

They were on duty but had decided to chat outdoors and allow the servants to sleep.

"How was she?" Bates, his hat pulled down to his eyes, the collar of his long black woollen coat pulled up, a soft scarf wrapped around his neck, jerked his head towards the servants' carriage.

"Like them all." Jane sighed. "Scared and grieving for all she has left behind her – not knowing what is in front of her."

"I am, at times like this, ashamed of being born male." Bates was proud of the help he was able to offer to the BOBs, but he wished sincerely that it was not necessary.

"Oh, whist!" Jane Morgan tightened her hold on the safety bar she clutched. "It is not only the fault of males that such things happen. Women too must be held accountable, you know." She sighed deeply. Too many people – men and women – looked aside and allowed atrocities to occur. "The world we live in needs to change. Too much is given to too few in my opinion. Every man and woman need to stand up and be heard. They need to speak out against inequality and injustice. Until that happens – well, people like you and me – we help. What more can we do?"

"You are a rebel, Jane Morgan."

"And proud of it, Simeon Bates."

"Are you really happy in your little house in Clover Close?" Bates looked down fondly at the woman who had fought so hard to improve her own and others' lot in life.

"I am." Jane smiled up into his face. "You have never been able to understand, Simeon, but that little house, as you call it, was like a palace to me when I first arrived in Dublin. I thought I was a princess and Mrs Keegan was my Fairy Godmother – I still miss that old woman." Jane shook her head sadly.

"The kindness and care you gave her was remarkable." Bates smiled. "I daresay she lasted longer – thanks to your care – than anyone expected."

"She was a wonderful old lady." Jane smiled fondly to remember the woman who had taken her into her home when the BOBs helped her escape the fate planned for her by the people who should have been protecting her. "I owe her everything."

"Not many people of your station would have known to look to the BOBs for assistance." Bates had always been curious about Jane Morgan but had not liked to ask her how she came to be in Dublin. The darkness and the reassuring noise of the train wheels turning seemed to be inviting confidences.

"The BOBs!" Jane laughed in sheer delight. "I had never heard of them or indeed even dreamed such an organisation existed."

"Then how could you know to turn to them for help?"

"I didn't." Jane laughed again. "I was determined to escape the fate planned for me by my brothers." She tried very hard not to think back on those nightmare days and nights but something about the clacking of the wheels on the rails and the silent darkness that surrounded them gave her the courage to share her story with a man who had always treated her with kindness.

"I was fortunate, I suppose, in one way," Jane said into the darkness. "My brothers argued about selling me to the highest bidder," she ignored his sharp intake of breath, "but they didn't know how to go about it. Then again, they argued they needed my help with the farm animals and the land. I was the one who kept them all fed – they didn't want to lose the unpaid labourer they had made of me but, at the same time, the talk of making a great deal of cash from selling me to the flesh pots they frequented was tempting them."

"How old were you?" Bates felt he had known this woman for a very long time.

"I was twelve years old." She felt tears fill her eyes but fought them back. It was as if she were crying for a stranger. So much time had passed and so much had happened to her in those years.

"Dear Lord!"

"I was becoming a woman." Jane shrugged. "I thought I was so grown up." She laughed softly at her own remembered innocence. "I waited until they were all lying drunk abed and with a blanket to cover my threadbare boy's clothing – they never bought me anything to wear so I wore what they had discarded," she waved that aside, "I crept out of that ramshackle house and through the filth of the yard and, with my head held high, wearing old boots only fit for the muck heap, stepped out to meet my fate."

"Merciful Father!" Bates shuddered.

"Well, someone was looking after me all right." Jane hadn't thought of those days in so long. "I walked until I could go no further and buried my aching body in a leaf-filled ditch. I settled down to rest having no good idea of what I was going to do when the morning came – only knowing I needed to get far, far away."

"What happened?" Bates prompted when Jane fell silent.

"I awoke to find myself in the middle of the local hunt." She threw her head back and laughed. "The charging horses fair rattled the ground I was lying on – the baying of the hounds – the blaring sound of the hunt horn – I thought it was Lucifer himself coming to find me where I lay shivering in that ditch."

Bates just stared at her, unable to imagine laughing at such a thing.

"The hounds jumped into the ditch with me, I was terrified, sure I was about to be torn limb from limb. The magnificent horses – groomed to within an inch of their lives. The red coats of the male riders, the bright flowing fabrics the lady riders sported – all was lost on me as I huddled there in the muck and shook. A lady rider – not a member of the hunt – but one of the mounted observers – came to investigate what the hounds had found – thankfully." She shook her head, amazed still at her great good fortune. "Lady Jocelyn Guinness."

"*Aah*," Bates said softly. The woman was a well-known supporter of the BOBs.

"As you say, Simeon, as you say." Jane had listened – without understanding – to the almost barked instructions of the lady. "That woman's servants moved like a well-trained army unit. They had the hounds away from my shivering body and me thrown into the back of a donkey-pulled cart. I lay there shivering with cold and shaking with shock, awaiting my fate." She looked into his eyes. "If I had known the wonderful fate that awaited me – why – I daresay I would have danced for glee."

"Wonderful fate?" Bates stared. "Slaving away under the command of a cantankerous old woman in a miserable cottage sitting cheek by jowl with the Dublin docks!"

"They say 'beauty is in the eye of the beholder', Simeon." Jane had had this argument with him before. He could never accept that she considered herself one of the luckiest women in the world. "That little house was warm and clean – something I had never experienced before. I had ample food to eat — another wonder. I was trained to keep that house and myself clean. I had my own bedroom — after sleeping on flea-infested straw all my life. Simeon, I thought I had reached the gates of heaven."

They remained silent while the train trundled through the darkness.

"It is becoming too cold to remain out here." Bates spoke softly.

"I made us a flask of hot chocolate earlier." Jane turned carefully on the jiggling little platform formed by the lip of the two carriages. "Shall we step inside and enjoy it in comfort?"

"After you, Mrs Morgan," said Bates with a smile.

Chapter 22

In Dundalk – before the train had come to a complete stop – the occupants of the two carriages were rudely awakened. The exterior of the carriages was being beaten forcefully. Shouting and curses carried into the carriages from the station platform.

"In the name of God!" Bates jumped to his feet.

"*Sir, sir, please, sir, you have to stop!*" A shouting voice could be heard over the banging against the side of the carriage.

"*Unhand me!*" a cultured voice barked.

"*Sir, please!*"

"*You!*"

A loud bang that Bates was afraid would damage the exterior of the carriage sounded. "*You in there, I wish to speak with you!*" Another vicious bang.

"*Stop that!*" Bates was pushing his arm into his coat, struggling to get the door open and step out onto the platform all at the same time.

Heads appeared under the curtains over the beds – sleepy servants wondering what was going on.

"Let me help." Jane opened the door with one hand, holding Bates' coat so he could push his arm into the sleeve with the other.

Rebecca had her hand forced into her mouth, holding back the cry of fear that wanted to escape – had she been discovered?

"Cease and desist!" Bates roared, while stepping out onto the platform, closing the buttons of his coat as he went.

"Mr Bates may need help." Jane closed the door behind Bates, waving her hands at the servants who were practically hanging off their beds. "You footmen, put on some warm clothing and get out there!" She lowered the half window in the door and hung out, watching the action.

Bates faced the tall magnificently dressed individual who continued to beat the silver head of his cane against the carriages.

Two uniformed railway guards danced ineffectually around the figure, afraid to lay their hands on him.

"Have you lost the run of your senses?" Bates roared at the man. *"Cease and desist, I have said! You are harming private property!"*

"Who the hell are you?" The man finally turned to pay attention to something other than his own rage.

"I, sir, am Bates, butler to the Dowager Duchess of Westbrooke whose carriages you are assaulting." Bates let his disgust for this behaviour show on his face and sound in his voice. "Do you have a reason other than insanity for attacking the ducal railway carriage?"

While this was happening, Constance, Letitia and Georgina were on their feet, wondering what on earth was going on. The three women listened to the sounds carrying clearly from the platform.

"I wish to speak to someone travelling on these two carriages." The man's educated tones and expensive clothing established him as a gentleman.

"I would suggest – strongly – that you leave this station and never approach Her Grace again." Bates stared down his nose. "Your behaviour, sir, is not that of a gentleman."

"See here, my good man," the gentleman blustered, "do you know who I am?"

"No, sir, I do not." Bates glared. "Nor do I care – you, sir, are no gentleman."

"How dare you!"

"I dare, sir, because you, sir, attacked, without provocation, the private railway carriages of my mistress the Dowager Duchess of Westbrooke – like an untrained cur." Bates was conscious of footsteps behind him and turned to look. He had hoped it would be someone official offering assistance but instead it was his own footmen still buttoning their uniform coats.

"*I wish to speak to someone from these carriages!*" the man shouted. He looked around the station. Spotting a uniformed station worker who was standing with his back pressed to the station wall – he gestured imperiously. "*You there, come here!*" He pointed to the platform at his feet. "*Are you deaf, man? Come here, I say!*"

The man remained as if glued to the station wall, his eyes staring, mouth hanging open.

"You there!" the man used his stick to nudge quite forcefully at the shoulder of one of the railroad guards who had attempted to stop his attack on the carriages. "Go get him, at once." He again used his cane, pushing so forcefully the guard was forced back a step. "I want that man brought before me. *At once!*" The last was roared.

"Sir," one of the guards stepped forward bravely, "if you could inform us of what this is all about?" The guard's face was pale, sweat globules forming on his skin.

"That man ..." Again the cane swung, causing several people to step out of its way. "That guard informed me that someone ..." he hit the head of his cane off the nearest carriage which happened to be the one carrying the Dowager Duchess and friends, "had expressed an interest in a notification I had placed on your noticeboard – at great expense, I might add – some female seemed to know something of the matter. I merely wish to see this woman and question her. My ward has been missing for some time and I seek information as to her whereabouts." He again struck the carriage. "I merely wish for answers to my questions. As you can plainly see, I am frantic with concern for my ward. I gave no thought to anything else when I heard that something of her whereabouts might be known by an occupant of these two carriages."

"Oh, dear Lord!" Georgina slapped a hand to her face. "I know what this is about." She turned, frantically seeking the place where the servants might have put her coat. She couldn't go outdoors wearing the skirt and blouse she had changed into for comfort while she travelled. She was not wearing her stays!

"Georgina?" Constance stared.

"This is all my fault." Georgina shook her head, warning Constance to ask no further.

"You will need your coat." Letitia hurried to open a long cupboard, revealing the outer wear. She held the ground-sweeping black overcoat open while Georgina quickly stuck her arms inside.

"I need my bonnet." Georgina felt sick to her stomach. If she was not very much mistaken she was about to face the monster who had kept Flora imprisoned and at his command for years.

"Here!" Letitia pulled the bonnet from a shelf, holding it out by its black ribbons.

"Georgina, there is quite a crowd gathering – matters might become troublesome out there – I cannot be happy with you facing that madman alone," Constance said.

"I am sure I will be safe with Bates." Georgina was not sure of any such thing, but she needed to go out there. She had to convince that man demanding answers that she knew nothing of his ward. It was imperative. She could not lead him to Flora – she simply could not.

"I will keep watch at the door." Letitia helped Georgina button her coat and settle her bonnet on her head. She turned to take something from the depths of the coat cupboard. "Here, it is always best to go armed when facing an angry man." She held out an ebony cane with a silver mallard head for a handle. "The bird's beak can do quite a lot of damage." She pressed the cane into Georgina's trembling hand.

"Go carefully, Georgina!" Constance said.

Georgina didn't react to her words – instead, stick in hand, she prepared to step out of the carriage and confront a man who terrified her.

"Bates!" Georgina called, stepping through the door Letitia held open for her. "Bates, I had words with that guard earlier. Perhaps I can be of assistance?"

"*That's her, milord!*" The stunned guard still at the wall suddenly came to life, shouting and pointing at Georgina. "*That's the very woman! She was fair staring at your notice! She even called her friends over to have a good look at it!*"

"Is this true?" The irate man began pushing people out of his way to get close to Georgina.

Georgina watched the man approach. She had no intention of demanding an introduction. She wanted to give this man no information of any kind. He must not be able to make enquiries about herself or those she protected.

"I, sir, have no notion of what is happening," she said. "I was sound asleep when you began to brutalise the carriage I was travelling in. I have stepped outside now merely to see if I can have you removed from this station. You asked about someone speaking of a notice? I thought perhaps I might be able to shed some light on the matter and spare everyone the abuse you are offering."

"I beg your pardon?" was practically spat in her face.

"And so you should," Georgina snapped, thankful no one could see her knees were knocking. "Your behaviour, sir, allow me to tell you, has been disgraceful."

"I do beg your pardon, madam." He finally remembered to raise his hat. "I was overcome with emotion when this guard," he flung his arm around to point to the guard now approaching, "contacted me, to inform me that someone, yourself it would seem, madam, had made much of the notice that I have had affixed to every noticeboard, in every railway station of the east coast. I am desperate for news of my ward. My attitude has been past all bounds of civility. I do beg your forgiveness."

Georgina looked at him and wondered why she couldn't see the monster hiding behind his pleasant face. Should he not have horns and a tail?

"I have no notion of which notice you mean, sir," Georgina said. "While waiting for our train to be refuelled I was merely passing time." She looked around at the gathering crowd. "It is something to do to pass the time, is it not – one peruses one's surroundings."

"You must remember!" The guard had reached their side. "You were staring right at it." He could almost feel the money of the reward in his hand.

"I am sorry, but I truly do not know what you are referring to." Georgina hoped her face was as innocent as she was desperately trying to portray.

"Perhaps if you looked once more at the noticeboard?" The irate and demanding gentleman had suddenly turned into someone of sweetness and light, smiling and gesturing towards the noticeboard attached to the station wall.

"I will do that, sir, but under protest." Georgina allowed herself to be harried over to the noticeboard, the crowd following at her heels.

173

"One should not reward such uncivilised behaviour."

He ignored her words, this suddenly charming gent. "See if anyone or anything looks familiar."

Georgina stood for some time, examining the tattered and torn notices. This man's notice stood out for its superior quality and pristine condition.

She exclaimed suddenly and pointed. "Is this the notice that concerns you?" She pointed to the image of Flora that had so disturbed her when she had first seen it.

"Yes, yes, that is my ward. You have seen her somewhere? You know something of her whereabouts?"

"I am most dreadfully sorry." Georgina turned from the noticeboard, shaking her head sadly. "It was the skill of the printer I remarked upon." She played to the crowd that had gathered, "I am something of an artist myself. I create images of flora and fauna that I am pleased to say appeal to a great number of my female friends. I have tried to reproduce my drawings – as offerings to kind friends – don't you know. Sadly, it would appear I do not have the skill needed to recreate my own work for prints – it is quite a skill, you know. It was the sheer skill of the printer which drew my attention to your notice. I drew my travelling companion's attention to this very matter." She pointed. "See how wonderfully skilled the printer has been in reproducing what I can only assume is a portrait painting of the lady. Truly, it is quite impressive."

She turned sharply on her heels.

"Now, sir, if you will excuse me. I have given you far more attention than your attitude deserves." She marched off towards the train with her heart in her mouth, always fearing that man would dare to hold her back. She did not breathe easily until the train pulled away from the station.

Chapter 23

"What river is that?" Rebecca asked, almost panting while being pulled along the cobbled gas-lamp-lit streets of Dublin.

"The Liffey." Jane pulled on the elbow she held, trying to get the young woman to move her blasted feet. Could she not walk any faster?

"What —"

"Look," Jane didn't stop walking, "could you keep your questions until we are behind closed doors? Now, for goodness' sake, pick up your feet!"

Rebecca tried to obey, but the boots she wore were stiff, ill-fitting and awkward on her feet and she was not accustomed to walking along cobbled streets.

When the train pulled out of the Dundalk train station after that rather unseemly display on the platform, Jane had thrown the fisherman's outfit Rebecca had been wearing when she arrived in Newcastle under the curtain that hid her from view and onto the bed platform. She ordered Rebecca to put the outfit on once more. Rebecca had struggled in the limited space to remove the dress and push her limbs into the under-britches and vest, trousers, jumper, stockings and boots. She was thankful for the additional warmth provided by the heavy clothing.

Rebecca had feared their arrival in Dublin – imagining everything that could possibly go wrong. She need not have worried. Bates and Mrs Morgan handled the matter with great skill. When the train passed through Balbriggan, under Bates' command the servants had swung into action, restoring order to the carriage.

It was the early hours of the morning as the train pulled into Dublin. In the servants' carriage everyone, apart from Rebecca and Jane Morgan, were sitting in their outer wear, wicker hampers packed and ready to be off-loaded.

Jane Morgan put on a long dark coat, swung a dark knitted shawl around her head and shoulders, rolled up the curtain over Rebecca's hiding place, pulled Rebecca to the floor in front of her, opened the carriage door and pushed Rebecca out onto the platform. It had appeared to Rebecca's wide-eyed stare that the woman had done it all without a wasted movement.

Now they hurried along cobblestone streets, following the river towards a bridge that was brightly illuminated by tall gas streetlamps. There were people working even at this hour – giant packages littered the docks.

Sailors stumbled along, drunk and singing, frightening Rebecca who had never seen the like.

"There is a seaman's mission along the way," Jane explained, pulling on Rebecca's elbow. "We should not attract too much attention." They turned onto the bridge. "But keep your head down."

"Here we are!" Jane wanted to break out in song. She opened the gate leading into her front garden with one hand while searching with her gloved hand in the deep pocket of her coat for the key to her house.

She opened her front door and pulled Rebecca over the threshold. "Stand there." She shoved her to one side, closing the door and locking it. "It is too dark for you to stumble around. I know every inch of this house." She hurried down the flagstone hallway. She would normally have used the rear entrance, but that way was darker and she'd been worried that Rebecca would fall over her own feet.

"Let there be light!" Jane amused herself by saying, taking a packet of long safety matches from the mantel over her range. She had cleaned out and set all the fires before she left that morning – or was it yesterday morning – she didn't know and just this moment she didn't care. She struck the match and applied the flame to the rolled-up paper in the range. She lit two gas lamps.

She stepped out into the hallway, where light from the kitchen now beamed out over the flagstones. "Come along!" she said.

Rebecca stood frozen like a statue inside the door where Jane had left her.

Jane sighed. "Come along. I've lit the fire in the range. I'll put the kettle on and make us both a sup of tea. Are you hungry?"

"Are there no servants to handle such chores?" Rebecca said as she moved towards Jane. She had never been inside such a small dwelling. She had, of course, seen workers' cottages on the land her family owned but she had never been invited inside one.

"The only servants in this house are thee and me." Jane shook her head. The poor waif. She had many shocks awaiting her. She took Rebecca by the elbow and towed her into the kitchen. "Leave your coat on, it's a bit chilly in here yet." She pulled a chair away from the kitchen table and almost forced Rebecca to sit down out of her way. She wanted to get the kettle on – she'd murder a cup of tea.

"Am I to remain here?" Rebecca looked around what appeared to her eyes a tiny kitchen. It was spotlessly clean, the few surfaces gleaming. Two large armchairs were sitting on the flagstone floor close to the range. The wooden table she sat at was covered in some sort of brightly coloured waxed fabric. A tall dresser pushed against one whitewashed wall held dishes, teacups hanging on hooks on the lip of the top shelves. The whole space was only marginally bigger than a doll's house to Rebecca's dazed eyes.

"Let me get organised." Jane took two teacups off their hooks. She began to set the table for tea. "Are you hungry? You never did answer me."

"I have no idea." Rebecca lifted green eyes to Jane's face, silently begging her understanding. She didn't know if she was on her head or her heels.

"I'll make us some boiled eggs with soldiers." Jane had been where this poor lost soul was. She had survived – so would Lady Rebecca. "You can make the toast. The bread won't be any too fresh but toasted it will be fine."

Rebecca put her elbows on the table and rested her chin on her clenched fists. She watched Jane move around her kitchen. It was like a beautiful dance. No movement was wasted. When she put out a hand, the item she needed seemed to dance to her fingers. She was much in her element here and it showed.

"Do you know how to toast bread?"

Rebecca shook her head. It had been many years since she toasted crumpets at the nursery fire. She doubted she remembered how – at this moment and in this place she was finding it difficult to remember her own name. She had truly travelled to a strange new world.

"Here!" Jane held a long brass toasting fork, a slice of bread attached to the prongs. "Come, I'll show you."

Rebecca slowly moved to obey the orders and instructions given to her. As she toasted the bread, Jane whizzed around getting everything they needed for a late night – early morning? – snack.

"Am I to remain here?" Rebecca asked again when they were seated across from each other at the kitchen table. "It must be obvious to you that I am completely useless in this environment."

Jane used the back of her spoon to break the top off her egg. She looked across the table to see Rebecca do the same. At least she could feed herself. What were the gentry thinking to turn their children out with no knowledge of how to survive without the constant attention of servants?

"Rebecca … I am not going to address you as Lady Rebecca or milady – while you are under my roof we are equals." She waited to see if there were any objections and, when none came, she continued. "The BOBs have no idea what to do with you." She laughed when Rebecca stared at her – shocked.

"I have been pulled and pushed from pillar to post and now you tell me these women, who seem to have taken over my life, have no idea what to do with me?" Rebecca was trying not to raise her voice.

"Ah, but did you at any time dig in your heels and shout no, enough?" Jane raised her eyebrows and waited.

"I did not." Rebecca turned her attention to her egg, not willing to meet the cunning grey eyes of the woman opposite her. "I obeyed every command given to me without question."

"That was your first mistake," Jane quipped, trying to lighten the mood.

"I thank you for all your help in escaping from what I was assured would be a life of bowing to men wishing to control me." Rebecca didn't like to think that men who were related to her by blood saw her only as a means to access her funds – but she'd been forced to concede the point. "I thank you for offering me a roof over my head … but, Jane," she stared intently across at the woman who seemed so assured, "it must be painfully obvious to you that I will be a shocking burden to you. I have nothing and no-one. I sit here eating your food, in clothing that is unfit for me to appear in public wearing – what have you been burdened with? It is not fair to expect you to open your home to me."

"It will all appear better in the morning." Jane was glad now that she had made up the bed in her spare room. She had thought to have made bed-making Rebecca's first lesson but looking at the bewildered face of this young woman she was thankful she had ignored her own instincts and made the bed. "We will eat and drink now. I have the kettle on to heat water for bottles to warm our beds. There is no point lighting the fires in our bedrooms. We will be beneath the covers and hopefully asleep in minutes. This house has a strange layout that I will explain to you in the morning. In the meantime, eat up."

While Rebecca was struggling along the cobbles of Dublin, a carriage carried Georgina to her home. She could not determine what the trip to the north of the country had gained her, but she had done it – she had faced society with her head held high. Perhaps now she could get on with her life.

She worried about that poster of Flora. How many people had seen it? There was a reward for information offered. The only thing that reassured her was that in the painting Flora's cheeks had been much more pronounced and the irate man shouting his worries and care to the world had forgotten he had cut off all of Flora's glorious hair. She looked different now but to anyone who knew her that portrait in the poster was very true to life.

Georgina smiled at the man standing ready to help her from her carriage. One of Billy Flint's many Smiths or Joneses. It reassured her to have these men to keep watch on the household. She stepped from the carriage, gave her overnight bag to the waiting man, paid the driver who with a tip of his whip to his hat jerked on the reins and drove off.

"The front door is locked tight, missus," Smith or Jones said. "The back door is unlocked."

"Thank you." Georgina followed the man. She was home and all she wanted right now was her bed.

"Billy Flint asked if he could meet with you at your earliest convenience," Smith or Jones said.

"You may inform Mr Flint that I will send for him." Georgina stood by the back door and held out her hand to take her overnight case. It wasn't heavy. "At this moment in time I wish nothing more than to sleep the sleep of the just. When I awaken, I will send for Mr Flint but do warn him that it will not be early in the morning."

"Yes, missus." The man opened the back door of the house for her and passed her bag into her hand. "I'll tell him."

Chapter 24

"Rise and shine!"

The sudden explosion of light and the cheerful voice woke Rebecca from a restless sleep. "We have places to be and things to do. Time to be out of bed and doing."

"I'm awake," Rebecca groaned into the pillow.

"Barely." Jane laughed. "Come along, there is a po behind that screen you can use. The necessary is down the back. I brought up hot water for you to wash. You can refresh yourself, come downstairs and have a cup of tea while we make plans for the day. Come along, half the day is gone."

"What am I supposed to put on?" Rebecca, her golden hair spilling out about her head, asked.

"I suppose you didn't notice the two great big trunks sitting against the wall?" Jane stood with her hands on her hips.

"Those are mine!" Rebecca had last seen those trunks in the Daniels' home. She used her forearm to push her hair out of her face. "How did they get here?"

"They were delivered days ago. The keys are hanging over them."

A black cord, key dangling from it, hung from a nail in the whitewashed wall. "Do you have anything in those trunks that you could wear today?"

"I don't think so." Rebecca remembered her impression of this little house last night. Nothing she possessed would suit. "Why don't you open those trunks and have a look while I use the po?" She jumped out of bed, wearing only the undergarments she'd worn under the fisherman's jumper and trousers. I daresay you will have a better idea of what is suitable than I." She hurried behind the screen, desperate to relieve herself.

"In the name of all that is good and holy!" Jane exclaimed over the sound of Rebecca relieving her bladder. "They're all bright colours, lace and frills!"

Rebecca stepped out from behind the screen to see Jane sitting on her heels, the two trunks open, staring at the contents. She walked to the jug and washbasin sitting on a stand, a towel draped over its rail. She poured the hot water from the jug into the basin.

"I can't even take this lot down the market and trade them in for more suitable clothing." Jane groaned. "No one around these parts could make use of such useless garments. Black, brown, or navy blue – that is what we wear, not lemon and peach." She stood up. "You can't wear anything of mine – I'm rounder and shorter than you." She pushed her hands through her silvering hair. "You will have to put on the trousers and jumper you wore before until we can find you something to wear. I only pray none of the neighbours pop in to pay a visit. I'll go down and put the kettle on. Hurry up – I let you sleep half the morning away."

Rebecca waited until Jane left the room. She fell to her knees in front of the trunks. With a silent prayer on her lips, she pulled the clothing out of one of them. She used her fingertips to feel around the bottom of it. There was a pop when she found what she was seeking. In the concealed drawer she found a heavy embossed leather pouch. It was her grandfather's golden-sovereign pouch, bulging with coins. She also discovered a wallet packed with white five-pound notes. She would be able to pay her way at least. Silent tears fell from her eyes while she clutched the leather pouch to her chest. She could not believe her grandfather had parted with an item he cherished. She ignored the small boxes she recognised – her jewellery inherited from her mother. Those too could be turned into cash if necessary. She returned the items to the hidden drawer and listened carefully for the sound of the pressure lock engaging.

She turned to the second trunk and added the clothing from it to the pile on the floor. Her breath caught in her throat when she found diaries belonging to her maternal ancestors in its hidden drawer. The books held the secret to the success of the fruit, flower, and vegetable business her ancestor established. Her grandfather had given her his treasures. She bent over the trunks, sobbing as if her heart would break.

In the kitchen, Jane heard the sobs and shook her head sadly. She'd let her cry it out. The tears were better shed.

It was some time before Rebecca joined Jane in the kitchen. She was wearing the trousers and fisherman's jumper, her feet bare.

"Jane, would it be permissible for me to look around this house and grounds? I looked out of my bedroom window – it appears you have a smallholding that is flourishing. I saw the chickens and goat out there. Then, when I stepped out of my room, even in the short walk down the stairs and hallway so many attractions caught my eye."

"It is a little place of magic, isn't it?" Jane was pleased she'd noticed. "The woman who owned this house, Mrs Roseanna Keegan, was an artist. She dabbled in so many art forms and many of them are built into the bones of the house."

"I was tempted to linger at so many little wonders – the coloured glass, the carved panels, the weavings, so much beauty and all under one roof."

"You will need something on your feet if you want to venture outdoors. I have a donkey too, so underfoot can be treacherous at times." Jane pulled the kettle over to the hottest part of the range with a sigh. "I don't know what we are going to do about your clothing though." She could consult the BOBs for funding, she knew, but the girl needed something now.

"You have a dog?" Rebecca asked over the sound of thunderous barking from outside the kitchen door.

"Indeed, I do not." Jane walked over to open the door. "*You do.*"

A bundle of brown and black fur exploded into the kitchen, barking madly, yipping, and crying.

"*Dandy!*" Rebecca screamed, falling to her knees to hug the hound she thought she'd never see again. "*How did you get here?*" She raised her chin to escape the frantic tongue that was trying to cover every inch of her face.

Jane stood watching them with tears in her eyes. At least the child could have one thing from her old life. The dog continued to yip frantically. Jane couldn't understand a thing it was yipping but that didn't matter. It was obvious the dog's young mistress understood every yip and bark.

"How?" Rebecca sat on the cold flagstone floor, her beloved dog in her lap.

"He kept running away from wherever they put him," Jane said. "I was asked if I would take him and you. I said yes for my sins."

"I can never thank you enough!" Rebecca buried her face in Dandy's neck fur and hugged tight. "It broke my heart to think of poor Dandy wondering where I was. To have him with me now! What can I say except thank you – from the bottom of my heart *thank you?*"

"You are most welcome." Jane smiled. "Now, wash up and come get something to eat and drink. The day is half gone and we have achieved nothing."

"I call her Muggins." Jane pulled on the donkey's rough forelock. "She is full of mischief, but she pulls the cart that carries me around the streets of Dublin. The nanny goat," she grunted when the goat gave her a hefty nudge, "I call many things – a lot of them swearwords – but officially her name is Boots."

"Because of her four white feet?"

"Because she has always been too big for her boots," Jane said. "As in bossy." She moved out of the way of another nudge.

They were walking around the grounds to the back of Jane's whitewashed cottage. Rebecca, with Dandy a constant shadow at her heels, walked around the ground admiring the planning that had gone into packing the most into the small space.

"This I know." Rebecca turned on her once-more-booted feet. "The land, the growing of fruit and vegetables. I know about these things."

"Just nothing about feeding yourself or taking care of a house?" Jane had shown Rebecca how to boil a kettle, rake out the fire in the range, wash dishes, tidy a table, take out the rubbish. She had even shown her how to make her bed – and pick up the clothing she had left trailing about her room.

It had been an education for both. Rebecca wanted to stop to examine every inch of the house, fascinated by the unusual home. Jane, however, insisted they take care of household chores first. Time and plenty to examine the artwork that hid in every nook and cranny.

"Why am I here, Jane, do you know?" Rebecca looked at the

thatched roof on the white-washed building standing in a large patch of green ground. The house was unlike anything she had ever seen before. It was larger and more substantial than a worker's cottage. The gleaming white wall of wattle and daub were of a bygone age. The thatched roof with a straw rooster crowing on top was whimsical to her eyes.

Perhaps if she had been raised as a true lady of the manor, she would have visited workers' cottages and seen something similar. She had lived on a large estate – in a manor house – that sat cheek by jowl with her paternal family's extensive estate and her great-aunts' forested grounds. She had been surrounded by a sea of green grass, trees that sometimes seemed to stretch to the sky, trees that spread wide their branches, blossoms and blooms. She had been happy there and never travelled far from home. Now she was in a world that was almost painfully foreign to her.

"Rebecca ..." Jane sighed and, with the donkey and goat following her, walked over to a bench. She sat and patted the wooden laths alongside her. "Sit down a minute and I'll try and explain." She waited until Rebecca sat and Dandy draped himself over her feet.

"I have told you the BOBs don't know what to do with you." She looked up into the denuded branches of an apple tree. "You have not yet reached your majority but, even then, you will not be safe." She sighed. "The BOBs help women who find themselves in difficulty. Some of whom want to escape a life of genteel poverty – living with relatives as the poor relation. None of which is you." She sighed, wondering how to explain to this innocent some of the dangers out in the big bad world.

"I am angry at the situation I find myself in," Rebecca prompted when Jane fell silent.

"You are a strange case for the BOBs." Jane laughed. "I too was a strange case in my time, so someone high in the BOBs decided to throw us together."

"What are your normal duties for the BOBs?" Rebecca asked curiously.

"I carry messages around the city." Jane reached out and slapped the donkey's neck affectionately. "Muggins here carries me all around. I sometimes hide a warm body in my cart and take it between meeting or moving points. A donkey and cart are easily overlooked, I find. I am usually the one called on to move women from point to point – keeping the line moving is important. Sometimes the young women freeze and endanger all. It is my job to see that does not happen. I do whatever is asked of me."

"And you give people shelter in your home?"

"Not usually, no. Rebecca, there are so many options open to you, but you must make the decision. The women who call on the BOBs are desperate to escape their old life. They are willing to turn their hands to anything. We move them and find them somewhere they can survive and hopefully flourish. They are homeless and penniless when they come to us. That is not your case. You have choices but you must make them. You must be free to make those choices and not under some man's thumb. The BOBs are offering you that chance."

"How?"

Jane had been well briefed on Rebecca's case. She needed to make the girl realise the danger that surrounded her. Any man could grab her, force his attentions on her and force her to marry him. It was frequently done. Jane sighed and spoke slowly while trying to find the words needed to make this young beauty start to think for herself.

"Your grandfather, a man who has always protected you, believes he is not long for this life. His son, your uncle, plans to destroy the family business – a business you have been involved in for years – as soon as he inherits. You are not welcome in his home – the home that is all you have ever known. Your titled father has gone to his Maker, leaving you a wealthy young heiress. There are so many dangers out there," she gestured past the tall wattle-and-daub walls that surrounded her little kingdom, "in the big bad world. I have been asked to help you navigate your new world while you learn your own tastes and wants."

"How is it possible to reach the age of nineteen and know so very little?" Rebecca leaned down to pet her dog who was frantically pawing at her, sensing her upset. She pulled him up onto her lap, needing the comfort of his weight on her.

"I came to this house," Jane gestured towards the white walls shining in the winter sunshine, "when I was twelve years old and an uneducated savage."

"Twelve!"

"I knew nothing – less than nothing. Roseanna Keegan –"

"A relative?"

"Indeed not. Mrs Keegan performed the same duties for the BOBs that I do now. She was an amazing woman – a free spirit and much ahead of her time. She thought it would be amusing to train me up to be a housemaid." Jane shrugged. "She never could teach me to keep my opinion to myself and bend my knee. She did however teach me to read, write and do basic mathematics. She taught me to appreciate the world around me. She taught me to think for myself – form my own opinions. She was the most wonderful woman I have ever met."

Chapter 25

"Good morning, Cook." Georgina walked into the basement kitchen.
"Good morning, Ruth."

"I thought I was going to have to serve you breakfast in your bath,
Miss Georgina." Cook tutted. "You spend so much time in that bath
you won't have a drop of natural oil left in your body."

Ruth, hands covered in flour, turned, dipped a knee, and mumbled
a good morning before returning to her work.

Georgina had no need to ask where the rest of her household were
– she had heard them working and talking around the house as she
came downstairs. The large kitchen with only two people in it made
the lack of serving staff glaringly obvious. This house demanded a
great deal of care.

"Will I serve you something to eat in me alcove, Miss Georgina?"
Cook fretted that she had no one to carry trays about. Her young
mistress had had neither bite nor sup and the morning half over.

"Thank you, Cook." Georgina smiled at the old family retainer,
aware that the woman needed to feed her charges. "But I have asked
Flora to bring Billy Flint to the servants' dining room. I can eat and

meet with them at the same time. If you wouldn't mind serving me in there, that is?"

Georgina had spoken with Flora while in her bath. She had warned her of the posters placed by the man who had named himself her master. Flora promised to take extra care while out and about, but she refused to flee from the home she was making for herself with Georgina's help.

"It will give you indigestion, having meetings and eating," Cook grumbled. "Can you not sit down and enjoy your meal in peace?"

"Morning, Miss Georgina." Billy Flint, his arms laden with thick, long, leather-bound ledgers came through the back door. "Sorry, Cook, I couldn't knock – me arms were loaded down, and I didn't want to kick your door."

"The dining room, please, Billy." Georgina pointed.

"This is only the first of the lot." Billy walked towards the dining room. A thump was heard as he put down the books. He was soon back in the kitchen. "I'll fetch the next lot."

"Am I to feed him and all?" Cook sighed.

"Not at all," Georgina said. "All that is needed is a pot of tea – a large pot made in a metal teapot if you would – we can keep the tea warm on one of our spirit stoves and serve ourselves as needed."

"Did you want toast?" Cook did not want to ask Ruth to stop her work. They needed to brown off those pie bottoms before filling them.

"Could I please have some of your fried egg with fried bread?" Georgina knew that was less work than someone standing holding a toasting fork out to the flames while someone else fried eggs.

"That's not enough to keep body and soul together," Cook grumbled, taking a heavy cast-iron frying pan from a cupboard.

"Can I help you in any way, Cook?" Georgina knew the old woman hated to ask.

"Flora won't be a moment." Billy Flint passed them again with more of the heavy ledgers. "She is gone to fetch her notebook, pen, and pencils. That woman is never without a notebook to hand. She's a caution."

"If you'd get out of me way, Miss Georgina," Cook put a spoonful of goose grease into the pan warming over the heat in the range. "I'll get about my business, and you get about yours."

"I have been cloistered …" Flora began.

"Wait!" Georgina felt an electric charge run down her spine. "Say no more. I need to make a note."

They were gathered around the table in the servants' dining room. Billy Flint had set up the spirit stove to keep the tea piping hot. The brew stood ready for them to serve themselves. Billy and Flora sat at one end of the long table with the ledgers spread across it. Flora had her notebook, pencils and her marvellous new fountain pen in its metal box sitting close to her hand.

Georgina, a cup of tea and a plate of beautifully presented eggs and fried bread in front of her, sat far away from the ledgers. She did not want to get grease on the books.

Flora selected a well-sharpened pencil from her supply. She did not select the fountain pen – while a marvellous invention, it did tend to leak at inopportune moments. "If it is not a private matter, tell me and I will make notes." She opened her notebook to a clean page and, pencil in hand, waited.

"Note to Goldenbridge Convent, re convenient time for visit." Georgina rested her knife and fork on her plate and wiped her mouth with her napkin. "Request a cheque from Richard Wilson. I will need to make a generous donation to the nuns, I have no doubt."

"The clergy are overly fond of the pound, shillings and pence."

Billy grunted under his breath.

Georgina pretended not to hear his words. "Billy to provide horse and carriage for my journey. That is all for the moment." She did not want to visit the Goldenbridge Convent, but she must obey her great-aunt's final wishes and there was a chance that she might have left something pertinent to Bridget's situation in that box. "If you will pass me the note, please, Flora. I will take care of those matters."

"I will hold on to the note, Georgina." Flora closed her notebook, the note still inside. "If I give it to you, you will put it in your pocket and forget all about it."

"True," Georgina picked up her knife and fork, "but do please remind me to carry out my own instructions." She looked at her plate in surprise. She had eaten far more than she had thought she would. "Now ..." she looked at her two companions, "tell me all."

"It is as I have said." Billy Flint looked at the ledgers, admiration shining in his eyes. "The three businesses are little goldmines."

"As I started to say before I was interrupted, Georgie," Flora said, "I cloistered myself in your office yesterday and made an in-depth study of those ledgers. The three houses – under Elias Simpson's financial guidance – are run very much as a proper business. Invoices are written, statements sent, and taxes paid. If one were not aware of the nature of the services offered in these houses, one would never guess from the ledgers." She put her hand on one beautiful leather-bound ledger and shook her head in admiration. "It is very inventive book work."

"I gave what time I could to the books." Billy had been in awe of Flora's understanding of everything written in the ledgers. "I thought the overheads and staff salaries were overpadded, but Flora assured me that all was as it should be."

"Do you both believe these three houses should be allowed to continue as they are?" Georgina was still not comfortable with the services offered by the three houses. However, she had not been appointed as the conscience of the nation. Houses such as these had been around since time immemorial.

"Yes." Flora would like to meet Sally Mulligan and discuss the three houses with her. She had questions she wanted answered. She would not endorse a business that abused women. But the businesses were sound and did indeed bring in a small fortune monthly.

"Yes," Billy said.

"Very well." Georgina wiped her lips and fingers on her napkin, wishing for a fingerbowl. The meal had been delicious but greasy. She stood, picking up her plate. She cleared what she had used from the table, putting everything on the sideboard. She poured a fresh cup of tea and returned to her chair.

"Here is what I have decided. I intend to leave the running of those three businesses to you both. You will both run them and take the profits as your own."

She waited for their objections – convinced they would believe she had lost her mind.

Billy Flint stood abruptly and, with his hands flat on the table, stared at her. He opened his mouth several times as if trying to speak.

Flora had paled and collapsed back in her chair. She too stared open-mouthed at Georgina.

"Sit down, Billy, and listen to me – both of you," Georgina said when they remained silent. "You two have much in common." She held up a hand when they looked like objecting. "You are both young and penniless. You both come from a less than ideal background. You both wish to succeed in life by your own efforts. I admire that ambition in you." She pressed her fingers to her eyes. "I cannot and will not be involved in the running of those three houses. It is against everything I believe in. However, I am not fool enough to ruin what is clearly a going concern." She paused to sigh deeply, silently cursing her late husband for leaving her in such a difficult position. "What I suggest is this – initially I will allow you to run those houses free of rent for a six-month period – that should give you time to learn the trade – so to speak." She tried not to blush. She was mortified to think of what the stock-in-trade of those "businesses" was. "After that period, all going well, you will be in a position to pay rent and –"

"Miss Georgina," Billy interrupted, "you would be robbing yourself blind."

"Georgie, Billy is right," Flora said. "It is a great deal of money. The cash flow from those businesses is astounding." There was no need to mention the vast sums of money that had been withdrawn by the Captain and spent on jewels and expensive gifts, racehorses and other such items that she was sure Georgie knew nothing of.

"I want nothing to do with them," Georgina said. "However, I will begin to charge rent on all three properties when the six-month period has passed. I am not giving you the buildings. That is not to say that you could not purchase them from me in the future."

"I think I am going to act like a maiden aunt and faint." Billy Flint knew what she was offering him. The start of his fortune. A start in life that he could never even have dreamt possible.

"Put your head between your knees," Georgina said unsympathetically.

"Georgie, are you sure?" Flora was breathless at the opportunity Georgie was presenting to her. "It is so much money."

"Money I have." Georgina shrugged. "I want to be able to sleep easy at night. Those three houses conduct business in an area that is something outside my experience of life – I am happy to be able to say – but they obviously serve a need and, as such, why should you two not profit from them?"

"Miss Georgina!" Billy fell to his knees by the side of her chair. He took one of her hands and pressed a fervent kiss into it. "I will never be able to truly thank you." He was not going to be fool enough to pass up this golden opportunity.

"Hush, Billy." Georgina pressed her free hand to the top of his head. "You have been by my side through my most difficult days. Now do stand up." She smiled into his tear-soaked eyes when he looked up.

She waited until he had returned to his chair, blowing his nose into the handkerchief he took from his pocket. He surreptitiously wiped tears from his cheeks at the same time.

"When we leave this room the business structure of the three houses will never again be discussed between us. You will both have to agree on how you shall go forward. May I suggest that the books show that the company of ..." she looked between them, "Billy, you will be seen as a clever fellow so can use your legal name of William Armstrong on business letterheads – Flora, however ..." she sighed, "that is a different matter entirely. You, Flora, will be seen as a harlot, my dear. You need to choose a nom de plume for your own use. It too must appear on the letterheads."

Flora, after staring for a moment at the other two, started to laugh. She fell about in her chair, laughing until tears streamed from her eyes. The other two stared at her, wondering if she had lost her senses. Sometimes good fortune was more difficult to accept than bad.

"I know exactly the name I shall use." Flora clapped her hands, a smile so wide on her face it had to hurt. "It just came to me – out of the air – like a gift. I shall become Mrs F. Pomeroy. Is that not a splendid name? Yes, indeed, Mrs F. Pomeroy shall be business partner to Mr William Armstrong – and gladly, even joyfully."

"Why that name?" Billy asked. "There is obviously something about it that tickles your fancy."

Flora began to laugh again. They had to wait until she had gathered her composure.

"Are you able to explain now?" Georgina asked when Flora had calmed.

"Madame de Pompadour was mistress to a king. It is rumoured that she supplied the king with pure young maidens for his pleasure. Do you not see?"

The other two stared at her blankly.

"That is my new name. It has meaning to me that will escape most people."

"It escapes me," Billy Flint said.

"Me too." Georgina nodded.

"My business nom de plume – Pom for Madame de Pompadour and the French for king is Roi, so I put them together and I make Pomeroy. The F. is indeed my initial, but it is also slang for a very naughty word." She continued to laugh with sheer delight. "Every time I see that name in print, I will be basically telling the world to –"

"Yes," Georgina stopped her before she could go further, "very clever. Although one hopes that those bearing the actual name of Pomeroy will never become aware of your interpretation and use of that name."

"So …" Billy did not care what the name meant to her or anyone else. He held out his hand to Flora. "The company of Pomeroy and Armstrong has been born?"

"Armstrong and Pomeroy." Flora took the offered hand. She was a businesswoman now. She could shake hands just like the big boys. "Let us keep the name correct – alphabetically."

Chapter 26

Two weeks later, on a Monday morning early, Georgina, dressed in a navy-blue suit, without stays or bustle, an outfit suitable for travel, the ensemble covered by a long woollen coat of the same navy, stepped out of her front door. She stopped and stared, astonished to see a strange horse between the traces of her old carriage. The bay mare danced impatiently between the traces while Billy Flint stood at its head, holding tightly to the bridle. Two men, Smith and Jones she supposed, sat on the box awaiting the off.

"Come ahead, Miss Georgina!" Billy called when Georgina stood at the top of the granite steps – staring.

"What on earth, Billy?" Georgina walked slowly down the steps, staring at the strange horse.

"I am afraid your old horse is only up to standing in her stable eating." Billy shook his head sadly. "I did not want to put her up to pulling the carriage. That old mare needs to be pensioned off, Miss Georgina."

"Where did this beauty come from?" Georgina stood at the horse's head with him, admiring the mare's solid lines.

"I borrowed her from the livery in The Lane," Billy said. "Truth to be told, Miss Georgina, you could do with a new carriage too. The springs on this old one are shot." He had not wanted to raise the issue, fearing it would look like he was trying to make space for himself and his men in the carriage house. Without the horse and carriage, he would certainly have a great deal more space available to him.

"It seems everything and everybody around me is aging," Georgina said sadly. "I have not time to discuss the matter of horse and carriage right now, Billy. But one thing I will insist on – my old mare – she will not be sent to the knacker's yard – I could not bear to think of her being turned into dog food and glue. She has served me well for many years."

"Understood. Climb aboard, Miss Georgina." He signalled to one of the men on the box. He watched the man jump down and hold the door of the carriage open for Georgina. "Smith and Jones will see you safely on your way. You might think about what you want to do about the horse and carriage when you are out and about." He slapped the horse on the neck with his open hand, releasing the bridle. "This little beauty will get you where you need to go a great deal faster than you are used to." He closed the door of the carriage once he was sure she was safely inside.

"Thank you," Georgina said weakly – one more thing for her to worry and wonder about. She sat back in her seat, confident that Smith and Jones knew where she was heading. Billy Flint would have seen to that.

"Would it be possible for me to visit my great-aunt's final resting place?" Georgina had spent an extremely uncomfortable hour being ruthlessly quizzed by Reverend Mother Augustus, the new leader of the Goldenbridge Convent. She had been offered no refreshments nor had her coat and hat been taken. It was vastly different to her previous visits to this house.

She had been interrogated about Ruth and Sarah, the two orphans from this convent that she had taken into her home. She began to feel as if she should admit to a terrible crime of some nature – what, she had no idea. It was a blessing that Bridget was never mentioned. Her great-aunt had indeed hidden her charge well. It hurt Georgina's heart to see another in her aunt's place. The brown-paper-and-twine-wrapped package, with bright splashes of red sealing wax splattered about it, sitting on the floor beside the desk, was a visible reminder of her absence.

"The Reverend Mother rests in our private chapel." Sister Augustus smiled sweetly. "We do not allow visitors."

"Could I bring flowers?" Georgina wanted to do something to show her great love and loss. Say a private and final farewell.

"I am sorry, no." Again, the sickly-sweet smile. "However, a financial donation towards the care of the gravesite is always welcome."

"Of course." Georgina withdrew the cheque she had Richard draw up for this very purpose from her pocket. She knew she could not leave without offering what she thought of as a bribe. The sweet smile she received when the nun read the numbers on the cheque made her want to slap the woman's face. Did the woman practise in front of a mirror. She knew she was being unreasonable, but it hurt.

She stood with great relief – the meeting at an end. She wanted to be out in the fresh air away from reminders of days past. When she tried to pick up the sealed box, she found it almost impossible to move. She knew what the package contained. She'd had no notion that the chest had rested in her great-aunt's care. She had heard tales of it all her life.

"Oh, dear, whatever can my great-aunt have left to me. It is inordinately heavy." Georgina could see the curiosity in the woman's eyes. If she thought Georgina was going to open the package here, she was sadly mistaken. "Would it be possible to ask my coachman to step inside and carry this box for me?"

"I am sorry – that is not possible." Augustus smiled. "You should perhaps empty the box and carry the items out individually?"

"Never mind." Georgina was tempted to flex her muscles. "It is most likely filled with books and if I drop it – well, what harm?" She mentally prepared to struggle from the room. "Excuse me just a moment, won't you?"

She did not wait for a response but walked swiftly out of the room across the black-and-white-tiled foyer to the front door. She opened the door wide, shouted for Jones to stand ready by the door and returned the same way to smile down sweetly at Reverend Mother Augustus.

"I shall take it from here. Good day to you, Reverend Mother." She wrapped her fingers under the twine and, almost buckling at the knees, heaved the heavy package up. Bent almost double from the weight, she began to carry it towards the open front door.

"In the name of Jesus, missus," Jones whispered as he took the heavy article into his arms, "what have you got in here?"

"Who knows?" Georgina waved regally towards the waiting carriage. "Put it in the carriage, please." With her head high, she walked to the carriage and got in. The package was taking up space at her feet. There it could stay. "*Drive on!*" she put her head out of the carriage window to shout.

Georgina sat back in the carriage, glad of the chance to simply breathe deeply. That had been a very unpleasant experience. The Reverend Mother had appeared to believe that Georgina was some kind of "devil's handmaiden". She had questioned her closely about her late husband. She had demanded details about Ruth and Sarah in a manner that struck Georgina as excessively offensive. She would not be returning to that convent if she could prevent it.

The young horse moved along at a much faster pace than she was accustomed to travelling. She had hoped for more time for simple contemplation. Jones shouting *whoa* and the slowing down of the carriage surprised her. She looked out the carriage window, wondering if they had really reached their destination. The door to the white building opened and a smiling woman stepped outside. This must be the place.

"*Mrs Whitmore?*" the woman called as soon as Jones had jumped down from the box and held the door of the carriage open.

"Mrs Morgan?" Georgina returned the greeting while accepting Smith's hand to step out of the carriage.

"Thank you so much for responding to my invitation, Mrs Whitmore." Jane Morgan held open the gate to her garden. She had sent a missive to this woman requesting her immediate attention. She had made a reference to the BOBs but kept the missive brief.

"One moment, please, if you will, Mrs Morgan." Georgiana turned to Jones on the box. "If you would take the package from the carriage and deliver it to my house. You could carry it up to my sitting room." She waited for his nod before continuing. "Then return here for me in …" She turned to Mrs Morgan with a raised eyebrow.

"Two hours?" Jane Morgan hoped they would have concluded their business in that time.

Georgiana turned to Jones on the box. "Two hours, please."

"As you wish, madam." Jones tipped his hat with his whip and as soon as Smith joined him the carriage moved off.

"I cannot thank you enough for agreeing to meet with me." Jane Morgan led the way into her house.

"I am always willing to help with anything that furthers the interest of the BOBs," Georgina followed her hostess into her home, trying desperately to see all of the carvings practically hidden in the wooden panelling and supports. "I must confess myself bemused by your request to see me. I can't imagine how I might help you?" It was only the slight mention of the BOBs that had moved her to visit.

"Please come through to the kitchen. It overlooks the garden, so I can keep an eye on my charge." Not to mention it was the warmest room in the house.

"I seem to spend all of my time lately in the kitchen." Georgina liked this woman.

"Let me take your coat." Jane took the coat and hung it up.

"Oh, how delightful!" Georgina exclaimed, examining the shy fairy hidden in the carving of the hallstand.

"This is a treasurehouse of secret delights, Mrs Whitmore."

"Please, do call me Georgina." She hated to be addressed by her late husband's name.

"I am Jane. Follow me, please."

Georgiana was enchanted by the well-laid-out kitchen – so much smaller than her own – but none the less functional.

"Please take a seat." Jane pulled a chair from the kitchen table.

"Why have you sought me out, Jane?" Georgina sat, speaking to the woman's back.

"I consulted the BOBs." Jane poured boiling water from the kettle into the teapot while she spoke. "The Dowager Duchess mentioned you." She put the kettle back on the hob before she turned. "I hope you don't mind."

"Not in the least. I owe a great deal to the BOBs," Georgina said.

"I have a charge, as I may have mentioned." Jane took a seat at the table while the tea brewed. She sat for a second before jumping up again and beginning to set the table. "I understand from my work with the BOBs that you have taken young ladies into your home and trained them in household skills, such as making beds, cleaning tables, preparing food."

"I have not." Georgina smiled sympathetically at Jane's obvious dismay. "My staff, however, have certainly done something of the sort."

"My charge is a young woman – a titled lady – she has the attention span of a flea when it comes to housework but step into the garden – there she knows something about everything." She gestured towards the lace-covered window of the kitchen. "See her." Jane pointed to a tall figure throwing a stick for an ecstatically barking dog. "I have had her in my charge for only two weeks. In that time, I have become very fond of her. But I have no experience with youth. I have spent a great deal of my life taking care of the elderly."

"What is she wearing?" Georgina stared.

"That is yet another thing. She travelled here from the north of Ireland in trousers and a fisherman's jumper. I was sent her chests, but they contained the most ridiculous garments. Everything was lace, frills, and ribbons, in colours such as lemon and peach." Jane held out her own deep-brown woollen skirt. "We wear black, brown, or navy in my world. I neither know nor care a jot about fashionable attire. I had thought to purchase some garments at the local market for her. " She jerked her chin towards the window. "But everything I bought was too short or too wide – she is tall and slim and I have no skill for judging garments or any real skill as a seamstress. She insisted I buy her trousers and jumpers down the market until we have suitable garments to hand."

"My poor woman!" Georgina was trying not to laugh. "Pour the tea."

"*Oh, me scones!*" Jane suddenly shouted. "*I forgot all about them! The arse will be burned off them!*" She turned quickly to open the door

204

of the range oven – using her skirt to protect her hands she removed beautifully browned scones from the oven.

"Jane," Georgina sat again, patting the table, "what do the BOBs have planned for your charge?" She poured the tea herself. "I know they must have something in mind."

Jane sat and accepted a cup of tea. "The BOBs want to set her up in a cottage of her own, with discreet servants, on someone's estate."

"How ridiculous!" Georgina sipped her tea. "The loneliness alone would drive her insane and is she to become invisible to masculine eyes? The BOBs will have to reconsider their options."

"Do you think so?" Jane asked.

"Has your company come yet?" The door to the kitchen opened and a tall young beauty wearing trousers, a dog at her heels, stepped inside. "I could murder a cup of tea." Rebecca loved that expression of Jane's.

"Lady Rebecca Henderson!" The words slipped between Georgina's lips. The resemblance to Bridget was startlingly obvious.

"Do I know you, madam?" Rebecca was trying to remove her muddy boots.

"My husband was with your father in his carriage when the train crashed." Georgina hadn't known of the plans the BOBs had made for this young woman.

Chapter 27

"Before you sit down," Georgina wanted the attention away from her blunder. How could she explain her instant recognition of Lady Rebecca? They had never met. "You need to fetch a cup and saucer for yourself."

Jane stared between the two, wondering what was going on. There was more here than met the eye. She kept her mouth shut and her eyes open – you learned more that way, she had found.

"While you are on your feet," Georgina continued, "perhaps you could serve us those delicious-looking scones that Jane has been good enough to prepare."

Rebecca stood with her hands on her hips, green eyes sparkling in a face that shone with health. "Has Jane been telling tales about my utter failure as a housewife?" She too was happy to ignore the mention of her father's death. She had heard the rumours of this woman's husband and another woman – how could you not? – the rail crash had been a subject of conversation and servant gossip for weeks and would continue to attract interest for a long time. Under the watchful eyes of her companions, she placed the scones on a long serving dish, butter and jam on the table and side plates with butter knifes close to each person. With a cup and saucer in hand, she joined the others at the table.

"It is very disheartening, madam." Rebecca looked across the table at the woman Jane had failed to introduce. "I watch Jane move around this kitchen and it is very much like watching an elegant dance – but when I try I feel like a veritable elephant."

"Do call me Georgina." She reached for a scone. "I have no doubt that you both have heard rumours concerning my late husband. I find myself cringing when addressed as Mrs Whitmore – after all, most believe I am dead because the woman killed on the train was reported as being Mrs Whitmore – so for this moment in time let us all use first names. I am Georgina."

"Thank you, I am Rebecca." The rules of society she had been taught seemed to fly out the window in this house.

"Now that we have that out of the way," Jane was convinced she was missing something, "can you offer any advice at all to me and Rebecca?"

"Looking at you, Rebecca," Georgina split her scone and spread butter as she spoke, "the most pressing need appears to be suitable clothing." The girl could not walk around dressed as a boy – no matter how attractive the outfit might make her.

"I am loving the freedom trousers give." Rebecca popped a piece of buttered scone into her mouth and chewed.

"You cannot go around the place dressed like a boy," Jane objected. "I have told you that until I am blue in the face."

Georgina looked at Rebecca with raised eyebrows.

"Yes, I must agree. I am in need of a complete wardrobe suitable for my new life. In the past I spent my days, usually, tending to my family's grounds. I wore dark serviceable clothing." She would not explain to these women that the articles in the chests her grandfather had sent were simply camouflage – used to disguise the true treasure that lay in the concealed chest compartments. She touched a hand to her breast, feeling the solid comfort of her fob watch under her shirt. She could not wear it openly for the moment but knowing she had it and touching it from time to time gave her solace. It was a gift given in love by her grandfather.

"Very well." Georgina looked at Jane. "Do you have boxes available to you? Something unobtrusive that would hold the clothing that was sent with Rebecca?"

"I would normally pack things up in tea chests, but the fabric of those dresses is far too fine. I would be afraid of ruining it," Jane answered.

"Do you have a means of transport available to you?" Hopefully she had something other than her feet for transportation.

"I have a donkey and cart."

"Very well." Georgina gave a decisive nod of her head. "Here is what I suggest you do about clothing." She had their complete attention. "There is a *modiste* – she is truly French – not one of the phony French that proliferate – Madame Emmanuelle – you need to take the clothing to Sackville Street –"

"She can afford a premises on the main thoroughfare!" Jane interrupted. She couldn't imagine parking her old donkey and cart outside a fancy shop.

"No, no." Georgina was trying to think of how to give directions. "There is a lane."

"Isn't there always in Dublin?"

"Emmanuelle is a truly skilled modiste. She has women working for her. She even has the latest in sewing machines."

"I hate to give up my trousers," Rebecca sighed.

"Lady Sutton often wears split skirts," Georgina smiled. "Not out in public but on her estate. She finds them extremely comfortable. You could ask Madame to make you something of that nature."

"What has this to do with all of that fancy stuff upstairs?" Jane waved a hand towards the ceiling in the direction of the bedrooms.

"I suggest you pack up all the clothing that is not of use and offer it to Emmanuelle. She can make use of the fabric if not the actual dresses." She went on before anyone could interrupt again. "Emmanuelle keeps a supply of readymade dresses on hand – mostly in black for funerals – but she may have something that Rebecca could use immediately. She would accept the items on hand in part exchange."

"I have money." Rebecca had told Jane she had funds available – just not how much. "Paying for the garments will not present a problem."

"That is all well and good," Georgina waved a hand from Rebecca's head to the area around her feet, "but while you look like that, you are a prisoner between these walls."

"Won't this modiste have a canary if I turn up at her door in me donkey cart?" Jane could not imagine any fancy establishment being happy to see her stop outside their business.

"I suggest you approach Madame Emmanuelle first on foot since money is not a problem and you will not have to carry the clothing you wish to exchange." Georgina pressed her fingers into her eyes for a moment. "Jane, Rebecca, under normal circumstances I would throw myself at your convenience – but – for the next seven to ten days – my days will be filled with so much toing and froing that it is making my head spin – the BOBs, don't you know."

The other two nodded in understanding.

"Jane, I suggest you ask Emmanuelle to fashion clothing for you

209

too – something like a maiden aunt would wear to escort her young charge around town …"

"I have such clothes available to me," Jane put in. "The BOBs, don't you know."

"Now …" Georgina began.

"Let me make another pot of tea," Jane stood up. "This one is stiff."

"Jane, we must continue to communicate by post," Georgina said to Jane's back. "Slightly ridiculous since we are not that great a distance from each other but for the moment safest. I have three ladies arriving any day now who do not need to hide away. They will be fitting company for Rebecca in her movements around town. Also, I have a distant relation living with me, a young woman who would be a good companion for Rebecca, but she too is enormously busy in the coming days."

"It sounds like you have your hands full." Jane sat to wait for the kettle to come to a boil.

"Jane," Georgina shook her head, "I have a severe shortage of trained staff, yet my house will soon be bulging at the seams. I want to assist you in any way I can but there is only one of me and at this moment in time I feel pulled in all directions. I will assist – that I promise you – but for the moment it will have to be by post."

"Have you any suggestions as to how I can take this one," Jane waved a hand at Rebecca, "to see this modiste without shocking the natives."

"Honestly," Georgina was frantically trying to think of a way she could offer help, "no."

"I am not comfortable leaving Rebecca in the house on her own." Jane stood to make tea.

"Do I really need to be hidden away?" Rebecca asked.

"Until we have something to dress you in," Jane put the lid on the teapot, "yes."

"I know!" Georgina snapped her fingers. "I will send my housekeeper to you. Lily Chambers has spent years measuring servants for uniforms. She can take Rebecca's measurements to Emmanuelle. They know each other. That will allow you to stay with Rebecca, Jane, and if Emmanuelle has something on hand that will fit Rebecca – well, all to the good. You can trust Lily Chambers. She is the soul of discretion."

That evening sitting around the table in the servants' dining room Georgina found it difficult to believe it was still the same day. She had achieved a great deal but there was still so much to do in the coming days. She needed to follow Flora's example and make notes of whatever was needed.

"I wish to thank all here for their kindness," Agatha Hancock suddenly said into the silence. Every head rose to look at her. "I have decided to take the train from Kingsbridge Station on Wednesday and return to Limerick. My bags are packed, and I need only order a carriage to carry me there."

Georgina used her napkin to postpone saying anything. Really, what more could be said? The woman had dillied and dallied around long enough.

"I ..." she got no further before Helen began to wail – loudly.

"But that is the day my Ernest is coming to call!" Helen spluttered. "What shall I tell him? What shall I do? He is emigrating to Canada, and I will never see him again, and now you tell me that you too are deserting me. What am I to do?"

Georgina knew Helen was corresponding with young Ernest Cunningham, her red-haired baker, but no mention had been made to her of a visit from that young man.

"Helen …" Agatha closed her eyes so she would not have to look upon the face that so resembled her lost love. She longed to slap the silly young girl. "I am not responsible for you or your actions." Not anymore, she thought. "I have contacted the Babington-Hawthorns and advised them that the baby has taken well to the glass bottle and formula. My time here is done. I am returning home to assume my old position." It was not as if she had not told the girl this before – multiple times.

"What shall I do?" Helen sobbed.

The drama was providing entertainment to others at the table. Bridget, Sarah, Ruth, and Liam were looking on wide-eyed while continuing to carry food to their mouths. Mrs Chambers and Cook looked like they wanted to be elsewhere and who could blame them? Flora was ignoring everything, lost in her own world. Dorothy looked like someone who wished to deliver a sound beating – to both women. It was left to Molly Mulvey to reply.

"I know what I would do!" Molly snapped. "I would marry the lad and travel to Canada with him. It's not like you're short of a few bob in your pocket these days." She had advised the same before, but Helen seemed to enjoy being in the middle of a drama. Molly had had more than enough of her.

"I was not made aware that your young man was to visit you at my home, Helen." Georgina was annoyed by this lack of courtesy.

"Nor I." Lily Chambers was the housekeeper. She should have been informed of any visit.

"I knew nothing of this." Agatha wanted everyone to know that she had no hand in this matter.

"It would appear you have failed to make the visit of Mr Ernest Cunningham known to this household, Helen," Georgina said. "Is that fair to the young man?" She closed her ears to the wailing with a sigh.

Chapter 28

"Do let us know that you have arrived safely." Georgina stepped back from the hired carriage. "I would be interested to hear your news."

"Thank you for everything," Agatha looked towards the house, hoping to see Helen at least waving from the steps. When there was no sign of the girl she had nurtured and protected for years, she sighed. She gave the driver the order to move off. She must not miss her train. She sat back in her seat, happy to be returning to where she belonged. She would put this episode behind her once she was back in her own world.

Georgina watched the carriage until it was out of sight. She was slightly ashamed of her relief. Agatha had been moving around the house like a ghost for weeks. She wished her well in her return to her old life.

"Bridget!" Georgina called to the young girl polishing the staircase. "Have you seen Helen?"

"Not this morning, Miss Georgina." Bridget stopped to look down the staircase. She glanced towards the front door. "Did she not come to say goodbye to Mrs Hancock?"

"She did not." Georgina wondered what the young woman was up to. She had not joined them for breakfast. "I had better check on her." She would not have done something foolish – would she? With her heart in her mouth, Georgina passed Bridget on the staircase, hurrying to the room occupied by Molly and Helen.

The room stood empty. No sign of Helen, Molly, or the baby. What was going on?

Georgina went back down the stairs into the basement, thinking to find the missing members of her household hard at work.

"Ruth, have you seen Helen this morning?" Georgina asked as soon as she walked into the kitchen.

"Oh, you missed it, Miss Georgina." Cook was having a pot of tea in her alcove. "While you were busy with Agatha – that one came into my kitchen – bold as brass – dressed to the nines and commandeered poor Molly. They went out the back door as you were waving goodbye to Agatha at the front."

"Where is the baby?" Georgina looked around frantically.

"In the servants' sitting room," Cook answered. "We were informed he'd been fed and changed." She glared at Georgina. "That one had the cheek to order me to keep an eye on the baby. The nerve of it!"

A breathless Molly Mulvey almost fell into the kitchen. She looked unkempt and windswept.

"She's gone off, Miss Georgina!" Molly gasped the words out. "I could not talk sense into her. She practically dragged me over to The Lane. She is much stronger than she looks, I can tell you. She demanded I help her. I did not know what to do. Her eyes looked that wild – I was afraid to refuse her. She ordered a carriage from old Ryan in The Lane. Off she went to meet that fella. Not to Kingsbridge, the train station Mrs Hancock is leaving from, but the one where the train to Cork leaves from." She leaned against the wall gasping, a hand to her heaving chest.

"Has she indeed?" Georgina snapped. "Did she take anything with her?"

"No, because she would have expected me to carry her bags. Honest to God, Miss Georgina, I have never seen anything like it. You would have thought she was Lady Muck the way she was acting."

Ruth and Cook watched the goings-on, neither speaking.

"What is happening?" Lily Chambers, Bridget and Sarah at her heels entered the kitchen.

Before anyone could answer a baby's scream of displeasure carried down the long hallway into the kitchen.

"Bridget, see to that baby," Lily ordered, never doubting her order would be carried out. She waited to be told what was going on in her household.

"I think that is the last of it." Lily Chambers stood in the open doorway of the room Molly and Helen had been sharing.

"Mrs Chambers, Helen is going to be spitting fire when she gets back here," Molly almost whispered.

"What Helen Butcher has failed to understand …" Lily looked at the fascinated faces around her. She had ordered Liam, Sarah, and Molly to assist her in removing all of Helen's effects from the guest room up to an attic room. Bridget was taking care of the baby under Cook's watchful eye. "What she has failed to understand is that she is not a guest in this house. She has in fact no standing whatsoever in this house." Lily wanted to box the young woman's ears. She could not remember when she had been so angry.

"*Mrs Chambers!*" Georgina shouted up the stairs from the first floor. "*Can you spare Molly? I would like to speak with her.*"

"Molly," Lily jerked her head towards the stairs, "go see what Miss Georgina wants." She waited until Molly had run to obey. She looked at the other three, trying not to sigh. Her morning routine had been destroyed by the actions of a mule-headed young woman. That would not be allowed. "We will take a short break." She led her crew down the stairs towards the kitchen.

"Molly," Georgina looked across her desk at the young woman lounging in the chair across from her, "I have received a letter from the Babington-Hawthorns concerning you."

"Me?" Molly stared.

"Yes, indeed." Georgina touched a letter sitting open on her desk. "The letter must have crossed with Agatha Hancock's correspondence. They make no mention of her leaving."

"Yes, Miss Georgina." Molly wriggled on the seat.

"The Babington-Hawthorns wish to know if you would be willing to accompany them on their journey to England."

"Miss Georgina," Molly leaned forward, putting her elbows on her knees, "I told yeh and told yeh, I do not want to be a nursemaid. I do not want to go into service. I want to be a Harvey Girl. I have me heart set on it."

"Molly," Georgina slapped a hand on the letter, "look at you!" She waved a hand at Molly. "You would have been pinched black and blue by a governess by now. You have wriggled and almost danced on that seat. I do not know what you have done to your clothing, but you are a mess. We in this house want you to achieve your dream every bit as much as you do. But, Molly, you are in no way ready to be sent out to America ..."

"But –"

"Molly, you have worked hard at your studies. I know this –

216

everyone speaks very highly of you. But when you leave the classroom, you fall straight back into being Molly Mulvey from The Lane. That will never do. Mr Harvey would never choose you to work in his eateries. I am sorry."

"Miss!" Molly's eyes filled with tears. She had worked so hard. Harder than she had ever worked before in her life. She was doing good – she was.

"Molly," Georgina pressed fingers into her aching eyes. "Sit up straight, you are slouching, and I know that you know better than that. Sit like a lady, at once."

Molly jerked into position.

"That," Georgina pointed, "is how you must sit – always."

"But, Miss Georgina," Molly protested, "it is just us here."

"That is the problem, Molly."

"I don't understand, Miss Georgina. I try so hard."

"I know you do, Molly." Georgina sat erect very conscious of her posture. "I do not mean to hurt your feelings, Molly. But you know as well as anyone else that one is judged by appearance before one even opens one's mouth. Then the shaping of our words denotes our class." She made no mention of Molly's Dublin accent.

"You are saying I can never crawl out of my beginnings?" Molly tried not to cry.

"I am not saying that at all!" Georgina snapped. "I would never have agreed to give you false hope. You have settled down to learn everything we have taught you here. However, you do not apply that knowledge outside of the classroom. Your posture is frightful," she waved a hand to Molly's again slouching figure, "you pick up your skirts and run around like a hoyden. That is simply not ladylike." She stared a moment to see if the girl was taking in her words. "Mr Harvey employs only ladylike young women."

"You think I'm going to fail." Molly's chest hurt.

"Molly …" Georgina straightened her shoulders and continued. "You cannot travel to America alone, so at this time you applying to Mr Harvey is a moot point." She held up a hand when Molly opened her mouth. "I strongly recommend you accept the Babington-Hawthorn invitation to travel with them. You have vast experience taking care of young children – all learned at your mother's knee. Far more than anyone else in this house. The baby terrifies us all – we fear doing something wrong and hurting the child."

"I've never been away from Dublin." Molly felt sick to her stomach with nerves. How could she travel on a train and a ship for the first time under the watchful eyes of the Babington-Hawthorns – they were strangers to her.

"Molly," Georgina ignored her words, waving her arms about her, "this house is not at all like the home I grew up in. There is no rigid discipline between the servants. The people living here now are making the best of what we have on hand – but it is less than ideal – believe me. You have never seen behind the doors of a true home of the gentry. You need to understand the enormous gap between what you know and as a Harvey Girl what you will be expected to portray. In travelling with the Babington-Hawthorns you will experience a completely different slice of life. If you keep your mouth closed and your eyes and ears open, you will learn far more than we can teach you in class."

"You think I should go with them?" Molly sat erect. "Will you promise me that I can come back here and learn to be a Harvey Girl?"

"The journey with the Babington-Hawthorns should take perhaps as long as a month. I do not know if they intend to return to Ireland with you. But in the time you would spend with the family, you will be exposed to how servants are expected to behave. You will have the opportunity to observe Mrs Babington-Hawthorn and her family. I believe it will come as quite an eye-opener to you." Georgina leaned forward. "I believe it is vital that you learn all that you can. You are being offered a chance. Take it. You were brave enough to take the chance Dorothy offered to you – now I am asking you to take another chance."

"The very thought scares me spitless, Miss Georgina," Molly whispered.

"Yet you wish to travel to America?"

"That's different somehow." Molly shrugged. "I thought I would be in company with other girls like me – girls wanting a chance for something different. I thought at the beginning that it would be me, Flora and Helen sailing off to America together." She hunched into herself on the chair. "I'm stupid. I see that now."

"You most definitely are not stupid," Georgina objected. "You have something no one can teach, Molly – you have what I believe is called common sense – a most rare commodity, I do assure you. You have so much potential, Molly. I want you to succeed. But I am afraid it will take more work from you and a wider view of the world you wish to enter. The voyage to England will provide some of that knowledge." She smiled suddenly. "Did I forget to mention," she tapped the letter, "that you will be very well paid."

"You really think I can do this?" Molly was beginning to feel excited.

"Yes, I do." Georgina said. "Speak with Billy Flint about this – he too has travelled to England under somewhat similar circumstances. He will be able to offer advice."

"I didn't know that!" Molly wondered what else Billy Flint had been up to.

"Speak with Billy, ask his advice." Georgina sighed. "You will also need suitable nursery maid uniforms for your journey. I will speak with Mrs Chambers – we will see you are as prepared as we can make you."

Chapter 29

"No sign of that young woman." Georgina attired in a red-velvet dressing gown buttoned to her neck, tightly waisted and falling to her feet, entered the kitchen. Her hair was in a braid over one shoulder, the skin of her face and hands gleaming from her nightly application of moistening creams.

"Not a sign," Cook, busy at the stove, said over her shoulder. She too was prepared for bed in a striped dressing gown tightly cinched at the waist, her hair knotted in pipe cleaners – to encourage curls – sticking out in all directions.

"I sent Liam over to the livery." Lily Chambers walked into the kitchen from her downstairs bedroom. She had heard the two women while walking along the hallway to join them. "Helen Butcher sent the carriage away. She had the cheek to tell the driver to send the bill here." She too was prepared for bed in a navy-blue buttoned dressing gown, her greying hair pinned and covered by a hairnet.

"I refused to allow Molly to go out looking for her. I told her she was needed to care for the baby and should leave Helen to us." Georgina took a seat at the alcove table. "I dread to think what might happen to a young country girl out on the streets of Dublin alone – but where would we go to look for her? She has been missing all day."

"Do you believe that having that baby has turned her mind?" Cook carried a pot of hot drinking chocolate to the table while Lily put out enamel mugs. It was far too late, in her opinion, to worry about fancy table settings.

"We none of us have ever given birth." Lily gave Georgina's shoulder a sympathetic squeeze when she joined her at the table. She knew how much the young Georgina had wished for children. "Every woman in this house practically melted in sympathy when young Helen first arrived here. We were all prepared to bend over backwards to assist her, thinking 'There, but for the grace of God, go I'. Perhaps that was our error?"

"That young woman has never liked that little baby – not when she was carrying him – and not from the moment he was born." Cook buried her face in her mug for a moment. "It fair broke my heart to see that little thing looking up at her with his lovely eyes wide while she fed him – she never paid him a moment's notice." She shook her head. "It ain't natural."

"Perhaps it was the nature of his conception." Georgina who had prayed never to conceive a baby for her husband could somewhat understand. She feared the hold a baby would give her husband over her – feared what he might do to an innocent child. Nevertheless, she would have loved her baby no matter who its father was.

"Agatha told us many times that Helen's mother is a hard-faced harpy." Lily returned her mug to the table – leaving a chocolate moustache on her upper lip. "Mayhap young Helen is just now showing her true colours." She licked the chocolate from her lip.

"I don't know what to do?" Georgina said. "It is very late, and the worry is keeping us from our beds."

"I can be hard-hearted too." Lily yawned. "I am going to bed and won't let worry keep me from my sleep." She looked at her mug. "When I have finished my drink."

"Perhaps I should have added a drop of brandy to the chocolate," Cook said. "I don't think I will be able to sleep a wink."

"Will you both think me a terrible person if I tell you that my overriding emotion is anger?" Georgina said.

"No." Lily patted her hand. "You took her into your home without question. You have treated her fairly. If this is the thanks she gives you – well, I question her raising."

A sharp rap on the kitchen door frightened all three women. The back door was opened slightly, and Billy Flint's voice shouted. "*I am coming in for a moment, ladies!*"

The three women were mortified to be discovered by a male in their night attire.

The door to the kitchen was opened fully and Helen Butcher was pushed inside with a hefty shove that almost knocked her to the floor.

"This one," Billy knew the problems she had caused the house today, "was all ready to march up the front steps and bang on the knocker – waking the entire house – she says she has no funds to pay for the carriage she hired."

"How dare you manhandle me!" Helen stared down her nose at Billy. "Who do you think you are – you guttersnipe!"

The three women sitting in the kitchen alcove stared in wide-eyed shock. *How dare she!*

"That will be enough out of you," Georgina said through clenched teeth.

"How much is the fare, Billy?" Lily prepared to stand away from the table and fetch the money needed.

"I paid him." Billy turned to leave. "You can settle with me in the morning. Goodnight." He understood their embarrassment at being seen by him in a state of undress. He should have made the young madam bed down in the hay with the old horse.

"Thank you, Billy!" Georgina called to his back. She worried about him. Did the young man never sleep?

"I am going to my room," Helen stated. "It has been a long day."

"Do not move an inch." Georgina scooted out of the alcove. "How dare you enter my home without permission? Who do you think you are?"

"I live here," Helen turned to leave.

"No," Georgina grabbed hold of one arm, "you do not. You left this house without explanation or apology. So," she waved dramatically towards the kitchen door, "there is the door. You may go out the way you came in."

"Don't be ridiculous!" Helen stared down her nose at Georgina. "You are paid to lodge me."

"That is where you are mistaken." Georgina wanted to slap the sneer off the young woman's face. "You are of no further use to anyone in this house. You decided – in point of fact you demanded – to be allowed abdicate your role as wet nurse to a baby I am receiving funds to house. Therefore, you are of no further use to me." Georgina heard the gasps from her loyal retainers, but this young woman needed to be put in her place.

"I can pay for my lodgement." Helen tried to free her arm. "Send me an accounting."

"The barefaced cheek!" Cook gasped.

"I ask your sacred pardon!" Lily stared.

"I am not running a lodging house!" Georgina waved a hand in front of her nose, trying to dispel the odour of alcohol on the young woman's breath. "And I have no intention of housing such a disagreeable young woman. Your belongings have been moved to the attic for storage. Now," again the wave towards the door, "leave. There are a great many lodging houses in Dublin, although I daresay none of them will open their doors to you at this late hour. Perhaps you could find one of the rooms rented by the hour in houses familiar to the town's doxies."

"I shall go to a hotel." Helen's chin was up, her cheeks flaming red with anger. "I can pay my way."

"How many decent young women do you think are walking the streets late at night obviously intoxicated and looking for a hotel room? Without a servant to hand and carrying her own luggage? You will be refused admission to any decent hotel."

"Molly will come with me. She can carry my bags." Helen smirked, ignoring the comment about her drunken state. "I'll be taking the baby too. Ernest said I should have got a lot more money for the little brat. He reckons I should be in clover if I play me cards right. He has a good head on his shoulders, does Ernest."

"Obviously a match made in heaven!" Georgina clenched her fists. She had never wanted to punch a person before in her life. But she was tempted. "You have sold the baby once. I'm afraid that transaction stands. You have signed papers to that effect." She couldn't really throw this hussy out in the streets but dear Lord she was tempted.

"I want Agatha." Helen opened her mouth and yelled, *"Agatha!"*

Georgina did slap her face. She did not slap her hard, but she would not allow this girl to wake the sleeping household.

"Agatha," she said to the astonished young woman, "has left this house as you very well know. You made it a point to sneak out while Agatha looked for you to say goodbye."

"I did not," Helen argued. "I went to meet my young man. He is emigrating to Canada. He missed his train and we had to wait for a

224

later one. I have spent the day with my one true love." It wasn't sorrow that sheened her eyes but fury at being treated in this manner. Who did these old biddies think they were?

"That load of rubbish might well work on Agatha," Georgina was not hard-hearted but this young woman had pushed her to her limit, "but you have shown your true colours today. I want nothing more to do with you. However," she held up a hand, "I could not sleep if I threw you out in the streets at this late hour – much as I am tempted. You may spend what is left of the night in a servant's room in the attic. Tomorrow, I will have you and your effects taken to the train station. You will be returned to your mother in Limerick. I wash my hands of you."

"You can't do this!" Helen screamed. "I am not returning to be at my mother's beck and call! I'll tell that aul' duchess what you are really like. She will never let you keep any young women here – what will you do for money then, you aul' cow?"

"That is quite enough of that." Lily had heard all she wanted to. "I'll take her upstairs."

"Indeed, you will not," Flora entered the kitchen. "I was coming down for a drink of hot milk when I heard the shouting." She removed Georgina's hand from Helen's arm, replacing it with her own. She leaned in close, sniffing. "Have you been imbibing strong spirits?"

"Ernest had bottles of his daddy's home brew." Helen belched loudly, sending a stinking cloud into Flora's face. "We both needed something to help us deal with the pain of our parting."

The older women shuddered, each contemplating what might have occurred if the young woman had fallen into the wrong hands in her inebriated state.

"I'll take her upstairs and make sure she doesn't wake anyone. There are those of us in this house who rise early to work." Flora grimaced at the foul odour wafted in her direction. She practically pulled Helen out of the room.

The three older women remained for a moment simply staring at each other. They were shocked by what they had just seen and heard.

"Hard liquor." Cook shook her head.

"It has been the ruination of many young women." Lily nodded.

"It certainly explains her behaviour this evening," Georgina said. "She cannot remain in this house. I cannot be responsible for her actions."

"I don't think that young woman will return to Limerick." Cook shook her head sadly. "I've never seen the like. Does she not realise the position she is in?"

"There are lodging houses in Dublin that take in young women." Lily sighed.

"We will solve nothing here." Cook began to clear the table. "I'm away to my bed. I cannot believe we have all been worrying ourselves sick about that young madam. She is big enough and bold enough by what we saw here tonight to look after herself."

Georgina opened the kitchen door. Because of the acoustics of the house sound carried down the long staircase. She stood listening for a moment, expecting at any moment to hear shouting and banging. When all remained silent, she closed the door turning back to her old retainers.

"Flora seems to have the matter well in hand. Lily, I had a great deal I wanted to discuss with you but frankly, I am more than ready for my bed."

"I'm tired too, Miss Georgina." Lily felt every one of her years. "Let us see what tomorrow brings."

"Do you think I should boil up some milk for Flora?" Cook hesitated to leave.

"No, Cook," Georgina said. "Thank you. You go away to your bed. The morning comes soon enough."

The three women wished each other a goodnight and, with heavy hearts, each made her way to her lonely beds.

Chapter 30

"*I don't want to go!*" Helen screamed, her arms wrapped tightly around the handrail of the entry steps. Her few belongings had been packed and were sitting on the pavement. "I have told you. I can pay my way. Please don't make me leave. I don't know what to do."

"I am sorry, Helen," Georgina's heart was in her throat. She wanted to scream herself at the young girl's distress. She had thought to handle this matter herself. She couldn't expect Lily to dismiss this young woman who was neither servant nor guest in her home. What was she supposed to do in such circumstances? "I don't run a boarding house. I will have someone escort you to Kingsbridge Station and put you on the train to Limerick."

"*I am not going back there!*" Helen screamed wildly, her face red, sweat running in rivulets down her clammy face.

"Come along, miss." One of Billy Flint's Smiths or Joneses was trying to gently remove the girl's arms from their death-grip on the handrail.

"Helen," Georgina sat down on the granite step beside the girl, "you don't know what you want to do. You don't know where you want to go. I cannot be responsible for you taking off on your own and wandering the streets of Dublin. Do you have any idea of the upset you caused yesterday? What is it you want, surely you have some idea?" She had tried talking to Helen this morning, offering options, all to no avail. What in the world was she meant to do with the girl? She did not know how to help her.

"*Nooooo!*" Helen screamed, kicking her heels off the steps like a bold child when her arms were being removed from the handrail. "*Noooo!*"

"What in the world is going on here?" a strong voice demanded.

While all attention was being paid to Helen, two carriages had pulled up in front of the Percy Place house. A statuesque woman had stepped out of the lead carriage and now stood on the pavement, staring at the tableau on the steps.

"That young woman sounds as if she is being tortured." The woman was wearing an all-brown travelling costume, a large fedora hat shading her face and a swagger stick under her arm. "You there!" She pointed the short stick at the man trying to release Helen's grip. "Step away from that female. *This minute.* Someone, explain to me what is going on here."

"I beg your pardon," Georgina stood up and slowly walked down the steps. "I don't believe we have met."

"Petunia Wallace-Montford!" the woman barked. "You are expecting me."

"Georgina Corrigan-Whitmore, how do you do?" Georgina tried not to let the groan rising up her throat escape. What a first impression to make!

"Please, help me!" Helen was suddenly on her knees in front of Petunia Wallace-Montford, her arms raised in supplication. "They are trying to make me leave. I have nowhere to go. Please help me!"

"Oh Lord!" Petunia Wallace-Montford looked down at the pretty blonde and sighed. She had thought she'd left this kind of emotional drama behind. "You there," Petunia again pointed her swagger stick at the man standing on the steps, "take her back inside, get her a cup of coffee – though I suppose it is tea here – very well, take her inside and have someone make a pot of tea." She stared down at Helen. "Stand up, girl, there is no need to remain on your knees. Stand up this minute and accompany this man." She didn't wait for her order to be obeyed but reached down and pulled the reluctant Helen to her feet.

"Excuse me!" Georgina needed to stand up for herself or this woman would walk all over her.

"Petunia," a short blonde woman with a sweetly smiling face stepped from the carriage, "you cannot issue orders like a sergeant major here," The woman flashed deep dimples when she smiled. "We have discussed this." She turned to Georgina. "I am Susan Templeton. I believe you have been expecting us?"

"Yes, indeed." Georgina tried to smile. "One moment, please." She turned to the man standing waiting on the steps. "Smith," she addressed him – he was either Smith or Jones. "Take Helen around the house, please, and hand her over to Flora, then if you could summon some men to help with the luggage, I would appreciate it." She waited while the man took Helen gently by the arm and led her towards the rear of the house.

"What a marvellous first impression we have made!" Georgina grimaced. How could she possibly explain this morning's carry-on?

"We can discuss all of this, inside," Susan Templeton said. "Petunia, we need to pay the carriage drivers and allow them to return to their work."

"Yes, of course." Petunia turned. "Where is Thelma?"

"I am right here, Aunt!" a young voice called from inside the carriage. "Staying well out of the way of your swagger stick." A slim blonde stepped from the carriage. She had her aunt's height, but her figure was softly rounded.

"Nonsense!" Petunia barked. "You there!" she pointed her stick at the second man on the first carriage. "Give the other chap a hand getting our luggage out of his carriage. *Snap, snap*, come along. We do not have all day." She walked over to the driver of the first carriage. "Now then, what is the charge. Do I pay you for both carriages or pay each driver?"

While this transaction was being carried out, men began to appear from the side of the house. They needed no instructions but began to take the luggage from the well-packed second carriage and carry it up the steps and into the house.

"Where do you want this, missus?" One man, a chest balanced on one shoulder, stopped to ask.

"If you could carry everything up to the third floor, please." Georgina didn't want all this luggage blocking her hallway. She also did not want to ask her few staff to carry the items up the stairs. "Shout for Bridget when you go in. She'll show you where to put the luggage." She couldn't expect Mrs Chambers to hurry up all those stairs.

"Will do, missus," the man said. "Come on, lads, we have work to do." The men trailed after him, each with items of luggage either on a shoulder or under each arm.

"Do you have an army at your disposal?" Thelma Wallace-Montford watched as men seemed to appear and disappear.

"It sometimes feels as if I do." Georgina didn't try to explain but waited until the carriage had been checked and cleared of belongings, the drivers paid and the carriages moved off. "Please, follow me,"

231

she invited the three ladies. "Welcome to my home."

"I will understand perfectly if you should prefer to seek lodgings elsewhere," Georgina said.

The four women were sitting in Georgina's formal dining room. They'd had time to refresh themselves after their journey. They had been shown to their rooms and invited to join Georgina when they were ready. Tea, tiny sandwiches, and scones had been served by Bridget and Sarah. Over tea Georgina had explained her strange household and the reason for the upsetting scene they had witnessed this morning.

"Your mistake, if you don't mind me telling you, was giving the young miss multiple choices." Petunia sat back in her chair. Without her hat and concealing overcoat, she was a strikingly attractive woman. Her blonde hair and blue eyes lent beauty to her strong-featured face. "I have seen it many times through the years. A young girl told what to do, where to go, what to think, practically when to breathe and then we suddenly expect them to make life choices. Some rise to the occasion but many fall into despair and must be coaxed."

"Something that drives Petunia wild." Susan laughed and gazed at her companion with affection.

"Aunt Petunia has vast experience in dealing with young women." Thelma said softly.

"It infuriates me how the young of a certain class are treated," Petunia said. "Not only females but males – we raise them up to jump at our every command and then expect them to gaily sally forth and conquer the world. *Rubbish!*" She slapped the table.

"We cannot change the world, Aunt Petunia." Thelma had heard this speech many times.

"If you have some suggestions for how to handle the problem that is Helen Butcher, I would appreciate them." Georgina was upset after yesterday's drama and this morning's unpleasant scene.

"The BOBs are asking a great deal of you, Georgina, if you don't mind me saying so," said Petunia. I have heard a great deal about you from Arabella, Lady Sutton. We correspond regularly. I was with Arabella in Paris when we encountered the young American women who told us all about the wonders of working for Mr Harvey. The BOBs ran with the idea and arranged for you to train young women to travel to America and become Harvey Girls. A marvellous idea in my opinion but ... and it is a big but ... the BOBs have had many problems in the past with placing young gently bred females. It seems to me that you have handled everything asked of you with great aplomb. You have placed everyone who has come through your door with excellent results, according to what Arabella has written to me. Helen was never and should never have been your problem."

"Thank you." Georgina truly was grateful for the kind words.

"You said she was a maid?" Petunia didn't wait for an answer. "You are short of staff. Put her in the attic with the other servants and set her to work."

"Petunia ..." They had already agreed to be on a first name basis. They were to share a house after all. "I cannot employ someone who must be taken by the hand and guided through her day. I have not the time, the staff nor the patience for such," Georgina said.

"Is there no question of her young man offering for her?" Thelma understood the problem.

"That young man has set sail for Canada to make his fortune." Georgina shook her head. "Helen is the last woman I could see being a helpmate to a man on the rise."

"Then we must find her a husband," Susan said.

233

"This too has been suggested," Georgina said. "But how am I to go about such a thing?"

"You appear to have an army of men at your disposal," Thelma said.

"Those men come to my aid, thanks to the good will of Billy Flint – a young man leasing my carriage house from me – they are his army if anyone's." Georgina wasn't going to try to explain Billy Flint to these women. If they decided to stay in this house, they would meet him.

"Speak to this Billy Flint," Petunia said. "Explain the situation. This Helen was a maid – was she not? She will not expect to marry a man of means. But you tell me she has a dowry to bring to the marriage which already gives her a step up from the average maid. Approach this Billy Flint and ask if he has a man under his command who would wish to take on a helpless but trainable wife who comes with funds. You may be surprised."

Susan suddenly started to laugh. She looked at the surprised stares she was receiving and only laughed harder. "I am sorry," she said when she had regained her composure. "It just suddenly struck me as hilarious. We worried so much about staying in some gentle widow's home. We thought we would be strangled by rules and regulations. Bored to our back teeth, having to be always on our best behaviour. Georgina, you have given me hope." She started to laugh again.

"Well, certainly nothing is as I had been expecting if not exactly fearing," Petunia said. "I should have placed more trust in the Lady Arabella. She always was a bright spark."

"Georgina, we," Thelma waved at her aunt and her companion, "none of us like to be idle. I have been foisted onto my aunt …"

Petunia sat forward to glare.

"Yes, I have, Aunt, and we both know it. The BOBs have agreed to cover my costs, thanks to your stellar work on their behalf. I have been educated – again thanks in great part to you, Aunt – to a very high degree. If I can help you in any way while we are under your roof, do not hesitate to ask. I will not offer as I have no idea of your wants and needs. But I am at your disposal."

"Thank you, Thelma." Georgina stood up. "Let me take you down to the nerve centre of my home – the kitchen – and I will introduce you to the household."

"That would be delightful," said Petunia. "We can but put one foot in front of the other and hope for the best."

Chapter 31

"Richard, I feel reborn." Georgina, a glass of wine in hand, looked around the dining room of the Shelbourne Hotel which was packed with after-theatre diners. "Thank you so much for inviting me to join you this evening. I have always enjoyed Purcell's music."

They had enjoyed an evening of music at the Tivoli Theatre before dining at the hotel. It had been many years since she had enjoyed such a social outing and she was feeling quite giddy.

"A client offered me the tickets. I had not intended to avail myself of them." Richard smiled. "Then I remembered how much you have always admired Henry Purcell's compositions. I was delighted that you felt you could join me."

"Petunia and company have only been under my roof for ten nights but already I am desperately seeking ways to convince them to stay. They have imbued new life into my house. It was at their insistence that I accepted your invitation."

Petunia and company had settled into her home as if they belonged. They had Helen Butcher serving as an upstairs maid. The young woman showed no sign of resenting the orders barked out at her by Petunia. She in fact seemed happier being told what to do at all times. Lily Chambers had felt able to leave the house in Petunia's capable hands while she visited Lady Rebecca and the modiste Emmanuelle and took care of matters there.

"I had noticed this evening that you appear to have slightly less weight on your shoulders." Richard said. "It has done my heart good to see you out and about. You have been too long enclosed behind the walls of your house."

"Oh, let us not discuss my problems." Georgina wanted to escape her responsibilities this evening. "Let us enjoy our meal and speak of old friends."

"If you prefer." Richard was willing to go along with her wishes. The smile on her face gave him such pleasure.

They sat over their meal, waiters discreetly jumping to see to their needs, while they talked of days past. It was a light-hearted conversation between two people who had known each other for many years.

As the evening progressed into night Georgina relaxed in Richard's charming company. She hated to see the evening end, but it was getting late.

She leaned over the table and in a quiet voice said, "Richard, will you come home with me?"

"Georgina, it is late. We must think of your reputation." Richard almost swallowed his own tongue. Surely she was not suggesting something improper? "I will of course escort you to your door as a gentleman should. But it is late, my dear. I will not come inside."

"As a widow, am I not allowed a little leeway?"

"My dear ..."

"Richard," she covered his hand on the table-top, "I wish to speak with you without what sometimes feels like one hundred interruptions."

"Your household?"

"Will be abed. Please, Richard." She threw her napkin on the table.

"Very well." What else could he do but agree?

"Would you care for something to drink?"

They were behind closed doors in Georgina's sitting room. Richard had lit every gas lamp, much to Georgina's amusement. She wondered if he worried for his virtue.

"No, thank you." He had not removed his topcoat, his top hat sat on a table close to his hand, his white silk scarf bright against the dark of his clothing.

"I have told you that my great-aunt, the Reverend Mother has died?"

"Yes." That was not what he had been expecting to hear.

"She left me a package," Georgina gestured to the package that remained wrapped in brown paper and string sitting on the floor. "She wrote to me, saying it is a family heirloom – I believe it is a chest from my mother's side of the family. I am delighted to receive it." She turned to look at him. "If the antique iron chest concealed by that brown paper is empty, I have no worries. It is what it might conceal that concerns me. I have not been brave enough to open the package." She shrugged. "I fear what it might contain and did not want to be alone when I opened it. Do you mind?"

"Georgie, I am, as always, at your service."

"Thank you." She opened a drawer in her desk and removed a scissors. She went on her knees beside the package and with a deep breath cut the first of the twine.

Richard walked over to stand at her shoulder, his curiosity aroused.

"This iron chest has been in my maternal family since the sixteen hundreds," Georgina said as she struggled to remove the wrapping.

"I have heard tales about it but have never actually seen it."

"Is it a puzzle chest?" Richard dropped to his knees to join her.

"No, it is a treasure chest." Georgina removed all the paper to reveal a banded iron chest. "It is solid iron and was used, I believe, to keep coins and jewellery safe while travelling." She smiled. "I pity the poor servants that had to move the thing – even empty it weighs a great deal."

Richard watched Georgina ignore the bristling locks and snaps. She searched the packaging and with a shout held up a big, long, narrow, heavy key with an oval opening at the top. He had never seen anything like it. The key had a large iron spike hanging from it by a strip of leather. He waited for her to put the key in the front lock.

"I hope I can open this." Georgina looked at the chest. Ignoring the locks, she began to push at the many iron bands that wrapped the chest. "Found it!" She pushed one band aside to reveal a keyhole. Placing the large key inside – it sank almost out of view – she put the iron spike through the opening in the top of the key and turned. The snap of a lock could be clearly heard.

"Fascinating!" Richard longed to examine the chest in detail.

"Let us pray that it is empty."

"Do you wish me to open it?"

"Please, the lid is rather heavy or so I was told by my mother."

"So it is." Richard grunted as he forced the heavy lid of the chest up and open. "It is not empty."

"I am almost afraid to look." Georgina nevertheless leaned forward to see what the chest contained.

"Let us remove the contents and put them on your desktop." Richard stood, brushing at the knees of his trousers in an automatic gesture. He brushed his hands one against the other before offering one hand to assist Georgina to her feet.

"I am so glad that you are with me." Georgina accepted the hand he held out. "Thank you."

"I believe we may well need that drink after all." Richard had recognised some of the contents. If they were not high-class jewellery boxes, he would eat his top hat.

"What am I to do?" Georgina gulped the brandy Richard had poured as she stood at her desk. She was so agitated she could not sit.

The contents of the chest lay open on the desktop.

"If I am not very much mistaken," she pointed to the glittering contents of the many boxes. "those are the Castlewellan emeralds. The diamond set is unknown to me."

Richard too had remained standing. He had removed his coat and scarf and thrown them over a chair. He was examining some documents.

He looked up at Georgina, eyes wide. "These are legal documents concerning ..." he shook the papers he held, "Bridget and her birth! She is the legal issue of the Earl and Countess of Castlewellan, as these prove!"

"I have always known that."

"Have you indeed?"he said, frowning.

"Oh, Richard, please do not behave in that odious fashion." Georgina hated to see his displeasure. "How could I tell you that Bridget was our friend Eugenie's daughter? No one was to know. Eugenie insisted upon it."

"Even when she turned up at this house as Jenny Castle – planning to become a Harvey Girl – she never revealed by even a motion that Bridget was her child. How could she do that?" Richard was in shock. The smiling little maid was a titled lady! It was like something from a melodrama.

They remained standing staring at each other for a moment.

"We must lock all of this away again." Richard began to snap closed the velvet-covered, satin-lined jewellery boxes that littered the desk. "Put them back in the chest for the moment. It is as safe as we can make it. Lock everything away until we can think what we should do." He would not feel comfortable storing any of these items in his office safe. Should they be seen or discovered – there would be questions he could not and would not answer.

"There is more," Georgina said.

"How could there possibly be more?" Richard was on his knees, repacking the iron chest – a treasure chest indeed. He paused, staring up at her.

"Castlewellan's eldest child, a daughter, Lady Rebecca Henderson, is in Dublin under the BOBs protection. And she is the living image of Bridget."

"My dear, you are giving me a headache." Richard continued to pile documents into the chest on top of the velvet boxes.

"What am I to do?" Georgina practically wailed.

"We will sleep on it." Richard jumped to his feet. "That is all I am capable of suggesting at the moment." He picked up his coat. "Frankly, my dear, I am almost dizzy from the problems that chest has presented to you. I don't know what to advise. I am at a loss. We must both sleep on it and meet again to discuss the matter. Things must change but how to accomplish those changes – well, my dear, I am ashamed to say – I have not a clue."

Chapter 32

"Enter!" Georgina responded to the rap on her drawing-room door.

"May I come in?" Dorothy Lawlor put her head in the door opening. "If you wish to be alone, I will not be offended."

"I would welcome the company." Georgina smiled. "I feel it has been some time since we had the chance to hold a private conversation."

"Such a strange day, Sunday," Dorothy stepped into the room, closing the door behind her. "I never know quite what to do with myself after church."

"The house feels empty, does it not? With the servants on their afternoon off, without their chatter the house seems to echo around me – leaving me to my thoughts. The weather does not help. December, such a dark, dismal month."

"Sometimes being on one's own is a blessing." Dorothy took the armchair across the hearth from Georgina, staring for a moment into the roaring fire. "There are times, however, when one wishes to escape one's own thoughts."

"The factory?" Georgina knew that Dorothy was having difficulties being accepted into what was perceived to be a man's world.

"I've become accustomed to fighting for every inch of control I must wrest from the old men who have sat so comfortably in their offices for years." She shrugged. "It is what it is – I cannot change the world. No, it is my sons." She sighed deeply, staring across the hearthrug at Georgina. "I am beset by guilt because I have not yet found us a home in Dublin."

"I understood your sons would continue their education in Dublin while spending time at the family estate in Kildare." Georgina wasn't terribly surprised by this news. She had never thought that Dorothy's twin sons would be content to be separated from their sole parent.

"I was so angry with the world when I sought the assistance of the BOBs in seeking Dublin lodgings." Dorothy said. "It is so dreadfully unfair that my late husband could leave our home to his degenerate brother! It was my funds that kept that estate running, my skills that made a somewhat success of the stud farm – but none of that was even considered. My husband died and I was left to become the poor relation to my brother-in-law. It is a woman's lot I do know but it is so dreadfully – *wrong*!"

"Could you not have sought legal advice?" Georgina shook her head and answered her own question. "What am I saying? Of course you could not. The learned gentlemen of the courts would have crucified you for your daring."

"When matters were left as they were, I did consider fighting my husband's last will but after careful consideration decided I would merely be giving my limited funds to some legal gent – all to no avail. We women will never win in the law courts – not as things stand. There must and will be change but perhaps not in our lifetime."

"One gets a frightful headache from banging one's head against the wall," Georgina said. "And this is a delightful conversation for a Sunday afternoon."

243

"It is certainly not why I sought your company." Dorothy shrugged. The world was as it was.

"Why did you?"

Before Dorothy could answer Georgina, a knock sounded on the drawing-room door.

"I appear to be popular this afternoon," Georgina remarked before shouting permission to enter.

"May we come in?" Petunia opened the door wide. Susan stood behind her, smiling.

"Please do," Georgina gestured to a settee placed close to the fire. "Take a seat and join us. We are solving the problems of the world."

"Ah, a gentle ladylike Sunday afternoon conversation," Petunia said as she sat.

"We are at a loss as to what to do with ourselves," Susan said.

"The downstairs is deserted," Petunia added. "The young are out and about. They will be wet and cold when they return, I daresay, but such is youth. Lily and Cook are in their rooms having a well-deserved nap."

"I was just about to tell Georgina why I had sought her out," Dorothy said. "If you would care to listen?"

"If it is private," Petunia prepared to stand, "we can leave you."

"I would not have invited you to join the conversation if such was the case," Dorothy said. "I am seeking advice and mayhap you both can offer some insight into what I should do."

"We are all agog." Petunia settled back into the comfortable cushions at her back.

"I came to this house a furiously angry woman. I had been disinherited by my late husband. I had the factory my father willed to me, but I had never managed it personally. I was determined to wrest some control of my life back into my own hands." She looked at the other women. "In doing so, I feel I have deserted my twin sons whom I care for greatly. My taking rooms in this house has left my sons at the mercy of their uncle – a man I detest."

"This man – the uncle – he is abusing his position?" Petunia asked.

"He is a drunken degenerate!" Dorothy snapped. "I should never have listened to my sons. They assured me they could manage their uncle and protect their inheritance."

"Do you wish to return to your husband's estate?" Georgina asked.

"*I most certainly do not.*" Dorothy glared. "I refuse to step backwards."

"Laudable," Petunia said. "What then do you want to do?"

"I wish to provide a home for my sons. A safe haven. But how can I?"

"Is it a question of finance?" Susan asked softly, not wishing to give offence.

"Not entirely," Dorothy said. "I had a notion that my husband planned something that would punish me for what he saw as my forward thinking – my unnatural ways as a woman – if you will."

The others nodded in understanding. They too had been considered unnatural women.

"While my husband lingered in his final illness, I removed items of value from the estate. I sold those items under an assumed name and placed the money I made into the hands of my father's man of business under my own name. I do not and did not consider what I did theft. My dowry and the money earned yearly from my father's business kept my husband out of debtors' prison. In living in this house, I have managed to save a great part of the salary I pay myself. My needs are not great. I have been excessively well looked after and at times entertained in this house."

"What then is the problem?" Georgina asked.

"I can afford to purchase a house," Dorothy said. "But to make it into a home for two growing men I need staff. It will take time and planning I simply do not have!"

Petunia and Susan exchanged a meaningful glance.

"Not to take away from your problems but perhaps what Susan and I have been discussing may help – it will certainly not hinder." Petunia squirmed slightly on her seat.

"Please, I will take any assistance I may." Dorothy had been running around in circles in her own head.

"As you may both be aware Susan and I found ourselves suddenly without our positions and without a roof over our heads. It is quite a shock to the system, let me tell you," Petunia said. "We came to this house, thankful for what we thought of as a rest stop. Time to plan the next move in our lives."

"Something has changed?" Georgina prompted when Petunia stared at her hands.

"Observing Lily and Cook during our brief time here has been like looking at our own futures." She looked up. "And, honestly, it is terrifying."

"Why so?" Georgina asked.

"We, Sally and I are decades younger than Lily and Cook, thankfully, " Petunia said. "Susan and I thought to seek positions with a retired or elderly gentlewoman. We were quite certain we would find employment – then we arrived here." She looked at Georgina. "What do we do when we are too old to work? It is not usual to house your servants when they are past their working lives, and everyone here knows that. You are quite unusual in your care of your staff, Georgina."

"Yes," Dorothy nodded. "It is shameful how people who have served one all of one's life are discarded – most end in the workhouse."

"We," Petunia looked at Susan, "have discussed requesting funding from the BOBs to establish an employment agency."

"I am unaware of such agencies," Georgina said.

"I too have never heard of – what did you call it – an employment agency?" Dorothy said.

"They are very popular in the larger cities." Susan thought she should make herself heard. "They even take advertising space in *The Lady* magazine."

"I have a friend," Petunia said. "A mature lady who has started one such agency in London. She informs me that she is earning a rich salary and is seeking others to work for her."

"That does not interest you?" Georgina asked.

"Again," Petunia said, "we would be employed by someone else. In fact, our employer would reap the rewards of our labours. Frankly, after speaking with Lily and Cook about the fate of servants known to them, we are alarmed. Neither of us wish to finish our days penniless if not homeless. I daresay Thelma – if she marries – or my brother would supply us with a roof over our heads. But," she slapped a hand on the arm of the settee, "we would end our days in a position I have fought against all of my life – that of the poor relation."

"So – we are considering setting up a business – an employment agency," Susan said.

"How would you earn an income?" Dorothy was fascinated.

"It is my understanding," Petunia said slowly, "that one takes a percentage of the yearly salary of each servant placed. One also charges the person seeking employment."

"You make money from both quarters!" Dorothy clapped her hands. "Delightful!"

"We have the disadvantage of being female," Georgina softly said. "We are not trained from birth to make or indeed earn money. If it would not offend your principles, Petunia, I would suggest consulting my man of business, Richard. He is a fervent supporter of the BOBs and may have some pertinent advice to offer. I am not at all sure but would the business you establish not belong to the BOBs if they put up the funds?"

"We have no other way of raising the funds," Susan said. "It is not as if we have items of value to sell or a rich inheritance."

"Perhaps you could interest investors?" Dorothy said. "I would be interested in investing in such a company."

"You would need premises in a good area," Georgina said.

"Is it an impossible dream?" Petunia felt beaten before she had even started. She had no funds to back her. She had only her own skills to offer.

"I do not believe so," Dorothy said. "But you should profit from your time in this house. It will give you the chance to investigate in depth what you might require."

"Why did you believe that Dorothy's situation might be something you could assist with?" Georgina asked before they could all fall into the doldrums.

"I had not thought of offering a complete package, so to speak." Petunia said. "But Dorothy is seeking a house, servants, a home. Susan and I could assist with that." She was feeling quite excited by the idea. "What of people making their home in Ireland for the first time? Surely a complete home set-up would be an attractive package to offer? Those who could afford it would pay – and pay well – would they not?"

"It is certainly worth thinking about," Georgina said. "Not to mention people such as myself who desperately need staff."

"It could be a richly viable concern if approached properly," Dorothy said. "I would certainly pay for someone to remove certain worries from my shoulders. I believe you have a good idea, but you must learn to present it as a business plan. I too believe you should approach Richard. You need a business brain until you have been trained to think in a certain way that is not what you have now. I hope you will not think I am disparaging you both. You will need help."

"We had no thoughts of becoming businesswomen when we came to this house," Susan said. "We had thought simply to continue as we were. Meeting with Lily and Cook, well," she gestured between herself and Petunia, "a cook and a housekeeper, you can see how that might affect us. We were able to look into our own future and did not like what we saw."

"Richard offered the women who came to us courses in handling their own finances," said Georgina, "which was beneficial to all. There may well be books you could study. You are neither of you stupid. You can learn. But approach this cautiously, so that you may succeed from the beginning."

"You will need to learn to deal with gentlemen who do not have your best interests at heart," Dorothy said. "I know of what I speak. Seek assistance and learn. Do nothing until you feel confident you can carry out your plans. We ..." she waved between herself and Georgina, "will give you every assistance."

"You have both given us a great deal to think on," Petunia said.

"I believe we have reached a conclusion," Susan said. "I have created some French fancies in Cook's kitchen. Would anyone care to try them?"

Chapter 33

"What are you going to do, Georgie?" Richard carefully stepped over a horse deposit of manure. It would not remain on the path thankfully. Some of the barefoot children scavenging along the barge towpaths for dropped pieces of coal or wood would soon clear it away to take home for burning.

"Concerning …?" Georgina, warmly wrapped up for the weather, her arm through her escort's, was watching her step on the bare earth of the towpath that ran along the side of the Grand Canal. She had invited Richard to accompany her on an afternoon stroll. It was a brisk cold day but the fresh air and winter light, what little there was of it, was a welcome relief from the enclosed space of her home.

"Richard, I am awaiting the arrival of my Fairy Godmother with a magic wand …"

"Georgie …"

"Richard, I invited you to join me so I could escape my home and the people who constantly appear to have a need of my counsel and advice." Georgina's voice was a sibilant whisper. There were people about on the towpath and sound carried – who knew who might overhear her words. "I have a king's ransom in jewels kicked under the desk in my office. The Babington-Hawthorns requested the use of my home for a consultation with Granny Grunt and Molly Mulvey. They are even now having that meeting in one of my drawing rooms." She took a deep breath. "I have Flora and Billy Flint studying in order to take over the running of houses of ill repute. I have nuns looking at me as if I am some sort of degenerate and to top all of that I have the legitimate daughter of an earl – a titled lady by birth – making the beds and dusting the furniture in my home. My housekeeper is at this very moment helping another daughter of that same earl hide in plain sight! An older girl. I close my eyes at night and the problems of the day haunt me until I am unable to sleep." She kicked a stone from her path into the flowing water of the canal, missing a foraging duck by inches, receiving an indignant quack and an irritated flutter of tail feathers for her action. "So, to answer your question, dear Richard, I have not a notion of what I am going to do."

"I regret asking." Richard tried not to laugh. But really Georgina with only her eyes peeping over the navy-blue woollen scarf wrapped around her neck between her very fetching bonnet and coat collar was a delight to his eyes. He had more sense than to mention that fact. He had the feeling she would kick him into the canal after that stone if he so dared.

"I am sorry, Richard. I should not take out my ill humour on you." Georgina hugged his arm to her in an unconscious gesture of affection.

"Are two daughters of the Earl of Castlewellan truly in Dublin?" Richard leaned in to ask.

"They are indeed." The pair stepped off the path to allow a horse to pass. They waved at the barge folk, remaining silent until the barge was out of earshot. "The BOBs have concealed the eldest with a lovely lady in her home near the docks. They had planned for me to take her, but she is the spit and image of Bridget. The Earl, for all his faults, bred true – they are both fashioned in his image with not a sign of the females who bore them in their features."

"That does cause problems." Richard stepped back onto the path to continue their stroll.

"Indeed."

"Bridget must be told," Richard said. "The child deserves to know her beginnings before she discovers matters for herself. She is very curious and keenly intelligent as we both know."

"How does one begin to explain the drama and indeed the horror that surrounds Bridget's birth? The decisions made by the adults involved at that time? I fear I do not have the skill or the words to explain something of that nature in a manner that will not damage Bridget's bright spirit."

"But we are agreed that she must be told?" He pressed her arm to his side. "Are we not?"

"I am unsure of the method that could be used to pass along such information." And if she were being honest, she resented the need for her to be the one to tell the child. She'd had nothing to do with hiding the poor girl away! "There is another matter I have not discussed with you, Richard, purely because I was bound to secrecy. The Reverend Mother left a doll with me. A doll fashioned by Eugenie. I was given instructions to keep the doll safe until Bridget reached her eighteenth year. I was also informed that there are papers hidden inside the doll's soft body. Perhaps it is time to reveal what has been concealed."

"Such high drama." Richard shook his head.

"To protect an innocent."

Georgina reached for the door leading into her basement with great reluctance. She looked over her shoulder at Richard who had refused to join her — claiming a need to return to his own work. With a gracious nod of her head in his direction, she opened the door and stepped into the hallway.

"There you are!" Flora hurried down the long hallway to join her. "I have been watching for you." She began to help Georgina remove her outer clothing. "The Dowager Duchess has sent you a message. Her servant is waiting in the kitchen for your reply." She leaned in as she removed Georgina's bonnet and whispered, "I refused to allow anyone to search you out." Then in a normal voice she said, "When you have attended to that matter, the Babington-Hawthorns request your company."

Georgina resisted, barely, rolling her eyes.

"I will take your outer garments upstairs while you attend to the Dowager Duchess's messenger." Flora began to open the many large buttons that ran down the length of Georgina's tweed overcoat.

"We need a mirror placed in this hallway." Georgina allowed her coat to be removed. "If I am to be accosted as soon as I step inside it would be convenient to be able to check my appearance."

"I will make a note of it." Flora, the coat over her arm, said.

"Of course you will." Georgina walked towards the kitchen. What now?

"Here she is now," Cook announced.

The male servant jumped to his feet as soon as Georgina entered the kitchen. He had been enjoying a cup of tea and a scone while he waited.

"Madam." The servant offered a courtly bow and, after removing a missive from his inside pocket, offered it to the lady who had just entered the kitchen. He had been informed this was an unusual household – but really – the gentry in the kitchen – what was the world coming to? He barely supressed a sniff of displeasure. Such would not be allowed in the house he served. "My employer, the Dowager Duchess of Westbrooke, has asked that you read this as soon as may be." He passed the sealed envelope over. "I am to await your reply."

Georgina knew better than to thank the servant. She had seen his attitude towards her clearly. "Flora, if you will accompany me upstairs you may carry my reply when it is ready." She walked swiftly from the kitchen with Flora hurrying at her heels.

"I'll take care of these." Flora raised the arm holding the overcoat. The bonnet and scarf hung from the hand of the opposite arm.

"Thank you." Georgina stepped into her office leaving the door open at her back. Before opening the envelope, she hurried over to the fire to warm herself. It had been chilly walking by the canal.

"Did you see that servant's face?" Flora laughed as she stepped into the room, closing the door behind her. "I do not think he approved of your strange household."

"His attitude is the least of my worries." Georgina walked over to take a silver letter opener from the top of her desk. "I wonder what the Dowager Duchess wants now."

"You will have to open her note to find out." Flora took a seat by the fire without waiting for permission.

"That thought had crossed my mind," Georgina agreed wryly.

She opened the letter, reading the few lines swiftly then reading them again. She dropped into the chair across the hearth from Flora.

"She is asking to meet with me tomorrow morning on a matter that need not concern the BOBs."

"Well, at least you will not have her usual parade of titled ladies and their servants to contend with," Flora offered.

"Just the Dowager Duchess and her entourage. I would love to refuse – simply to enjoy her reaction. Do you think anyone has ever refused the Dowager Duchess?"

"It would take a braver soul than you or me to do something of that nature." Flora smiled.

"Yes." Georgina took a seat at her desk and muffled a laugh.

"What has amused you?"

"I am tempted to simply write, 'YES' at the bottom of her missive and return it to her servant."

"That would be in very bad taste." Flora laughed. "But tempting, I agree." She watched Georgina remove writing paper and an envelope from one of her desk drawers.

In no time at all the short acceptance letter had been written and sealed in its envelope.

"If you would give that to the servant, Flora," Georgina stood, "I would appreciate it. I will now tend to the Babington-Hawthorns."

"Should I have Cook send up a tray of tea?"

"Has no tea been served yet?" Surely Cook would have seen to the matter?

"I have no idea." Flora had been studying business papers in the staff dining room when curiosity had drawn her into the kitchen upon the arrival of the Dowager Duchess's servant.

"I will ring down when I know more."

Georgina walked across the hallway towards the second drawing room. She opened the door to a scene of domestic bliss. The Babington-Hawthorns had arrived at the Percy Place house that morning to discuss removing the baby. The couple were seated together on a leather settee. Granny Grunt, at the couple's request, had agreed to meet with them there to offer advice on bottle-feeding and matters pertaining to baby care. The older woman now took pride of place in a comfortable chair to one side of a blazing fire – well covered by a fireguard. Molly, for the first time wearing a very fetching grey-and-white uniform, stood in one of the fireplace alcoves her hands neatly folded at her waist. She had been asked to meet with the couple to discuss future travel arrangements. The baby waved plump limbs about and took centre stage on a sheepskin rug – a rug Georgina did not recognise. All of this Georgina took in at a glance.

"My dear Georgina," Ethan Babington-Hawthorn jumped to his feet at her entrance, "thank you so much for offering us the use of your drawing room. We both – Lavender and I," he looked down at his wife who smiled sweetly and nodded, "thought we should meet with Molly here where she is most comfortable. There is so much to discuss and plan. Without ever meaning to, we have quite taken over your drawing room, I am afraid." He smiled charmingly.

"We cannot express our thanks for all of your help during this difficult time, Georgina," Lavender said. "I am sure all here will miss Molly but I am delighted to tell you that she has agreed to leave this house for the time needed to assist me. I assure you we will take good care of her. I would be quite lost without her assistance."

Georgina smiled and gave a nod of acceptance of their words. "Has no tea been served?"

"Tea was offered." Lavender clapped her dimpled hands. "I was – for the very first time – feeding the baby his bottle – under Molly and Granny's eagle eyes. I had images of disaster occurring with hot tea flying all of its own accord around the room while I concentrated on the baby." She laughed gaily. "So, we declined the kind offer."

"A cup of tea would be much appreciated," Granny piped up. She was gasping for a cup and not about to refuse the chance to be served in comfort.

"I'll just take his lordship out of here," Molly said. "He has been fed and what goes in one end comes out the other." She gripped the sides of the white apron she wore over her grey uniform skirt and top and shook it. "I'll tell you something for nothing, Miss Georgina, whoever came up with the idea of a lacy white apron for looking after a baby needs their head examined."

Molly didn't notice the amused stares she was receiving from all in the room at her outrageous behaviour – she was a servant after all – even the baby appeared to laugh.

Molly bent to lift the baby off his rug. "Open that door for us, Miss Georgina." The baby was gurgling in delight at the sudden movement. "I'll tell Cook to send up a tea tray."

The others in the room waited until Georgina had closed the door before they began to laugh.

"She is delightful!" Lavender held a hand in front of her mouth while laughing aloud. "I am sure I will want to keep her with me forever. There would never be a dull moment if only Molly would agree to stay with us."

"She is certainly entertaining," Ethan said.

"Do sit down, Ethan." Georgina walked around the sheepskin rug and took the chair across the hearth from Granny. "I am afraid Molly has made her feelings on entering into service crystal clear. She has no desire to be a servant of any kind, I am afraid. It took all of my powers of persuasion to get her to agree to accompany you to England when you decide to travel."

"Since you have raised the subject, Georgina, you will no doubt be pleased to learn that the Babington-Hawthorns are about to remove themselves from Dublin," Ethan said as he took his seat. "That is one of the primary reasons we asked to meet with Molly and Granny today."

"Decisions have been made?" Georgina prompted when the couple just sat smiling at each other.

"We have been greatly blessed since we travelled to Dublin," Lavender said. "We have been staying with friends of my family in their home on Fitzwilliam Square since the turn in the weather dashed our pleasure in being 'barge folk'."

"Yes," Ethan said with a grin. "It drove us to return the barge to its owner and seek alternative accommodation."

Lavender laughed. "It is convenient to have friends living so close to this house," she said. "I have made it my business to speak at length with the family's nanny. The woman is truly a wonder – Nanny Grace she is called – the woman has been with the family for simply years and has so much knowledge she has been willing to share with me."

"My wife has quite pestered the poor woman and taken copious notes." Ethan smiled fondly.

"I tried to steal Nanny Grace away from the family, but she refused to budge," said Lavender. "She has been with the family for so long she is almost part of the furniture." Lavender had hoped to employ the experienced woman but had accepted her refusal to leave the family she obviously loved. "I have met so many wonderful women here that I would like to take back to my husband's estate," she sighed. "Sadly, I have been refused on all sides."

"Have plans then been made?" Georgina asked while pouring from the silver tea service Bridget had delivered to the drawing room.

Bridget, in her best uniform, stood ready to pass the tea poured by her mistress.

"We have been somewhat fortunate." Lavender accepted the delicate china cup of tea and saucer from Bridget's hand. "Nanny Grace has agreed to tend to our child in the nursery of our friends' home while we arrange the journey to England."

"That is good of her." Georgina passed Bridget the cup and saucer for Granny before preparing Ethan's tea after enquiring about his preferences.

"Yes, indeed," Lavender said. "I have asked Molly to meet with

Nanny Grace to discuss travelling with a baby. I have no knowledge of the subject."

"I too am sadly lacking in such knowledge." Ethan wished for something stronger than tea but gladly accepted the cup and saucer from the maid's hand. "We are in dire need of servants who can handle the new responsibilities that have fallen upon our shoulders. It is astonishing to me how much planning and preparing goes into caring for such a young child."

"It would appear that we are all in dire need of capable servants," Georgina remarked.

"A senior maid serving in our friends' home informed us that she wishes to return to her home in England," Lavender said. "She has offered her services to us for the sea crossing in return for us paying her passage."

"Has she training in the care of a child?" Georgina enquired.

"None at all." Lavender sighed. "Molly will be in charge of the baby at all times but as we have seen," she smiled with genuine pleasure, "Molly is not at all what one expects from a servant – of any nature. The maidservant travelling with us will be able to guide her in how to travel aboard trains and ships – one hopes."

"Will Molly encounter much difficulty in your home, Lavender?" Georgina poured tea for herself.

"Not at all. I have written and warned my family of Molly and her – shall we call them – eccentricities?" Lavender sipped her tea.

"I have advised Molly to observe your home and servants most carefully," Georgina said. "The girl has dreams of travelling to America to become a Harvey Girl."

All present in the drawing room knew of the chance being offered to young women by Fred Harvey, the Englishman making a name for himself in America.

"That would be a difficult transition for someone of Molly's background and education, would it not?" Ethan had made a point of enquiring about Harvey and his enterprise after hearing about the work of the BOBs and their hopes for the future opportunities for the women they helped. "It is my understanding that this Harvey chap seeks young women of good education and from families of rather better than good homes." None of which Molly appeared to have to his eyes.

"Molly has a bright and enquiring mind," Georgina said. "We are training and educating her – despite all signs to the contrary – in how to behave in polite society. She excels in her studies." She ignored the muffled laughter. "However," she added her eyes shining with suppressed laughter, "she refuses to apply what she has learned to everyday life – to my despair."

Granny Grunt sipped her tea, content to sit back and let the gentry speak. She'd speak out if she had something to say and, after all, she was being well paid for her time. She had spent a great deal of time with Lavender, advising her on female health care. She had even supplied the young woman with instructions on making some of her special tisanes. The pair – while being charming – had also been a great source of income to Granny. She could afford to sit with her feet in the fire and listen.

"Molly has agreed to prepare the baby for his journey to our friends' home this afternoon." Ethan refused more tea. "It is my intention to try and persuade her to spend some time in the nursery there with Nanny Grace."

"We are aware and grateful for Molly's – shall we call it – hands-on experience?." Lavender too hoped that Molly could be persuaded to stay under Nanny Grace's eagle eye until they were ready to leave on their travels. "She has learned a great deal about dealing with babies at her mother's knee but there are matters that were perhaps not covered in such ..." she paused delicately wondering how to voice her concerns without insult, "close-lived quarters." Molly had made no secret of the fact that her large family lived in one room. A state of affairs that had shocked the Babington-Hawthorns.

Time passed as the Babington-Hawthorns filled Georgina in on their plans to remove the baby from her house that very day. She tried not to sigh with relief when she realised that matters for the family were moving along with speed.

Bridget stood ready to serve tea or pass biscuits while taking in every word of what was being said. She envied Molly the chance to travel to England.

"Bridget, you may return to the kitchen," Georgina said. "Please offer Molly any help she may need in preparing the baby. I am sure all of those below stairs will be sad to see him leave but we wish him well on his journey into his new life, do we not?" She knew Bridget spent a great deal of time caring for the baby while Helen, the woman who gave birth to him, ignored him at all times.

"Yes, miss." Bridget bent her knee and took her leave.

"Georgina," Ethan said as the couple stood in the open door of the Percy Place house, ready to leave. "It is rather indelicate. I feel we owe you a debt of honour, but you have also dispensed a great deal of coin on my son's needs and care. I would like to reimburse you."

"That is most gracious of you, Ethan – but entirely unnecessary. You could, however, if you are so inclined, make a donation to the BOBs." Georgina had, in fact, been charging the BOBs for the needs of young Master Babington-Hawthorn.

Two carriages waited in the street below the house, horses stomping their hooves impatiently. Molly was sitting in the second of the carriages, a broad beam on her face, silently hoping someone she knew would see her up in her own carriage sitting like a bloomin' duchess! The baby in her arms had been fed, washed, and changed, so with any luck the little man would sleep while she enjoyed her first carriage ride. He had better not throw up on the first coat she had ever owned, or she'd be livid. It might be grey and part of this silly uniform – but it was hers.

"I cannot thank you enough for everything you have done for us." Lavender was inclined to tears. This was such a momentous moment for her. She would finally have the baby she had always wanted – after so much heartbreak and loss, the resprehensible actions of her husband's father had given her the gift of a child – a son. She was both terrified at the responsibility and giddy with joy. "We will write, of course, but we shall not see you in person for some time, I think."

Georgina would not be a hypocrite and say it had been a joy to assist her, but she could send her on her way with a smile and best wishes. "Lavender, take care of your little family and do keep in touch. I will be happy to hear from you."

"Come along, my dear." Ethan took Lavender's elbow and, with a nod of his head towards Georgina, walked down the steps towards the waiting carriage.

Georgina waited until the carriages moved off before closing the door. She returned to the warm drawing room.

"They're off then."

"Granny!" Georgina put a hand to her chest. "I had quite forgotten you were here. You've been awfully quiet."

"Hadn't got anything to say." Granny smiled. "Besides, I'm enjoying meself sitting in your comfortable chair, burning your coal and being served tea I didn't have to make meself."

"There is that, I suppose." Georgina laughed softly.

"That's another lot off your hands." Granny wondered if there was any chance of more tea. She'd make her way down to the kitchen soon, but she was comfortable where she was. "What are you going to do about the mother of that baby?" Granny shifted in her chair, suppressing a groan. Growing old was painful. "Not that she has a mothering bone in her body where that poor baby was concerned. Still, I suppose that was for the best too."

"When I think of the life the orphans in my own home have lived, I can't help but be delighted for the future that little boy will enjoy." Georgina didn't sit down. She had matters to attend to and today seemed to be running away from her. She began to return the soiled dishes to the trolley.

"Still, it might not be ideal," said Granny, "but the nuns do give them young ones a roof over their heads and food in their bellies. They train them up to go out in the world too. They are not running the streets barearsed and shoeless like so many I know."

"You should have seen the place!" Molly had a captive audience. She'd had Liam put a match to the fire in her bedroom. Far from it they were raised but she could grow to love the luxury of it.

Bridget, Ruth, and Sarah sat on one of the two beds in the room, hanging onto her every word.

"Honest to God, I thought this place was huge but it's only half the size of the Fitzwilliam Square house – and servants – coming out of your ears they were!" Molly was packing a bag to take to the home of the Babington-Hawthorns' friends. She could learn a lot from that Nanny Grace.

"They have a separate servants' staircase in that house – can you believe it?"

"That's usual in the better class of house," Sarah said. "I hear the seamstresses complaining about carrying linens up and down those stairs." Sarah studied with a skilled seamstress twice a week.

"I won't be using those stairs." Ruth was being trained by a cook in the home of one of the families who were friends to the BOBs. "I'll be staying in the kitchen."

"You will be using them stairs to go to your bed and come down in the morning." Molly felt very important. Imagine her swanning around the place – packing a travel bag – if you please! "I nearly swallowed me heart at the thought of carrying that baby up those stairs. Talk about steep!" She looked over at her audience. "But I went up the main staircase if you wouldn't be minding. I followed Mrs Babington-Hawthorn up those stairs like one of the gentry. I wished me ma and da could see me."

"I'll tell them all about it, our Molly." Liam was sitting on the bedroom floor with his back to the bed the three young girls sat on.

"Here, Bridget," Molly suddenly said. "You like babies, don't yeh? You could maybe be a nanny or nursery maid. That might be something Miss Georgina would have you trained up in. That nursery was a sight for sore eyes, I can tell yeh for nothing."

"The nuns at the orphanage said Bridget was only fit for cleaning," Ruth said. "They would have given her training in a skill if they thought she was bright enough to learn."

"Don't you be giving Bridget ideas above her station." Sarah pursed her lips as she'd seen the seamstress training her do. "She has enough ridiculous ideas of her own, heaven knows."

"Well, aren't you two the little sourpusses!" Molly put her hands on her hips to stare down at the girls. "Bridget can do a lot better with her life than scrubbing floors and washing windows and so I would have told those old nuns if they had ever asked me. Shame on you two for not wanting the best for your friend!"

264

Liam buried his face in his knees, delighted his sister was giving those two what for. They were getting too big for their boots in his opinion.

"Maybe I could be a nursery maid until I am old enough to become a Harvey Girl." Bridget worried about her future.

"You should talk to Miss Georgina about it." Molly returned to her packing. Not that she had very much to take but just the act of preparing a bag to take with her was thrilling. "I tell you – that nursery – you have never seen anything like it. Toys as far as the eye could see." She giggled. "Nanny Grace let me have a ride on this big wooden rocking horse." She closed her eyes in remembered delight. "The bed for the baby was like something out of a fairy tale and the nursemaid had her own bedroom. I tell you, it was another world."

"I can't wait until I am old enough to work in one of the big houses," Sarah said.

"It will be nice to earn wages," Ruth agreed. It didn't seem fair that she worked so hard and the nuns received her wages.

"There you all are!" Flora pushed open the bedroom door. "Is no one going to their beds tonight?"

"We were hearing all about Molly's adventures." Bridget smiled brightly at her friend.

"That is all very well but you all have to be up and about bright and early in the morning. Time for bed."

There were grumbles but all obeyed the softly voiced order.

Chapter 34

"I am quite determined to visit the Americas."

The Dowager Duchess, with her personal assistant and constant companion Letitia McAuliffe, were sitting in Georgina's drawing room, enjoying hot chocolate. The women had arrived at the appointed hour and to this point had indulged in polite chitchat. Now that the servants had withdrawn, it appeared Constance was ready to discuss her reason for this visit.

"Constance has long been an admirer of Buffalo Bill Cody." Letitia shook her head fondly at her longtime employer and friend. "She devours those penny-dreadful novels concerning the American west and now this …"

"I met Buffalo Bill Cody when he put on a cowboy show before our own Queen Victoria," Constance, the Dowager Duchess, was almost swooning at the memory.

"The man put on the show for the Queen's Golden Jubilee." Letitia thought she should make a mention of that fact.

"It took my breath away." Constance put a hand to her breast. "All of those half-naked young virile savages running around screaming and brandishing their tomahawks. Why, I scarce knew where to look! It was the most wondrous experience. I so wanted to be one of the people in the stagecoach being attacked by the savages." She sighed deeply at the remembrance of the stagecoach being pulled by six horses racing around the open-air arena. The gunshots and powder exploding as Buffalo Bill on his mount charged in pursuit of the screaming savages to rescue the passengers of the coach. She had almost been unable to breathe with the excitement.

"Unfortunately, a duchess is outranked by a future king." Letitia's eyes sparkled.

"Yes, unfortunately. The evening I attended the show the stagecoach was occupied by three kings of Europe and our own Prince of Wales." Constance had been quite put out to lose the chance. "I had hoped when Victoria agreed to attend the show and even to take part in the stagecoach hold-up that my chance would come. Again, I was to lose out to others."

Georgina wasn't quite sure how to react to this anecdote. What had this to do with today's visit? She held her tongue, listening politely as a good hostess should.

"You are wondering no doubt what this has to do with my visit," Constance said.

Georgina stared a moment, shocked – was the blasted woman a mind-reader?

"Are we quite assured of our privacy?" Constance looked towards the door. She knew her own servants waited at doors to attend to her needs. It could be a nuisance when one wanted to speak confidentially.

"I am afraid that my household is such that no servants can be assigned to remain in the hallway awaiting instruction." Georgina understood her concerns. "Your own servants are no doubt in the kitchen enjoying a cup of tea."

267

"Letitia, have a quick peek," Constance ordered.

Letitia obeyed instantly, walking over to the door and even stepping out into the hallway. "We are alone," she said, returning to her seat.

"Very well." Constance leaned forward. "I hope you will agree with me when I say that young Bridget must be told of her beginnings."

"I –" Georgina began to speak.

"No, please, hear me out." Constance held up a hand. "Clive Henderson, the late Earl of Castlewellan is no more. That is a fact. The two young females he sired have been left more than comfortably situated financially, which is to his credit we must all agree." She sighed deeply, moving the bodice of her deep-purple gown. "However, young women of fortune, while much admired and envied are also in danger if they do not have a solid male wall of protection at their backs."

"Bridget, while being legitimate, is not nor has she ever been known to that family," Georgina stated.

"My dear Georgina, you have seen Rebecca, have you not?" Constance had lost much sleep worrying about this matter. "There is no denying the deep family connection between Rebecca and Bridget, that is a fact. Dublin is a small close-knit community with many travelling its streets and carrying information – how long do you think we can keep Bridget hidden away? The new earl will be actively looking for Rebecca and the missing Countess of Castlewellan – mark my words. He will have already put men on the hunt." She pushed out of her chair with difficulty – really the clothing women were forced to wear in order to appear fashionable! It hindered one's movements!

Letitia and Georgina exchanged glances. It was polite to rise when someone of a higher social rank stood. Letitia waved to Georgina to keep her seat. They were in her home, after all – supposedly enjoying a friendly visit – not a society gathering.

Constance stared out of the drawing-room window over the steps leading to the front door down to the public street and out to the canal. She paid close attention to the people passing by and those meandering along the two towpaths. Really – how was one supposed to keep an innocent safe when just anybody could stroll past one's home? She shuddered at the very thought. Her own Dublin residence had a high railing around it, keeping the undesirables away. The butler and strong footmen protected the inhabitants of her home.

"Georgina," Constance returned to stand beside her chair, "you are well known as a particular friend to the missing countess – as is dear Richard Wilson. You grew up together and remained friends. This is known, Georgina." She looked at the chair with displeasure. Really, she was old enough to become a rebel and throw away these dreaded stays which pinched and pulled at one painfully. She almost laughed at her own vanity, knowing well she would never relinquish something which gave her an enviable figure for a woman of her years.

"I was questioned closely when Eugenie first disappeared all of those years ago." Georgina watched Letitia rise to assist her friend and employer into her seat. "I made it perfectly clear at that time that I knew nothing of merit."

"Georgina," Constance stared at the younger woman, "this new Earl of Castlewellan cannot afford to allow Rebecca and the missing countess to apply for the funds that have been left to them by the late earl."

"I am sorry, but I am unaware of the details of the late earl's last will and testament," Georgina said.

"I had not expected you to be," Constance said. "Allow me to inform you that it has sent shock waves throughout polite society."

"I am sorry to hear that," Georgina said, simply because Constance appeared to be waiting for her to comment.

"Because of my friendship with the sister of this new earl and that lady being an ardent supporter of the BOBs – Lady Caroline

Wormsley, who was of course aunt to the late earl ..."

"Constance you are wittering!" Letitia snapped.

"Yes, well," Constance glared at her companion, "Lady Caroline has kept me up to date with everything that is occurring in and around the Castlewellan estate." She waved a hand. "But that is neither here nor there – one of the reasons I have called to see you today – well, simply put, Caroline sent a young man to me with all the latest news." She leaned back in her chair, wondering how to explain all that she knew.

"Do get on with it, Constance." Letitia had matters to attend to.

"While I enjoy, as everyone appears to know, reading the penny dreadfuls, it is not at all amusing to feel as if one is living in one of those stories." Constance sighed deeply. "To make what is a long and involved story as brief as possible, Caroline sent the young man to warn me of the danger both Rebecca and the missing countess – our friend Jenny Castle – are in from this new earl."

"*Danger!*" Georgina gasped.

"This new earl is a man of the cloth and piously pompous beyond belief – and he is all but penniless. The estate – if managed properly – will provide him with a healthy income but he has five sons and three daughters to settle into their new place in society. That cannot be done without a great deal of ready funds." Constance so disliked speaking about money but it must be done.

"The late earl never appeared to be short of funds." Georgina was confused.

"The late earl amassed a vast private fortune which he was free to bequeath as he pleased," Constance said. "The Castlewellan estate is entailed to the nearest male relative, but the late earl's private funds are not."

"Constance, you will be the death of me!" Letitia snapped. "You are going around in circles. What Constance is trying to say, Georgina, is that Lady Caroline Wormsley has informed us that Rebecca and the missing countess are in line to inherit all of the late earl's great wealth."

"Very great wealth," Constance added.

"Indeed." Letitia glared. "A sum of money has been set aside to fund a search for the missing countess. A vast sum has been set aside for the child that the late earl knew his countess conceived. The fear that the child may be male is keeping the new earl frothing at the mouth, to hear Lady Caroline's man tell it. After all, should the missing Countess have given birth to a male, that would disinherit the good vicar, would it not? The man would be forced out of his new accommodations at the very least."

"And what a man Lady Caroline has sent to inform me of all this," Constance sighed. "Tall, handsome as an angel, with broad shoulders and slim hips ..."

"Constance, control yourself!" Letitia snapped.

Georgina could only stare open-mouthed.

"Oh, do not be so hidebound!" said Constance. "If old men of eighty can drool over young girls of eighteen, why should I not indulge? I do not touch," she sighed again deeply, "I simply look and imagine."

"I should have left you at home." Letitia shook her head. One could not remain angry at Constance. "Allow me to tell you what has been tentatively, planned, Georgina. A man by the name of Thomas Cook set up a travel company which arranges tours for people wishing to travel in safety within a group. I have consulted this company in Constance's name, seeking information about the many requirements for such a venture." Letitia was speaking rapidly, not wishing Constance to interrupt. "I am awaiting their return post. What the Dowager Duchess suggests is that young Bridget be informed of her background. She should be introduced to her older sibling. In the new year they should both accompany Constance on her tour of America."

271

Letitia was almost breathless as she finished.

"Dear Lord!" Georgina said.

"It is ideal," Constance put in. "While we are travelling and enjoying the Wild West of America, we can have my man of business and Richard Wilson arrange the paperwork and establish a way that these young women can safely claim their inheritance."

"It all sounds so simple when you say it like that." Georgina knew it would be a nightmare. It was all very well for the Dowager Duchess to speak of the adventure of all of this, but the practicalities would fall on others' shoulders. She feared it might well be hers. How could she keep two young women safe?

"I cannot be involved at this time." Constance gave a put-upon sigh. "I have social obligations. I must be seen at the Christmas ball at Dublin Castle and then of course there is my own ball. I cannot disappoint my friends by not giving my much-anticipated ball. One must uphold one's place in society. And really, one would not wish to travel in winter – the very idea makes me shudder."

"Sit down, Lily."

Georgina was dining in solitary splendour in her dining room. She could not face the chatter of the servants' dining room, not while her mind was still spinning with all that Constance had told her.

"You look like you've been passed through the wringer, Miss Georgina." Lily had eaten with the servants.

"I feel like it." Georgina pushed her plate away from her.

"Cook isn't going to be happy seeing her good food returned." Lily pushed the plate back towards her mistress.

"I am not hungry." Georgina pushed the plate away again, leaned her elbows on the table and dropped her aching head into her hands. "How is Lady Rebecca?" she asked without lifting her head.

"That young woman is chomping at the bit to escape the restraints we have put on her." Lily waited a moment to see if Georgina would say more. "Bridget has been making enquiries about becoming a nursery maid. It would appear young Molly told her it may be something she would be good at."

The silence in the room grew as both women waited.

"That is all I need," Georgina finally said without raising her head. "The legitimate daughter of the late Earl of Castlewellan wiping babies' bottoms for a wage."

"*The child is legitimate?*" Lily had suspected there was a mystery around Bridget – but she had never imagined this!

"She is Eugenie's daughter."

"Eugenie!" Lily gasped. "The Jenny Castle who passed through this house on her way to America to become a Harvey Girl?" It beggared belief.

"That very woman." Georgina dug her fingers into her head, trying to force out the ache.

When she raised her head and opened her eyes, she saw that Lily was gazing at her in consternation.

"So, Lily, you now understand the immense problem we are facing."

"Indeed I do. And added to that, I am worried about Bridget – she is becoming deeply unhappy here. She has lost all her friends. Flora is caught up in whatever you have her and Billy Flint doing. Molly has moved out to stay with the Babington-Hawthorns. Ruth and Sarah are behaving like spoiled little madams. They consider themselves superior to Bridget now that they are being trained up for a well-placed position in what they imagine will be a great house. The girl deserves to know who she is and where she came from."

"So everyone keeps insisting." Georgina agreed. She just wished she did not have to be the one to tell her.

Chapter 35

"Richard," Georgina smiled at a group of passing officers, waiting until they had passed before continuing, "would you think me a perfectly unnatural female if I informed you that I do not enjoy these social occasions at all?"

Georgina and Richard were strolling around the perimeter of the Dublin castle ballroom. The annual castle Christmas ball was one of the social events of the season, Dublin Castle being the centre of power for the British Government and its forces in Ireland. Despite attending the ball last year and providing delicious gossip to the attendees, she had been surprised to receive an invitation.

The ballroom was ablaze with candlelight which, together with additional light from gas lamps, sent prisms of fire shooting from the jewels gleaming around the naked shoulders of the ladies in their jewel-toned ball gowns. The decorations on the red-coated uniforms of the attending officers shone, the gold braiding standing out brightly against the red jackets.

"That is because you do not enter into the spirit of the thing, Georgina." Richard bowed to a woman he knew slightly. "You need to sit around with the elderly harpies tearing apart reputations and dissecting what is being worn by all here. Then there is the younger crowd – gossip, my dear, fuels the interest of that bunch – and I am informed that this is the perfect venue to arrange assignations with officers who may enjoy a little dalliance while away from home."

"Why, Richard, I am surprised. You are a virtual mine of information." Georgina had been the subject of gossip among this set. The amorous advances – made to her at last year's ball – by smiling officers thinking to assuage her grief – she shuddered to think of it. She was being careful to cling to Richard this year. The gossips and interfering old biddies could make of it what they would. They did not control her life.

"I do what I can." Richard took her elbow while stepping aside to allow a party of ladies and smiling officers to pass. "Am I allowed to mention how splendid you look this evening?" He wondered who had dressed her. His Georgie was not normally a fashion plate.

"Petunia Wallace-Mountford insisted on overseeing my toilette for this event." Georgina unknowingly supplied the answer to his thoughts.

"Was it she who insisted on the tiara?" He admired the diamond and amethyst tiara worked into Georgie's very flattering hairstyle.

"That woman!" Georgina smiled thinking of Petunia and her barked orders and demands – which one could not object to as her obvious knowledge and caring heart were apparent in everything she did. "I refused to wear deep mourning. I will not be a hypocrite. Petunia declared that a dark purple – an acceptable colour for mourning – would be acceptable." She ran her gloved hands down the skirts of her silk ball gown. The bracelets, necklace and earrings of diamonds and amethyst complemented the relatively simple style of the beautiful gown. She had felt almost regal when she'd examined her image in the mirror before leaving home.

"You do realise that you will now have to improve on this evening's attire when you attend the Dowager Duchess's annual ball." Richard fought his smile.

"Oh, do stop, Richard!" Georgina used the back of her hand to gently swipe at his arm. "You know I dislike all this fuss and botheration. Thankfully, Petunia enjoys all aspects and delights in seeing to my suitable attire – she declared herself quite enchanted with making arrangements and then staying home with her feet up and a good cheroot and brandy to hand."

"I would prefer that myself, truth be told." Richard put a finger between his neck and highly starched white collar. "But one does what one must – shall we dance?"

"It would appear your household is not yet in bed." Richard opened the carriage door and stepped out. A bright light gleamed from behind the glass half-moon at the top of the door leading into the Percy Place house.

"Oh, Lord!" Georgina's feet ached from dancing. Her jaw ached from bestowing false smiles on the many officers who sought to attract the attention of the latest widow on the social scene. Her ribs ached from the tight lacing of her whalebone corsets. She had hoped to creep into her house and to her bed. "I hope none of the young servants are up and about. Their day starts so early." She accepted Richard's hand to step out of the carriage. "Do you know, Richard?" she held onto his hand. "I feel quite like Cinderella – this evening I was bedecked in silk and jewels being danced around a ballroom and now," she sighed, "I worry about my lack of servants."

"Does that make me your prince?"

"You have always been my prince, Richard." Georgina blushed at her daring. She removed her hand from his and ran up the steps to her front door before he could react.

Richard stepped back into the carriage when the door opened and then closed behind his Georgie. "Her prince, by gad!" he whispered to the empty carriage. "Am I indeed? Well, who would have guessed the evening would end on such a wonderful note?" He settled back into the leather seats to dream of the future.

"Petunia, you did not need to wait up for me!" Georgina said.

"You will need help getting out of that gown," Petunia, in a tweed dressing gown and leather slippers, said. "If I had not offered to wait for you, Lily was bound and determined to sit in the hallway for hours."

"Then I thank you." Georgina smiled tiredly. "Lily needs her rest." She turned for the stairs.

"Was the evening a success?" Petunia asked.

"I daresay it was." Georgina was almost dragging her aching body up the stairs. "One could hardly move for the press of bodies and, from the almost continual hum of voices that could be heard under the music, the gossiping matrons were having a wonderful time."

"They will all no doubt be served breakfast in bed by their staff around noon." Petunia followed Georgina into her room. "Will you be doing the same?"

"I do not think I have ever slept till noon in my life." Georgina held out her arms.

"I suggest you make tomorrow or indeed today the first time." Petunia opened the clasps of the bracelets that covered Georgina's long evening gloves.

"My house would come to a standstill." Georgina turned her back to drop the bracelets on her nightstand.

Petunia opened the clasp of the necklace.

With Petunia's help, Georgina was soon undressed. She promised herself a long morning bath, imagining she could still smell the many perfumes and strong colognes worn by her fellow guests at the ball. She was simply too tired tonight so, without bothering to wash, fell into her bed while Petunia stood with the covers pulled back for her.

"Are you intending to greet the morning before it's over?"

Lily's voice broke into Georgina's dreams. The sound of curtains being drawn back and the bright spark of winter sunshine caused her to drag the bedclothes over her head and groan.

"If you don't get out of that bed and be about your business, you will never sleep tonight," Lily continued without sympathy. Why, the day was half over! "I've been out and about since early morning and could not believe my ears when I returned for the noon meal and was informed that you were still abed."

"Lily," Georgina did not remove the bedclothes from her face, "before I dismiss you for your gross impertinence – please tell me you brought a pot of tea to accompany your abuse of my poor person."

"You won't know until you get your head out of that burrow you've made and open your eyes." Lily stood over her mistress hands on her hips.

"What time is it?" Georgina pushed back her bedclothes.

"You have a few minutes before the clock strikes noon."

"Indeed!" Georgina could not believe she had slept so late. She had been so sure she would be up and about at her usual hour. "Did you bring tea?" She opened one eye slowly and quickly opened the other when no pain attacked her. She felt sluggish. She never slept the day away.

"I did."

"Thank you – pour me a cup while I visit the toilet, please." Georgina struggled from the bed.

"Cook wants to know if you will be joining us for lunch!" Lily said to her retreating back.

Georgina merely groaned at the thought of a heavy meal on her delicate stomach. How did the gentry live like this? Out all night and sleeping all day. She couldn't do it. She slammed the toilet door behind her with relief.

While Georgina was being awakened, a stranger strolled around the side of the house and into the mews garden.

"Can I be of assistance, miss?" one of the men who lodged with Billy Flint stopped to ask. He'd never seen this young woman before. He knew this house was a safe place for a certain class of woman. This one was dressed in what appeared at first glance to be rough clothing – looks were deceiving. The quality of her tweed skirt and long jacket was better than that worn by the working classes. She might have a fringed dark tweed shawl pulled over her head instead of a hat, but she was no pauper. The leather gloves and shoes she wore would have been tempting to a certain type of rough customer. She was lucky she hadn't been robbed or worse walking the streets on her own.

"Does Miss Lily Chambers reside here?" the stranger enquired.

"She does, miss."

"I have a need to speak with her."

"If you would follow me."

"Thank you."

Rebecca was quite delighted with herself. She had managed to navigate the streets of Dublin with no problems. She had found her way to Percy Place. Really, what was all the fuss and botheration about? She was perfectly safe.

Liam caught a glimpse of their visitor from a kitchen window. "Cook, it looks like we have another lost lamb." He had become accustomed to strange ladies seeking their way to this house. It added a bit of excitement to his day. He ran to open the door before the stranger knocked.

"Just you hold on a minute there, young Liam Mulvey!" Cook shouted, hurrying after him. "Who made you master of this house?"

But Liam had pulled the door open.

"I am looking for Mrs Lily Chambers." Rebecca smiled brightly.

"Come in." Cook really had no other option but to invite the stranger in. "Thank you, Smith," she said to the man standing to one side of the young woman. "I will let you know if we have need of your services." Really, it was a comfort to have Billy and his band of ever-changing Smiths and Joneses at the bottom of the garden. You never knew when you might have need of a strong man about the place.

"Very good, missus." Smith or Jones pulled at his forelock before walking away whistling.

Rebecca stepped through the door thrilled with the success of her little adventure.

"You were wanting to see Lily, you said?" Cook asked over her shoulder as she headed back to her cooking.

"Yes, please." Rebecca followed the woman and boy into a large bright kitchen. Dropping the shawl from around her shoulders and head, she handed it to the young boy who was gaping as he offered to take it from her. She began to remove her gloves, vaguely aware of a young kitchen maid standing staring.

"Sit yourself down." Cook didn't know what to do. What was the world coming to with the mistress in bed till all hours of the morning, Lily disappearing hither and yon, never explaining herself? Now this young woman boldly walking the streets of Dublin on her own! She'd be fit for bedlam if this continued.

"Liam, run and fetch Lily, quick as you please." She returned to what she had been doing. The meal was going to be ruined if it was not served up soon.

"Ruth!" she snapped at the young kitchen helper who was standing stiff as a statue staring open-mouthed at the young woman who had not bothered to introduce herself. Had the BOBs sent her here? "*Ruth!*" she called again when the young maid made no move. "Whatever is the matter with you, child? The good food I've prepared is going to be ruined – *ruined!*"

"*Cook!*" Ruth croaked while pointing rudely at the visitor. "*Look!*"

"In the name of all that's good and holy, what is going on this day?" Cook wanted to collapse but she had duties to perform. "Have you lost the run of your senses, Ruth Brown?"

"*Cook!*" Ruth was still pointing. "*It's Biddy all grown up!*" Her eyelashes fluttered and the strength went from her knees. She collapsed onto the kitchen floor in a cloud of dark material.

"What is going on here?" Lily entered the kitchen on Liam's heels just in time to see Ruth fall to the floor. "Liam, give me a hand here!" She quickly crossed the floor, paying no attention to the others in the kitchen. "Whatever has happened, Cook?" She stood over the maid, fearing her knees would not allow her to rise again if she got down on the floor.

Cook couldn't respond as she stared at the newcomer, a hand to her mouth.

"Get up off the floor, Ruth," Liam grunted as he tried to lift Ruth up on his own. "You'll catch your death of cold."

Ruth's eyelashes fluttered. She hadn't really fainted – not all the way. She had just been shocked into collapsing, she reassured herself. When she caught sight of the stranger staring across the kitchen at her out of familiar green eyes, she tugged frantically on the hem of Lily's skirt.

"*It's the work of the devil!*" Ruth groaned dramatically. "*Look, Mrs Chambers! It's Biddy all grown up! We need a priest!*" She crossed herself frantically to keep evil away. "*Biddy must have sold her soul to the devil!*"

"Cook, can I help carry anything into the dining room?" Bridget walked into the kitchen and halted, staring at her friend on the floor.

"*Now there's two of them!*" Ruth's hand was a blur as she crossed herself repeatedly.

"*Who are you?*" Lady Rebecca Henderson stared at the maid who had just entered the kitchen. She had been enjoying the melodrama while not understanding anything that was going on. Now she stared at her mirror image, dumbfounded.

Chapter 36

Lily tugged her skirt free of the kitchen maid's hand. She stared at the young woman who had all unknowingly brought chaos to this house. She longed to close her eyes on the scene before her.

"Well now, young madam, you have certainly put the cat amongst the pigeons," she said.

The people in the kitchen stood almost frozen in place. No one knew quite what was happening or what to do.

"Ruth …" Sarah stepped into the kitchen and cried out in shock when she caught sight of her friend lying on the floor. She had just stepped outside to leave a load of soiled linen in the outdoor washroom, after a morning spent changing all the beds in the house with Helen. She paid no attention to the stranger in their midst, too concerned for her friend.

"Sarah, Bridget, help Ruth up off the floor, for goodness' sake." Lily looked around her, wondering how she could make this situation disappear. With a sigh she realised the cat was well and truly out of the bag. "Liam, run and get Miss Georgina. Sarah, take Ruth to the bathroom and help her tidy up. Cook, start putting the food on the table. I daresay the youngsters are hungry. Look at the time – it won't be long before the rest of this household wanders in to be fed."

Bridget, without taking her eyes off the stranger with her face, side-stepped over to hold out a hand to help her friend off the floor.

"Biddy, do you think it's your mother?" Ruth whispered while grabbing onto the offered hand but making no effort to rise.

"Who ...what?" Sarah asked.

"There!" Ruth still on the floor, afraid her knees wouldn't hold her up, jerked her head in the direction of the stranger.

"Merciful God!" Sarah gasped. "Where did she come from?"

"Is that Biddy's mam?" Ruth hissed.

"No, she is much too young, I think." Sarah stared, hardly able to believe what her own eyes were telling her. "But, Biddy, she must be a relation of yours, don't you think? You couldn't look so much alike without being related, could you?"

"How should I know?" Bridget was afraid to even imagine that she might have found a relative.

The three young orphans stared and whispered, each afraid to even say what each was thinking. That one of them might have discovered that most cherished of dreams – a relation.

"Girls!" Lily Chambers clapped her hands. "Cook needs help serving the meal. Do get up off the floor, Ruth! Sarah, do as I have instructed and help Ruth tidy up. Bridget ..." What on earth could she do with Bridget? And where was Helen? Really, that girl! She did the work set out for her, but she had a nasty habit of not being available when needed.

"Mrs Chambers ..." Lady Rebecca began.

"I'll deal with you presently." Lily held up a hand as she watched as the two young maids reluctantly leave the kitchen.

"Lily Chambers!" Cook opened her mouth to berate her long-time friend.

The raised hand silenced her also.

"What possessed you to come here, Lady Rebecca?" Lily demanded.

"You left your purse on the hall table when you left Jane's house this morning." Rebecca removed the item from one of the deep pockets in her skirt. She had her own money safely pinned to a pocket in her bloomers. "I did not want you to think it had been lost on your walk home."

"So, you decided to return it, did you – out of the goodness of your heart?" Lily was aware of Cook and Bridget hanging on their every word. She had received a note in the post from Jane requesting her advice. She had decided to answer Jane Morgan's note in person that very morning. Lady Rebecca's wardrobe was being created at speed in the modiste's workshop. The girl was already in possession of several garments suitable for daywear. Items of intimate apparel however needed to be purchased from local stores of which Jane, in her note, freely admitted her ignorance. "Does Jane Morgan know what you are about?"

"Jane was down the garden when I left." Rebecca dropped her eyes. Was what she had done so wrong? She could not remain hidden away. "I did not think to disturb her. I did leave a note on the kitchen table."

"What in the world is going on now?" Georgina's voice could be heard before she stepped into the kitchen. "Liam informs me that we have an emergency. Has the house caught fire?" She was wearing her night attire, having no intention of dressing before she had her promised bath.

"We have a visitor," Lily said simply, gesturing towards Rebecca as she spoke.

"Lady Rebecca!" Georgina shook her head. "You are all I need today! Does Mrs Morgan know where you are?"

When Rebecca didn't answer quickly enough, Lily said, "She

informs me she left a note on the kitchen table before escaping the house."

"Liam –"

Before Georgina could give instructions Cook banged a large pot on the kitchen table.

"Is no one in this house to eat today?" she demanded just as the two maids returned. "Before I know where I am, I'll have Flora, Petunia, Thelma, and Susan under me feet demanding to know why the food is not on the table!"

"Ruth, Sarah," Georgina glanced at the kitchen clock, "assist Cook in getting the meal on the table. Bridget, Rebecca, sit over there in the alcove out of the way. Liam, run across the garden and fetch a Smith or Jones for me. I need someone to carry a message down to the docks."

Liam ran from the kitchen.

"Miss Georgina –"

"Not now, Rebecca. I must deal with one thing at a time. Mrs Chambers, if you would kindly write a note to be carried down to Jane's house. Jane must be informed that her charge has arrived here safely and will be escorted back to her later in the day. Have you eaten, Rebecca?"

"I had breakfast with Jane." Rebecca wanted to demand an explanation.

"Ruth, set an extra place in the staff dining room." Georgina clapped her hands to get everyone moving. "Come along, everyone, the day has been disrupted quite enough."

Bridget and Rebecca stared at each other, neither knowing quite what to say. Rebecca had wanted a little adventure. It would appear she received more than she had bargained for.

Rebecca finally allowed herself to be seated in the kitchen alcove.

She was aware of the activity around her, but her eyes were almost glued to the young girl taking a seat across the table from her. There was a painting of herself as a young girl hanging in her grandfather's house. This little maid could have sat for the artist. They were so alike it was uncanny.

"I am Lady Rebecca Henderson. Who are you?"

"I am Bridget O'Brien, the downstairs maid."

Rebecca almost gasped. A downstairs maid. How was this possible? The girl was surely a relative of hers. "Where are your family?"

"I am an orphan." Bridget knew nothing about herself and her origins. She didn't know what to tell this stranger. "I was sent to this house with my friends Ruth and Sarah — we are all three of us indentured here until our sixteenth birthday."

"Indentured — indeed?" Rebecca, in spite of herself, was amused by the girl's wordage. She knew that quite a few servants had their quarterly wages sent to their parents. She had never thought of them as being indentured. She had heard of some who borrowed money and agreed to work off the debt by being indentured servants — primarily those wishing to travel to the colonies and not possessing the means to pay for their travel. "You borrowed a vast sum of money, did you?" she asked, trying to bring a lighter tone to the conversation.

"No. What would you call it?" Bridget had learned the word through her studies with Flora. She believed firmly that all three of the orphans in this house were indentured to the orphanage. "We are required to work for four years while the monies we earn are sent to the orphanage to reimburse them for our raising. Is that not indenture?"

"I daresay it is." Rebecca was impressed by the clarity of Bridget's response.

"Ladies …"

287

Both young women jerked in surprise. They had not noticed Georgina standing outside the alcove.

"I have some of the answers you both no doubt seek." She put both hands on the table and leaned over to them. "However, I have left my bath water cooling and this," she gestured around the busy kitchen, "is neither the time nor the place to talk. I am returning to my no doubt tepid bath while you, Bridget, may escort Rebecca into the staff dining room. I strongly suggest you keep any thoughts you might have about this situation firmly behind your teeth until I am free to meet with you both."

"If you know something you need to tell us now," Rebecca insisted. "We are the innocents in whatever this is." She waved a hand between Bridget and herself.

"I agree. But now is not the time and this is not the place to speak of such matters." She turned from the alcove, furious at the position she found herself in. It was not her place to reveal family secrets. But if she didn't do it – who would? "I will meet with you both as soon as I have had my bath and gathered my composure."

"Miss Georgina, you need to eat something!" Cook called when her mistress looked like leaving the kitchen. "You need something to hold body and soul together."

"If you would be kind enough to keep something for me in the warming oven, Cook, I would appreciate it." She left the kitchen to have what would now be a quick bath and in some way try to prepare mentally for what she could say to help the two bewildered young women who had found themselves in a situation not of their own making.

"What have we missed?" Flora, with Petunia, Susan and Thelma at her heels, entered the kitchen from the garden. She'd met her companions in the street outside the house. They had all been out and about early this morning and were now returning to enjoy one of Cook's hearty meals.

"Just more of the drama to be found in this house," Lily waved to the kitchen alcove where Bridget and Rebecca were staring out at the sudden appearance of the four women.

"There is never a quiet moment in this house." Bridget was glad of the diversion. She had no idea what to say to the woman sitting across the table from her.

"*Well, bless my soul!*" Petunia exclaimed. "I thought you looked familiar, young Bridget!" It had been teasing her mind ever since she'd seen the young maid. Susan had advised her – in the strongest of terms – to leave the matter alone but it had teased at her mind in moments of reflection nonetheess.

"Aunt Petunia …" Thelma nudged her outspoken aunt with her elbow.

"*Petunia!*" Susan snapped, deeply afraid of what her sharp-tongued friend might say.

"Ladies, allow me to introduce you to Lady Rebecca Henderson," Lily said.

Bridget and Rebecca stood and stepped out of the alcove.

Lily introduced the others to Rebecca and there was much bowing of heads and mutterings of "Charmed" and "How do you do?".

Lily then hurried to her office to pen the note to be delivered to Jane Morgan. Whatever happened in this kitchen now was out of her hands.

"Rebecca Henderson! You would be the late earl's child," Petunia said and turned to Susan. "Do you remember, Susan? Some years back the late Earl of Castlewellan came to the academy in Paris – he was considering sending his daughter to us and wanted to examine the school personally." The man had set off all of Petunia's inner alarm bells. She had kept young Thelma well away from him. "Such masculine beauty was rarely seen inside the academy walls." She had never understood how he – a single gentleman – without a prearranged appointment – had gained entrance to their very private property. "He was rather difficult to forget." As was the way he had examined the young students who had giggled and blushed when passing him in the corridor. She'd been mortally afraid the man would make a nuisance of himself.

"Petunia, I despair of you." Susan remembered that man very well. They did not have many males of his calibre pass through their doors. Men who did visit the academy were primarily older gentlemen, fathers, and guardians to young women. She had thought the Earl a vision of masculine beauty on first sight. But he had sent shivers down her spine for some unknown reason.

Thelma had seen the man under discussion and thought him wonderfully handsome.

"Well," Petunia pointed to the matching pair staring with wide green eyes and open mouths, "if those two are not of the Earl's begetting my name is not Petunia Wallace-Montford!"

"This is all very interesting," Cook said with a snap in her voice, "but can I ask you all to wash up and come to the table before my meal is ruined completely?"

While the others hurried away, Flora stood for a moment staring at the girls before shaking her head and walking away.

"It would seem I am not the only one who thinks we are closely related," Rebecca whispered to Bridget.

"I am lost for words." Bridget didn't know what to say or indeed what to think. Was it the done thing to recognise someone like herself who was so obviously born on the wrong side of the blanket? The nuns had always maintained that the girls in their care were born of sin and sorrow. Was the proof of this standing before her?

"Do you believe Georgina can explain the resemblance between us." Rebecca waved vaguely in the air between herself and Bridget. "Can you truly be my sister as Petunia proclaimed?"

"The plot thickens," Bridget said dramatically. "Come! I will show you to the bathroom." It should be vacant as the three who had just entered would return their belongings to their rooms and make use of the upstairs bathroom, she hoped.

"The plot does indeed thicken," said Rebecca as she followed her.

"Flora will sometimes take me to the afternoon showing at the local theatre. I heard that expression used on stage. I have never had the opportunity to use it before," Bridget said over her shoulder as she led the way to the bathroom.

Chapter 37

Georgina, her hair coiled neatly at the back of her head, opened the front door of her home and simply stood staring outside but not really seeing. The navy skirt and high-neck pale-blue blouse she wore were not warm enough to allow her to stand outdoors for any length of time, but she dismissed the chill. She needed air. How was she to handle this latest situation?

She consulted her fob watch and calculated the time. The servants would have finished their meal and be restoring order to the basement rooms. She'd receive a tongue-lashing from Cook, but she really couldn't eat a heavy meal at this moment in time. Not with her stomach roiling with nerves. She took a deep breath of the cold air and stepped back into the house, closing the door at her back.

With her shoulders back and head high she went down the stairs to the basement.

"Is the kettle boiled, Cook?" Georgina stepped into the kitchen, asking a silly question. The kettle was always on the boil in this kitchen. She was pleased to see she had timed her entrance perfectly. The kitchen was a hive of activity as dishes were being removed from the servants' dining room. "I'd like a pot of tea and a slice of your bread and butter." She held up a hand and shook her head when Cook appeared ready to deliver a lecture. "Bridget, leave what you are doing and carry a tray to my drawing room when it is prepared. Mrs Chambers, Bridget will remain with me for some time. Please give whatever chores she is responsible for to another." She turned back towards the door leading upstairs. She could feel the eyes of all in the kitchen on her back.

"Should I come too?" Lady Rebecca asked.

"No. I will speak with you presently, Lady Rebecca," Georgina said without stopping. She went at speed up the stairs and across the hall into her private drawing room.

She put a match to the prepared fire in the hearth. Liam kept all the fireplaces cleaned of ash and set paper, sticks and small nuggets of coal in the empty grates first thing every morning. She gripped the mantel and stared at the flames licking at the tightly rolled newspaper until the dreaded knock sounded on her drawing-room door. She longed to climb out the window and run but instead shouted permission for entry.

Bridget opened the door, the tray held steady on one hand. "Cook asks that you allow the tea to brew a minute, Miss Georgina." She entered and put the tray on top of a small table.

"Take a seat, Bridget." Georgina waved towards one of the pair of chesterfield chairs framing the now brightly burning fire.

"Miss Georgina?" Bridget froze in shock. She now knew from the many lectures Helen delighted in giving to the three orphans that this was a strange household. She had been aware of course that matters were not as they should be in this house but one thing she was sure of — a maid did not sit in the presence of her mistress — not in her private drawing room!

"This is far from a normal day, Bridget." Georgina shook her head at the young girl and smiled. "We can safely throw all the rules out of the window. Give me just a moment to pour myself a cup of tea. I need it." She needed something a great deal stronger, but tea would have to suffice.

"You no doubt have many questions you long to ask." Georgina poured tea, waiting for the avalanche of questions to pour forth. Bridget always wanted to know why.

"I cannot think of where to start, Miss Georgina." Bridget had eaten a meal, aware of everyone staring from her to the stranger in their midst. The food had almost lodged in her throat. She didn't know whether to laugh or cry.

"Your mother, Bridget," Georgina added a little milk to her tea, "was a childhood friend of mine." Did that sound as if her friend was deceased? Oh, confound it, she couldn't second-guess every word out of her mouth. She had thought to remove the doll given into her keeping from her desk and give it to the child, but she had her orders. Bridget must be eighteen before coming into possession of that dratted doll. She could not ignore the wishes of her late aunt the Reverend Mother.

"You know who my mother is?" Bridget's green eyes almost popped out of her head, they were opened so wide. "You know where I came from?"

"Bridget, I knew nothing of you until the late Reverend Mother of the Goldenbridge orphanage demanded that I take you into my home …"

"Demanded?" Bridget gasped.

"The Reverend Mother was my much-loved great-aunt." Georgina smiled in remembrance of that redoubtable lady. "When that woman spoke, you jumped to obey."

There was silence for a moment. Georgina sipped her tea, trying to think of how best to phrase what needed to be said. She had thought about this moment while she'd bathed and dressed but, now that it was here, she was having difficulty finding the needed words.

Bridget sat and waited, afraid to open her mouth for fear of saying the wrong thing.

"Your mother, Bridget, was married to your father. You are no baseborn orphan." Georgina knew something of that nature would be important to the girl. "Your parents were married with great fanfare. I was one of the many guests at the affair. I lost contact with my friend soon after the wedding – something I believed to be perfectly acceptable – we lived far from each other after all, and I believed my friend to be occupied setting up her new home." She was struggling. "I had no idea your mother had fled her marriage. It was not until an investigator knocked on the door of this house that I discovered your mother had disappeared. I was shocked and worried, unable to supply any information."

"My mother ran away?" Bridget thought it sounded like the plot for one of the stage dramas Flora was so fond of. She clenched her hands into fists, surprised her hands were not visibly shaking – her body shivered and even with the fire she did not feel warm. The nuns had discouraged, rather forcefully, the orphans from asking questions. But she had to know. "Was my father truly the Earl of Castlewellan as Petunia said when she saw Lady Rebecca and me in the kitchen?"

"You are indeed the daughter of the late Earl of Castlewellan." Georgina felt sick to her stomach. She could not discuss the Earl and his unnatural behaviour with this innocent.

"I don't understand." Bridget's teeth were chattering – her bones felt as if they were shaking apart. What did all of this mean? "Surely if my mother had made such an advantageous marriage she would have no reason to run away? Is that not what every female expects – a marriage and family?" It wasn't what she wanted. She wanted to be a Harvey Girl but she knew she was different from most other females.

Georgina hadn't been aware Petunia had mentioned the possibility of a relationship between Bridget and the Earl of Castlewellan. Did that help or hinder what needed to be said here? She drew a deep breath and proceeded. "Bridget, I am sorry to have to tell you … but, your father while being all that was deemed manly in appearance and manner, had a hidden flaw … he much enjoyed harming, both physically and mentally, the women he should have been caring for."

"That is terrible." Bridget looked shaken. However, she was no protected innocent – physical chastisement was not unknown to her as an orphanage inmate. "He was what Cook calls 'a street angel and a house devil' then?" She had heard that expression while listening to Cook chat with Billy Flint.

"Very much so." Georgina wanted to end this conversation. It was most unseemly to be discussing such things with a young girl, but what could she do? Bridget needed to understand at least in part what had caused her mother to behave as she had. She gathered her composure. "I knew none of this at the time, as I have said. It was the Reverend Mother who informed me of the circumstances of my friend's flight and your birth. And, Bridget, your mother paid the nuns handsomely for their care of you."

"She did?" Bridget stared, wondering if she could possibly ask the question trembling on her lips. Had her mother survived her birth? If so, where was she? She had seen the women who sought out the BOBs – they wanted to disappear without trace – had her mother been one of those? Did Miss Georgina know – surely she would tell her if she did? Imagine – a mother!

"Indeed, she did. She was injured before her flight and was barely hanging onto life when you were born. You were given the name Bridget O'Brien for your entry into the orphanage books – B.O.B. – which would tell any who knew that you were under the protection of the BOBs. She wanted you cared for – hidden away – I am afraid, now Lady Rebecca has discovered you, we will have to rethink your situation."

"We *are* related then?" Bridget didn't know what to say or think. She'd longed for a relative, but something told her it was not going to be a case of 'they lived happily ever after'.

"You share a father with Lady Rebecca as Petunia apparently pointed out. Therefore she is your half-sister."

"A sister – imagine!" Bridget wondered if she could withstand any more shocks. Miss Georgina had known that her father was a member of the nobility – there was far more going on here than she knew or understood.

"I have tried – without drawing attention to you – to prepare you for the wider world, Bridget." Georgina poured more tea. "Hoping you could perhaps one day take your rightful place in society."

"Is this why you have allowed Flora to educate me?" Bridget stared at her clenched fists sitting in her lap. She had never wondered about the opportunities offered to the three orphans in this house. She had been willing to believe it was a matter of human kindness, whatever Ruth and Sarah had said. "And encouraged me to learn to ride and believe I could better my situation in life?"

"Bridget, I was placed in an impossible position. You are the daughter of my dear friend. You were in my home. I was expected – for your own safety – to treat you in no way different from any other maid – I could not do it. I tried to improve your life a little. I could not do all that I wanted. I tried to open your eyes to the world around you – the possibilities."

"Does this mean I may never become a Harvey Girl?" Bridget's green eyes filled with tears at the possible loss of that cherished dream.

"Is that what you wish to be – a Harvey Girl?"

"I want to travel. I want to see what is out there." She waved towards the window overlooking the canal. "I believed becoming a Harvey Girl would be the first step on my travels."

"Bridget," Georgina closed her eyes for a moment, "any conversations concerning your future must wait. You are very young. It will be years before a firm decision concerning your future needs be taken. At this moment in time, we must discuss the changes that having Lady Rebecca turn up so unexpectedly have caused. Please pull the cord and summon a servant. We need to include Lady Rebecca in this conversation. I had hoped by telling you a little about your origins first it would seem a little kinder."

She watched Bridget slowly stand and walk across to the tapestry bell pull.

"While we wait, I will try to force this slice of bread down and finish my tea." Georgina wanted to put her arms around the obviously befuddled young girl.

They waited in silence for someone to respond to the bell.

A knock sounded on the door of the drawing room.

"*You rang, madam!*" Helen called out from the hallway, waiting for permission to enter. She was desperate to know what was going on. This house became stranger by the day.

"*Send Lady Rebecca to me!*" Georgina called out.

"*Yes, madam!*" Helen put her eye to the keyhole, wondering what they were talking about. There were not even whispers about these strange goings-on downstairs. That was so strange – servants always gossiped about their betters.

"Have you dropped something, Helen?" Petunia was standing in

298

the open door of the stairway leading down to the basement. She had followed Helen, sure she would be up to no good. She was sorry she had encouraged Georgina to keep this one on. It was time and past they found a husband for her and got her away from this house.

"I was just checking my shoe." Helen stood without a blush at the lie. "Madam requests the presence of Lady Rebecca." And that was another thing – why was a titled lady sitting in the servants' quarters? And what was that Bridget doing in with the mistress? There were secrets in this house. She could smell them!

Petunia turned and shouted down the stairs. *"Lady Rebecca!"*

Susan was standing at the ready at the bottom of the stairs. It did not take long for Rebecca to respond to Susan's summons. She went past Susan, up the stairs and through the door at the top that Petunia held open for her.

"If you please, Helen – this way." Petunia commanded, giving the maid no opportunity to delay her return downstairs. Trusting Susan to see that Helen could not return upstairs, Petunia walked with Rebecca to the drawing-room door.

She rapped her knuckles against the door and, at the shouted permission to enter, opened it.

"If you are to have a conversation of a private nature," Petunia stepped into the drawing room on Rebecca's heels, "you may want to keep your voice down and remain vigilant." She took a man's handkerchief from the pocket of her skirt and bent to stuff it into the keyhole. "Young maids with curious ears and loose lips are about." She stood, unaware and uncaring of the stares she was receiving from the three others in the room. "That will muffle any sound." Without a word more she left them to it.

"Helen!" Georgina and Bridget said together, sharing a glance of understanding.

"Lady Rebecca, take a seat," Georgina gestured to the settee that faced the fire. "You have caused – all unknowingly, I will admit – a great deal of problems with your sudden appearance at my door."

Rebecca took a seat without speaking. She could not apologise. She would not mean it.

"Bridget, as I have just informed her – is your sister." Georgina stared at the matching beauties. "You share a sire. Bridget is the daughter of your father's second marriage."

"The missing heir?" Rebecca had known this day had to come. The talk of the missing heir had been part and parcel of life in the area around Castlewellan. How strange to think that she might be the one to put an end to years of conjecture! She patted the cushion beside her. "Come sit with me, little sister. If we need to keep our voices down, it is better we be close." She waited until Bridget joined her on the settee and took her hand. She was proud of her own stoicism but then her life lately had been one shock after another – what was one more? "Our father was not a nice man. I know not how you came to be here – and a maid at that – but I can make some guesses."

"I have been made party to this brouhaha very much against any inclination of my own." Georgina did not wish to speak about the life of the late earl and his peculiarities. "We are now left with the consequences and must attempt to deal with the situation. Bridget, Lady Rebecca is in Dublin under the auspices of the BOBs."

Bridget's head snapped around to stare at her mirror image. "You are to disappear? The BOBs are to help you find a new life? You are to become a Harvey Girl?" The words came so fast it was a wonder they were even understandable.

"No, no," Rebecca was quick to assure her.

"Bridget," Georgina hated to see the girl in such distress, "Rebecca is not like the other women who have passed through this house. She has not found herself homeless and penniless. I have no knowledge of the workings of the BOBs in cases such as Rebecca's. I know only that she is to be kept hidden until the BOBs know what they are going to do to assist her."

"I have the great misfortune to be very wealthy." Rebecca grimaced towards Bridget, then her green eyes widened, her free hand went to her mouth, as she turned and stared at Georgina. "Dear Lord, I have just thought …"

"What?" Bridget looked from one woman to the other.

"Yes, indeed." Georgina nodded towards Rebecca. "Bridget, Rebecca is in danger because she is a wealthy spinster. The BOBs are attempting to keep her hidden while they work out how to protect her."

"Yes?" Bridget prompted. She wasn't stupid. She had heard and seen a great deal since coming to this house.

"You too are in danger now, little sister," Rebecca said sadly.

"Me!" Bridget was astonished.

Rebecca waited to see if Georgina would explain further. When she remained silent, Rebecca took a deep breath. It would appear explanations would be up to her. She was the elder sister after all. No matter how strange the circumstances appeared to be.

"Bridget, for much of my life I grew up listening to the servants whispering about the Earl of Castlewellan's missing heir …" she began.

"Me." Bridget felt faint.

"Indeed, so it would appear." Rebecca nodded and looked to Georgina but the good lady simply gestured to her to continue. "The servants and the Castlewellan estate workers would often discuss 'the missing heir' whenever there was a neighbourhood gathering. One could not help but hear." She paused for a moment to think. She was getting off track.

"What has this to do with me being in danger?" Bridget was waiting for someone to tell her to leave the room – this could have nothing to do with her – was she dreaming?

"I was forced to run away from home." Rebecca tried again. She would keep it simple. "The new earl – the man who has inherited the title and land – is not someone with vast sums of money at his disposal. Our father on the other hand was a man of great personal wealth. The new earl fears that with our father's death you and I will inherit that wealth. The new earl needs the funds he fears we will inherit."

"Bridget," Georgina said, "if news of your whereabouts should become common knowledge the new earl would be within his rights to demand we present you to him. He would be perceived to be your guardian."

"He has already tried to demand my return to the Castlewellan home," Rebecca said. "That I think is primarily why my grandfather insisted I should run away." There was no need to enter into further explanation of her own plight.

"I am having great difficulty thinking of myself as anything other than an orphan." Bridget shook her head. "This new earl would be my relation – a great-uncle?"

"He has eight children of his own and no wife." Rebecca could see the dreams of having a family in Bridget's eyes. She tried to find the simplest explanation. "He needs you and me under his thumb so that he may make free with our monies."

"So," Bridget said, "I would be like the women who have travelled through this house. This man could use any monies I might have, then reject me."

"I am sure he would keep you under his heel as a poor relation eventually," Rebecca said.

"I have a great deal to think about, do I not?" Bridget felt there was still a great deal about this situation she didn't understand.

"We will seek guidance from the BOBs." Georgina was out of her depth. "It is all I can think to do at the moment."

The three remained silent for a while, each lost in her own thoughts. Georgina stared into the fire. Bridget was lost in the feel of her hand being held by an actual relation – a sister. She was quite breathless with the wonder of it all. Rebecca too stared into the fire. She had no solution to offer.

Chapter 38

"What was it like growing up with a family?" Bridget asked at length. It seemed, even if she had found a family, it was not as she'd imagined and dreamed about.

"If you mean a mother, father, sisters and brothers," Rebecca shrugged, "I am afraid I have no idea."

"You don't?"

"Bridget, my mother was not brave enough to flee our father." Rebecca wished she could tell her newfound sister a tale of love and wonder but she could not. "My mother was carried from our father's home by the woman who became my godmother, Mrs Daniels. Now, the Daniels family have what some might see as the perfect family. I have been considered a part of that family from the moment of my birth. But I am afraid it was a case of being on the outside looking in. Despite my grandfather's caring, I have never truly felt part of a family. I know that I am fortunate to have people who care for me. But …"

"Are you to become a Harvey Girl?" Bridget wanted to change the subject. She did not like to see the sadness in eyes that were so like her own.

"I have no idea what a Harvey Girl is, though I dread to think." Rebecca's thoughts ran to women who were forced into a life of shame. She had heard of the demi-monde and had no wish to be a part of it.

"I will leave you two to discuss matters." Georgina had been listening with half an ear to the conversation of the other two. "Bridget, I will tell Mrs Chambers that you are to remain with Lady Rebecca until I return."

"Miss Georgina?" Bridget jumped to her feet, a frown on her face.

"Remain here, Bridget, until I return. I shan't be long." Georgina hurried from the room.

Georgina made her way down to the basement. She was delighted to find the kitchen occupied only by her old retainers. Cook and Lily were sitting in the kitchen alcove enjoying a gossip.

"Lily, has a note been despatched to Jane Morgan?" Georgina took a seat beside Lily on one side of the table.

"It has, Miss Georgina," Lily shook her head. "A right kettle of fish this is."

"Lily has been telling me a little about where this Lady Rebecca came from." Cook stood. "She never said a word about the young lady until she turned up here." She didn't want anyone to think her friend had been speaking about matters that were private.

"Sit down, Cook." Georgina put out a hand to stop the older woman from leaving the alcove. "You have been on your feet since early morning and deserve a rest."

"I am going to get you something to eat, Miss Georgina." Cook pulled away. "I can practically see the pain behind your eyes. It will be hunger that's causing that." She nodded her head emphatically.

"I couldn't eat." Georgina pressed a hand to her stomach. "The very thought of food makes me feel ill."

305

"A slice of toast and a lightly poached egg will soon settle your stomach. I daresay Liam will be glad to eat the plate of food I set aside for you." Cook ignored her mistress. She knew what was best.

Lily wanted to offer to make a pot of tea, but she couldn't leave the alcove unless Miss Georgina stood aside.

"Where is everyone?" Georgina looked around the kitchen that seemed three times larger than usual without the bustle of servants and guests.

"Thelma was kind enough to offer to oversee the maids," Lily said. "I had the beds stripped this morning, never thinking the house would be put into yet another uproar." She shook her head. "The beds need to be made with fresh linen. Ruth is upstairs lending a hand."

"And the rest of our strange household?"

"Petunia and Susan are having a business discussion in their room. Flora is out and about. Liam has run across to The Lane to visit his family. Cook gave him leftovers from our midday meal to take to them. I daresay they will be glad of them."

"I had hoped to encourage Petunia into taking a stroll in the fresh air with me." Georgina closed her aching eyes for a moment.

Left alone in the drawing room, Bridget and Rebecca stared at each other, neither knowing quite what they wanted to say.

It was Bridget who broke the uncomfortable silence.

"You don't have to answer me if you do not wish to, but why are you here?" She waved a hand about. "In Dublin, I mean. Why did the BOBs send you here? I mean, most of the ladies who have come through this house were left penniless by their relatives. They did not wish to become the 'poor relation'. Or else they had no choice but to flee cruel husbands and ended up homeless and penniless. Georgina said you are different. What is your story if you would not mind sharing it with me?"

"I have tried to explain to you the problems facing me because I am considered wealthy. I have not done a very good job of it. Truthfully I have been confused since the moment my grandfather told me I must flee everything I knew," Rebecca said.

"Had you really no idea of the peril you were in? After all, you must always have known that you were wealthy and you are old enough to understand your situation." Bridget thought you knew everything when you were an adult.

"I never gave the subject of wealth a thought." Rebecca hated to disillusion the girl staring at her with such belief in her eyes. How could she tell this girl, who had been cast into an orphanage for heaven's sake, that she had given no thought to her own future.

"But the BOBs —"

"Bridget," Rebecca held up a hand when it appeared Bridget had yet more questions she was unable to answer, "I am not an expert on the workings of the BOBs. I have heard of them vaguely while growing up. It was others who decided I must be carried away from everything I knew, not I. I was whisked away from the only home I have ever known. I had to leave my grandfather – the only parent I had ever known – my friends – even my horse – a gift from my godmother – was lost to me."

"I have learned to ride." Bridget was desperate to discover something she shared with this sister. "Lady Arabella invites us to her country home. We learned to ride astride …"

"You never!"

"Yes, indeed. The ladies who were here before needed to learn skills that will carry over into their new lives. The life of a Harvey Girl. It was all very exciting. We wore what Lady Arabella referred to as divided skirts. They are all the fashion for ladies of adventure. I did enjoy learning to ride. I miss it now that winter is here."

"But, my dear little sister, that is not at all ladylike – riding astride for a female is quite frowned upon by society. But how intriguing!" Rebecca wondered what it would be like to have the freedom to ride astride and at speed.

"I have never been a part of society," Bridget said simply.

"I am afraid that if news of you is made known all of that is about to change." Rebecca regretted the changes her very presence here would bring to the young girl. "I do wish people would not keep so many secrets! Surely, of everyone, we two have the most reason to know and understand what is happening that concerns our very lives?"

"I am frightened," Bridget whispered.

"So am I, sister," Rebecca put her arm around the trembling girl's shoulders. "So am I."

In the kitchen, Cook and Lily had metaphorically stood over Georgina until she had consumed the lightly browned toast and poached egg, with tea to wash it down. Now the pair were insisting that Georgina return to bed and rest in a darkened room with a moist towel over her eyes.

"I need to speak with Petunia!" Georgina protested. If anyone knew the secrets of society, Petunia Wallace-Montford was such a one.

"You can talk to Petunia while you rest," Lily insisted. There was no need to check if the linens had been changed on the mistress's bed. The mistress always came first.

"There are so many things I need to take care of," Georgina objected weakly.

"I daresay whatever needs doing will wait for you." Cook wanted to slap the table but didn't. She hated to see her young mistress so worn down.

"I do not know how people can dance the night away then rise to handle their affairs the next day."

"They do not." Lily encouraged Georgina to stand. She was trapped in the alcove until her mistress moved. "The gentry enjoy their amusements without care. It is the servants who take care of the household. You have simply forgotten how things are done. It has been many years since you were free to enjoy a day without cares."

Georgina allowed herself to be almost pushed out of the alcove, through the kitchen and up the stairs. She kicked off her shoes and fell onto her freshly made bed, enjoying the scent of fresh linens while Lily drew the bedroom curtains closed. She groaned aloud when a moist cloth was placed over her aching eyes.

"I'll ask Petunia to visit you." Lily pushed Georgina back onto the pillows when she tried to raise her head. "You remain as you are."

She whisked out of the room and up the stairs to request that Miss Wallace-Montford visit her mistress. When that was done to her satisfaction, Lily returned downstairs.

"Georgina," Petunia rapped softly on the bedroom door before opening it. "Are you awake?"

"I am awake." Georgina didn't move. "Do come in. I am under orders to remain as I am."

"Ah, servants!"

Petunia stepped inside the room, holding the door open to allow the light from outside to show her the way before she closed the door and crossed the room to sit on the side of the bed.

"You wished to speak with me," she prompted when Georgina remained silent.

"I am unsure where to turn and am hoping you may guide me somewhat, Petunia."

"This has to do with the uncanny resemblance between your downstairs maid and Lady Rebecca Henderson, does it not?"

"Bridget," Georgina raised one side of the cloth to look at her companion before dropping the cloth again, "is the legitimate issue from the second marriage of the Earl of Castlewellan."

"The missing heir." Petunia put her hand on Georgina's shoulder for a moment before removing it. "The second child was a female?"

"Bridget."

"This will put society abuzz. There has been talk of the missing heir to the Earl of Castlewellan for many years. How have you kept the child a secret for so long?"

"It was not of my doing, believe me." Georgina was glad of the cloth that covered her eyes. "I knew nothing of the child until my great-aunt who happened to be the Reverend Mother of the Goldenbridge girls' orphanage demanded that I take Bridget into my home as a maid and help conceal her."

"Well," Petunia said, "this is truly fact resembling fiction. Have you read that novel by Mark Twain, an American writer who pens delicious novels that appeal to the masses – *The Prince and the Pauper*?"

"Oh, dear Lord, the Dowager Duchess will be delighted. She loved that novel and spoke incessantly about it." Georgina groaned. "The woman will be beside herself thinking she is involved in a situation that resembles the plot of Mr Twain's novel. I daresay she will want to write to the man and discuss the matter."

"Constance is a lovely lady. I am very fond of her. However, she does appear to leave the solving of the problems she helps create to others."

"Does she not!" Georgina said.

"So, if I understand your concerns," Petunia shook her head, "you have the two legitimate children of the late Earl of Castlewellan – two vastly wealthy young chits – in your drawing room."

"I do."

"I can appreciate the reasons for your headache."

310

"Thank you." Georgina raised the cloth to stare through the gloom. "What am I to do?"

"Pass the problem back to the Dowager Duchess!" Petunia snapped. "She has the staff and the means to handle this matter."

"Bridget is the daughter of my childhood friend," Georgina said softly. "I would have taken her into my home and raised her as my own if matters had been different." She had no wish to revisit her own problems. "Constance wishes to travel to America and explore the Wild West with both girls by her side."

"The woman has lost what little wits she has!" Petunia gasped. "Those two will be a magnet for every fortune-hunting mama and rascal in the world."

"So I would have thought."

"Nothing can be done about this matter until after the Dowager Duchess's Christmas ball." Petunia's thoughts were whirling. "She will have no time to tend to the problem until the ball has proved yet another success. She takes her Christmas ball and its duties very seriously."

"But, in the meantime, I have two young girls I cannot wrap in cotton wool and lock away in my drawing room," Georgina said.

"Lady Rebecca cannot continue to reside with Jane Morgan," Petunia stated. "Jane is a dear, but she lives too close to the docks. That would make stealing Rebecca and getting her from our care too easy. A boat and willing crew could get the girl away to where we could never find her. What were the BOBs thinking of?"

"Hence my dilemma."

"Has anyone actually asked Lady Rebecca what she would like to do with her life?" It was not the done thing to allow young ladies to decide their own fate, she knew. But surely the chit had some idea of what she wanted from life. She encouraged her young students to plan for their own futures.

Chapter 39

"I insisted Flora allow Bridget to accompany her today," Petunia said.

Georgina and Petunia, wrapped in long heavy woollen coats, hat, scarf and gloves to protect them from the cold of December, walked together through the streets of Dublin. Petunia had her swagger stick – something she never left home without – under her arm. The two women had left the Percy Place house unfashionably early to visit the home of Jane Morgan. It was not a socially acceptable time for calling on someone, but they hoped to find visiting early would ensure they found her at home.

"I had to intercede rather forcefully last night when Helen tried to interrogate young Bridget on matters that are none of her business. She was demanding answers to questions the poor maid could not and would not give." Petunia's breath made clouds in front of her mouth. "I have wanted for some time to apologise to you, Georgina, for insisting you retain Helen in your home. The girl is a troublemaker for all her angelic looks. I would suggest we find her a position in another household with all haste. The girl has a loose tongue and there are secrets within your home that need protection."

Georgina remained silent. What could she say? The girl had revealed her true nature in recent months. It was yet another headache the BOBs had gifted her with.

"We are almost to Jane's house." Georgina was glad to see the familiar street. "I do hope she is there."

"Nice little house." Petunia was willing to allow the subject of Helen to drop.

They remained silent while opening the gate and walking through Jane's small front garden to her door.

Petunia used her swagger stick to rap sharply on the wood of the front door.

The door was opened in a very short time.

"Well, bless me!" Jane Morgan had never expected to find Georgina and a stranger on her doorstep so early in the morning. "I thought it was the redcoats come a-calling." The sharp rap on her door had startled her.

"May we come in, Jane?" Georgina asked.

She stepped through the door, Petunia on her heels, when Jane wordlessly opened the door wide, allowing them entrance.

"Have you met Petunia Wallace-Montford?" Geortgina gestured to her companion.

"I have not had the pleasure." Jane looked at the stern figure. "I have heard a great deal about you, however." She smiled at her unexpected guest. "You are quite the legend, Miss Wallace-Montford, with the ladies of the BOBs." She closed the door against the bitterly cold wind that was blowing off the River Liffey.

"Call me Petunia, do."

The two women were busy removing their layers of outdoor clothing.

"Come into the kitchen." Jane was never one to stand on ceremony.

"Bring your outerwear with you. We can put them over a chair to warm. You will appreciate the warmth when you need to step back out into that day. If I had known you were to visit, I would have put a flame to the drawing-room fire." She led the way to the kitchen as she spoke.

Her two guests, their outerwear over their arms, followed her to the kitchen.

"Is Rebecca not about?" Georgina almost groaned when she stepped into the welcome heat of the kitchen.

She and Petunia draped their outdoor clothes over kitchen chairs.

"You cannot keep that one indoors." Jane pulled the steaming kettle from the back of the black range which was pumping heat into the kitchen and put it over the hottest part of her range. It wouldn't take a minute to come to the boil. "She is outside playing with her dog and tending to my outdoor chores. Take a seat, both of you. I'll have a pot of tea on the go in a minute."

"Thank you." Petunia waited to see if Georgina would ask to see Rebecca immediately.

"It is best if we leave her there for the moment." Georgina took a seat at the kitchen table.

"I heard all about the ructions she caused at your house yesterday." Jane used the sleeve of her jumper to lift the heavy kettle over the teapot standing close to hand on the range top.

"We are still feeling the effects of her visit." Georgina watched Jane make the tea.

"That will take a minute to brew." Jane sat down at the table across from the two women, her back to the range.

"We believe it would be safer if Lady Rebecca were removed from your home, Jane," Georgina said with a nod towards Petunia. "Do you have any objections?"

"I would be happy to release her into your care." Jane appreciated the two women – far above her in society – asking her opinion. Also, she had been told by Rebecca in greatest secrecy of the appearance of the 'missing heir'. She had no wish to have anything to do with that kettle of fish, thank you very much. "As I have told you before, Georgina, she needs more adventure and company than I can give her. But what about her dog? That girl will not leave the animal behind again. It is old and the two are devoted."

"A dog." Georgina wanted to bang her head against the kitchen table. "That is all I need."

"One moment." Petunia put her hand on Georgina's arm and smiled almost evilly. "I have heard Helen complain long and loud about her previous master's hunting dogs and house hounds. Perhaps this dog will help solve one of your problems, Georgina." She laughed. "Helen has said many times when lecturing the young maids that she will never stay in a house with a dog again!"

"I'll get the tea." Jane jumped up.

"How on earth do you hear so much household gossip?" Georgina stared at Petunia.

"I check frequently on the work of the maids." Petunia felt no shame at listening in to the maids' chatter. "Helen likes to lord it over the three young maidservants in your home – all while doing as little as possible herself. If that young woman put as much energy into carrying out her duties as she does avoiding them – she would be the best worker in Ireland, I have no doubt – I like to keep an eye on her whenever possible. I try to save Lily Chambers the many journeys up and down the stairs as is needed to keep the house running efficiently."

Jane set the table, using her best china tea service. She put out the cups and saucers, a filled sugar bowl and milk jug while listening. She put a silver teaspoon on each saucer. She had no knowledge of

Georgina's home so could add nothing to the conversation. She listened with interest, however.

"That is kind of you, Petunia," Georgina said.

"I feel responsible for Helen Butcher remaining in your home." Petunia sighed. "I jumped into a situation I had no knowledge of with both feet – something my friend Susan lectures me against frequently. I am afraid I was over-weary and grimy from prolonged travel and wished only to reach our destination in peace. I saw a problem and as is my fashion declared a solution without consulting anyone. I can only apologise."

"Helen Butcher had been a problem long before you ever arrived, Petunia." Georgina pulled the empty cup and saucer that Jane placed on the table towards her. She toyed with the spoon on the saucer.

"But you were removing her from your home when I stuck my nose in!" Petunia too pulled a cup and saucer towards her.

"Was I? I wonder." Georgina put milk in her cup from the china jug. "Let us speak of something else. We need to speak of Lady Rebecca. Helen, I have no doubt can wait until another day. One problem at a time."

Jane carried the teapot over to the table. "I have no knowledge of this Helen but tackling one problem at a time seems a sensible solution to me." She poured tea into the three cups before putting the teapot on the trivet she'd already placed on the table and covering it with a knitted tea cosy. She took her seat and waited.

"Jane," Georgina shook her head, "Lady Rebecca cannot remain here. Her outing yesterday brought too much attention to my home."

"In what way?" Jane prompted, knowing well what was coming: the appearance of the 'missing heir'. Would that she could tell her friends and cronies about this! She made no mention of the fact that Rebecca had already given her this titbit of news.

"I have in my employ a young housemaid. One of three orphans placed into my care by the Goldenbridge orphanage." Georgina ignored Jane's sniff of disgust. The care of orphans was not well viewed by the public. In Georgina's opinion, orphanages might not be ideal havens of bliss, but they supplied a need and at the very least the children were housed, clothed, fed, and educated somewhat. "Her name is Bridget O'Brien ..."

"The BOBs." Jane instantly recognised their handiwork.

"Indeed," Georgina said without giving details. "Bridget is Lady Rebecca's sister. Her father's child by his second wife."

"The missing heir?"

"Ah, you have heard about that," said Petunia.

"How could I not? The gossips had a field day with such a delicious item of gossip." It had set society on its heels when a well-connected countess ran from her marital home.

"Well, Rebecca and young Bridget are as alike as two peas in a pod," said Georgina. "Neither of them knew of the other's existence. In fact, we had been compelled to keep the truth of Bridget's past from her. It had been hoped that we could keep the two girls apart, but that cat is well and truly out of the bag after Rebecca's visit yesterday." Georgina sipped her tea, her mind still trying to come up with impossible solutions to the problems she saw ahead. "It is vital that we remove Rebecca from your home."

"Have you spoken to the BOBs about this?" Jane earned her monies working for the BOBs and had no wish to lose that connection.

"The Dowager Duchess and everyone connected with her, it would appear, are knee-deep in the final preparations for the Christmas ball," Petunia said. "If there should be any problem about this matter with the BOBs, refer them to me."

"That is very reassuring." Jane smiled. "I provide a great many of my own needs from my smallholding out back. My home is my own but there are times when cash is the only option. I earn what cash I need from my work with the BOBs."

"Understood." Petunia said. "Truthfully, I cannot imagine what the BOBs were thinking of putting a pretty young female so close to the docks. The white slave trade is still flourishing, whatever anyone may like to think."

"I have tried to instil fear of that danger into Lady Rebecca's mind, but the chit is stubborn," Jane sighed. "As we all were at that age, I suppose."

"Very true." Petunia refilled her cup. Thoughts of the people who profited from stealing young girls and boys and selling them into a life of degradation hurt her heart and soul.

"It would be best, I believe," Georgina didn't want to give even a minute's thought to the horror of the white slave trade, "if Rebecca returned to my house with us this morning. A carriage will be coming in an hour or so – that should give her time to pack up her belongings – yes, that includes the dog," she said when Jane looked ready to speak. "I have no idea what will happen to the girls in the future but, for the moment, thanks to my – I don't know what to call Billy Flint and his motley crew – but I have a team of men to hand if they should be needed."

"Lady Rebecca needs to be outdoors." Jane didn't know who this Billy Flint was and didn't care to ask. "I have never seen anyone so constrained by being kept indoors. She needs to keep her faithful companion, her dog, by her side but honestly – she is useless around the house."

"It is winter," Petunia stated as if they were not aware. "There is little to do outdoors as far as I am aware."

"We will have to face that problem when it becomes necessary."

CHERISH THE DREAM

Georgina too filled her teacup. "The most urgent matter for the moment is to remove Rebecca to my home. We can discuss any solution that might present itself with Rebecca at our ease."

"There is still the problem of Bridget," Petunia said softly.

"I will leave the problem of this Bridget to you two." Jane glanced at her kitchen clock. The day was wasting. "I'll call Rebecca in."

She went to the back door, removed a heavy shawl from a nearby nail and wrapped it around her head and shoulders, removed her slippers, and pushed her stocking-covered feet into the wellington boots that sat under the nail, before stepping out into the cold day.

Chapter 40

"My dear Georgina," Letitia McAuliffe was speaking before she even set foot over the threshold of the Percy Place house, leaving the ornate carriage with the shield of the Duchess on its door standing in the street, a young man holding the horse's head. "You are quite out of favour with Constance. What were you thinking of to send a note declining the invitation to her Christmas ball? Constance is extremely displeased."

"I am amazed she even noticed I was missing from the guests." Georgina took Letitia's coat and hung it over the hook in the hallstand. "The Dowager Duchess's balls are always such a crush." To her mind it was a delight when one was first on the social scene — a young girl with her life in front of her — to dance the night away, attend the breakfast gathering and then be escorted home by red-coated soldiers to ensure one's safety. She almost sighed aloud, quite frankly she would rather be by her fire in comfort. Was she becoming old and staid? "Is the carriage to wait for you?" She had not been expecting this visitor.

"Yes, I shan't be here overlong." Letitia followed Georgina into her drawing room. "I have been sent on an errand of some urgency." She walked to the fire and stood with one hand searching in the deep pockets of her brown woollen skirt. "The Dowager Duchess has sent me to deliver a missive she has received, addressed to your guest, Lady Rebecca." She held the white vellum envelope high.

"You knew I had her removed to my home then?" Georgina had not yet sent a note to the BOBs informing them of her movements. She supposed Jane Morgan had taken care of the matter. Jane after all was dependent on the goodwill of the BOBs.

"I did not. I went first to Miss Morgan's house and was informed that Lady Rebecca had been your guest for several days."

"Indeed." Georgina walked over to join the other woman before the fire. "I don't wish to meddle, but it is my understanding that it is imperative Lady Rebecca remain hidden. Who on earth would know to send a missive to the young woman in Dublin?"

"It is not my place to question my employer." Letitia said. "I merely carry out the duties she has set me. I was ordered to deliver this missive into Lady Rebecca's hand with all haste. That is what I am attempting to do."

"As you wish." Georgina pulled the embroidered cord to summon a servant.

The women remained standing while waiting. At the knock on the drawing-room door Georgina opened it to discover Helen.

"Have Lady Rebecca attend me," she ordered, shutting the door in the maid's face. "Do take a seat. I have not offered you refreshments, Miss McAuliffe – would you care for tea or perhaps coffee?"

"Nothing for me, thank you." Letitia took a seat, perching on the edge of the comfortable chair. She had matters to attend to this morning and she did so hate being lectured by the coachman when he was obliged to keep his horses standing.

Rebecca knocking on the door and entering after permission broke the uncomfortable silence.

"You sent for me?" Rebecca looked between the two women.

Georgina and Letitia stood.

"May I introduce you to Miss Letitia McAuliffe, companion to the Dowager Duchess of Westbrooke," said Georgina. "Miss McAuliffe, Lady Rebecca Henderson." Should she leave?

"Lady Rebecca," Letitia bobbed a curtsy before holding out the envelope in her outstretched hand, "I was asked to put this missive into your hand."

"For me?" Rebecca accepted the envelope.

"You will find a letter opener on my desk," Georgina said when it appeared Rebecca was simply going to stare at the envelope.

"Thank you." She crossed the room to the desk and picked up the silver letter opener. She put the sharp silver blade under the lip of the envelope and jerked upwards, splitting the envelope open. Without a word she took the letter out of the envelope and stared first at the signature.

"Aubrey!" she gasped, holding the letter to her chest. She turned to stare at the woman who had passed her the envelope. "Aubrey Whittaker is in Dublin? How on earth did he know to find me here?" She didn't wait for an answer. "Oh, let me read what he has written!" She was almost bouncing in place. "Aubrey, I cannot believe it!" She had grown up with Aubrey, following in his footsteps while he led them into adventures. He would have been the first person she contacted when ordered to flee her home but he had been overseas.

She gave her attention to the letter in her hand while the other two women waited patiently.

"Aubrey Whittaker is staying with the Dowager Duchess of Westbrooke?" Rebecca's green eyes were practically drilling into Letitia

McAuliffe as she demanded an answer. "How on earth has that come about?" She was sure Aubrey would have told her if he had an acquaintance with the Dowager Duchess – but then again – perhaps not.

"Mr Whittaker has been a welcome guest of my employer for some weeks." Letitia had no intention of claiming greater knowledge.

"Georgina, I must speak with him." Rebecca looked down at her simple navy skirt and white lace blouse. It would serve. She had to speak with Aubrey before he sailed out of her life forever. He had written of his plans to seek position on a ship. What was he thinking of? He was a man of the land.

"I have a carriage outside." Letitia had been warned by Constance that something of this nature might occur.

"Georgina!" Rebecca beseeched, holding the letter clutched to her breast.

"Fetch your coat and bonnet," Georgina said. "You will be safe in Miss McAuliffe's company and I daresay the Dowager Duchess will see to your safe return."

"Thank you!" Rebecca was running from the room as she spoke. "I will be but a moment!"

"You expected this?" Georgina said.

"Constance did forewarn me," Letitia agreed.

Georgina stood in the open doorway, watching the carriage pull away. She wondered briefly if she had reached a stage in her life when she was past being surprised. She shut the door when the carriage disappeared from sight.

"Who is supposed to look after that hound now that Lady Rebecca has gone gadding about, I'd like to know?" Helen's whining voice carried down the house.

Georgina shook her head. She really needed to do something about Helen Butcher.

"This is the strangest house I have ever worked in," Helen continued to gripe.

"I understood you had only ever worked in one house before coming here," Bridget's soft tones answered.

"Don't you take that attitude with me, young Bridget O'Brien! Just because you look enough like the Lady Rebecca to be her sister, you needn't be putting on any airs and graces around me. If you are related, I daresay it is something for you to be ashamed of."

Georgina wondered how the poor child kept her tongue behind her teeth. How she must long to shout about who and what she was, but now was not the time. There were no plans yet in place to handle this situation. She sometimes felt as if she were sitting on a boiling cauldron, the lid rattling dangerously, waiting for an explosion.

"I saw a letter for you from Canada, Helen," Sarah's voice now echoed down the staircase. "Are you really thinking about emigrating?"

"I am." For once there was no whine in Helen's voice. "My Ernest writes that I will have to wait until the winter is done. He is up to his rear-end in snow, if you can believe such a thing. He writes the world is all white and a body can freeze to death walking from one house to another."

Georgina, still standing in the hallway listening, prayed that Ernest Cunningham was indeed serious about having Helen join him in Canada. If she knew she only had to bear with Helen's company for another few months, well, it would be a blessing having an end in sight. She shook herself slightly while walking towards the stairs leading to the kitchen. She needed company and a pot of tea.

"Georgina, do you have a moment to spare?" Petunia ran down the stairs, catching Georgina just as she put her hand on the door leading to the staircase.

"Is the matter private?"

"Not in the least," Petunia said.

"I was just going to ask Cook to make a pot of tea." Georgina opened the door.

"I will join you if you have no objections." Petunia followed on her heels.

Georgina watched the activity in the kitchen for a moment before speaking.

"Cook, is it possible to have a pot of tea served in your little alcove?"

"Ruth, see to it," Cook said without taking her attention away from the mixture in the large bowl she was holding under her arm against her body.

"Yes, Cook." Ruth hurried to obey.

"Should we ask Susan to join us?" Georgina asked as the two women walked across the large kitchen towards the alcove.

"There is no need." Petunia took a seat to one side of the table. "I merely wish to bring you up to date on our activities." She glanced around quickly before leaning forward to whisper. "Did you hear that Helen is thinking of emigrating to Canada?"

"I overheard her say something of the sort just now. I thought of offering to row her there!" Georgina joked as she took a seat opposite Petunia.

"She is a trial to the nerves." Petunia shook her head.

"What news did you wish to share?" Georgina leaned back to allow Ruth room to set the table.

"I believe we have found a suitable house for Dorothy," Petunia announced. "Susan and I have been walking the streets of Dublin, inspecting property like ladies of wealth." She laughed.

"What of your idea of setting up a service to secure property and

325

provide staff for gentry moving to Dublin?" Was she ready to go ahead with her daring plans?

"Everything has fallen into place in a fashion Susan and I could never have dreamed of. We entered into discussion with the Graham family and –"

"Not the Graham family on Upper Mount Street?" Georgina interrupted.

"The very people. Do you know them?"

"The Graham family have lived in that house for many years. They were friends of my parents. I knew them vaguely socially." Georgina shook her head. The house was only across one of the canal bridges from her own home. It would be very convenient for Dorothy and her daily journey to her factory. Then too it would suit her twin sons who were students at Trinity College.

"The family are emigrating to America," Petunia leaned in to say. "They are not making any formal announcements yet. I was told of it through a connection of the Dowager Duchess. It was fate."

"America?" Georgina waited until Ruth had placed a teapot on the table before continuing. "Are they not rather old to be thinking about emigrating?"

"They have a son in America." Petunia busied herself serving the tea. "He writes frequently apparently, telling them of the glorious sunshine available year-round to them. I believe he went prospecting for gold in California. He has since set himself up with a mercantile and, to hear his parents tell it, is making money hand over fist."

"Is that not a rather large house for Dorothy and her sons?" Georgina hoped and prayed for the sake of her old neighbours that their son was telling them the truth when he wrote of his riches. It would appear everyone who left these shores became a rich person almost overnight – a mathematical impossibility. "It has been some years since I visited the Grahams in their home, but I do remember it was of an impressive size."

"Yes, indeed, and that is the beauty of it." Petunia clapped her hands, she was so pleased with her findings. "The house is of such a size that we are considering asking Dorothy to rent the basement to Susan and me for our offices and living accommodation. It is centrally located and would serve us rather well, don't you think?"

"You have been busy," Georgina stated admiringly.

Chapter 41

"Aubrey, my dear," Rebecca said when the pair finally managed to escape the demands of the Dowager Duchess, "are you not a trifle old to be threatening to run away to sea?" He had made mention of this notion in his note to her. They had not seen each other in two years, Aubrey having been in Europe studying methods of estate management in different countries.

They were standing by the window of one of the many drawing rooms in the Dowager Duchess's Sandymount home. The view was uninspiring, but it did not matter. The pair were too busy examining the many changes that had occurred since they last saw each other. An elderly relative of the Dowager Duchess occupied a chair drawn close to the fire. They had been assured that their elderly chaperone was practically deaf but keen of mind.

"You have certainly grown, Rebecca." Aubrey took both of her hands in his and stared, delighted to have found her. He had wanted to take his leave of his many friends before he sailed away – perhaps forever. The Daniels family had been helpful but cautious when he expressed a wish to see Rebecca. It was only when it was established that he would not be returning to Castlewellan that they issued him with her particulars – swearing him to secrecy. "Although the ensemble you sport does not flatter, my dear."

"*Tut, tut, tut*, a little decorum if you please!" Their chaperone clicked her teeth.

The pair didn't hear, too fascinated with their perusal of each other.

"You have been too long in Paris." Rebecca laughed, not in the least insulted. Who cared what she wore? Aubrey had returned and sought her out! He was even more handsome if that were possible. He had been prettily beautiful at sixteen when he attracted the attention of all the women of their neighbourhood. He had matured through the years since and grown so tall. The masculine beauty of his face and firm body were a sculptor's dream – his thick chocolate-brown hair was the height of fashion and his pleasure at the sight of her shone from his icy grey eyes. He was truly breath-taking.

"Come," still holding onto her hands he turned her from the window, "let us sit and speak of what has brought us both to this moment." He released one hand to lead her over to a sofa in plain view of their chaperone. He waited until Rebecca took a seat at one end of the long sofa before tugging on his trouser legs and taking the seat furthest from her but still in comfortable conversation distance.

"You first," Rebecca said. "What on earth is this nonsense about running away to sea? You are a man of the land, Aubrey Whittaker."

"I have no land that is my own, Rebecca." Aubrey could not take his eyes from the young beauty across from him. His friend Rebecca – all grown up.

"But ..."

"I returned from my travels to discover your father had died." He did not offer condolences on the loss of her parent. He was aware of Rebecca's relationship with the man. "I became immediately embroiled in assisting my grandfather in packing up a lifetime – much to my shock as you can imagine."

"Packing – what on earth do you mean – your mother's family have been managers of the Castlewellan estates for generations. Your grandfather educated and trained you to take up that position. It is the reason he took you in."

"So I had always believed." Aubrey had been shocked by everything he discovered on his arrival at the place he called home. "I don't know the relationship of the present earl to you – uncle, cousin, it is immaterial. The man is a fool. He intends to put one of his sons into the estate manager's manor house and in full charge of estate matters. It was believed – I cannot imagine why – that I would be willing to train the youth. I was not polite in my refusal." He was silent for a long moment, thinking of his grandfather. "Grandfather has made plans to move into his sister's large home on the seafront in Newcastle, which is quite close to the Castlewellan estate. She will make much of him, no doubt. She has been a widow for years. The pair are planning to whittle down the multitude of memorabilia that has been amassed by the family over the years they served as the Castlewellan estate managers."

Rebecca stared open-mouthed. Had the new earl no idea of the training, education and sheer hands-on knowledge needed to run such a vast estate? Obviously not. "It would appear we are both now landless vagrants. We have spent our lives caring for and nurturing land that will never be ours."

"It was rather ironic." Aubrey knew how much she loved her fruit and flowers. "While I visited with her, Mama lectured me until I felt my ears would bleed on the folly of working for another. I do so dislike when Mama is correct."

"But running away to sea, Aubrey?"

"I have funds, Rebecca." Aubrey did not want her to think he had pockets to let. "Mama, Papa, and Grandfather are all that is generous. But money is soon spent and must be replenished. I want land of my own. Somewhere I can make my own life. I thought time spent on the sea would give me the opportunity to reflect on the changes I am facing."

"Aubrey ..." Rebecca shook her head.

"Mama did suggest," he switched to the French language knowing she would understand, "that I could make a fortune selling this," he gestured from his hair to his toes with one long-fingered hand. "I have always been rather beautiful, no?"

They both clearly heard the shocked gasp from the chaperone whom they had been assured, by the Dowager Duchess, spoke no French and was hard of hearing.

"A trifle vain, perhaps?" She loved the mischief sparkling so clearly in his eyes. He had always been able to make her laugh.

"I need to be outdoors, Rebecca." Aubrey ignored her jibe. "You of all people know that." She too flourished in the outdoors. "Be that on sea or land."

"I have a proposition for you, Aubrey." Rebecca had been thinking deeply ever since she had seen his signature on the note he sent. She took a deep breath, looked into his eyes and before her nerves could fail her, said, "You could marry me."

"My dearest Rebecca," Aubrey smiled sadly, "nothing would give me greater pleasure, but it is impossible — and you know why. You of all people know the problems of my birth. We have discussed it often in secret between ourselves."

The scandal of his birth was not well known in Castlewellan, but enough people knew that his mother had fled the estate to escape the attentions of Rebecca's sire. She had fallen, at fifteen years old, into the hands of a much older married French roué – an aristocrat who kept her close for years. After giving birth to the son she was forced by circumstances and her aging lover into leaving with her father, Martha Whittaker had taken matters into her own hands. Under an assumed name, she was now one of the most infamous Parisian courtesans. She owned a great deal of property she rented to others in Paris. She was an acknowledged leader of the French demi-monde – making her fortune profiting from the men attracted to her beauty of face and figure. Aubrey – while he could never speak of it openly – was proud of his mother. She had taken adversity and turned it to her own advantage. He wished to do the same – how could he not?

"Aubrey," Rebecca moved along the sofa, wishing to be close enough to touch when they were discussing a matter so intimate and life-changing, "I have been pushed hither and yon ever since the death of the Earl. I am warned repeatedly of the danger I am in as a wealthy young woman. I have been forced to leave everything I have ever known. I fear I have reached my limit." She hit her chest with a clenched fist. "I too long to feel the land beneath my feet – *my* land."

"*Tut, tut, tut,* this is most unseemly," their elderly chaperone was standing over them, glaring and clicking her tongue against her teeth. "You must maintain a respectable distance from each other – I insist."

"I am trying to propose marriage to this man!" Rebecca snapped. "It is difficult enough without you interrupting. Please return to your seat until I have this matter settled."

"*You young hussy!*" the old woman barked but she returned to her chair by the fire. She had her orders from the Dowager Duchess.

"Aubrey," Rebecca dared to take his hand in hers, "in the house where I reside at the present moment, the talk is all of America. There is much excitement and discussion of making a new life in the colonies. I have never given any thought to emigration." She took his hand in both of hers and squeezed as hard as she could. "We could marry, travel to America and no one would know where we come from or who we are. We would be free to write our own history and work towards our own destiny."

"You have given this matter a great deal of thought!" Aubrey could not believe the words coming from her mouth. He wanted to bang his head to be sure his ears were working as they should.

"None at all." Rebecca delighted in the shock she could see on his face. "Aubrey, we have a great deal in common. We have known each other since childhood. We were both raised by our grandfathers to love the land. A land that could never be ours and from which we are now exiled. We have been cast adrift from our moorings. I have no wish to continue to be pushed and shoved by the whim of others. We ran free together when young. We have a friendship I have always cherished. I want to take my own destiny into my own hands – with you by my side – will you at least consider my proposal?"

"Well, Mama is to be proved correct once more." Aubrey sighed dramatically, gesturing from his head to his toes again. "It would appear I am selling this after all."

"Aubrey!" Rebecca released his hand to punch his shoulder.

They fell against the back of the sofa and laughed like lunatics, the spirit of adventure fizzing in their veins.

Chapter 42

Richard ran up the steps of Georgina's home and into the house. Liam was holding the door open for him. He pushed open the drawing-room door without knocking.

"Georgie, whatever is the matter?"

"I have no idea." Georgina turned from her desk and shook a piece of paper in the air. "The Dowager Duchess demands I present myself for her pleasure. She further demands that I be accompanied by Bridget and your good self. She is sending her carriage. A rider delivered the message." She stared wide-eyed at Richard. "First Constance's companion arrives at my door and carries Lady Rebecca off – now this."

Richard almost sagged against the doorframe. When Liam had run to his place of business and demanded he attend Georgina immediately his mind had whirled, trying to anticipate the latest disaster. "When a duchess, dowager or not, demands your presence, well, my dear, all one can do is obey."

"I need to change." Georgina looked down at what she was wearing. "I have already sent Bridget upstairs to dress." She looked at

Richard. "You too, Richard – we must present a dignified appearance at the very least." She knew Richard kept a change of clothing to hand at his city office.

"Whatever you say, my dear."

Georgina, Richard, and Bridget stood in the elegant hallway of the Dowager Duchess's house trying not to fidget under the stern glance of the butler. A maid had taken their outer wear from them, and they now stood waiting to be allowed into the presence of Her Grace.

Bridget, in a green skirt, high-neck cream blouse with lace trim, hair brushed until it gleamed, stood trying not to stare around her. She had never seen such wealth. She needed to take everything in to report back to a very curious Ruth and Sarah. She had entered by the front door!

The butler opened the door. They waited while he formally announced each name before stepping into a gold-and-cream ornately furnished brightly lit room.

"My dears, thank you so much for coming at such short notice," Constance said from a chair that resembled a throne. "There is a matter of some urgency to be discussed but first let me make you known to Mr Aubrey Whittaker."

The introductions were conducted, and everyone performed their social duty beautifully. Bridget was rendered almost speechless at being introduced. With the introductions out of the way they took a seat and waited to be told why they had been summoned.

"Rebecca and Aubrey are to be married." Constance threw out her arms to announce. When she did not receive the expected gasps of surprise, she continued. "They wish to marry with all haste. I have been made to understand that this is the perfect solution to dear Lady Rebecca's every problem."

"Is the lady not underage?" Richard worried about legalities.

"I have in my possession a legal document duly authorised from her grandfather, allowing me to approve of the match if Rebecca should find someone she wishes to marry." Constance bowed her head graciously.

"Before we go any further," Aubrey stood to address a matter that concerned him, "there is a matter that needs to be discussed."

Bridget held her breath. Was this very handsome man going to ask what she was doing in such company? She had noticed him staring at her in surprise. He did not question her close resemblance to Rebecca, much to her relief. She did not know why she had been invited to join this company. She sat back in her chair and waited to see what would happen next.

"For those of you who do not know, Rebecca and I grew up together. My grandfather is or I should say, was, the manager of the Castlewellan estate. I am aware there is a great disparity in our fortunes. I am not penniless, but I am certain I am not as wealthy as my intended. For that reason, I wish papers drawn up that will protect Rebecca's inheritance from me. Her money is her own and will be passed to any children we might have. It does not matter to me if this is not known to others, but I will not abuse the trust Rebecca is placing in my hands."

"My dear boy!" Constance practically danced on her seat. "How wonderful! A man of convictions and honour. Such a rare find in today's world!" She felt her eyes fill with silly tears.

"I have been given to understand by Her Grace," Aubrey ignored the Dowager Duchess and addressed Richard, "that you, sir, have the knowledge and the means to oversee this matter?"

"Aubrey, there is no need," Rebecca objected.

"There is every need, Rebecca." Aubrey took her hand. "You must be protected at all costs, and I will do all in my power to see that you are."

"I salute you, sir." Georgina said what all were thinking. "That is a very fine thing you are doing."

Bridget was breathless at the romance of it all.

Rebecca listened without surprise while the others marvelled at Aubrey's suggestion.

"Georgina," Constance said, "Rebecca will stay with you while the modiste works on an extensive wardrobe. I have been giving some thought to the matter of the wedding ceremony. Lord and Lady Sutton have a large estate not too distant from Dublin. It would be an ideal venue for the wedding. The Suttons have a private chapel. I am certain dear Arabella would not object."

Georgina exchanged glances with Richard. The Dowager Duchess was a force to be reckoned with when she was planning the lives of others.

"Aubrey is a welcome guest in my home and so it shall remain," Constance continued. "Richard, you can oversee the paperwork needed to protect Rebecca's inheritance?"

"I will first need to see a copy of the late Earl of Castlewellan's last will and testament." The young man impressed Richard.

"We have much to do." Constance clapped her hands. "I do so dislike the ennui of life after the Christmas and New Year balls but now I have a wedding to plan and a young couple to launch on their new path in life. Is it not delightful?"

All agreed it was delightful but quite a few could see there were problems ahead.

Chapter 43

"How are matters progressing in your home?" Richard questioned Georgina while strolling through the gas-lamp-lit Dublin streets. It was three weeks since their visit to the Dowager Duchess's home. They had been to the theatre and were enjoying the chance to stroll through the somewhat smoky air and the rare opportunity to speak without fear of interruption.

"There are a great many plans afoot," Georgina, her arm entwined through Richard's, said. She was not being unseemly – they needed to remain close in the dim light, she assured herself. "January is usually a dreary month to my mind but behind the doors of Percy Place the month has been a veritable hive of activity. Molly Mulvey has not yet returned from England. The girl writes such entertaining letters giving her impression of all that she has seen and done. Dorothy and her sons have been to visit the Grahams. It would appear they like the house – talks are ongoing. Petunia and Susan have diagrams of their plans for the basement of the house well in hand."

"And the bride?"

"Lady Rebecca," Georgina laughed softly, "I have never met a lady so disinterested in what she will wear."

"Except perhaps yourself," Richard did not wait for her to react to his words. "It was kind of Lady Sutton to agree to the use of her Kildare estate for the wedding."

"Aubrey and Rebecca, always with Bridget in tow as chaperone, have been taking a barge from Dublin to the estate in Kildare. It is fortunate that the Sutton estate has a landing pier for the barge within its grounds. The plans are moving ahead at a speed that leaves me gasping. Thankfully all I need to do in the circumstances is listen while I am informed of the latest marvel." Georgina said. "Lady Sutton, Arabella has offered the couple the use of her guest cottage until they are ready to leave the country." She had seen the 'cottage'. A five-bedroom private dwelling on its own grounds – with servants!

"Are they still planning a move to America?" Richard asked. "Surely – when they marry – Lady Rebecca will have the protection of his name and can no longer be considered in danger from unscrupulous fortune-seekers or indeed her relatives?"

Richard, with his father's aid, had drafted the papers needed to protect Rebecca's fortune.

"They have been advised to wait out the cold weather before travelling. The pair are quite determined to emigrate. I have supplied the particulars of Euphemia Locke-Statton." Mia was one of the women sent to Percy Place by the BOBs. "She married a Mr Josiah Huffington-Bridges and resides in New York. The man is a cowboy from Texas according to Mia's letters."

"The elegant and snobbish Euphemia Locke-Statton married to a cowboy! My dear Georgie, that beggars belief."

"Eleanor Anderson, the lady who was everything that was helpful to me, and the ladies sent to America, assures me that Mr Huffington-Bridges is in fact an extremely wealthy Texas rancher." Georgina smiled. "I supplied Eleanor's particulars too to Rebecca and Aubrey. The letters are fairly flying from New York to Dublin. They are being carried special delivery at great cost."

"I must make time to visit with Aubrey," Richard said softly. "I would be very interested in what he has learned about American business affairs, as no doubt my father would be too."

"You have an interest in emigrating to America, Richard?" Georgina gasped.

"Not at all," Richard quickly reassured her. "But with travel between the two countries becoming so swift and efficient – think of it, Georgie – only five days to travel from Cork to New York – why, the idea fairly makes me dizzy. There is much that could be achieved by promoting business interests in America."

"The sheer scale of the country boggles the mind," Georgina said. "Dear Bridget's map gives one only a rough idea of the size of America. I am afraid I cannot imagine a nation so immense."

"That is what makes the idea of doing business with these Americans so fascinating." Richard was excited by the very idea.

"You and Billy Flint!" Georgina shook her head slightly. "He is extracting every bit of information he can out of Aubrey."

"That same Billy Flint has retained my firm as his financial advisors." Richard nudged her lightly.

"Billy Flint!" Georgina again shook her head. "That young man will go far. He has re-instated his physical self-protection training for Rebecca, Thelma, Flora, Bridget, and anyone else who cares to join. He was vastly impressed by Petunia's skill with that swagger stick she is never without. The woman is quite lethal with her weapon of choice and has been giving demonstrations to the group."

"I cannot quite envision you sporting a swagger stick, my dear Georgie." Richard laughed at the image in his head.

"And you never shall see such a thing."

"However, the idea of young ladies learning to protect themselves is all to the good, as I have said before. Did you not tell me that Mia has found someone in New York to continue the training she started with Billy and his men?" Richard was one of the many who read the letters from America with fascination.

"Yes, indeed." Georgina had been surprised to learn it. Mia had even insisted her young stepdaughters learn all that they could. "Mia is determined to never again be at the mercy of another. The young women who pass through my house are learning to be as independent as possible."

"That is all to the good. One needs to have the ability to protect oneself." He nudged her gently with his shoulder. "Has Eugenie been notified of how matters stand here?" He knew Georgina was in correspondence with Jenny Castle, the Harvey Girl who was once the Countess of Castlewellan and Bridget's mother.

"Richard, I am beyond furious with Eugenie." She simply could not think of her friend as Jenny. "I have asked her advice on the matter of Bridget. I have practically begged her to return home so matters concerning her daughter may be put right. She refuses. She claims there is nothing she can do." If Eugenie were in front of Georgina at that moment, she would be tempted to do violence to her.

"Matters cannot be allowed to continue as they are." Richard put his hand over Georgina's hand where it rested on his arm. "The new Earl of Castlewellan needs to receive official notification of the fact that there is no 'missing heir'. That the child born to Eugenie was female. It is not my place to take charge of such a notification but, my dear Georgie – someone needs to take care of the matter."

"As soon as that notification is put in the post – Bridget is in danger

– she will become as much a pawn as Rebecca." Georgina had thought of little else in the dark hours of the night.

"As you say, my dear." Richard sighed.

They continued to walk in silence, lost in their own thoughts.

Chapter 44

"*We are not speaking to you!*" Ruth's voice hissed. "*Until you tell us.*"

"*You are keeping secrets. We are supposed to be your friends.*" Sarah's sibilant whisper.

"Leave her alone." Liam's deeper masculine tones.

"*It is not right to keep secrets from your friends.*" Helen's sanctimonious hiss.

Georgina, her bedroom door slightly open, her hand on the doorknob, froze in place. She had been about to open the door for a dash to the nearby toilet. She had not realised it was the hour the servants would be leaving their attic rooms to begin their day.

She listened to Bridget being harangued by her fellow servants. She wanted to step into the hallway and box ears. She noisily opened the door wide bringing silence to the group frozen on the stairs. She stepped into the hallway, making no motion to indicate that she had either heard or seen the servants. Closing the toilet door at her back, she leaned against the door for a moment. This could not continue.

"You are up and about early this morning, Miss Georgina." Cook

343

stared when her mistress, washed and dressed for the day, stepped into her kitchen.

"I am indeed, Cook." Georgina glanced at Ruth. The other servants were around the house carrying out their duties. "I am wanting a pot of tea for two and a quick nourishing snack. In my office, if you please." She turned and left the kitchen.

"Ruth." Cook did not need to give any instructions. The girl had ears. She wondered what had put the fire in Miss Georgina's eyes.

Georgina hurried up the stairs, following the sound of whispering voices.

"Bridget," Georgina did not step into the bedroom, "leave what you are doing and come with me."

"I cannot release Bridget from her duties," Helen said. "I will send her to you when I no longer have need of her."

"*I beg your pardon?*" Georgina was surprised smoke was not coming from her ears and nose. "Are you under the impression that you hold a position of authority in this house? A position that supersedes me!" She did not wait for a reply. "Bridget, with me – *now.*"

With Bridget on her heels, she hurried down the stairs, across the hall and into her drawing-room office.

"Close the door, Bridget," Georgina said when the younger woman stepped into the room. "I have ordered tea and a snack from cook. Sit down while we wait." She had put a match to the fire and lit the gas lamps before going to the kitchen.

"Miss Georgina …"

"Bridget, I must apologise to you."

A knock sounded on the drawing-room door.

"Bridget, open the door, please." Georgina glanced at the mantel clock. Were the hands frozen in place? Surely eons had passed since she first awoke!

"Do you want me to move the table closer to the fire, Miss Georgina." Bridget stepped away from the now open door.

"It is fine where it is, thank you, Bridget."

Ruth glared at her friend – it was her job to deliver trays – not Ruth's.

"Put the tray on that table, Ruth." Georgina waited until Ruth had left the room before beckoning Bridget over to the oval table under the long window. "Join me."

"Miss Georgina," Bridget did not move, "what am I doing here? I am neither fish nor fowl lately and being in here with you like this is only going to cause trouble."

"We have all treated you shamefully, Bridget." Georgina pulled out one of the two wooden chairs tucked under the table. She removed items from the large tray setting them around the table. "Sit down, please."

Bridget remained standing, her stomach rumbling.

"Please, join me." Georgina took a seat. "We can speak while we break our fast." She raised a silver dome from one of two plates, revealing poached eggs sitting proudly on thickly sliced toasted bread. "Sit down Bridget, do."

Bridget sat – what else could she do? She was rendered speechless when Miss Georgina began to serve her.

"I am so dreadfully sorry, Bridget," Georgina poured tea into two cups. She waited while Bridget put milk and sugar into her tea. "I informed you that you were of noble birth, introduced you to your sister then blithely expected you to return to your duties as a maid in my household. Do eat something."

Bridget picked up her knife and fork, wondering if she could force the food past the lump in her throat.

"Bridget, I am about to share something with you." Georgina had spent the long hours of the morning thinking about this. "Your mother left a doll she had made for you with the nuns. The doll was passed to me with the instructions that I was to give it to you when you reached your eighteenth birthday. I have no idea why your mother chose the age of eighteen, perhaps she thought to give you time to arrange your affairs before you reached your majority. However, I am going to ignore my orders and give you the doll now. I believe there are papers inside the doll. Perhaps the papers will help us decide how best to allow you to claim your birthright."

My dearest child, I know not if you are male or female. I know simply that I love you and pray for your health and happiness. I do not yet know if I will survive your birth. I feel so dreadfully weak. The women who surround me are doing all that they can.

Bridget read the words through tears. She had been unwilling to rip the seams of the yellow-haired rag doll, but Georgina assured her the doll could and would be repaired.

While Bridget read her letter Georgina examined the other papers found inside the doll. She gasped when she read them. She needed to consult Richard. Could she ask him to be a party to the wild and perhaps illegal schemes running through her head?

A sharp rap on the door sounded and the door began to open.

Georgina stood stiffly in front of the contents of the doll spilled over her desk. She breathed a sigh of relief when she saw who was seeking her out as Flora's head appeared in the opening.

"Flora, come in." Georgina gestured towards her desk. Bridget, she noticed was paying no attention to her surroundings.

"What is all of this?" Flora stared at the wads of stuffing and scattered papers.

"Bridget's mother created this doll for her," Georgina stated simply.

She held out some handwritten pages attached to an official document.

There was silence in the room while Flora read the notes left by the Countess of Castlewellan.

"Georgina," Flora raised her head, "do you wish to open this particular kettle of fish?"

"I cannot ask her," she nodded towards an oblivious Bridget,

"But Eugenie is not dead!" Flora whispered, shaking the official document in her hand – the last will and testament of Eugenie Henderson, Countess of Castlewellan.

"She might as well be!" Georgina snapped. "Who will deny that the child's mother died in childbirth – you? There is no way to prove Eugenie Countess of Castlewellan still lives – quite to the contrary. That will," she pointed to the document, "states that if anything should happen to Eugenie Henderson, the child she carried be placed in the care of Georgina Corrigan," she pointed to her chest, "which you must agree is me."

Flora had not been present for a great deal of the happenings in this house recently. She was engaged in studying the chance of a new life Georgina had gifted her. She had ears however and heard a great deal of gossip and whispering about Bridget and Lady Rebecca.

"That child," Georgina pointed to the silently weeping Bridget, "has been treated abominably. She deserves better from all who should have been seeing to her needs."

"Georgina, I do not like the gleam in your eyes."

"I am in possession of the Castlewellan emeralds." She nodded at Flora's wide-eyed stare. "I have that!" She rapped the official document with her fingertips. "I believe it is time to put matters in motion."

"I'm sorry but I cannot advise you. I will return to the kitchen."

Flora left the room and as soon as the door closed at her back she tore her jacket from the hallstand – pushing her arms into the sleeves while running from the house. She crossed the nearest canal bridge.

Richard eased his way into Georgie's drawing room, uncertain of what he would find. Flora seemed to believe that Georgie needed him urgently. He found a scene of calm. Georgie was sitting across the fire from a sleeping Bridget. She turned her head when he entered.

"Richard," she said without a great deal of surprise in her voice, "Flora ran to you, did she not? I saw her leave."

"What is going on, Georgie?" He leaned against the door, unwilling to let anyone enter.

"I am going to use the Castlewellan emeralds to blackmail the current earl into allowing me to raise Bridget as my own." Georgina stood, crossing the room to her desk. "I have the last will and testament of the late Countess of Castlewellan." She picked up the legal document and pressed it to his chest.

"Georgie …"

"I do not care, Richard." She threw her arm out, pointing to Bridget. "That child cried herself to sleep after reading a letter from her mother. Enough. Eugenie refuses to involve herself so I am going to manage matters as I see fit."

"Think about what you are saying, Georgie." Richard had never seen her like this. "You would be breaking more than one law."

"I no longer care!" Georgina snapped. "I have obeyed the law. I have behaved as a well brought-up woman should. Well, no longer. I am taking matters into my own hands as I should have done from the moment I met Bridget." She gave an emphatic jerk of her head. "Even if it means fighting the new earl for my rights as guardian," she slapped the paper on his chest, "a guardianship passed to me by the child's mother. Should it mean leaving this house and travelling to America to keep Bridget by my side, I will do it. I will no longer stand by and watch Bridget being punished for a sin that was never hers."

Richard stared for a tense moment without speaking.

"If you are about to become a desperado on the run in America, my dear Georgie …" He pulled her into his arms. "Might I suggest you take me with you?"

"Richard!"

Bridget stopped pretending to sleep and cracked open her eyelashes to look at her mistress being soundly kissed by Richard Wilson.

"Will you marry me, Georgie?" Richard whispered against her damp lips.

"You find outlaws attractive?" She pulled back to look up into his beloved face.

"I have always found you attractive, my dearest Georgie."

"I am quite determined on this course of action."

"Blackmail and forgery?" Richard could not imagine anyone less likely to commit such crimes. But his love was correct — something must be done about Bridget O'Brien. For the moment, however, he had the woman who had held his heart in her hands for years in his arms. He pressed his lips to hers. This was his moment, everything else would wait.

THE END